continued . . .

SHADOW
SILENCE

~

YASMINE
GALENORN

JOVE
New York

A JOVE BOOK
Published by Berkley
An imprint of Penguin Random House LLC
375 Hudson Street, New York, New York 10014

Copyright © 2016 by Yasmine Galenorn.
Penguin Random House supports copyright. Copyright fuels creativity, encourages
diverse voices, promotes free speech, and creates a vibrant culture. Thank you for buying
an authorized edition of this book and for complying with copyright laws by not
reproducing, scanning, or distributing any part of it in any form without permission.
You are supporting writers and allowing Penguin Random House to continue to
publish books for every reader.

A JOVE BOOK and BERKLEY are registered trademarks and the B colophon
is a trademark of Penguin Random House LLC.

ISBN: 9780515156256

First Edition: October 2016

Printed in the United States of America
1   3   5   7   9   10   8   6   4   2

Cover art by Tony Mauro
Cover design by Danielle Mazzella di Bosco
Book design by Laura Corless

To my agent, Meredith Bernstein,
who has had my back for many a year.
Thank you.

ACKNOWLEDGMENTS

I have a usual list of suspects to whom I owe a great deal when I'm writing a book. To my editor and agent, for encouraging my vision and supporting it. To my husband, Samwise, who is one of the most supportive men I've ever met. To Andria and Jenn, my assistants who help make it possible for me to write three books a year and stay sane. To my readers, who buy the books and support my fan base—without enough readers buying the books, authors wouldn't be getting contracts. And lastly, to Ukko, Rauni, Mielikki, and Tapio—my spiritual foundation.

You can find me on the web at Galenorn.com, and all the links to my newsletter and my social networks can be found there. If you want to contact me, please e-mail me through the contact page on my website.

Dear Reader:

And so, we come to the second Whisper Hollow book, Shadow Silence. *I hope you enjoy this book as much as I did writing it—the world of Whisper Hollow is very near and dear to me, and it haunts my dreams and thoughts.*

I hope to be writing far more Whisper Hollow stories in the future, though it will be through another venue. Be assured, I have new books and new series coming out, but you will need to check my website to find out what publisher/venue through which they will be available. If you sign up for my newsletter on my website, you will be assured of finding out about all my future releases. I do promise—no matter what—I will have more books to share with you.

Brightest Blessings,
The Painted Panther
Yasmine Galenorn

Under the water it rumbled on,
Still louder and more dread:
It reached the ship, it split the bay;
The ship went down like lead.

SAMUEL TAYLOR COLERIDGE,
"THE RIME OF THE ANCIENT MARINER"

Some places speak distinctly. Certain dark gardens cry
aloud for a murder; certain old houses demand to be
haunted; certain coasts are set apart for shipwreck.

ROBERT LOUIS STEVENSON

Advice for Visitors to Whisper Hollow

1. If you hear someone call your name from the forest, don't answer.

2. Never interrupt Ellia when she's playing to the dead.

3. If you see the Girl in the Window, set your affairs in order.

4. Try not to end up in the hospital.

5. If the Crow Man summons you, follow him.

6. Remember: Sometimes the foul are actually fair.

7. And most important: Don't drive down by the lake at night.

Whisper Hollow:
*Where spirits walk among the living,
and the lake never gives up her dead.*

THE MORRÍGAN

The Morrígan, Night Mare Queen and Goddess of Sover-eignty, Queen of Shapeshifters and Mother of the Fae, culls the dead from the battlefield and gathers them to her, under the embrace of her feathered cloak. She is mother to the Bean Nighe and the Bean Sidhe, the sirens of the spirit world, who warn of death to come by vision and by song. She is mother to the Crow Man, who haunts the woodlands of the world, surrounded by a murder of crows, carrying her messages to those to whom she would speak. The Crow Man walks before the goddess, announcing her appearance. He speaks through the raven and the crow, and to ignore his summons is to ignore the gods. Do so at your own risk.

But not all dead wish to stay in their shadowed realm, and not all dead understand the reality of their situation. And in some lands, the energy of the Veil is so strong that the dead can walk freely between the worlds. So it was that the Goddess of Crows engendered nine great families—the bloodline passing through the maternal side—of women born to drive the wandering dead back into their graves, to stand between the dead and the living as protectors. The Morrígan's daughters, known as the spirit shamans, are charged with these duties.

To each spirit shaman, a match is born—a shapeshifter

by birth. He will be her protector and guardian. They will be forever bound. And to each spirit shaman, a lament singer will arise—a daughter of the Bean Sidhe—who will work with her to complete the triad. Together, they will protect the portals of the world that lead into the realm of Spirit, and keep the dead from flooding the land of the living.

CHAPTER 1

—❦—

The Cold Moon brought the winds, rushing in off the Strait of Juan de Fuca to whistle through tall fir and cedar and snake through the thick undergrowth, rattling the windows as they surrounded Whisper Hollow. Catching the town up in their icy embrace, they danced through the long December night. Up on Hurricane Ridge, the snow was clouding the Olympics, blanketing the peaks with a thick layer of powder. Down in the shadow of the mountains, the storms were bringing rain and sleet, and perpetual gray clouds that swept through on the atmospheric river.

I adjusted my coat and blew on my fingers, trying to warm them as I inscribed a band of runes in charcoal paste on the headstone. I was sitting on the grave, straddling the freshly mounded earth that covered the pine casket bearing Hudson Jacks's mortal remains. Saturday, he had left this world, dragged down into the lake by the Lady. She was ravenous lately, it seemed, and Hudson had been in the wrong place at the wrong time.

As I inscribed the runes, Ellia played in the background, her violin keening through the night as the wind picked up her notes and tossed them willy-nilly, almost as if the song and storm were doing battle. Her music strengthened my magic, as we bound the dead man to the deep dark of the graveyard. Penelope was waiting in her tomb to take his spirit with her into the Veil, my gruesome Gatekeeper who was terrifying and beautiful. *Death's maiden.*

To the side, Bryan stood watch. My protector and guardian shifter, he kept on guard for those who sought to disrupt me when I was too far into the magic to protect myself. He was also my lover. Fiercely protective, he crossed his arms as he surveyed the graveyard.

Behind me, the sound of the tomb opening told me Penelope was ready.

I stood and pointed my dagger at the headstone. Twin serpents coiled around the hilt in silver, and a crow was engraved on the pommel. The sigils on the blade began to glow as I whispered the chant of summoning I had found in my grandmother's journal.

"From the depths of your grave, I summon thee.
From the dark night of your death, I call thee.
From the icy grips of the Lady, I wrest thee.
Hudson Jacks, I command thee, stand forth in my
*   presence."*

I shuddered, wondering if I'd ever get used to the weight of the dead pressing in on my shoulders. I could feel them watching through the Veil. Those who still walked this world watched silently from their graves, waiting for their own chance to wander.

A moment later, there was a rush of energy as Hudson shimmered into sight. His form was translucent, and he looked as he had in death. Coiling vines draped around his neck where the Lady had taken him into her arms and dragged him below her icy surface. Hudson had been wandering since his body washed up on the shore, and twice now he had appeared outside his brother's window. The Lady's spirits often turned into Haunts, dangerous and hungry. Ellia and I needed to put him to rest before he became trouble.

I held out my hand to him. I had only been doing this for a little over six weeks, but I was learning fast. He gazed at my fingers, then at me, cocking his head to the side.

"You cannot refuse me. I am Kerris Fellwater, the spirit shaman of Whisper Hollow. I'm a daughter of the Morrígan and you are bound to obey me. Let me lead you to the Veil, where the Gatekeeper awaits." The words themselves were a charm, strengthened by the strains of Ellia's song and the power of the Morrígan.

Hudson paused. If he bolted, we'd have our work cut out for us. But a glimmer of relief appeared in his eyes and he held out his hand, placing it in my own. His fingers were like bees stinging my palm; the energy crackled and snapped, sparking against my skin.

I held fast, ignoring the discomfort and turned, leading him toward the tomb, where the double doors were open. Ellia fell in behind, still playing as her cloak fluttered in the wind, and Bryan followed, silently guarding our backs.

Penelope's mausoleum glowed from within, the blood of her chalice lighting the night. As the wind keened like a Bean Sidhe, merging with Ellia's violin to knife through the air, we approached the base of the knoll where Penelope had been laid to rest. Her crypt straddled the line dividing the modern graveyard from the Pest House Cemetery, where more dangerous shadows lurked. Built of cinder block buried deep into the shroud of grass and mounded dirt, the crypt was stained from time and weather.

A plaque affixed to the side of the door glimmered in the light emanating from inside. I knew the words by heart. *Here*

Lieth the Mortal Remains of Penelope Volkov, Guardian of the Veil, Gatekeeper of the Graveyard. Enter and Despair.

As I entered the crypt, the crystal chalice stood on the dais, the crimson liquid within churning like a kaleidoscope. My own blood was in there, along with the blood of other spirit shamans, lament singers, and guardians who had held their posts during Whisper Hollow's history. It was rumored that every Gatekeeper's chalice contained a drop of the Morrígan's blood, as well. This is what kept the glass intact and the liquid within in a perpetual motion, a glowing, whirling vortex. I dipped one knee in front of the chalice, acknowledging the Gatekeeper.

And there she stood, to one side. Penelope in all her gruesome beauty. Dark veins of black blood trailed out from the raccoon mask that shrouded her eyes. She looked fragile as porcelain, fragile as a picture from long past, ready to dissolve at the first whisper that touched her. Her hair was upswept in a chignon, blond tendrils coiling down to her shoulders.

Penelope towered over me, six feet tall and gaunt in a black dress that fell to her ankles. The dress shimmered with sequins, the sheer material revealing the bones that thrust against her alabaster skin. But jutting out from her body from within, as if she were a voodoo doll turned inside out, were the tips of long nails, surrounded by glistening splotches of dried blood. She looked as though some crazed inner carpenter had gone mad with a nail gun.

She glanced at Hudson's spirit, a hungry look filling her eyes, then back at me. "He reeks of lake water and *her* scent. We will cleanse him and remove her binding."

"Yes, he was taken by the Lady a few days back. She gave up his body fairly quickly, though. I don't know why." Usually the Lady kept them longer, tying them to her while she fed on their spirits before she loosed them back into Whisper Hollow.

"Perhaps he was not to her taste." Penelope laughed,

making me shiver. I had gotten used to her appearance by now, but she still scared the hell out of me. I had no clue as to how extensive her powers were and I wasn't sure I wanted to know. The fact that she was Ellia's older sister didn't help any, either.

I let go of Hudson's hand, and he glanced at me, a fearful light in his eyes.

"Go on, it will be all right." I gave him a gentle nod.

Penelope held out her own hand, and he reached out to touch the nails jutting from her wrists. He glanced up at her—he was not a tall man—and she gave him a soft smile and took hold of his fingers.

"Welcome to the Veil, Hudson Jacks. Take my hand, love, and join my dark kingdom."

It was the same greeting each time, and each time, the spirit would smile dreamily and follow her into the Veil. As I watched, she gave me another nod. I turned and walked out of the crypt to where Ellia and Bryan waited for me. The doors behind us swept shut with a thud, and that was the end of Hudson Jacks.

We returned to his grave, Ellia still playing. I had one last spell to weave before we were done for the night.

I pressed my hand against the charcoal rune stream, and sprinkled Rest Easy powder on his grave. As I stood and circled the grave, deosil—clockwise—with my dagger pointing out, I invoked the charm that would, with all luck, keep Hudson by Penelope's side until he was ready to move on from the Veil to . . . wherever it was that spirits wandered after they left this world.

> "Do not rise. Do not wake. Do not the Veil, now
>   forsake.
> Do not whisper. Do not walk. Do not dance and do
>   not talk.
> To the Veil, you shall remain, within the Gatekeeper's
>   domain."

As I finished, there was a hush, and then the sound of crows echoed through the graveyard. The charm had taken. The Crow Man was watching.

I turned to Ellia. She switched to a tune that made me weep no matter what mood I was in. I had learned over the past weeks that it was customary for the spirit shaman to weep over the dead, to mourn them even as she drove them to the Veil. It was an honor, my duty to remember them. I knelt, my tears falling on Hudson's grave, as I filled a little jar with graveyard dirt and labeled it. Then we were done. I wiped my eyes and stowed the jar in my bag along with my dagger and other tools. Ellia slowly lowered her violin.

Bryan silently crossed to my side and held out his arms. I leaned into his embrace. Each spirit had a personal story. Each spirit left a legacy and a family behind, even if we never knew what that legacy was. I was the last to bid them farewell as they crossed between the worlds. Sometimes, I would be the only one to *ever* remember them. Whether beloved, or lost and forlorn, they all faced the spirit shaman last—all over the world, we were often the last mortal the spirits would see before crossing into the Veil.

I rested my head on Bryan's shoulder. He was familiar, he smelled of safety and love and passion. Like me, like Ellia, he was a child of the Morrígan. As he leaned down and pressed his lips to mine, I glanced over his shoulder. The moon had broken through the clouds. She was shimmering against the grass, and as I watched, a murder of crows flew past the silver orb, winging their way toward us and over our heads.

"The Crow Man is walking," I whispered. "Something's going to happen."

As I spoke, the clouds rolled in again, and a hail of rain broke over our heads. As we raced for my car, I glanced back at Penelope's tomb, where a faint light shimmered from the knoll. The crows had landed on the tree over her mausoleum. Yes, something was up, and I had no doubt the Crow Man would make sure I was right in its path.

* * *

Our work done, we sped through the night to Lindsey's Diner, the hot spot for Whisper Hollow residents who wanted a late-night snack. Peggin, my best friend, and her new beau—Dr. Divine—would meet us there. I still wasn't sure what to think of *Deev*, as he had told us to call him, or *D-D* as Peggin called him. An artist, he had been drawn to Whisper Hollow like a moth to a flame. The town was like that. If Whisper Hollow wanted you, you would somehow find your way here to stay. If the town *didn't* like you, it spit you up and out, and if you resisted going, it would feed you to the Lady or one of the other spirit beings that lurked in the shadows.

As we pulled into the parking lot, I saw Peggin's car. I eased into the spot next to it. As I turned off the ignition and stiffly stepped out of the driver's seat, I glanced down at my jeans. Dried splotches of mud dappled the denim, but at this point I didn't care. I just wanted something to eat, and to catch up with Peggin, who had been swamped at work the past week.

Bryan wrapped his arm around my waist as we headed into the diner. "You okay? You sure you're up for this? We could go home and I could make you something to eat there."

I caught my breath. His touch sparked me off no matter how tired I was, and I flushed just looking at him. He was five eleven, with dark brown eyes that shifted color depending on his moods, and his hair grazed the top of his shoulders, tousled strands the color of wheat. Bryan Tierney looked to be in his thirties, but he was actually over 140 years old—he was my protector, a wolf-shifter guardian, a son of the Morrígan.

"No, I want to see Peggin. It's been over a week since we last got together."

He laughed. "You two are inseparable. I love that you have her for a best friend."

"She's your friend, too. You know that anybody that has

my back is good as gold in her book." I glanced over my shoulder.

Ellia was two steps behind us as she checked her phone for texts. The older woman was over seventy but looked timeless and was as fit as anybody I knew. She was tall, with long silver hair that flowed over her shoulders. She was wearing a pair of linen trousers, a button-down blouse, and the flowing floor-length green cape that she always wore when we went out to tend to the dead.

I pushed through the door as we came to the diner, and the smell of burgers and fries assailed me, making my mouth water. The restaurant was open till two A.M., and Lindsey had remained true to her mother's vision. It was outfitted in retro-fifties style, but updated and clean. The menu had more choices, and they even made specialized dishes for allergy sufferers, but overall, it was still Mary Jane's Diner, under her daughter's name.

I started to look for Peggin but Debra-Su, who worked the night shift as a waitress, pointed me toward the back corner booth. She knew who I was looking for. She handed me three menus after seeing who I was with.

"I'll be there in a moment. They haven't ordered yet." She winked.

"Thanks, Deb." I took the menus and threaded my way through the tables toward the booth.

Peggin heard my voice and was instantly on her feet. My best friend—and the only one I had kept in touch with on my fifteen-year sabbatical from Whisper Hollow—she was a firecracker. At five seven, she was a few inches taller than me, and stacked in all the right places with a plump hour-glass figure. Her rich coppery hair was natural, and she was one of those wisecracking brainy women who caught you off guard, flouting the stereotypes. She was about as athletic as my cats, she dressed like a fifties pinup girl, and she carried a gun with which she was a deadeye shot.

"Get your ass over here, chica." She hugged me first, then

gave Bryan a quick hug. Ellia, she did not touch. *Nobody* touched Ellia—it was too dangerous.

As we swung into the other side of the booth, I saw that Dr. Divine was there. He had lived all around the states, he said, but could never seem to remember where. It was as if he had just appeared full-grown on Whisper Hollow's doorstep one day, ready to rock. He turned heads wherever he went, but for him, his appearance was as natural as breathing. Tonight was no exception.

Dr. Divine looked like a steampunk aficionado on steroids. He was probably about five nine, but he wore platform sneakers that sent him past six feet. His top hat was made of purple velvet, encircled by a black leather hatband with an intricate brass clockwork design on the front. Thin black braids dangled down past his ass—there must have been fifty of them.

Deev was pale as moonlight, but I wasn't sure what color his eyes were because he always wore clockwork goggles that looked like they were out of some mad scientist's lair. He was in blue jeans and a button-down denim shirt, over which he wore an ankle-length patchwork duster of denim and velvet and leather and a kaleidoscope of prints.

He also had an open-carry license and strapped what looked like an antique flintlock pistol—a blunderbuss—to his thigh. I asked him once if it really worked. He answered by pulling it out and promptly shooting a can of cola that was sitting on a picnic table. Apparently, he had put the semiautomatic together himself from antique parts and updated it, just like he had made the rest of his outfit.

But there was nothing *precious* or prima donna about him. He was dead serious about his art. When we first met, I wasn't sure whether he was just odd or scary-crazy. Turns out, a little bit of both. But he was as sane as anybody who lived in Whisper Hollow.

"Hey, Deev," I said, sliding into the booth. Bryan followed, and Ellia swung a chair around from one of the tables to sit at the end. "How goes it?"

Deev cocked his head to the side. Somehow, he always managed to keep his hat on perfectly straight. "Jokney got out today. I still haven't found him."

Bryan cleared his throat and I could tell he was trying not to laugh. Jokney was a sculpture of a doglike creature that Deev had built from shiny chrome scraps, black leather, and some sort of fur that he'd gotten off an old fur coat from the vintage clothing shop.

At times, Dr. Divine's artwork took on a life of its own and went wandering around the town till he rounded it up and carted it back to his house. This usually didn't present a problem, except when it was some nightmarish vision he'd had. Those, he usually kept locked away against the chance that they, too, might decide to wake up and go out for a little walk.

"Have you tried the dog pound?" Ellia asked, her eyes twinkling. She liked the man, that much I could tell from the very beginning.

"Not yet, but that's on my list for tomorrow if he hasn't come home." He leaned back, wrapping an arm around Peggin's shoulders. At first she was skeptical when Bryan offered to fix them up, but after the first date, they had become an item. They fit. Together they made a startling duo. His crazy met her twisted in a wonderful, weird way.

I leaned back in my seat and opened the menu, staring at the choices. Everything looked so good. I was starving, as I always was after a night in the graveyard.

"You've been chasing down spirits in the graveyard?" Peggin was studying her own menu.

"Yeah, we had to make sure Hudson Jacks didn't go gallivanting around. You know what happens to the ones taken by the Lady. They tend to wander. Usually they become Haunts, or in some cases, the Unliving, and right now, we don't need any more of either type around town."

There were five paths of the dead.

My grandma Lila—the spirit shaman of Whisper Hollow

before I took over when she died—had drilled me on the lessons from the time I was little.

The Resting Ones were those who had died, but not yet passed through the Veil. They quietly waited for Penelope to come for them and caused no trouble.

The Mournful Ones were more memory than anything else, reliving their deaths time and again as though on a movie screen. They could be disturbing to watch, but usually had no truck with mortals.

Wandering Ones wandered far from their graves, traveling the byways, but they, too, ignored humans for the most part. All three of these were rarely a problem, although I did my best to release them so they wouldn't be caught forever on this side of the Veil.

The dangerous spirits, though, were another matter. Haunts were active troublemakers and liked to make life uncomfortable for human beings. They were the poltergeists and the spirits who could occasionally shove people down staircases.

And then, there were the Unliving. The Unliving returned on a corporeal level, and could cause serious harm. They weren't zombies, not in the movie sense. No, the Unliving were smart and cunning and highly dangerous, especially when rogue. Veronica, the local Queen of the Unliving, kept a tight rein over those she summoned. At some point, I was going to have to visit her lair. All spirit shamans were expected to make some sort of connection with the royalty of the dead.

"Honestly, your night sounds more fun than mine." Peggin made a face. "I've got to move in less than thirty days."

It was my turn to frown. "What's this? Why? I thought you loved your place?"

She shrugged. "I do, but the landlord called me last night. She's going to move back into the house. I have until the end of the month to find a new place to live."

"Aren't you on a lease?"

"No," she said. "Once the initial lease was up, the arrangement fell into a month-to-month agreement and I just forgot about it. My landlord is seventy-two, and up until this week, she seemed to be very happy living with her daughter. But apparently the two had a major tiff—which I heard all about—and that sealed that. No warning, nothing. Just a big bomb dropping." She made a whistling sound, then, *"Poooooophhh . . ."*

"What are you going to do?" I knew how hard it could be to find real estate in Whisper Hollow, and I knew Peggin didn't have enough money saved up to buy a house. Her job was secure but she didn't make very much.

She cleared her throat, staring at me over the top of her glasses. "I think I've found a place. I went out looking today and stumbled on a house that would be perfect. I haven't been inside, but I'm going to check it out tomorrow. It's a fixer-upper, but I'm not afraid of a little work."

Deb returned. "Ready to order, folks?"

I handed her my menu. "Double cheeseburger, fries, and a chocolate shake. Also—coffee. Lots of it."

Peggin laughed. "It's almost midnight. But coffee for me, too, and I'll have the grilled cheese with bacon. Chips, pickles, and cherry pie."

"How you two can consume so much caffeine and still sleep at night confounds me," Bryan said. "I'll have chicken strips, fries, and no coffee. A Sprite, please."

Dr. Divine asked for loaded potato skins and a plate of calamari, and Ellia ordered a bowl of chowder and extra rolls.

After the waitress left, I turned back to Peggin. "So, where is this house? I hope you have room for a garden. I know how much you love hydrangeas."

She gave me a long look. "Promise you won't argue?"

That rang an alarm. Peggin wouldn't say something like that unless she knew I wasn't going to approve. "All right, let's hear it. Where is it?"

Peggin glanced at Dr. Divine. He just stared at her silently. "On Fogwhistle Way, across from the pub. It's one of those abandoned houses near the Pier in the Foggy Downs subdivision."

Fucking hell. "You have to be kidding. Are you *insane*? You can't move there." I leaned across the table, staring at her.

Ellia chimed in. "That's prime territory for the Lady. What on earth prompted you to think of moving there? The subdivision's been abandoned for decades."

Ellia was right. The Foggy Downs subdivision was all but abandoned. Too many people had met with accidents, been lured into the lake by the Lady, or had otherwise fallen into general misfortune of one sort or another. There were about ten houses in the neighborhood—all from around the turn of the twentieth century—and they were right next to the Fogwhistle Pier, which had been abandoned as well, given how many deaths the Lady had engineered from there.

Peggin stared at us. "If you two are done scolding me? Listen, you know as well as I do that there aren't many houses for rent in Whisper Hollow. I can't live in an apartment—I can't stand the idea of being cooped up. And the houses in safer neighborhoods are far too expensive. This house is rent-to-own, and if I fixed it up, I think it would be pretty."

Peggin could be a little bullheaded when she thought she was being ganged up on, and if we continued to argue with her, it would only make her more determined.

I wanted to reach across the table and knock some sense into her, but since that wasn't an option, I decided to try another route. "Will you at least let me come look at it with you?"

She held my gaze for a moment, then relaxed. "All right. I've got an appointment with the Realtor tomorrow. Come with me if you like. As I said, it has a rent-to-own option and it's in my price range. I've had enough of people yanking my life out from under me. If I can reclaim the house, if there's not a fortune to invest, I'm planning on buying it. I have to go somewhere."

Bryan turned to Deev. "What do you think about this plan? Have you seen the house?"

"I have." Deev regarded him from behind the clockwork goggles. "Peggin's an adult, she can make up her own mind." But he didn't look happy. He glanced at Peggin. "I just want you to be careful. The Lady eats who she will, and she's been hungry lately."

Peggin laughed. "Don't think I'm unaware of that. But I promise you, I won't hang out at the lake. I'm not the sun-bathing type, which is probably why I live here and haven't moved away to sunny California." She sobered. "To be honest, I don't know what it is about this house, but I feel . . . it needs me. And I need a place to call my own."

Deev gave a quick shake of the head. "I told you, you can always move in with me till you find a safer home."

I blinked. That was a quick offer for him to make, considering how short of a time they had been together. But then again, if I were in his shoes, given the option of having Bryan move into a house next to a monster's lair, or letting him come live with me, I'd pick the latter, too. And Bryan and I had only been together about five or six weeks, though it felt like so much longer.

But Peggin was having none of that. "Thanks, but I need my space. I learned the hard way that I have to make my own way in this world." She ducked her head. "I know you're trying to help, but I . . ." She paused, looking over at me for support. "*You* understand."

I let out a slow breath. "Yeah, I do."

And I did. Peggin's childhood had mostly consisted of ridicule for her choice in clothes, for her weight, for her lack of interest in getting married. Her older sister, Lisha, had become a family icon. The "normal" one, she was blond, trophy-wife thin, had gone to college and—after earning a bachelor's degree in art history—had married into a family filled with lawyers and doctors. Peggin, on the other hand, was a size 12, had no interest in joining the upwardly mobile society set, and so her parents told her she could either study law or business in college. Anything else and she'd have to pay for it herself. She had turned them down and found herself a job, saving enough to take an online medical transcription course.

A year after Peggin graduated from high school, Lisha got pregnant, and her parents moved to Seattle so they could see the baby more often. Peggin had stayed behind.

After she earned her certification, she went to work for the hospital. Now she worked for Corbin Wallace, one of Whisper Hollow's best doctors. She had managed everything on her own. Peggin was used to taking care of herself and if she was wary of anybody offering help, it was because it had always come with strings attached.

Deev seemed to sense her resistance because he gave her a little squeeze and backed off. "Well, if you need a place, you know you've got one. Just keep it in mind in case you don't like the house and can't find something suitable by the end of the month."

I decided to change the subject. Peggin was looking far too tense.

"Agent H caught a mouse today and decided to drop it on my bed for when I woke up." Agent H was one of my Maine Coons. I had three. The other two were girls— Gabrielle, better known as Gabby, and Daphne, named after Daphne du Maurier, one of my favorite authors. They were all huge, basically walking Tribbles on legs.

Peggin snorted. "Sounds like Frith. He likes to bring me garter snakes that get in the house. Folly's too lazy."

"I love your ferrets." Dr. Divine grinned then. He didn't smile often, but when he did, it was a trickster grin, a heady, sensual smile.

Bryan let out a laugh. "Have you ever let your ferrets visit Kerris's cats?" He slid an arm around me as the conversation eased into a comfortable chat and we wound down from the day.

* * *

I was standing in the field near the lake. I recognized that I was dreaming—or rather, that I was out on the astral in my dreams. The field was open with no shrubs or trees except for the knee-length grass that whistled in the wind. As I stood there, my arms stretched to the moon that rode high in the night, the faint cawing of birds echoed through the air.

A murder of crows came winging in, landing around me. The vast flock settled, their blue-black feathers shimmering under the silver moonlight. They formed a circle, with me at the center. And then, I heard it. A slow processional filled the night, accompanied by violins and panpipes and the ever-present bodhrans beating the steady rhythm.

The Crow Man is coming.

I shivered, exposed and vulnerable in the Dream-Time. The ground around me quaked with his footsteps as the giant approached, clouds of blue fire swirling around him. An indigo cloak flared around him, the stars reflecting in its folds as he walked. A fur shawl encircled his shoulders, and atop his head rested a headdress—a giant crow's head with eyes that glowed red, and a piercing beak. His hair was long and black, falling to his shoulders, and his eyes were slits of white fire. In one hand, he carried a wand of silver, with a glowing crystal on top.

I slowly settled to the ground, overwhelmed as I always was by his presence. Each time, his power seemed to have grown stronger, perhaps because I was far more attuned to his Mistress than I had been the first time we met. Or perhaps he was just opening himself to me. Whatever the case, I just wanted to curl by his feet and stare at his beauty.

He did not speak, but held out his hands. As I looked into his palms, a mist began to rise, coiling like a serpent. It bade me to follow it, and I was flying through the night, the Crow Man by my side. He winked at me, but his smile vanished as we spun through the stars. Then, without a word, we landed again, by the shores of the lake. The Crow Man pointed to the waves and I gazed out over the dark surface of the water.

The winds rose as the flock of crows thundered overhead, shrieking their anger. I glanced back at the water and there she was. Rising from below the surface, a figure cloaked in pale white, dripping with water. She reminded me of a skeleton, clad in a layer of waxen skin. Her hair draped around her shoulders, long strands of seaweed and vines, and her skin was the color of gray mud. Through of hollow sockets, dark as the raging depths of the waters, she looked straight at us and began to laugh as she held out her arms.

"Come to me. I promise you peace of mind. You will find joy in my embrace, and all that you've ever longed for will be yours. Let me give you a taste of my magic." Her voice was as silken as smooth brandy, and my first instinct was to answer her call.

But the Crow Man clasped a hand on my shoulder. "Listen to her song, so you will recognize it when you hear it again. The words may not be there, but the call is always the same."

At that moment, a scream echoed through the clearing. *Peggin!*

I whirled, looking for her, but all I could see was the Lady, standing on the water, laughing as she held Peggin in her arms, unconscious. The water churned as the Lady began to slowly sink below the surface, dragging Peggin with her. I began to scream as I wrenched myself out of the Crow Man's grasp and raced forward. Overhead, the crows went winging by, screeching so loud their cries filled the night air, as the Lady and Peggin vanished from sight.

CHAPTER 2

~

The paw woke me up. It was furry, calico, and belonged to Daphne. All twenty pounds of her were perched directly on my shoulder, and I groaned, trying to roll over under her weight. As she reluctantly climbed off me, I struggled to sit up, blinking the nightmare away. A glance at the clock told me it was four A.M., and I reached over and flipped on the light. Bryan hadn't been able to stay—he had an early-morning meeting—so we had called it a night at the door.

I pushed myself back against the headboard and wiped my eyes. They were wet and I realized I'd been crying in my sleep. The next moment, the dream came flooding back and I panicked and grabbed my phone, about to call Peggin, but then I stopped myself. I was slowly learning which dreams were portents, which were reality, and which were just the messed-up carousel of my thoughts.

As I thought back over the components, I examined what my gut was trying to tell me. Fear, yes, and worry, but we had been talking about the Lady during our late-night dinner, so that could account for my dream.

You know I was there.

The voice echoed in the back of my mind. It was the Crow Man's voice, smooth and tempting, with that touch of danger behind it. He was a crafty one, a trickster, but he never lied. He might manipulate and play games, but he wasn't out for his own agenda. He was the messenger for the Morrígan. And I knew better than to ignore him.

I let out a slow breath as Daphne curled up on my lap. Ever since we had moved back to Whisper Hollow, Daphne had become my dream guardian. She woke me from nightmares, she kept an eye on the house. As I stroked her fur, smoothing the long hair that swirled in a medley of orange and black and white, she looked up at me and let out a soft mew. Gabby, in all her shining black glory, was snuggled with Agent H on the bottom of the bed.

"All right, pumpkin, I'll listen." I gave her one last pat on the butt and then, after settling down under the covers, I closed my eyes and tried to get back to sleep. I'd listen and watch, and do what I could to look out for Peggin.

So yes, I'm Kerris Fellwater. My father disappeared before I was born, and my mother went missing when I was three, so I had lived with my maternal grandparents. But my grandfather was an emotionally abusive son of a bitch. When I was eighteen, I left Whisper Hollow. My grandmother, a spirit shaman, had begged me to stay and learn what destiny had signed me up for—it was my duty to take over from Grandma Lila when it came time. But I couldn't stick around and subject myself to Duvall's emotional abuse.

Fifteen years—and what felt like a lifetime later—my grandparents were taken by the Lady. That was two months ago. I returned home to take up my grandmother's post, and promptly discovered that my mother hadn't abandoned me, but had been murdered. With Bryan's help, I tracked down her killer and took up as spirit shaman. I was still shaky in my training, but with Grandma Lila's journal, the help of Ellia—my lament singer—and the guidance of Bryan, who turned out to be my protector—I was learning. And I had the Crescent Moon Society to back me up, a secret society that tried to keep the spirits of Whisper Hollow at bay.

If you live in Whisper Hollow, you know the rules. And they are just that: *rules*. Not suggestions. Not guidelines. Oh, sure, you can break them if you want, but don't be surprised if you meet me as I escort you to Penelope's realm. Because breaking the rules in Whisper Hollow is quite often the last thing you'll ever do. There are only seven of them and they're easy to keep, but they cover most contingencies.

1. *If you hear someone call your name from the forest, don't answer.*
2. *Never interrupt Ellia when she's playing to the dead.*
3. *If you see the Girl in the Window, set your affairs in order.*
4. *Try not to end up in the hospital.*
5. *If the Crow Man summons you, follow him.*
6. *Remember: Sometimes the foul are actually fair.*
7. *And most important: Don't drive down by the lake at night.*

Keep to the rules and there's a good chance you'll make it through alive.

Whisper Hollow is on the northwest side of Lake Crescent, over on the Olympic Peninsula in western Washington. Not many people know we're here, because the town likes it that way. Across the highway from the junction, the Olympic National Park takes over. Ancient growth—so tall you can't see the top of the timber when you look up—comprises most of the forest, the trunks of the fir and cedar plush with dripping moss, lichen, and mushrooms. The park receives over one hundred forty inches of rain during the year, and in winter, snow usually blankets the peaks, especially up on Hurricane Ridge, where the winds rage at hurricane strength and bend the trees and vegetation into a permanent state of deformation.

Spirits run rampant on the peninsula. Not just ghosts, but odd creatures, strange beings, and dark shadows whom you really *do not* want to encounter. But with the Morrígan riding over my shoulder, and my friends and family by my side, I'm starting to learn what it really means to be a spirit shaman. It's in my blood. It's in my soul.

C ome morning, I dragged myself to the espresso machine. I lived in the home that I had grown up in, my grandparents' home. When the Lady killed them, they had left it to me. Actually, I say *grandparents* but the truth was, the man I had grown up thinking was my grandfather wasn't actually blood-related. In fact, my real grandfather—Aidan Corcoran—was also a shapeshifter. Unlike Bryan, Aidan's a lionshifter. In fact, he's the king of a clan. To say that my background was confusing is an understatement.

But I was slowly straightening things out, and I was happier than I had ever been. Whisper Hollow was my home, and I loved the house and felt safe within its walls.

I fired up the espresso machine, which I had nicknamed Fred. While the machine was heating up, I fed the cats, who were milling around my feet. Three giant Maine Coons versus me meant their breakfast was served up first.

"You aren't starving and you know it." I snorted, placing their dishes on the tray I kept for them. Gabby liked to pull food out of the dish with her paw and eat it off the floor, so the tray kept the floors from getting dirty. After they were set, I pulled four shots of espresso, added hazelnut creamer, and popped a couple of slices of bread in the toaster, then pared off a piece of cheddar and munched on it while waiting for the bread to toast.

The phone rang. I still had a landline—Grandma Lila had one and I hadn't bothered to disconnect it. When the power went out, it worked, and since the storms made that a regular occurrence, I figured I might as well keep it. I used my cell phone so much that I was always having to charge it, so it was nice to have an available dial tone when I needed it.

"Hello?" I was hoping it was Peggin, and I wasn't disappointed.

"You are talking to a woman who spent the night being thoroughly fucked." Her voice was luxurious, and she sounded more relaxed than I had heard her in a while.

"It sounds like the doctor has the cure for what ails you." I grinned. Peggin was a sensual woman. In fact, men gravitated to her like bees to a flower. She had an Aphrodite vibe to her and the kicker was, she was totally unaware of it. Oh, she knew when guys were hitting on her, but Peggin's sex appeal was as natural as her quirky style. And she had a heart of gold, even though she was nobody's doormat.

"I really didn't expect this, not when Bryan offered to fix us up. I'd seen D-D around town, but he's always kept to himself and he's never indicated that he was even remotely interested in hanging out. At least with people. He's obsessed with his art."

"That reminds me. Did he find Jokney?"

"No, but we've alerted the chief of police, and she's keeping an eye out. Anyway, you ready to meet me out at the house?" Her voice took on an edge, and once again I felt the wall of resistance go up.

Hoping that the place would be an absolute disaster so she'd decide to back away on her own, I cleared my throat. "Yeah, I'm ready. I'll meet you there. Ellia can't make it. When Bryan and I dropped her off, she reminded me that she has a formal tea today—the Matriarchs are meeting in

Port Townsend for tea and shopping. And Bryan's off at a business meeting this morning. So it's you, me, and Deev."

"Oh, D-D can't make it either. He stayed for half the night, then got up at two A.M. and took off for his studio. He's in the middle of some major creative explosion and it's better if he works than having him pace around for half the night."

Maybe this was a good time to try once more. "I know it's way soon to be thinking of moving in, but if you were staying at his house, he wouldn't have to leave in the—"

"Stop. Kerris, you know my answer to that. Don't even go there." But I could hear the faint smile behind her words. "Thank you for caring."

I decided to play my trump card. Taking a deep breath, I said, "I had a dream last night."

"What about?"

I opened my mouth, but then stopped. I was ready to tell her everything, about the Crow Man and the Lady dragging her under, but I couldn't get the words out of my mouth. They stuck in my throat, and though I wanted to speak, I couldn't force my lips to move. A cawing out the window alerted me and I glanced over to see a crow perched in one of the bushes by the house, staring in the kitchen window. So the Crow Man had shown me the dream, but he wasn't going to let me tell her about it. I let out a long sigh.

"Nothing . . . it was . . . nothing. I'll see you there. Text me the address and I'll meet you in about half an hour. I need to stop at Ivy's and pick up some things she found of my father's that she wants me to have. She has to leave by ten for the Matriarchs' tea." Ivy was my paternal grandmother, whom I hadn't met until I returned home to Whisper Hollow.

"Sounds like all the Matriarchs are gathering," Peggin said with a laugh. "All right, I'll be at the house by nine thirty. The Realtor will meet us there."

And with that, she was off. I finished my breakfast and picked up the wet food the cats hadn't eaten—a few nibbles left in the bowl. I set down their free-feed dry kibble, and rinsed out the dishes and put them in the dishwasher. Then, gathering my purse and coat, I gave one last glance around the kitchen.

"Bye, Grandma Lila." My grandmother's spirit hung around. Every now and then she appeared to me, but I always felt her near.

One of the cabinet doors opened gently, then closed. Her way of saying good-bye and be safe. With a soft smile, I headed out for Ivy's.

Ivy looked only slightly older than I was, though she had forty-two years on me. She was a shapeshifter—a wolf like my father, Avery, had been. It had hit her as hard as it hit me when we found out he had been murdered, but at least we were able to lay both Avery, her son, and Tamil, my mother, to rest together.

Ivy was waiting for me, her eyes crinkling into a smile as I entered her kitchen. It was just too odd to call someone "grandma" who looked only a little older than me, so we settled on just "Ivy" and she was good with that.

I gave her a quick hug. "Hey, Ivy. You look gorgeous!"

She was wearing a flowing tea dress that looked right out of another era, and had all the matching accessories—pale blue clutch, ivory afternoon gloves, and even a hat to match. She gave me a quick twirl and laughed.

"Every year, we have this tea shortly before the holidays. In time, you and Peggin will join us. But for now, it's restricted to the older . . . influential . . . women in the town, with one or two exceptions."

I wrinkled my nose. "Starlight?"

Starlight Williams was the leader of the Crescent Moon Society and was as close to a social rich bitch as I'd ever met. We clashed upon first meeting but had to work together, so we made an effort to maintain civility. That was about as far as we could manage.

"Yes, Starlight. She *does* deserve to be at the tea, regardless of what you think of her, child. But you two will have to figure out your own differences. For now, I think you're both making the effort to keep out of trouble." She slid on her gloves, then nodded to the counter. "The box is over there. Anything you don't want, bring back and I'll send them to Avery's father." She paused, then let out a long sigh. "I'm still getting used to thinking of my son as dead. All these years, I knew he was lost to me, but there's always that spark of hope. When the bones actually come home, there's no denying it, is there? And you, dear one, never even got to meet him. I think you would have been friends. You are his daughter, that much is for certain."

And with that, she slid on her coat, buttoning it against the chill fog that blanketed the morning, and headed for the door. I picked up the plastic tub, trying to peer through the sides. But my curiosity would have to wait. Ivy walked me to my car and kissed me on the cheek, then headed off for her tea. As I slid the box into the back hatch of my CR-V, I thought how odd it was to find family where you thought there was none, and to lose the family you had hoped to find.

The Foggy Downs subdivision was old, turn-of-the-twentieth-century old. Built with the highest hopes in mind, it had taken a nosedive from the beginning. Ten houses in a cul-de-sac, now eight of them were empty and had been for some time. I wasn't sure who lived in the two that were still occupied, but whoever they were, they didn't keep up their yards very well. Both houses—side by side—had overgrown lawns and a lot of dead brush around them. The windows were covered with heavy drapes, and the outer walls were weathered, with peeling paint.

The subdivision sat in a half circle with the lake to the back. A line of trees—about one hundred and fifty yards of forest—separated the back of the center lot from the water. Not enough for comfort. Not at all. The undergrowth was sparse—unusual for this area, and it looked like at one time, the subdivision had tried to turn the greenbelt into a park but it had long been abandoned.

Peggin was waiting for me. She was leaning against her car, parked in the driveway of the house at the very end of the cul-de-sac, which meant she was closest to the copse and, by default, to the lake. *Too close.* I eased into the driveway beside her, squinting through the trees at the silvery sheen of water. The morning was cloudy—overcast as usual—but the rain was holding off, though the temperatures were only in the mid-thirties. We could potentially see some snow by nightfall, though it probably wouldn't stick.

As I stepped out of my car, the house caught my attention and I found myself mesmerized by the sight of it. Like the others, it had the same abandoned air and weathered siding, but there was something about it, something that invited me in to say hello. I suddenly understood why Peggin liked it—it reminded me of a lost orphan, looking for a new mother.

But as I stood there, staring at the three-story Victorian, I became aware of a shiver snaking up my back. Whatever lingered here didn't want me to look too hard. A bevy of crows circled overhead, cawing loudly, and I glanced up at them, trying to read what they were saying.

"Are you sure you want to go inside?" I didn't intend that to be the first thing I said, but apparently my mouth was working on autopilot.

Peggin nodded. "I have to. I need to see what's in there. I don't know why, but this house calls out to me." She whirled on me, her arms crossed against the cold. "I know I should be frightened because of the proximity to the Lady, Kerris. *I know that.* But I can't help myself—I want to bring this house back to life. I can't explain it, but . . ."

I gave her a soft nod. "I do understand," I said, and truth

was, I did. I could smell the stench of loneliness wafting off
the old house. It was reaching out, trying to find someone
to heal whatever wounds it had garnered over the years.

"Are you *sure* you want to go in? We could just turn and
walk away. I know that you promised yourself you'd look
but . . . if you want to go, we will." I tried one last time.

Peggin looked back at the house, and a flash of indecision
washed over her face, but then she resolutely shook her head.
"No, let's go inside."

I bit my lip, but motioned for her to lead the way. As we
entered the gate cordoning off the yard, I thought I could
hear a *click* as it swung closed behind us, as though something had sealed the path we were on. I swung in behind her
and followed her to the porch.

The sidewalk was broken, with grass growing through
the cracks, but the porch still looked to be in fairly good
shape. There were no broken boards or rotted patches that
I could see. As we clambered up the front steps—there were
seven of them—we reached the wide veranda. The porch
was enclosed by a half rail running the length of the front
of the house.

I found my dread growing. I didn't want to go inside now,
or ever. The allure had seemed to vanish and all I could
think about was that I would rather be anywhere but here.
It was hard to force myself to keep from heading back to
my car.

"Who were the last owners?" I asked, more to hear some
noise than because I really wanted to know.

"I'm not sure, to be honest. The owner is selling it as is.
They didn't even bother with a security lock like most for-
sales have, my Realtor said. Apparently most of the local
kids are too frightened by how close it is to the lake to bother
coming around Foggy Downs."

She paused by the newel post that attached to the stair
rail, stamping her feet against the cold, then leaned against
the column and shook her hair out of her face.

"I want to tell you something, so you'll understand why I am so set on buying this house."

"I'm listening."

"Here's the deal. I like D-D. I like him a lot. I like him so much that I don't want to screw this up. I'm not sure what the future holds, Kerris, but for me, to be able to find somebody I click with? It doesn't happen very often. *Almost never.* I know you think guys are always checking me out and yeah, they are, but not the way I want. Most of them just want to sleep with me, or grab my boobs. They aren't interested in me as girlfriend material. Or even for a friendship."

I stared at her. "I never thought about that, to be honest."

"I don't know how or why, but I magnetize guys by their balls, not their hearts. But Dr. Divine . . . Kerris, when Bryan hooked us up, I expected either a total brush-off or the usual. But you remember what happened, right? He took me up to Hurricane Ridge for a winter picnic. We ended up making snowmen, having a snowball fight, making snow angels—which I don't mind telling you, look freaking strange when your date wears a top hat. And then, we had dinner and drinks in front of the fireplace in one of the cabins. It just got better from then on."

"I remember."

She had called me, ecstatic, but sounding frantic. *I'm not used to this, how the hell do I act?* she had asked me. I told her to just be herself. Apparently, it had worked on both their parts.

"He's eccentric as hell, but we can talk. He has a sense of humor that's hidden behind all those braids and goggles, and he makes me laugh. And all the weird gadgets and gear? That's who he is. It's not an affectation. I don't want to endanger that. Do you understand? It's too new, too soon to make any sudden moves. I'm afraid . . ."

And then, I did understand. "You're afraid that if you move in with him till you find a place, that something will go wrong."

She nodded. "I'm not ready to give up the fantasy yet. Reality sets in at two in the morning when you're puking your guts out from the flu. Or when you've got cramps so bad that you're cursing your goddamned uterus. We spend the night together a lot, yes, but I'm not ready for the blinders to entirely disappear."

I had a feeling that Dr. Divine had left his blinders on the doorstep, but I decided not to press the matter. I understood what she was saying, because even though he was my protector, bound to me by the goddess we both served, Bryan and I were still new enough that I had some of those same fears myself.

"I get it. Okay, I won't push you to stay with him. I'm sorry, I'll try to be supportive. I'm just . . . this area scares the fuck out of me."

She pressed her lips together. "Honestly? Me, too, but there are ways to counter the Lady. I'm looking into charms and wards. And I'm sure that between you and Ivy, you can help me do whatever is necessary. Now, come inside with me? My Realtor will be here soon."

"Lead the way." I wanted to be as supportive as I could.

Peggin inserted the key and unlocked the door. "Jack brought me the key this morning. He'll be along in about twenty minutes. He had to drop his kids off at preschool after he left the key at my house." She opened the door and a soft *hush* rushed out. Oh, it could have been my imagination, I suppose, but by now it didn't matter. Imagination or reality, I didn't like this house and I wasn't about to pretend I did.

We entered the foyer and she toggled the light switch, but nothing happened. "No power. I should have figured. Okay, at least it's daylight and we should be able to see."

"Thank gods for small favors." I wanted more than anything to tell her about my dream but I knew that the words wouldn't come, even if I tried again. For some reason the Morrígan and the Crow Man were keeping me silent. "I wish Bryan could have come with us."

"What do you expect to find? *Ghosts?*" She laughed.

"Who knows? Maybe. Maybe nothing. We know for sure what's living out in that lake."

She paused, then let out a long sigh. "As I said, I know what's out there. And I'm fully aware that there are ghosts here. I figure you'll be able to help me guide them on their way."

I reached out to see if I could sense any lingering ghosts that might be around. The house had a spooky feel anyway, given that it was old and abandoned, but even beneath the dirt and the cobwebs, I could tell we were being watched by spirits. In fact, I would have been surprised to find the place clear. This area had seen a lot of deaths. Whether any of them had happened in this house, I didn't know, but the spirits were awake and wandering.

The foyer was a long, narrow hall with doors on either side, and a staircase leading upstairs just beyond the door to the left. It reminded me of a lot of houses that were this age. Sure enough, when I opened the door to the right, the room was small—probably a parlor of some sort—and cramped. The ceilings were high, the windows cracked in several places, the hardwoods still in decent condition.

"Look," Peggin said, pointing to the fireplace. "I love the mantel."

I joined her. The mantel was gorgeous, I had to admit that. Carved from what looked like a single piece of wood, it was thick and chunky, and I wasn't certain just what kind of wood it was, but there was something about it that set it apart from the rest of the room.

"I have to admit, this is a beauty. And the fireplace looks like it probably still works, though you'll want an inspector in here to check it out. Probably needs a good cleaning." I rubbed my hand across the wood of the mantel, wiping away the layer of dust that had accumulated. Beneath the grime, the gleam of highly polished grain appeared. A spark rippled through my fingers, startling me. It wasn't static electricity, that much I knew.

"This room could be so beautiful." Peggin was looking out the window. "Can you imagine this space, clean and spruced up? Heavy velvet drapes . . . a fainting couch and a piano? This would make such a wonderful library!"

I could hear the wonder in her voice and knew that, unless we found something horrible, she was lost to the house. While I loved my grandparents' house, I hadn't become intensely attached, and I wondered if I ever would. I felt comfortable in my home, but given all the baggage I had from my childhood, there were times I still cringed.

We moved on to the room opposite the hall, which appeared to be some sort of office. Then, before going upstairs, we continued along the foyer. A powder room was tucked in beneath the stairs, then the hall opened into the kitchen, with a formal dining room off to the right. The dining room had wide bay windows overlooking the backyard with a prime view of the lake.

The kitchen was large, with an eat-in breakfast nook, though it needed a thorough updating. It looked like the last time anybody had done any upgrades was during the sixties, because the appliances were the pale pink of the fifties, the countertops were laminate, and the cupboards were painted a sage green enamel.

"Um, complete gut job. I know you like retro, but this . . ." I looked at the floor, which was a hideous black-and-white-checkerboard pattern. Well, it worked in Lindsey's Diner, but here, it just looked jarring against the rest of the pastel décor.

Peggin snorted. "You think? I agree. I like retro in my clothes, but with an updated edge. In my kitchen, I want stainless appliances, and either granite or quartz counters. And I prefer dark wood to this. But . . . the cabinets don't look in that bad of shape." She opened one of the cupboards, eyeing the hinges. "Strip the enamel, sand and stain . . . new hardware . . . it would take some time but I could do it myself. I'm handy. I could buy new appliances."

"You'd need an electrician to verify that the place is up to code. I'm betting on the need to rewire the whole place." I frowned. "Are you sure this would be worth it? I foresee a ton of renovations."

She shrugged. "Let's look upstairs. The cosmetic stuff can wait; I can tackle it as I go. The kitchen, wiring, and plumbing might need an immediate overhaul. I have enough in savings to manage that, I think."

"Make certain you want the place before plunging that much into it, especially on a rent-to-own basis. I'm just saying." But I had to admit, from what we had seen so far, there appeared to be no mold or water damage, and the bones of the house seemed fairly solid, at least from a cursory examination.

We headed up the stairs. They were narrow, but not terribly steep, and the banister and railing seemed secure enough. Other than the occasional squeak, the wood seemed to be solid beneath our feet. The stairwell made a turn to the right, and then we were in the hallway. Here, it was obvious somebody had renovated the design. It wasn't the typical layout for a house as old as this one. There were four rooms on this level. One of the doors led to a full bath, though it was on the small side. The other three were bedrooms—one of them a large master suite with a spacious bathroom, though it looked right out of the seventies. Another stairwell at the end of the hall led to the third floor.

I stared into the master bedroom. "Okay, this has to be a reno. Masters were never this large in these old houses. And very few master bedrooms had their own bathroom. My guess is that the master bath and bedroom were originally two smaller rooms. The design here looks to be circa 1975 . . ." I paused, staring at the heart-shaped tub. At least it was big.

She laughed. "Yeah, that tub is a little bit on the cheesy side, but it will work. I could live with it for a while. And if they updated the plumbing when they built this bathroom, maybe the renovations won't be so extensive." She walked back into the master bedroom. The window overlooked the backyard and the lake. "I admit, it's creepy . . . the view. I can almost see Fogwhistle Pier from here. But . . ."

"Peggin, are you sure you're interested in this place? I have to admit, there's a lot of potential here, but . . ." I stopped. It was no use. She was in love with the house and there was nothing I could say to make her change her mind. "I can tell by that look on your face that no matter what I say, you're going to buy this house. So will you at least let me do what I can in order to make it safer for you?"

She glanced around the room once more, then let out a slow laugh. "Yeah, I will. I promise. And I'll have you over here helping so you can keep an eye out for the spooks."

I glanced out the window. "There are two walking through your backyard right now." Even from here, I could see the bedraggled-looking ghosts wandering through the yard. Whether they were friend or foe, I wasn't sure, but one thing was certain: I'd find out, and find out as soon as I could.

Peggin's phone buzzed. "Jack's here. He's out front. Let's go downstairs and see what he has to say." And with that, we headed out of the bedroom, and into Peggin's future.

CHAPTER 3

⌒

"Jack, this is my best friend Kerris. Kerris, this is Jack Walters. He's from Walters Realty. We've known each other for a long time. And he's going to tell me what it will take for me to buy this house." She turned to him and gave him a wide smile. "I love the place, though I need a full inspection to see what I'm getting myself into here."

Jack, who looked like a fairly mild-mannered accountant type, chuckled. "I think you'll be pleased to find out that when I agreed to take on this property, I had a full inspection done. That was two months ago. I can show you the results and then, if you want another, we can proceed from there." He motioned toward the door. "Shall we go in? And do you have any questions to begin with?"

"How old is this house?" I decided that his invitation to ask questions extended to me as well. And even if it didn't, I was going to anyway.

"The house was built in 1920, by Herschel Dorsey. So the place is pushing ninety-plus years old. Over the years,

it's been renovated several times, the last being in 1976."
He paused, frowning. "I think I should tell you that there
have been twenty-three owners. And I don't know how many
renters."

I blinked. *Twenty-three people had owned the place?*
"What is this? Amityville?"

He shrugged, looking mildly uncomfortable. "I'm not certain what happened. I only have the list of owners and rebuilds
done on the house. I don't know why anybody left. I do know
that the original owner—Dorsey—died in a nasty accident
only a few years after he built the house. He was starting to
cut down a tree in the front yard—that old oak out there—and
something happened with the ax. It slipped, slicing into his
leg, and he bled out before anybody found him. You can still
see the gashes in the trunk, even though they've healed over."

Peggin glanced at me. "Maybe he's one of the ghosts you
saw wandering the property?"

"Could be."

Jack cleared his throat. "Even though there's no require-
ment that we disclose supernatural activity, my firm feels
that . . . well . . . this is . . ."

He looked so pained that I couldn't help myself, I started
to laugh.

"This is Whisper Hollow, right?" I grinned.

He tilted his head, scrutinizing me for a moment before
snorting. "Yeah, you got it. So yes, there's a history of supernatural activity here. I don't know exactly what kind, but there's
a notation that a few families who rented this place just up and
left. In fact, two of the families actually left a number of their
belongings behind, refusing to come pick them up. Most of that
stuff is stored in the attic and comes with the house."

He led us into the parlor. "The chimney is in need of
repair, but the fireplace works. It does need to be cleaned.
The windows are all original and I would recommend
replacing them with double-pane as soon as possible. That's
about it for this room."

The office received a pass, too. The powder room was the next stop.

"All plumbing was upgraded in the mid-seventies. I don't think anything has been touched since then, but the inspection showed that most of the pipes are still in decent condition. The house is on a septic system and you'll likely need a new one within the next two or three years. That can be quite an expense and the seller is considering that in the purchase price." He motioned to a closet door. "The water heater is in there. It will need replacing in about five years, I'd say. The furnace, which is in the basement, is actually fairly new. The old one died on the current owner, so he replaced it about three years ago."

"Well, that's something. The plumbing will be okay for now, and the furnace is fine." Peggin frowned. "How much will a new septic system run me?"

"Between ten to twenty thousand dollars, depending on what permits the city requires." He consulted his clipboard. "While we're at it, one other thing you can check off your to-do list is the wiring. It was upgraded about fifteen years ago and should still be good. The circuit box is still in good condition, according to the inspection that I had done."

I wasn't sure whether to cheer or sigh. That was one worry off her list and one less impediment toward buying the house. But at least she'd be safe from stray fires. "What about the roof? How's it holding up? And any water damage or mold noted?"

If Peggin was upset with me for asking questions, she wasn't showing it.

Jack consulted his clipboard again. "Roof has about ten years left on it. Needs a few patches but it's still good. The inspector found no sign of mold, which honestly surprised me and I'd have that test run again, just in case. No water damage found. Chances are that the place has asbestos but it wasn't uncovered during the inspection. It might come up during renovations or repairs, though."

As we entered the kitchen, Peggin pointed to the floor. "What's underneath the linoleum? Hardwoods, by any chance?"

"I don't know on that one. One thing I can tell you is that all the upstairs renovations were permitted. The records are there." He leaned against the counter. "So, do you think you might be interested?"

Peggin glanced at me, but I kept my mouth shut. After a moment, she nodded. "What's the asking price, and it would have to be rent-to-own, so what would that entail?"

Jack let out what seemed to me was a relieved sigh. "Asking price is seventy-five thousand, and that's negotiable, depending on the terms. Let's go back to my office and talk. Of course, you can rent it without the to-buy option, but if you want to make any substantial changes in the near future, you'll have to go the other route. Meet me in about twenty minutes?"

"Twenty minutes it is."

He walked us to the door, locking it behind us and pocketing the key. "I'll see you in a little while, then." And with that, Jack returned to his car and eased out of the driveway.

I glanced at the lot. There were plenty of creatures walking this land that weren't visible to the naked eye. But if Peggin had made up her mind, there wasn't much I could do, and given that the Crow Man wasn't allowing me to tell her about my dream, I figured that I might as well do what I could to help her.

"You want me to come with you?" I asked.

She frowned, then shook her head. "No, I'm just grateful that you're here. I think, given the repairs needed, if I can get them down to sixty thousand, that will be a good place for me to be. I've some savings, but that will have to go into fixing up the necessities."

"Let me know what happens. Meanwhile, I'm joining Bryan for coffee when his meeting's over, and I want to do some shopping. At some point this week, I'm going to buy a tree."

I hadn't celebrated much of anything while I'd been away

from Whisper Hollow, but the town valued its winter holidays. Christmas, Yule—Solstice—Hanukkah, Kwanzaa . . . they were celebrated town-wide, and the town turned into an extravaganza of lights and decorations starting the weekend after Thanksgiving. Whisper Hollow seemed to welcome the cheer.

"Oh, good. I'll call you later." She gave me a quick, tight hug, whispering, "Thanks again, for being here. Trust me, I'll be careful."

As we both pulled out of the driveway, a gust of wind hit hard, and beyond the house the lake churned. I stared at it silently, thinking that sometimes, careful wasn't good enough.

W hisper Hollow was a beautiful town, regardless of the dangers inherent within it. With a nouveau-Victorian feel to it, the town might as well have been the oldest living member of the community. While Whisper Hollow had its abandoned lots and houses, most of the town was well-kept and tidy. People took pride in their homes, in their businesses, in the community. Brick and stone comprised a good share of the buildings, and Whisper Hollow had a number of Painted Ladies. San Francisco might have its Postcard Row, but Whisper Hollow was a postcard unto itself.

While there were only about five thousand people in the town, it was compact and the downtown area was definitely centralized. The shops were as colorful as the houses. The Broom & Thistle Coffee Shop was the local coffee hangout. The Herb & Essence apothecary was run by a gothic-looking gentleman I knew only as Prague. The Harlequin Theatre served as both cinema and stage. All were beloved members of the community.

So was the Vintage Bookstore on Cedar Street, owned by Trevor Riversong, a member of one of the Salish tribes. Trevor was also a member of the Crescent Moon Society. He brought his tribal knowledge of the area to bear in our meetings.

A block over, and a few blocks further north on Main Street was the Whisper Hollow Town Square, a mini-mall, and the Crescent Moon Spa, a full-service day spa. Other little shops dotted the main drag, boutiques that catered to both specific interests and general browsing.

As I drove through the streets, looking for a parking spot, I spied one next to Beacon Park, on the corner of Third and Main. The park was across the street from a sports field, the community center, and the town pool.

Beacon Park had a gazebo and plenty of benches scattered around, as well as a playground area for children. In the center was a large tiered fountain. For eight months out of the year it ran, but from the beginning of November to the end of February, it sat silent, except for the period starting on the Winter Solstice until New Year's. Then, it sparkled with colored water spray, providing the temperatures cooperated. Towering firs and maples guarded the park, along with a couple of old oaks, and a giant cedar. Smaller bushes and ferns graced the park floor, but for the most part, the undergrowth was kept in check.

I eased into the spot and turned off the engine. Parking was cheap; I could park all day here for five dollars compared to cities like Seattle. As I fumbled in my purse for quarters to feed the meter, a tapping on my window jolted me out of my thoughts and I found myself staring at a fit, pulled-together-looking woman with skin the color of deep umber. Her short, spiky pompadour was bleached red. What always stood out to me, though, were her eyes. They were luminous, coffee brown like my own.

"Nadia!" I quickly found my quarters and then opened the door, stepping onto the sidewalk.

Nadia Freemont was near my own age, although you could never tell ages in this town, and she owned the Mossy Rock Steakhouse, the most upscale restaurant in Whisper Hollow. She was a genius with food and her meals were rumored to have sparked more than one romance in town.

Nadia was in the circle of friends Peggin and I had known in high school, and she, too, was part of the CMS. I had seen her a couple of times since returning to Whisper Hollow, but we hadn't had a chance to catch up yet.

Nadia gave me a quick hug. "I saw you parking there and couldn't resist. I don't have a lot of time, but wanted to clue you in on something." Her eyes twinkled and she winked at me. "Women have to stick together."

"What's up?" I pulled my coat tighter. The wind had picked up, and the temperature felt like it was dropping.

"That man of yours? Bryan Tierney? He's made a reservation for Sunday night and he asked me to make a special dessert. I'm not going to tell you what, but I have the feeling something's up, so make sure you let him surprise you. Don't make any other plans." She leaned against my car, shivering. "Damn, it's cold. I expect we may be in for a dusting of snow. Hurricane Ridge is getting massively dumped on."

I glanced at the sky. There was a faint whiff of ozone in the air—like right before a snowstorm or thunderstorm. "I can smell it. Whether it's snow or rain, I think the weather's going to hold nasty for a while."

"I think you're right. Anyway, I have to run. I just gave a talk over at the high school about what it's like to be a chef and own a restaurant. Career day, I gather. Now I'm headed to the steakhouse to make sure dinner prep is under way." She blew on her hands, then, briefcase in hand, headed toward her car, which was parked a couple of spots up the street from me.

I said good-bye and briskly headed the other way, toward the center of the downtown area.

Whisper Hollow was alive and bustling. Regardless of the small population, the town never seemed empty. It had its share of regular ghosts. I could sense and see them walking the streets. Most, I never bothered with. My grandma Lila had let them roam, as well. They weren't doing anybody any harm, and seemed content to meander through the town without upsetting anybody.

I ran over my shopping list in my mind. I wanted to find gifts for Bryan and Peggin, obviously, but also Aidan—my grandfather—Ivy, Ellia, Deev, and a few other people. It felt good to have friends again. When I had been living in Seattle, managing a coffee shop, I had acquaintances, but never anybody to really hang out with.

And I had rarely dated. Once guys found out that I could speak to their dead mothers and girlfriends and find out just what kind of people they really were, they seldom asked me out again. Or they just wanted an easy lay, and the fact that I wore an F-cup bra never failed to bring in a certain group of fetishists as well.

That reminded me, I needed new bras. Big boobs meant a lot of wear and tear on the support system, and I went through bras every six months, even though I treated them with loving care. I was passing Elsa's Lingerie & Lux Shop, so I dropped in for my first stop of the day.

Elsa was in her eighties, but she was also still as pulled together as she had probably been every day of her life. She never went anywhere without her coral lipstick, her gloves, and her Dior handbag.

"Kerris, how are you?"

I smiled and leaned on the counter. "I need new bras, Miss Elsa. Did you get in the brand that I like?"

"Right here—Elomi, 38F. Are these the styles you wanted?" She showed me two different choices, and I bought two of each.

Purchase in hand, I gave her a little wave and headed for my next stop. Peggin's gift was easy. I knew she had been eyeing a new dress, but had bemoaned the cost. She wouldn't be able to buy it now, not if she was going to buy the house, and I also knew what shoes she wanted to go with it. The vintage shop where she had found it also carried new retro designs. The dress had a flared skirt, fitted bodice, and was printed with a gothic floral design in plum and black. The shoes were chunky heels, also a plum color to match. I asked the clerk to box up both and, shopping bags in tow, headed for the coffee shop. Bryan should be there by now.

The Broom & Thistle was one block over from the vintage clothing shop, on Third and Cedar. I pushed through the doors just as another bone-chilling gust of wind swept past. Shivering, I glanced around the shop, hoping to see Bryan. He was there and he jumped up when he saw me, hurrying to take my bags.

"What do you want? Sit down and get warm while I order your drink." He pressed his lips against mine while maneuvering me back to the table.

"Triple-shot hot mocha, heavy on the chocolate and whipped cream. And a slice of cherry cake, too." I hustled into the chair, taking the bags back from him to set by the wall. We were next to a window, but the shop was well insulated. Even so, I could still feel a slight chill radiating through the glass. This winter was going to be a cold one.

As I waited for Bryan to return, I saw Nelly bussing tables. The Broom & Thistle was owned by the Brannons—Nelly was also a lounge singer and took part in the local theatrical group, and Michael was an excellent swordsman, as well as a member of the Crescent Moon Society. Michael was Irish through and through, and Nelly also had Irish roots.

Whisper Hollow was steeped in three ethnicities—Irish, Russian, and Native American. And the three backgrounds jostled with each other to attempt to create a comfortable mix of heritages.

Bryan returned, drink and cake in hand. "For you."

I cupped the mocha with my hands, grateful to feel the heat radiating off of it. "I'm so cold. It's icy as hell out there and blowing a good one."

"So, did you go with Peggin this morning?"

I let out a long sigh. "Yes, I did. And I don't like the place at all. She's going to buy it, though, and I guess . . . I understand why. I quit fighting her about it, because once she's gotten an idea into her head, she's not going to let go. The best we can do now is make it as safe as possible, but there are spirits walking that house, Bryan. And I don't think all of them want to be there. And the lake . . . it's too close. The Lady's out there and hungry. She's riled up this winter, and I'm not certain if it's because of . . ." I paused.

"Magda?" Bryan's tone dipped. He held my gaze.

I hung my head, not wanting to talk about her, but then nodded. "Yeah, Magda."

Magda Volkov was Ellia and Penelope's mother. The woman was well over 115 years old, but she was going strong. Back in Russia, Magda had been a foe of the дух мастер, the spirit masters who worshiped the goddess Morena. Basically, it was the same idea as the spirit shamans and Morrígan. Magda had been a dedicated witch in the service of Baba Volkov— Mother Wolf Witch, a forest crone–goddess powerful in the ways of shadow magic and necromancy.

Even though they had immigrated to the United States, Magda had wanted her daughters to follow in her ways, but both had repudiated the sinister magic and so Magda had killed Penelope and had cursed Ellia, effectively writing off both daughters. Penelope had become the Gatekeeper, and Ellia—a prodigy from birth—had been called into service by the Morrígan as my grandmother's lament singer.

Magda had retreated to the woods of Whisper Hollow, and had integrated herself into Cú Chulainn's Hounds, the mortal enemies of the Morrígan and her servants. Now, the Hounds and Magda were railing against the town, for control and dominance, and it was up to the Crescent Moon Society and me to stop them from succeeding.

"I don't know if Magda's behind the Lady being so hungry, but I wouldn't put it past her to stir up things. As it is, I need to talk to Veronica. I've put it off as long as I could, but I need to curry her favor. There are too many spirits walking, too many of the Unliving going rogue."

"When do you plan on doing this?" He frowned. "You

aren't going anywhere near her without Ellia and me in tow. We're a team, remember?"

I smiled softly. It felt good to have protection, and even though Bryan couldn't guard against everything that came at me, it helped bolster me up knowing that he was ready and able to follow me into the darkest shadows if need be. Even if we hadn't been pulled together as lovers, he would have made an incredible friend.

"I remember, and I promise. I'll talk to Penelope. In fact, maybe I'll stop by her tomb this afternoon. Even if she doesn't show herself during the day, she'll know I'm there and she'll hear me." I leaned back, basking in the warmth that blasted through the heating ducts. "You know, it feels like a lifetime ago that I returned to Whisper Hollow, yet it's only been a couple of months. How does that happen? My life in Seattle seems like a long dream that I just woke up from."

"You knew you had to return. Somewhere in your heart, you knew that it was your destiny, and so you were just marking time there." Bryan leaned across the table to take my hands in his. His skin was warm and protective, and he brought my fingers up to his lips and kissed them gently. "I'm so glad you came home. I didn't realize how lonely I've gotten over the years." He paused, then added, "My daughter's coming to town after the first of the year. Do you mind that she'll be here?"

That was enough to wake me out of my lazy haze. "Juliana's going to be in town?"

Bryan had been married once, back in 1950, by order of his pack. Arranged marriages were common among shifters, especially in wolf clans. Though Bryan and Katrina weren't a good match, they had a daughter together. Katrina had died in childbirth. Juliana lived in Boston. In her sixties, she looked mid-twenties. Shapeshifters aged far more slowly than humans. I had spoken with Juliana on the phone a couple of times, but never for any length, and I wondered if she would resent me.

I must have looked askance, because Bryan laughed and kissed my fingers again. "It will be fine. Don't worry yourself over it. Juliana's glad that I found you, and she accepts my role under the Morrígan as any good Tierney daughter should. She knows what our family's duty is, and she honors that duty. She'll never be called to serve, given she's a female shapeshifter, but one day she may bear a son promised to be a protector. And I would be proud if she is chosen to be one of the Sacred Mothers."

I had never heard that term before. "Sacred Mothers?"

"Any woman who bears a child destined to be a shapeshifter guardian, a spirit shaman, or one of the lament singers is considered one of the Sacred Mothers. All spirit shamans, if they have children, are Sacred Mothers."

"Then my mother and grandmother and great-grandmother . . ."

"Yes, they were part of the honored ones." He smiled gently, and then said something that I had not been expecting to hear. "When we have a child, if it is a daughter, you will join them."

I blinked. I had barely gotten used to being in a relationship, let alone thought of having children. But before I could say a word, he shook his head.

"No, don't even say it. We'll talk more about it later. We have plenty of time. So what do you want to do the rest of the day?"

"I have more shopping to do, and then I'm going to stop at Penelope's tomb on the way home. By then . . ." My phone rang and I glanced at the caller ID. Peggin. "Speak of the devil. Hold on one second."

As I answered, Bryan cleared our table and shrugged into his jacket.

"Peggin? How did it go?"

"I'm a homeowner!" She sounded so excited that I couldn't help but smile, even though I was cringing inside.

"We've worked out an arrangement. Contingent on another

inspection, I'm getting the place for fifty-five thousand. They're anxious to unload it and with needing a new septic system and the other repairs, the owner caved at our first offer. I'll be paying them five hundred a month, with three thousand for the option fee—that will go toward the purchase price after a year. Three hundred of the rent each month will be put toward house payments. After a year, they'll raise that to four hundred. Of course, if I change my mind, none of that's considered equity, not until I've paid ten thousand total. In a year, I might qualify for a loan to pay it off, given I'll have put some money into the house and been there awhile."

I congratulated her. "So, when's moving day?"

"I was hoping you could help me on Saturday? I might as well get myself situated in there and start cleaning up the inside. My landlord has offered to let me out of this month's rent if I find a place soon enough." She sounded excited, so I decided to just roll with it.

"Of course I can help. Hold on." I muted the phone and motioned to Bryan. "Can you help Peggin and me this weekend? We're moving her into the house." I must have looked horribly grumpy because he stifled a groan.

"I'll be there. What do you think she wants as a house-warming present?"

"A new house."

"Something more practical."

I thought for a moment. "Well, she needs someone to repair the chimney and sweep it out."

"You got it."

I conveyed the information to Peggin. "Bryan says find someone to fix and clean the chimney as his housewarming gift."

She let out a loud squeak. "Tell him I adore him. I'll call around today. Are you going to the concert in the park tonight?"

"We were planning on it." I grinned. Everybody in town would end up at the concert. That was just a given.

"Then I'll see you there." And with that, she hung up.

I stared at my phone. "Well, it's a done deal. She's taking the house." I wanted to tell Bryan my dream, but once again, my lips wouldn't move and the words were frozen in my throat. So, instead, I said, "I want you to do me a favor. When we move Peggin into the house, pay attention to what you feel. There are things the Morrígan won't let me talk about—literally. I need to make certain that . . ." Once again, the words wouldn't come.

"I think I understand. All right. I have to get back to work. But I'll call you in a while. Dinner tonight at my house before the concert? I'll grill some steaks. You can bring dessert." He waggled his eyebrows and I let out a snort, the tension easing back.

"Oh, I'll bring dessert all right. And maybe something a little sweet as well as spicy." With a laugh, I leaned across the table to catch his lips with mine, easing into the kiss. He let out a soft "Mmm" and I wanted to climb over the table right then and there, but restrained myself. A moment later, I softly pulled away. "I'll see you later. All of you." And, pursing my lips, I blew him another kiss, then gathered my bags and braced myself for the chill of the outdoors.

Ninety minutes later, I had finished half of my shopping and was trudging back to my car, laden down with bags and boxes. As I reached the park and was stowing my purchases in the trunk, I heard a sound that was suspiciously familiar. I glanced over at one of the trees near the edge of Beacon Park. The old cedar soared into the air, so tall and wide that it could shelter the entire circle of benches that ran beneath the overhanging branches.

The trunk of the cedar was ringed by ferns, waist high, behind the benches. Something was scuttling from within the fronds. I could see the faint movement as they wavered, even though they were sheltered from the wind by the massive boughs.

I slammed the trunk shut and then slowly crossed the

sidewalk to the park, heading across the sodden grass toward the tree. "Who's hiding in there? I hear you. Come out."

No answer, but another shuffle in the undergrowth told me they had heard me.

"Come on, answer me. I'm Kerris Fellwater, the spirit shaman, and I know you're there." I kept my voice light but firm, and pushed a little magic behind it.

A moment later, the fronds on one of the larger ferns parted, opening to reveal an odd, misshapen face peering out. The creature was the color of sage, and about two feet tall, bipedal with long spindly arms and legs. Its head was flattened, its face lumpy with what looked like odd knots. Warts, maybe, but I wasn't betting on it. The creature's ears, though, were long and pointed, overhanging its head, and the eyes flickered with a pale lemon-colored light. *One of the forest Fae.* It had to be.

Nature spirits were part and parcel to the area—to all wild areas, actually—but I hadn't noticed them much till my return home. Then I began to remember that as a child I saw them, all around. Even into my teens, I had known they were there, though they were harder to see when my hormones hit and puberty kicked in. But now, the ability was coming back.

I was about two yards away from the creature when I stopped, not wanting to spook it. Kneeling down, I balanced myself by holding on to one of the benches. The creature winced and I realized that it recognized I was touching iron—the Fae hated wrought and cast iron, though they could and did touch silver and gold, and sometimes steel.

"Are you all right?" I got the sense that something was wrong. Forest Fae often wandered through the town, but they seldom brought themselves to our attention. They could so easily camouflage against the trees and bushes that most people never realized they were looking directly at them.

The creature crept closer, keeping a close eye on the bench as though it were an enemy ready to strike. After a moment, it was about a foot away from me.

It leaned forward and, in a tinny voice that was so faint it was hard to hear, it said, "The Forest Lord bade me come. Spirit Shaman, help is needed. The Screaming Tree has woken up but the Crone silenced its warnings. The Ankou are gathering in the forest. The Crone seeks to send them into the town."

I stared at the Fae. The Screaming Tree had not been awake in decades. Even during Grandma Lila's time, she told me the Screaming Tree had remained silent. It was a portent, which meant there was something deadly roaming the woods that even the natural spirits who lived there couldn't take care of. And if the Ankou were gathering, that could only mean danger for everyone who lived in Whisper Hollow.

"I'll come. I'll gather my people and we'll come." I stood, staring at the creature.

It—he, I suddenly had the feeling—nodded. "Do not tarry or the danger will be too great." And with that, he crept back toward the tree and vanished in the undergrowth.

I glanced up at the sky. The silver sheen of clouds took on an ominous cast, and my mood quickly slid south. Between worrying about Peggin, and now this, the jolly-holly holiday season was seeming anything but a joyful time.

CHAPTER 4

Before I went home, I stopped by the cemetery. It was only a few minutes' walk from my house, fewer by car. As I parked in the spot closest to Penelope's tomb, I saw another car nearby. I scanned the graveyard. Over by an empty spot beneath one of the towering trees, I spotted Jonah Westwood. He was kneeling on the ground, examining a patch of grass.

The current undertaker for Whisper Hollow, Jonah had taken over from his uncle. He made me nervous and I didn't know why. Perhaps it was that he always wore a solid black suit and what looked like a squat top hat. Or perhaps it was the way his cheeks were so gaunt that it made me think he was halfway to the grave himself.

And I knew for certain that Jonah had odd talents that didn't always sit well with the inhabitants of the town. For one thing, it was well-known that he liked to photograph the dead before they went to their graves. He said it was just tradition, like they had done years before. I personally thought it was ghoulish, but since he *did* ask permission from the families, there was nothing I could do about it.

I wondered if I could get away with ignoring him, but when he saw me getting out of my car in the graveled parking spot, he stood and headed my way.

Damn it. I really didn't want to talk to him.

"Kerris! How nice to see you." He doffed his hat, inclining his head as he walked toward me. "What are you doing out here on such a blustery day?"

I jammed my hands in my pockets so I wouldn't have to shake hands. "I have to talk to Penelope. I need to leave her a message."

His eyes lit up, and I realized that the prospect intrigued him rather than repelled him like it did most people. "I would love to meet the *mistress of the graves*. In my line of work, it seems like it would be a wise idea to know who's waiting on the other side for my clients."

There was just something creepy about him. "Well, Penelope asks who she will to enter her tomb. I suppose if she ever wants to talk to you, you'll get a message from her. Trust me, you'll know." I was hoping to stave off any requests from him. I could just see him asking to go with me, and that was the last thing I needed.

"Ah, well. Can't blame me for being interested. After all, death is my arena." Again the creepy vibe emanated off him like a bad case of BO. He glanced up at the trees. The boughs were whipping in the wind and once again the scent of snow filled the air. "We're up for some nasty weather, aren't we?"

I chafed, wanting to get away. "And it's only supposed to get worse. If you'll excuse me, I'd like to take care of my business and get home before the rain starts to pour again." I edged away, hoping he would take the hint.

After a moment he doffed his hat again. "Well, then, I bid you adieu for the day. Until we meet again, Ms. Fellwater." And with that, he turned and ambled back toward his car.

I wondered what he had been doing out here, but decided that I didn't really want to know. I waited until he drove off before turning back to Penelope's tomb. I had no desire to be locked in a mausoleum with him outside the doors.

Hunching my shoulders against the wind, I crossed the grass to the tomb.

The doors were shut and, being daylight, it would do no good to sound the knocker. There was, in a recessed cubbyhole against the side, a little knocker with which I could summon the Gatekeeper. When I was out here escorting souls to Penelope, I didn't need to use it. She knew when Ellia and I were up to our game. But when I needed to consult her about other things, if the sun had set I would knock on her grave and she would usually come out. During the day, I had to resort to other methods.

I gripped the great handles on the door. Closing my eyes, I whispered her name. "Penelope, I've come to talk to you. Open the door."

The double doors slowly swung open, and I let go of the handles. As I entered the tomb, a muffled silence overwhelmed me. Penelope was nowhere in sight, but I knew she was in her sarcophagus. I wasn't sure whether it was her choice to remain there or whether she was bound there till nightfall like the vampires of legend, but either way, it didn't matter.

I walked over and placed my hands on the stone lid, leaning down so that my mouth was close to the embellished stone. "Penelope, I need to talk to you. I need an audience with Veronica as soon as possible. Please, set one up and let me know when she will see me. Until then, peace."

And that was it. Penelope would hear me when she woke for the day. As I exited the tomb, the doors slammed behind me with a great thud. I headed back to the car as the clouds broke open, a shower of hail thundering down. The pea-sized pellets whipped against my hands and face, catching in my hair and clinging to my jacket. The ice stung as it hit my skin and I broke into a run, trying not to slip as the hail covered the grass with a coat of white.

"Snow would be better than this," I grumbled, fumbling for my keys. As I sat in my car, catching my breath, I once again looked over at the grassy plot that Jonah had been staring at. There was nothing remarkable about it. I supposed undertakers liked to hang out in cemeteries. Either that, or he was communing with the grass, looking for a new spot to plant somebody who had died. Either way, I was relieved to be away from him. I started the ignition and eased out of the cemetery, glad to be headed home.

By the time I got all my bags and the tub of my father's things into the house, I was thoroughly chilled and hungry. As I slid out of my coat, Gabby began rubbing around my legs and sniffing my jeans.

"Yes, I'm home. What have you been doing with yourself? Have you and your brother and sister been good babies?" I turned on the flame beneath the teakettle, then popped a couple of pieces of bread into the toaster. I glanced through the refrigerator, trying to find something quick and easy to eat with my toast. Finally, I opened a can of soup, poured it into a large mug, added a little water, and put it in the microwave. By then my toast was ready, and I buttered it and set it on the table. I poured the steaming water into the teapot and added raspberry tea bags, and carried that over to the table. Finally, my soup was ready, and I settled myself in a chair to eat, and poured a cup of tea.

I thought about the Fae creature. While the meeting was fresh in my mind, I called Ivy and left a message that I needed to talk to her, Ellia, and Oriel—they would be gone all day at the Matriarchs' tea. Then I went back to my lunch as the storm railed outside.

By the time I finished eating, I had finally warmed up enough to stop shivering. I carried my dishes to the sink, then turned back to stare at the tub of my father's effects. I wasn't sure what I was going to find in there, and I wasn't even sure how I felt about opening it. So much had happened in the past couple of months to change the way I felt about him.

I had gone from secretly hating him because I believed he abandoned my mother and me, to mourning the fact that he had been murdered. The shift was abrupt and difficult, leaving me with a massive dose of guilt about ever doubting him in the first place.

I approached the tub cautiously, circling the table. I knew that Ivy wouldn't give me anything to distress me, but I still felt like I was entering alien territory. Finally, I reached out and removed the cover. As I edged my way over to peek inside, I felt someone watching me. I turned around, and there, in my kitchen, was a glowing white wolf. Bryan was also a white wolf, but he was actually alive. This was a spirit—the spirit of my father.

"Avery, I didn't expect to see you." In fact I had seen him once, when he led us to the remains of my mother and himself. Since then, he hadn't been around. Or if he had, I wasn't aware of it.

He stared at me, his glowing eyes soft and warm like caramel. I felt invisible arms wrap around me in a gentle embrace, and I wanted to lean in and rest my head on whoever's shoulder was there. The embrace was protective and caring, and I realized that I was sensing Avery's spirit in more ways than one.

"Avery, I wish I could've known you. I wish you could have survived. My mother loved you so much. I'm sorry for what Duvall did to the both of you."

I realized then that I was crying, a trickle of tears tracing down my cheek. I eased into the chair next to the tub, and leaned my elbows on the table. I hadn't really cried for my parents since we found out what happened to them. But now, it was as if my feelings were a wall of water, and the dam couldn't hold them, crumbling as they lashed themselves against it. I rested my arms on the table and leaned my head against them, letting the tears come, feeling the wave of loneliness, fear, and abandonment from my childhood wash over me again.

The soft pressure of hands rubbed against my back, soothing me until my tears began ebb, and I glanced up to see my mother standing there, smiling at me. She vanished, fading gently, and I pushed myself back in my chair and wiped my eyes with my sleeve. I sniffled, and reached for a tissue from the sideboard, blowing my nose. It'd been a long time since I had faced those feelings and let them come, and now I felt like a weight had been lifted off my shoulders.

I glanced over at the wolf, who still stood there. "Thank you. I think I needed that. I hope you don't hold it against me—that I thought you ran away and left me and Tamil. I didn't want it to be true, that's why I used to pretend that you had run off and joined a secret government organization and that you would come back for me one day when you were allowed. I'm sorry that I never got to meet you in life, but at least I know that you didn't run away. That you would never have run away."

The wolf gave me a nod and settled down on his haunches to watch. At that moment, Agent H meandered over and stared at the spirit. Then, with an audible sigh, the cat turned and wandered away. That made me laugh. I finally returned to the tub and began taking things out.

There were the requisite pictures—a laughing young man dressed in jeans and a flannel shirt. In one he was standing by a pickup truck that I recognized from Ivy's driveway. In another he and my mother were snuggling on a porch swing. I set the pictures aside. The tub also contained a couple of medals and trophies. Apparently Avery had been extremely good at chess, so much so that he had won several statewide matches. Ivy had also included a few of his favorite books, and a few assorted trinkets from his room. In a shoebox, she had bubble wrapped a wood carving. It was of a wolf, carved from cedar. It still smelled of the wood, and as I ran my hand over the smooth and polished surface, I realized that Avery had made this. It had his energy all over it, in every stroke, in every chiseled feature.

"It's beautiful. You did such beautiful work." I skirted the wolf spirit to place the carving on the kitchen windowsill where I could see it every time I walked by. I returned to the tub and put everything else back inside until I could take care of it, then replaced the lid and set the tub aside. As I turned, the wolf spirit bobbed his head again and vanished.

That night, I dressed for warmth—given the concert we were going to was outside—fed the cats, and headed over to Bryan's. Bryan was my next-door neighbor, as well as being my guardian and my lover. His estate was large; the brick building could easily have been called a small mansion. When I was growing up the building was empty, but Bryan had moved in during the time I was gone. He had made friends with Grandma Lila, and while he had never told her, he was actually waiting for me to return.

The Morrígan had come to him when he was in Ireland, to tell him that he was to be the guardian of the spirit shaman in Whisper Hollow. From that moment on, every move he made was with the expectation of one day guarding the person who turned out to be me.

When I first returned Whisper Hollow, the backyard had been overgrown—unusual for my grandmother to allow to happen. Over the past month I had taken the gardens in hand, pruning them back and weeding them, culling out the dead plants until they were in check, and now the garden waited for spring to arrive again. The stone fence dividing Bryan's property from my own was falling apart in some areas, and a stone gate at the far front corner of the backyard provided access between the two yards. I left the patio light on as I trudged along the trail that we had created from my back door to the gate.

Bryan's house stood three stories tall, reminding me more of a school than a house, although I knew it had been built around one hundred years ago by a business mogul who had wanted to get away from the big city. While I had never been inside before I returned home to Whisper Hollow, by now I knew the layout well. The house had a basement with a wine cellar and a workout room. The basement also had a second kitchen, which had originally been for the servants. Three other rooms had been bedrooms, but Bryan had opened them all up into one great entertainment space.

The main floor with a chef's kitchen, formal dining room, a living room, and two parlors, as well as a bath served most of his needs. He had turned one of the parlors into an office, and the other into a secondary office and library.

It'd taken me a while to find out what Bryan did; at first he had said he owned a couple of international businesses, and that was true. But as to what they actually were, he had been more reticent. It had taken me a few weeks to discover that Bryan didn't actually *need* to work. His family had come into a great deal of wealth through the years, and he was due to inherit it at some point in his life. But he liked working, and so he had set up an antiquities business—which basically meant he hunted down rare objects that people wanted on commission. And he also owned a travel agency, where he booked tours of the United Kingdom, especially Ireland. He didn't head them up himself, but oversaw the agency. He had also made a fair amount in the stock market.

The second story of Bryan's house contained two full master suites, a morning room, and what had once been a nursery. And the third story, smaller than the other two, contained two bedrooms and an attic. Sometimes I wondered what he did with so much space, and whether or not it got on his nerves to wander around such a huge place that was empty except for him and the day maid. He told me he had thought of hiring a cook on several occasions, but he didn't feel comfortable having much staff around when it was only him.

The grounds of the estate were beautiful, with flower gardens and a topiary, and several fruit trees that were scattered among the fir and cedar. He *did* hire a groundskeeper, who came in twice a week to keep up with the two acres on which the estate sat.

The walkway up to the house from my gate was paved stone, and I moved at a quick pace. While the hail had stopped shortly after it began, the weather was nippier, and the clouds had socked in. As I dashed up to the front door, I was relieved to see that Bryan was home.

He answered, drawing me inside and taking my coat. "How was your day, love?"

But before I could answer, he wrapped me in his arms and pulled me in for a kiss. His lips were soft and I grew short of breath as his hands found their way beneath the sweater I was wearing. I pressed against him, wanting the kiss to go on and on. A moment later and he was pushing my coat off, lips still locked to mine. I could feel his heat rising and it sparked off my own need. He tossed my jacket on the nearest chair as I took hold of his shoulders, walking him back toward the sofa.

I was working at his belt buckle, trying desperately to free his belt, when both my phone and his set to jangling.

"Damn it," I whispered. "Ignore?" Then I stopped. What if it was Peggin? What if she'd gone out to the house and—"Crap." I pulled away and whipped my phone out of the pocket of my jeans. Bryan let out a little groan, but answered his, as well.

"Kerris? Peggin. D-D wants to ask a favor. Jokney's been spotted near your house. Can you go out and take a look? We'll be up that way in a few minutes. D-D's calling Bryan right now."

I repressed a sigh. "Bryan's right here. Where was Jokney last seen?"

"Out on Rainshadow Street, and he turned onto Blackberry Lane." She paused. "Oh no, we didn't interrupt . . ."

"Yes, you did but luckily we're still dressed. Heading out to find the critter now. We'll see you in a bit." I slid my phone back into my pants, glancing at Bryan with a rueful grin. "We can't just say no."

"Yes, we can and we should. But it's too late now. Come on, get your coat. I'm going to take a moment to . . . calm down." He pointed toward the front of his jeans, where I saw a remarkably happy bulge.

I laughed. "The cold will calm you right down, if you unzip your fly."

"No thanks, Cruella." But he snickered when he said it and, adjusting his belt, he grabbed his own jacket, which was near mine.

We headed out the front door, and Bryan motioned to his car. "It's too cold to be running around without a car. And too wet."   •

I slid into the passenger seat as he started up the engine, then eased the car down the driveway. I had a CR-V. Bryan had a tricked-out Jaguar, along with two other vehicles that were more practical, including an SUV. Tonight, he'd pointed to the sedan—an ultrasonic blue GS F Lexus. As we swung a left on Blackberry Lane, which bordered the front of both his property and mine, he turned the high beams on so we'd have a better chance of spotting Jokney if he was still in our area. A few seconds later, we were at the turn onto Bramble-wood Way, which led to the cemetery to the left, and toward town to the right. On the other side of the street was Bramble-wood Thicket, a thick and sometimes dangerous copse, and a little farther along, my grandmother Ivy's house.

I leaned forward, squinting to see if I could spot any sign of Jokney. The sculpture was clockwork—all gears and cogs and leather and fake fur and dials, but it looked like a tall metal dog, and it had gotten out before. Dr. Divine called Jokney a *he*—insisting the creature was male—but really, it was an odd mixture of gears and magic. I wasn't sure what kind of magic Deev had within him. Sometimes, his creations came to life—and not always the ones that you kind of wanted to see thrive. But Jokney was cute, and friendly, and all he wanted was a little TLC, even though Deev thought the world of him.

As a gust of wind rattled the trees, Bryan swerved onto the shoulder of the road. "There!"

"Where?" I scanned the area, then saw what he was pointing to. In a strip of grass in front of the thicket was the gleam of metal, and as the car lights hit it, they illuminated the shape of a dog, in skeletal steel form.

"Jokney. I swear, Deev needs to slap a leash on that thing when he gets here and keep it caged up." I eased my door open. "Let me try. Jokney's come to me before."

"Only when you weren't chasing him. Somehow, I have a feeling the taste of freedom's gone to his little metal skull." Bryan snorted, then quietly opened his door, flipping on the hazard lights to let people know we were there and stopped. There wasn't much traffic in Whisper Hollow, but given it was dark and stormy, and the road was slick, it paid to be cautious.

We slowly ambled across the street, acting like we weren't up to anything. Jokney paused—he had been "sniffing" a fern and now he turned, raised his leg, and aimed. Nothing came out, of course, but nobody could say he didn't give it the old college try.

"I think Deev puts too much of himself into his art," I mumbled, watching.

"His magic runs deep. I doubt if he even understands how it happens, but he has elemental energy. He's a creator in the truest sense of the word. He builds something, and the magic he subconsciously weaves into it brings it to life. I wonder how long he's had this talent." Bryan circled to the left of Jokney as I circled to the right.

"I don't know. I doubt even he knows. He seems to have no clue of his past prior to arriving in Whisper Hollow. He told Peggin that he rode in on the wind, on a stormy day, and opened his eyes and boom, here he was."

Sometimes, people who came to Whisper Hollow blended in so well that their former lives seemed like a dream. With Deev, I had a feeling it went even deeper. Whisper Hollow was the Bermuda Triangle of the Northwest. Some people could pass through without blinking and never remember they had ever been here. And others—others came to stay, even if they didn't realize it when they first arrived.

"Jokney! Oh, Jokney? Come here boy, come here." I whistled to the mechanical dog, snapping my fingers and leaning over. It wasn't like he was a robot, but he could still hear and understand me.

Jokney cocked his head, looking at me, and I could swear there was a curious expression on his face. Yes, he was made up of cogs and gears and metal and leather, but there was no electricity within, no battery to make him operate. The whimsy and magic of the situation hit me and I giggled.

"It's quite the thing, isn't it?" Bryan said. "I remember when I first came to Whisper Hollow. The entire town seemed like a playground to me. Sometimes a nightmarish one, but a playground nonetheless." He patted his leg, whistling to the dog. "Come on, Jokney. You don't want to be running around out here alone. Dr. Divine wants you back."

After another moment, while Jokney regarded us with deliberation, I picked up a thin stick and waved it in the air. "Do you want to play fetch, boy?"

At that, Jokney perked up and quickly trotted over to my side. He was wearing a red bandanna around his throat, and I gently reached out and grabbed hold of the knotted scarf. Jokney suddenly froze, and with one last look at me, he was once again a statue—as still as an ice sculpture. At that moment a pickup drove up behind our car, and Peggin and Dr. Divine jumped out of the cab.

"You found him!" Deev sounded relieved, a smile breaking out on his face. "I was so worried about you, Jokney. There are nasty creatures out in these woods. You need to stay in the barn with the others."

Peggin was smiling at me, her eyes twinkling. "Every now and then Jokney seems to get an itch, doesn't he?"

"Well, he can scratch that itch in the barn with the others." Deev gathered up Jokney in his arms and carried him to the back of the pickup, where he a fixed a chain around Jokney's neck. Part of me wanted to object, but then I had to remind myself that Jokney wasn't a flesh-and-blood dog and the chain wasn't going to hurt him.

"How did he get out in the first place? Don't you keep the door locked?" Bryan peeked in the back of the truck. It was filled with pieces of metal, rolls of leather, a humongous toolbox, and various other odds and ends.

Dr. Divine leaned against the side of the truck, one hand on Jokney's head. "I haven't figured out who can do it yet, but I've got somebody in there who can open the door. Every now and then someone escapes. I'm just grateful my Cthulhu sculpture hasn't hit the road yet. That would be a real nightmare."

I decided to take a chance on asking. "Do you know which ones are going to wake up? Is there something special you do to them that gives them that power?"

Deev shrugged. He reached up and scratched his forehead beneath the top hat. "I have no clue. When I create—when I'm driven to sculpt—all I can see is the vision in my head. I create, I build, I sculpt, I talk to them while I am creating them. And then, some just wake up on their own. I don't pick the ones that come to life. And once they do come to life, I never feel like I have the right to take them apart. Well, if something came to life and was very dangerous—if it put others in danger—then I would do what I could to deconstruct it. But Jokney, for example. He's become as much a part of my family as anybody."

"Did any of your creations ever come to life before you came to Whisper Hollow?" Bryan slid his hands in his pockets and stamped on the ground, his breath coalescing in the air as a puff of fog.

At that moment, a loud cawing of crows filled the air. Considering they usually weren't active at night, I tried to tune in to hear what they were saying. As I closed my eyes, I could feel the shadow across the sky chasing the crows as they tried to divert it away from Whisper Hollow. But it paused over the town, and I wanted nothing so much as to get under cover.

"We need to get out of here. It's not safe to be out away from crowds tonight. Concert should be fine, but we better go now." I turned to Peggin and Deev. "Are you coming?"

Peggin nodded. "It's the Whisper Hollow Snow Concert. Of course we're coming." They climbed back in their truck as Bryan and I headed back to his Lexus.

"What was that?" Bryan asked as he started the ignition.

"I'm not sure, but it isn't friendly. The crows were trying to lead it away from the town, but they weren't successful. Whatever it is, it's not friendly toward the Morrígan or the Crow Man. And that means it's our enemy as well."

My phone jangled and I glanced at the text. It was from Penelope—though how she had or used a phone, I wasn't sure. Whatever the case, she had texted: Veronica will see you Friday night at nine p.m. You may bring your guardian but leave the lament singer at home. Be on time and be polite. Stand by the entrance to her lair and she will send a guide.

"Looks like I'm headed to see Veronica," I said, reading the text to Bryan. "You'll go?"

"Of course."

We were quiet then as Bryan headed toward the community center. I stared out the window into the darkness, thinking about Whisper Hollow and all of us who made our home here. We lived on the edge of an ancient forest that was filled with dark creatures and spirits, and elementals from a time before humans walked the earth. There was no telling what it was that sailed overhead. But I had a feeling that we would be finding out before too long, and I didn't think any of us would be very happy about it.

CHAPTER 5

The next morning, after Bryan went back to his house, I received a call from Ivy.

"You needed to talk to us?

"Yes, I need to talk to the three of you. I found out something that the Crescent Moon Society might need to know about, but I wanted to talk to you guys first. Is there any chance you can meet me today, preferably this morning?" I was finishing up my coffee. I had gotten up early, and hoped to make an early start. Daphne jumped up on the table and nudged my arm. I absentmindedly began petting her as I waited for Ivy to answer.

"I'll call you back in five minutes." And she hung up. One thing about the Matriarchs of town, they got right to the point when need be.

I carried my cup over to the sink, rinsed it, and stuck it in the dishwasher. Then, I watered the hanging philodendron in the corner. I didn't dare leave plants around where the cats could reach them, because Gabby tried to chow down on anything that resembled vegetation. So what few I had indoors hung high up from the ceiling. Then, I picked up the dish that had contained their canned food, rinsed thoroughly, and added it to the dishwasher. After filling their kibble bowl, I was about to throw a load of clothes in the washer when my phone rang. It was Ivy.

"It's eight thirty now. Come over in half an hour and they'll be here." She paused, then added, "You get to bring the goodies this time." With a laugh, she let me go.

I headed upstairs. I had something to do before I went. There were two sides to the second story of the house, and each had its own staircase.

Beyond the kitchen was the master suite. Upstairs, above it, was my grandmother's sewing room, along with the attic. I had turned the sewing room into a ritual room, where I could focus on my spirit shaman training. Along one wall of the room was a hidden panel, leading to a large storage room where my grandmother had kept her secret stash of diaries and supplies. The room was tucked between the sewing room and the attic, and I had found it by accident. She kept the room hidden knowledge from Duvall, realizing that he had been an enemy. Now I didn't need a secret room. But it seemed wise to keep it hidden, nonetheless.

The eight-by-eight-foot room contained, on one side, a built-in workbench with cupboards overhead. On the other side stretched a wall of shelves, upon which rested 2,400 jelly jars filled with graveyard dirt, gathered by my grandmother and my great-grandmother down through the years. Every grave they had presided over was represented here, along with a handful I had already worked my magic over. Every jar had a label on it with the name of the deceased, and some of those jars had a dark *P* printed on the label as well. That meant that the grave would be found in the Pest House Cemetery, the darker and more dangerous part of the graveyard.

I sat down at the desk that had been my grandmother's. I had left Lila's desk where I had found it, overlooking the side yard leading to Bryan's property. I had pushed her sewing machine to the side. In the other part of what had been her sewing room, there was now a soft rug, an altar table dedicated to the Morrígan, and a bench on which I could sit and meditate. Now I bowed in front of the altar table, and then settled myself on the bench, resting my hands on my knees and closing my eyes.

"O Gracious Morrígan, Queen of Shapeshifters and Mother of the Fae, I call to you. Let my message find its way to you on the wings of the Crow Man." I paused, collecting my thoughts. "I'm not sure what we're up against; twice now I've felt a dark shadow hover over the town. Please guide me in what I need to know. Please guide us in finding out how to cope with the Ankou. As your daughter, and spirit shaman, I ask that you answer."

I knew better than to wait. The Morrígan would answer when she was ready.

I rose and gathered the upholstered doctor's bag that my grandmother had left to me with all her tools in it. It was time to go talk to the Matriarchs about the Screaming Tree and the Ankou.

My meeting with the Matriarchs didn't go exactly as I had expected. For one thing, Oriel—the Heart and soul of Whisper Hollow, in essence the gatekeeper of the town itself—had listened quietly as I explained what the forest sprite had told me.

After I finished, she turned to Ivy. "Have you seen much of the nature spirits lately?"

Ivy shook her head. "They've been quiet. But then, during autumn and winter, they tend to fall into silence. There's work for them to do during these seasons but it's more internal to the ecosystem. But I've sensed a general unease through my gardens."

"I felt a shadow—first the other day, then last night. It's like some great cloud has moved into Whisper Hollow and is watching over the town. It feels dangerous, and I found myself wanting to hide from it. I felt that if it saw me, it might . . . snatch me up or something." I knew that sounded ridiculous, but when I examined my fears, there it was. I felt like whatever I had seen was watching—looking for something, though not me in particular, and I didn't want to be on the other end of the microscope.

Oriel was first to speak. She was around fifty-five or so, the age my mother would have been if she had lived, and was a plump, earth-mother personality. A golden braid circled her head, and for some reason I kept thinking of her as Scandinavian, though I was pretty sure her roots lay elsewhere. She ran a boardinghouse, mostly for single men and passersby through the town, and she had a deep, elemental-based magic that seemed to hold everything together.

"The Gray Man."

Ivy jerked around. "You think he's come out again?"

Oriel nodded. "I think he may be reemerging. I doubt that has anything to do with the Ankou in the forest, but it would explain the feeling Kerris is getting."

"If so, we're in for a spate of missing people. We should warn the loggers, once we know for certain, along with their kin who live in the woods." Ellia picked up her teacup, her gloved fingers cautiously holding the delicate bone china. Ivy had made tea, but true to her word, they had looked to me to provide the goodies. I was glad that I'd stopped by a nearby doughnut shop for a box of éclairs and Danish.

I watched them for a few moments as they lapsed into silence. They seemed to be discussing this without actually saying a word. I could feel the crackle of energy running among the three. Finally, I cleared my throat.

"I'm afraid I don't understand whatever language you're not speaking," I said with a wry grin. "Is there any way I could be included in this conversation?"

Ellia let out a loud laugh and slapped her knee. "I told you she was a firebrand, Oriel."

Oriel lowered her glasses, peering at me over the top. "You're coming along fast, my dear. Your grandmother was keen with the Sight, but you—even though you've always had it, you've come so far since you returned."

I nodded. The fifteen years I'd lived in Seattle, I had found a way to use my abilities. Ghost hunting, for one, kept me active and kept the energy from backing on me, which could be dangerous. But since I had come back to Whisper Hollow, my abilities had exploded and I sometimes felt like I was walking between worlds, constantly aware of the expanded realities going on around me.

"Have you heard the legends of the Gray Man? Did Lila ever tell you about them?" Ivy stood, crossing to a bookcase near the table.

"No, I don't think so, though the name sounds familiar." I ran through all that I had read in Lila's Shadow Journal. I had my own now, and it began the way Lila's had, with one minor change. It read:

Traditions & History of the Spirit Shamans
Generation 50: Kerris Fellwater
Daughter of Tamil Fellwater
Daughter of the Morrígan

My grandmother was the forty-eighth generation. My mother would have been the forty-ninth, if she had lived. I hadn't finished reading the Shadow Journal—it was a lifetime of spells and rituals that I needed to learn—but so far, I hadn't seen anything about a "gray man."

Ivy returned from the bookcase, a slim volume in her hand. She offered it to me. "I don't want you taking this book out of the house—it's one of the few copies still in existence and I've got it heavily warded to keep any prying eyes from finding it. But you can read it when you come over."

I glanced at the title, *Gray Men and Black Mists*. A quick

vibration ran through my fingers, and I realized I didn't like holding the book. "What the hell?"

"You felt it, then?" Ivy leaned forward. "That book was written forty years ago by one of Whisper Hollow's residents. He vanished shortly thereafter, but your grandmother found the manuscript and had it printed off and bound. She owned a copy, I own one, Oriel and Ellia each own one, and the Crescent Moon Society has one in its library. Lila's copy should be somewhere in your house."

"I'll search for it." I flipped through the pages. A sketch caught my eye. It was a thin-bodied, long-necked creature, looking human and yet . . . not. He had a bald head and wide, rounded eyes, his nose was almost flat against his face, and his skin was somewhere between gray and the sepia of old photographs. My stomach lurched. Whatever this was, I didn't like it.

I stared at the image for a long while before asking, "What kind of spirit is this?"

"That's just it, dear," Oriel said, leaning forward. "We're not entirely sure, though we have speculated a lot. But his kind have been seen in the forest up near Timber Peak. Strange lights have been spotted in the sky there since the founding of Whisper Hollow."

I realized just what she was saying. "Are you trying to tell me we have . . . aliens . . . around here? On top of everything else? UFOs?"

Ellia shrugged. "I don't care what you call them, we just know they don't belong to our world. Though I doubt they come through on actual ships—at least not physical ones from our realm. The lights seem to coincide with when ley line activity flares, and when the sun sends magnetic storms our way. I personally think the Gray Man—or men—are interdimensional creatures and that they are able to cross over from their world to ours during those periods. The increased activity can create viable doors between worlds—doors through time and space."

I tried to take it in. It wasn't that I was skeptical. After all, I was a spirit shaman, I worked with ghosts and saw forest sprites and was the daughter of a goddess. But that we were also dealing with interdimensional creatures . . . it felt like too far, too much to comprehend. And yet . . . and yet . . . something about it resonated.

"What about Bigfoot? Is Sasquatch related to the Gray Man?" Over the years, Sasquatch had made himself known around the area and it never felt like this was his natural home, if that made sense. He felt . . . *other.* The way he came and went, appearing one moment and vanishing the next, led me to wonder if perhaps he, too, wasn't darting through doorways in time and space.

"You begin to understand," Ivy said. "We *do* think he's related to them, though how, we don't know. In fact, at times I believe the Gray Man hunts him. Sasquatch is volatile and unpredictable, and can be violent, but he bears no evil nature. The Gray Man? He's dangerous."

I let out a long sigh. "What about the mist? The black cloud? Why do you think—why does this book think—that they are connected?"

"Because when the black mist appears, it has the same feel as the Gray Man, and the lights up on Timber Peak begin to appear again. We're thinking it's possibly the doorway through which the creatures come."

I let that set in for a moment. The thought that we were being spied on made me nervous. "Do you think the mist itself has a consciousness? Because what I saw felt alive and very much aware. I really didn't want to be anywhere near it because I felt it might pick up on my presence."

Ellia took the book from me, cautiously avoiding my fingers even though she was gloved. She flipped through it till she came to the passage she was looking for, and then handed it back. "Read."

I scanned the paragraphs.

"The black mist often precedes a period of activity where

the Gray Man and the sky-lights are vivid and prominent. Members of the Crescent Moon Society have offered several possibilities for what this mist is. One, that it's actually the vehicle through which these creatures move—the portal between the worlds. Another, more favored speculation— and the one this author tends to believe—is that the mist is a scouting agent for the Gray Man/Men.

"That it precedes their appearance and seeks out the most likely targets. For what that purpose is, we don't know, but every time the mist appears, one or two humans vanish from the town. On rare occasions, they have been found, wandering in the woods alone, with no memory of what transpired during the time they were gone. The mist is usually accompanied by a feeling of dread, or fear—as though some calamity is about to befall the viewer. More than one witness has admitted to running for cover, in hopes of not being seen.

"One of the few discrepancies noted is the size and shape of the mist. At times it appears small and compact, moving like a dark circle against the sky. At other times, it's reported as a larger, hazier fog slowly rolling over the area. But it's important to note that regardless of the shape or size, the mist is always blacker than the sky, even at night, and blots out visuals of the stars and moon should it cross their path."

I set the book on the table. "Well, that sounds about like what I sensed. I can't tell you if I actually saw it; sometimes it's hard to discern between inner and outer sight. But I know what I experienced is the same thing described in this book."

Ellia glanced at Ivy, who in turn glanced over at Oriel.

"Well, we should make a trip up to Timber Peak for several reasons. And we do so while it's daylight. One, we need to check on the Screaming Tree and look for signs of the Ankou. Two, we look for any discernible signs that the Gray Man is returning."

"Are they related?" I asked her.

"I doubt it. The Ankou don't seem to have much truck

with the alien spirits around here." Oriel frowned then. "But we can't be sure. But given the Ankou are members of the Unliving, and that these seem to have escaped from Arawn, the god of the dead, I rather doubt it. I think, though, the energy of the Gray Man and the black mist can *exacerbate* the emergence of the Ankou. Like charging a general area with a massive battery. Anything in there, even if it's not related to the battery, becomes activated."

She stood. "Well, then, if we're headed up to Timber Peak, I'll go put on my walking skirt. Kerris, you're dressed for the woods already. Ellia, Ivy . . . bring your gear. I'll return in twenty minutes and we'll drive up."

I straightened my shoulders. "You mean you're going up there *today*?"

"Of course," Ivy said. "And you're going with us. There's no time like the present and it's vital we don't leave any chance of the Ankou invading the town for later."

I blinked. I hadn't expected them to immediately jump into action. In fact, I had thought that we'd sit around, talk about it, and then present the issue to the Crescent Moon Society. My consternation must have appeared on my face, because Ellia laughed.

"You really don't think we're going to fob this off on Gareth and his men, do you? Not until we know what's actually going on."

"I . . . I didn't know."

"The buck stops *here*, my dear." Oriel placed a gentle hand on my shoulder. "We're the ones who keep Whisper Hollow safe—well, as safe as we can. It's up to us to investigate threats. The last outbreak of the Gray Man sightings was . . . oh . . . what . . . thirty-two years ago? When you were just a baby. Something had to have happened for the mist to return. While I'm gone, Ivy, can you check the solar storm readings? Look for mega storms, especially those that caused any activity as far as the aurora borealis in our area. Look back as far as . . . oh, I'd say six months."

"Will do." Ivy headed over to her desk and fired up her laptop as Oriel excused herself.

As the door closed behind her, I turned to Ellia.

"I think . . . I'm a little bit afraid," I said.

She smiled. "You should be—the Gray Man is nothing to mess around with. But you'll be with us, and we have our ways of keeping out of his clutches. As time goes on, you'll meet more and more of the spirits who make this area their home. Oh, I know you've heard of a lot of them, at least you did when you were a child, but the fact is that the spirit shaman is responsible for a whole lot more than pushing the dead back into their graves. You're a *shaman*, a daughter of the Morrígan. You are called to her service to protect the people she watches over. And she is Whisper Hollow's patron goddess, regardless of what the Hounds may think."

"Oh look—there have been a number of solar storms within the past few months, any number of which have spawned off the aurora. I think we may be onto something." Ivy sounded far too excited for what we were talking about.

"Great. Lovely." I swallowed the lump in my throat and picked up one of the éclairs. If we were going to knock on the door of some alien interdimensional critter out there, I was determined to do so on a belly full of chocolate.

Timber Peak was named for all of the tall timber that had been logged from there over the years. Now it was protected land, and all of the trees and undergrowth had grown back. It was obvious where the clear-cutting had taken place—the trees were shorter there and all the same height—but the endemic flora was returning, and hopefully would be allowed to flourish and restore the area to its natural beauty.

The old logging roads were still in existence, used mostly by hikers, mountain bikers, and snowshoers to reach the backcountry. They could be precarious, though, washing out during rainstorms, and icing over during winter when snow reached the higher altitudes. There was also a main road leading to the lodge at the top of Timber Peak, although it, too, often fell victim to washouts and rock slides.

I had left my car at Ivy's. We were all in Oriel's SUV, a huge old tank of a vehicle. I had a feeling the SUV could ford a river and come out kicking. As I got in the backseat with Ivy, I glanced behind us into the cargo area and saw several blankets, what looked like a survival kit, a pair of snowshoes, a pickax, and a shovel. Nobody could say that Oriel wasn't prepared for the unexpected.

We passed the Unitarian Universalist church on Forest Drive, then Juniper Mall. Shortly after we passed Elkwood Lane, we turned left onto Timber Peak Drive. We were headed northeast, out of Whisper Hollow. The grade on the road steepened abruptly and within a few minutes we were surrounded by the forest on both sides.

The rain was holding off, although the ever-present clouds cast a pall over the town. I wasn't sure whether it was because I was in a car filled with women who carried strong magic, or perhaps my own abilities were heightened, but I could sense creatures from the forest watching as we passed by. It was an uncomfortable feeling, as though we were headed into territory that—while we weren't exactly unwelcome—wasn't ours in which to play. We were guests here, and the forest spirits weren't going to let us forget it.

"Can you feel them?" Ivy asked. She was watching me carefully.

I nodded. "Do you know who they are? Or what they are?"

"Forest creatures, sprites, Fae, the spirits of the loggers and miners that still live in these woods. Maybe Bigfoot himself. There are beings out here for which we have no name, beings that have never been human, and who never interact with humanity. The forest is alive; that's one of the first things I learned when I moved here."

"Every forest is alive," Oriel said from the driver's seat. "Some are older than others and they sleep. Some of the ancient forests are still awake, and they brood in their silent long thoughts. New forests are often young and playful, and may not understand how precarious their existences are. Some, filled with creatures like the pixies, are dangerous for the unwary. Timber Peak . . . this whole area . . . it's a chaotic area inhabited by volatile energies. The woods don't necessarily hate us, but they don't welcome us either. We're fair game, if we overstep our boundaries."

I listened, keeping my mouth shut. There was a lot I had to learn, and these women would help teach me if I let them. My grandmother might not be able to guide me in the intricacies of my post—that I had to learn from her journals and trial and error—but the three women in this vehicle could make my path so much easier.

"Aidan comes up to the woods a lot. He loves Timber Peak, he told me," Ivy said.

I stared at her, surprised. "You and Aidan talk?"

That my maternal grandfather was hanging out with my paternal grandmother was news to me. Since he had returned to Whisper Hollow, settling in quietly in Oriel's boardinghouse, I had slowly begun to forge a relationship with him. The Hounds still had it out for him, that much I knew, but we would do what we could to keep him safe from them.

Ivy blushed. "Well, he comes over for dinner now and then. We have a lot in common, you know. He lost his daughter and I lost my son. You *are* our granddaughter." There was a hint of defensiveness in her words, and I realized right then that there was more going on than just a harmless dinner here and there.

I eyed her, wondering if I should say anything—wanting to tease her—but decided to let them have their privacy for now. "I see." I didn't mean to imply anything by my tone of voice, but Oriel and Ellia burst out laughing.

"You can't keep much from this one, Ivy. Your granddaughter's special. Smart as a whip and far more talented

than either her grandmother or her great-grandmother."
Oriel chuckled. "And before you say a word, Kerris, yes,
you are. You just don't know the full extent of your abilities
yet. I think some aspects will be a long time coming, but
you are growing every day. You may not realize it, but you're
far stronger than you were even two months ago."

I paused, then hesitantly said, "I wish I felt more secure.
Every time I turn around, I realize how much I missed out
by Grandma Lila not being able to train me. I had my reasons for leaving, but I stayed away too long."

"Perhaps," Ellia said. "And perhaps not. There's a reason
and rhyme to most things, and my thoughts are that if you
returned too soon, you may not have discovered that your
parents were both murdered. You may not have been able to
lay them to rest. And by unwinding the mystery of their disap-
pearances, you're now able to heal from the thought that they
abandoned you. That will stand you well, as you move into
your power."

I thought about what she said. It made sense. Being
caught up in childhood hurts and old wounds that hadn't
healed—it blinded one to the truth. While it hurt to know
they were dead, the knowledge freed me to move on.

As we wound through the forest, the trees overcrowded
the road, especially the maple and birch, whose bare
branches wove a lacework canopy over the edges of the road.
Here and there, a bough from one of the tall firs had dropped,
and Oriel grew silent, focusing on skirting the danger zones.
Driving over a large branch could rupture something
beneath the SUV, or puncture a tire. There were also small
washouts to both sides, where the constant rain had eaten
away at the shoulders.

We passed through Hangman's Ravine, where the drop-
off on either side could prove deadly, should the car spin out
of control and tumble over the edge. The road was narrow
enough that we could see—far below—Miner's Creek tum-
bling along. While white-water season didn't happen till

spring, all the rain we had received over the past few months had engorged the stream, sending it thundering along with whitecaps and muddy water.

We passed through the ravine and out, and the grade steepened. I had no clue where the Screaming Tree was located, but Oriel, Ellia, and Ivy would know. I made it my business to study the route in case I needed to come back here on my own.

Fifteen minutes out from Whisper Hollow saw us fully into tall timber country. We passed a sign that read LUPINE VALLEY, and Oriel eased off onto the side road just beyond. The road was gravel, wide enough for one car with a generous shoulder, and led into the forest proper.

"The Screaming Tree is just beyond Lupine Valley Campground." Ellia glanced over her shoulder at me. "About a ten-minute walk from the campground's parking spot."

"I don't remember much about Timber Peak, or even Grandma Lila talking about it." My grandmother hadn't been remotely interested in camping, and neither had Duvall, one of the few things they had in common. Grandma had married him to keep the love of her life—Grandpa Aidan— safe. When she snuck away to visit Aidan some years later, she returned pregnant with Tamil, my mother.

"Your grandmother didn't like coming out here. She was too tuned in to the energies and it always disturbed her." Ellia hesitated, then added, "We had a friend in high school . . . his name was Yancy. He was taken by the Gray Man. Lila and I found his body, ripped to shreds, in Lupine Valley. What the creature did to him was . . . it was beyond description. It was savage, worse than any animal would ever inflict. Part of him was gone, bones found in the area had vicious bite marks on them. The Gray Man has an appetite for flesh and blood."

I let out a long breath. "Cannibal?"

"How can it be cannibalism when it's not your own species? No, but predator, and carnivore. And cruel. The medical examiner verified that Yancy had been eaten while still alive. I'm not sure how he knew, but he was able to figure that out." Ellia's voice drifted into silence as she went back to staring out the window.

As we rumbled along the gravel road, mud puddles began to appear, but Oriel drove the horse of a machine over them. Another ten minutes and we turned again, onto a dirt road by a sign that read LUPINE VALLEY CAMPGROUND. NO HUNT-ING. Camping spots branched off from the main drive, to both right and left. A few more miles and we swung into a large circular parking lot next to a wide expanse of open grass. Picnic shelters and tables dotted the area, along with restrooms and a playground area.

"How many people come camping, given the stories about the Gray Man?" It boggled my mind to think that anybody would bring their kids here if they even remotely believed the tales.

"More than you'd want to think. But they come in groups—there *is* safety in numbers, you know." Ivy pointed at one of the picnic tables. "That's where they found Yancy. I wasn't with Ellia and your grandma, but I came out here for the memorial."

Oriel parked, and we climbed out of the car. I winced as I stretched, my knees glad for the break from sitting down. As I walked over toward the table that Ivy had pointed out, I closed my eyes, trying to tune in to the lay of the land.

It started with a whisper—just a faint one. I couldn't quite catch what was being said, but there was something riding the wind, a nuance or secret or some hidden thing. I tried to catch what it was saying, but every time I got close, it slipped away again. The feel, though . . . the feel reminded me of the Shadow Man, and I knew the Ankou were here.

"I can feel them. The Ankou." I turned to Ellia. "It's like the Shadow Man, only there are more of them."

When I first returned home, I'd been attacked by one of the Shadow People—creatures that were from the land of the dead. They belonged in the Underworld, and when they ventured into our world, they were dark shades in human form, black silhouettes with neither faces nor features. The Ankou attacked and drained the energy from the living, bringing fear and pain to their victims. Often, they went after children, who were helpless.

My first encounter with the Shadow Man was in my childhood, when one had attacked me in my bed. But they could—and would—attack anyone. When in their proper place, the Ankou served as soldiers in the service of Arawn, Celtic Lord of the Underworld. But if they escaped their servitude and entered our realm, they roamed at will. Technically members of the Unliving, the Shadow People had stronger powers than most Unliving, because they sourced their power directly from Arawn.

"The question is, are they serving the dark lord, or were they summoned here to serve . . . another?" Ellia lowered her head, frowning. I knew she was thinking of Magda, her mother.

"That's what we're here to find out," Oriel said. "Let's hie ourselves to the Screaming Tree before anything comes out of the woods at us."

And so we set off, onto a trail leading into the forest from the back of the campground. All through the ten-minute walk through rain-sodden undergrowth, the silence of the forest seemed to grow. As water dripped with a steady cadence from the boughs above, I fell into the rhythm of the forest, reaching out with every step, trying to fathom the depths of those creatures who made Timber Peak their home.

CHAPTER 6

Oriel slowed. She was surprisingly quick and nimble in the forest, and blended in as though she thoroughly belonged here. She led the way, following a path that disappeared after the first couple of minutes, but always seemed to know exactly which direction to turn. We followed, first Ivy, then me, then Ellia behind us. I noticed she had taken off her gloves and was hanging back a few feet away from me. If she fell, she wouldn't be in danger of touching me. Ellia had been cursed by her mother. Her hands held madness in them—her touch would drive a person into a world of perpetual pain and confusion.

True to what she had told me, after a ten-minute walk out of Lupine Valley Campground, we broke through the thick tangle into a clearing. In the center sat a tree. Or rather, what remained of the tree. The trunk was still upright, at least forty feet of it, though it was obviously dead, but it wasn't a widow-maker. It looked like it had been petrified—the bark was almost shiny.

I wasn't sure what kind of tree it had been, but it was old and tall—the top of the tree looked like it had at one time been toppled by a lightning strike. About six feet off the ground were three openings, in the guise of a screaming face—two eyes and the mouth. The opening to the "mouth" was jagged and dark, and I had no desire to stick my hand in and find out how far back it went or what might be in there.

Oriel paused. "The Screaming Tree is dampened. Can you feel the energy?" She glanced around, a suspicious look on her face.

Ellia and Ivy closed their eyes.

After a moment, Ivy sighed. "It's coming from deep within the woods. Dark and almost formless. Whatever it is, it's disrupting the energy field of the tree. We have to put a stop to it so we can figure out what's going on."

Oriel glanced at me. "You can be the anchor."

"Anchor?" Now I *was* confused.

"When we do work like this, if we're out in the woods where there might be danger, we always have an anchor. Someone grounded, not part of the ritual, to keep their eyes open. Like Bryan acts for you—though we won't rely on you to protect us, just warn us. So don't be worried about that." The way she said it almost made me think that they were giving me make-work, to keep me out of trouble, but given that we were in territory known for dangerous spirits, I decided not to be so hasty in my assessment.

"All right. I'll sit over here on this log to keep out of the way." A nurse log near the Screaming Tree was covered with moss. The rain had saturated the moss, but I found a spot where I could peel it away, exposing the wood, and settled down on the damp log. It suddenly occurred to me that our safety would depend on my alertness, and any concerns about being a fourth wheel vanished as I took my post.

Ivy, Oriel, and Ellia spread out to form a triangle around the tree. Their arms, outstretched, still couldn't reach around the tall timber but I had a feeling that wasn't going to matter.

They began to back away in unison, one step at a time, until they were about ten steps from the tree on all three sides. A hush settled over the area, the silence broken only by the echo of birds, warning that rain was coming.

I shivered as the chill settled through my coat. Everything seemed muted and distant. My head suddenly felt full of fog as though I had a cold or was exceptionally tired. Instinctively, I knew that whatever force was causing it was the same thing that was dampening the powers of the Screaming Tree. I shook my head, trying to keep from falling into a trance. I needed to remain alert and aware, rather than giving in to the pull the magic in the forest was exerting.

Oriel raised one hand, holding it toward the tree, palm facing forward. Ellia took up her violin and put it to her chin. Ivy spread both arms out as though she were waiting for someone to drape coats over them. She lowered her head as Ellia began to play. The notes that reverberated out of her violin were low, almost grating, but I could feel them resonate through the forest, as though they were being absorbed by the trees and plants. I tried to keep my focus from being swept into the magic that the three women were weaving by analyzing what was going on.

Oriel was generating the energy—I could sense it radiating off her outstretched hand. Ellia was picking it up with her music and moving it around to Ivy, who was taking it in through her own hands and . . . I squinted, trying to figure out what was happening. Then, in a blink, I could see it. Ivy was transmuting the energy; she was feeding it through the trees, through the ferns and ivy and huckleberry. Together, the three of them were saturating the area.

The fog in my head started to dissipate, rolling back, and I realized then that they were clearing the forest, fighting back whatever magic held the Screaming Tree silent. As Ellia's playing ramped up, Oriel was sourcing more energy, feeding it to Ellia at a rate so quick that I could almost see the waves ricocheting through the air toward the lament singer. In turn, Ellia caught them up with her bow and violin, turning them toward Ivy, who sent them reeling through the forest. Mesmerized, I watched the interplay, wondering if I'd ever be able to control the magic like they could.

A sudden noise caught my attention. I jumped as someone brushed past me. I was on my feet in an instant, but then I realized that it was my grandmother standing there. Grandma Lila was watching them work. She glanced over her shoulder at me and smiled, and I once again longed to be able to throw my arms around her and give her a big hug, but it didn't work that way with spirits. Then, she pointed behind me, a worried look on her face, and I turned.

There, behind a nearby tree, was something tall and hairy watching us. The moment it saw me looking, it turned and vanished, as if it had never been there. I blinked. Whatever it was had been quick and big. A bear? Maybe. Another thought flirted around the outside of my brain, but I wasn't ready to entertain it. I started in that direction but Grandma Lila appeared in front of me, shaking her head and pointing back to the fallen log.

I was about to ask her why she didn't want me to go look, but then decided I didn't want to take a chance on disrupting the magic Oriel and the others were weaving. I let out a slow breath, returning to the nurse log. But this time, I quit trying to focus on the energy and, instead, kept my eyes peeled.

Another five minutes and the silence shattered as the Screaming Tree let out a long, piercing shriek, startling me so much that I lurched backward, almost falling off the log. I caught my balance, steadying myself so that I was sitting upright again.

Oriel, Ivy, and Ellia lowered their hands. Ellia carried her violin back to the case where it sat on a dry patch of ground beneath one of the cedars. The tree was awake again—I could sense it.

"It screamed." I struggled, trying to remember the history of the Screaming Tree.

"It always does when there's danger coming to the town, and I hear it," Oriel said. "That's why the forest sprite who talked to you was so worried. He knew that I didn't realize there was magic up here dampening the tree."

I hesitantly approached the tree, keeping my hands to myself until I knew whether it was safe to touch it. "How did it get its name? And who . . . how does it know to scream?"

Ivy joined me. She nodded at the tree. "You can touch it. If you try to hurt it, the tree will scream, but if you approach it with no ill intent, it will allow you to touch its trunk."

As I reached out, gently placing my hands on the trunk, Oriel continued.

"When Whisper Hollow was first founded, the first Heart of the town came out here and left offerings to the forest folk—peace offerings, so to speak. A horrible storm came in off the Strait of Juan de Fuca. It rolled over the slopes, toward the town. It was a horrible night, with wind gusts raging past eighty miles per hour. The forest took the brunt of it. The Screaming Tree was fully a hundred and fifty feet high then, and it became the focal point for the lightning to vent its wrath. A jagged fork split the tree, toppling the top two-thirds of it. The offerings had been placed beneath its trunk. Something happened—some magic in the lightning strike or the energy behind the offerings, I'm not sure what, but the tree trunk woke that night. After that, every time the town's been in danger, the Screaming Tree screams, and I—or whoever the Heart of the town has been—has heard it."

"So, the lightning storm sort of . . . made the tree the town's sentinel. I wonder if that would have happened without the offerings?" But I knew the answer already. Because the Heart of the town had offered an olive branch to the forest spirits, they—in turn—returned the favor. Another thing struck me. I always knew that Oriel was the Heart of Whisper Hollow but I hadn't realized it was an official post.

"So . . . the Heart of the town. How did you end up getting assigned the job?"

She flashed me a cagey smile. "My dear, we're born to it. Like you're born to be a spirit shaman. We travel till we find the town that needs us and then we settle in. I happened to be lucky enough to be born in the town that I was meant to serve."

"So there was another Heart before you?"

"Of course. Ever since the founding of Whisper Hollow, there's been a Heart. Manae died when I was young, but she knew the day I was born that I would replace her. She taught me about Whisper Hollow from the time I could barely walk. I grew up learning the town's moods and whims. My father was a member of the Crescent Moon Society, so it was easy. The CMS knew I was destined for this post. They brought me in at a young age, and helped me find my way. Old Manae was quite the woman. She, herself, had been born in Wales."

I nodded. There was still so much history I needed to learn, so many of the town customs with which I wasn't familiar. "There are things watching us." I told them about the creature I had seen. "I'm not sure if it was a bear or Bigfoot or what."

"It could be Sasquatch, though he tends to make his presence known. Bear? Also possible. The Ankou can't come out in the daylight. I suggest we erect the wards around the area to keep the Screaming Tree from being enchanted again, and then head back to town. We can't meet with the Crescent Moon Society till Saturday night. There's just too much chaos in everybody's life right now due to the holidays, and this isn't an emergency. Not yet." Ivy shook her head. "I wish this hadn't happened right now. It's not a good omen."

"It's *never* a good omen when somebody tries to silence the Screaming Tree," Oriel said.

They worked silently, affixing their wards around the area, and as I watched I began to appreciate how strong these women were. They were part of a legacy that had been passed down from the Morrígan, as was I. It made me want to be strong in my own right, and I realized—I didn't want to disappoint them, even more than not wanting to disappoint myself.

* * *

Thursday went by uneventfully. I had slept deep after our trek through the woods, and it was a relief the next day to have an entire day spent with nothing but errands and shopping. I bought groceries, did laundry, cleared out part of the garage—though I had no desire to dig into Lila and Duvall's store of cobweb-encrusted boxes just yet—and spent an hour on the phone, convincing Peggin she was not allowed to move into her new house or even go over there by herself till we were there to help her. I still didn't like the thought of her living there, but there wasn't much I could do about it. So I just gritted my teeth and made the best of what I still thought was a bad situation. Bryan was out of town for the day, so I spent the evening curled up with a good book and the cats.

But come Friday, I was jittery. I knew it was because I was due to head out to Veronica's at dusk. Facing the Queen of the Unliving wasn't anything to laugh off. People went into her lair and never came out again, and very few knew the workings of her mind. I wasn't sure what it entailed to become a member of the royalty of the dead, and I had no clue how the kings and queens of her shadowy realm were chosen, but I was smart enough to recognize the power inherent within them. I didn't delude myself that I could do anything to stop her, once she set her mind to something. The spirit shamans could control the general members of the Unliving, but I had never heard of one controlling a king or queen of the realm.

As I dressed for the evening, I took extra care. I was meeting royalty. Perhaps she wasn't alive, or a recognized monarch by most people, but she would notice if I showed up looking like I had just rolled out of bed. I chose my best black jeans, and paired them with a beautiful blue embroidered V-neck sweater. I almost fastened a silver belt around my waist but then remembered that she might have an

aversion to the metal and chose, instead, a black leather belt.
I slid on black velvet ankle boots, and brushed my hair back
into a neat ponytail.

Bryan had taken as much care—he was dressed all in
black, wearing black jeans, a black button-down shirt, black
leather duster, and platform boots. With his scruff of a
beard, and the tousled hair that coiled around his ears, he
looked like he had stepped out of some European vampire
movie. In other words: *hot*.

I turned to him. "Are you ready for this?"

He set his jaw and shrugged. "Do you think we'll ever
be ready for this?"

"Not exactly, but I guess we don't have a choice, do we?"
I sucked in a deep breath and looked at myself in the mirror.
"Do I look too . . ."

"Soft? Yes. But if you wear the leather jacket you bought,
it will help. And braid your hair—it looks more severe that
way. You don't want to show weakness to someone like
Veronica. She may play ball with the customs, but she'll be
watching you for any chink, any crack. Remember: She's
one of the Unliving, and as their queen, she's going to have
an ego to match." He slid his eyes over me. "Damn, you're
hot. I want to fuck you right now."

Even his voice set me off. I caught my breath. "If we
could get out of this, I'd happily stay home and fuck your
brains out. But we have to go. It's time . . . and I don't want
the Hounds to somehow swoop in and curry her favor before
I get a chance to meet her and cozy up to her. I don't know
if that could happen, but I don't want to take a chance on it."

He leaned against me as I turned to the mirror to check my
makeup, pressing his body against my back, spooning me. I
could feel him, hard and erect against me, and I groaned, wanting him, wanting to strip off my clothes and crawl into bed.

With a low chuckle, he wrapped his arms around my waist
and leaned down to whisper in my ear. "Can you feel me?
Can you feel how much I want you? How much I need you?"

"Yes." My words caught in my throat. His breath was hot on my neck, his voice rough. He nuzzled my neck with his lips, brushing back my hair with his face to kiss the skin beneath. I squirmed, heat rising between my legs as I let out a ragged breath.

"You're making it hard for me to concentrate."

"You're just making me hard in general. You always do. I love the way your body fits against mine." He caught my ear with his teeth and tugged gently, avoiding my gold hoops.

Most men had wanted to fuck me because of my boobs—they were huge—and then they had complained about the rest of my size. I wasn't stick thin, by any stretch of the imagination. So Bryan's adoration of my body came as a welcome relief. But more than that, he respected me, and he loved talking to me. The combination was irresistible.

"If we don't get a move on, we won't make it out of the bedroom, you know," I murmured, turning to wrap my arms around his neck. I tugged on his lip with my teeth, then kissed him, full and deep and dark as he moaned into my mouth. But I managed to catch hold of myself and I pushed him back. "Later. After. I'll probably need it to take the edge off the worry. This isn't going to be a cakewalk, you know."

"I know. Come on, killjoy. Reject me and then make me go out hunting through a moldy old graveyard." But he grinned when he said it, and held out his hand. I took it and, gathering our jackets and my purse and bag of goodies, we headed out to the car.

I had thought of asking Peggin to go with us, but decided the last thing she needed was a trip into the land of the Unliving. Ellia stayed home, given Penelope's warning. We drove down to the cemetery, even though we could have easily walked—too many times after my encounters with the dead, I found I needed to get my ass into a diner or a bar or anything to touch base with the living again, to remind myself that I was still a living, breathing woman.

Veronica's lair was at the back of the Pest House Cemetery,

against the base of a high grassy butte overlooking the lake. The lair was located within the hillock, and from what I knew, was a labyrinth of tunnels. The Pest House Cemetery was the oldest part of the Whisper Hollow Cemetery. During the 1800s, a network of institutions had sprung up around the country, meant to house those with TB and other communicable diseases that were, at that time, incurable. The patients were usually quarantined to protect the community, though it really meant incarceration, and they were left to die in squalid conditions. In most cases, they were buried in cemeteries next to or near the Pest House.

The Pest House Cemetery was located directly behind the old Pest House, which I had not braved a look-through yet. The Pest House was dilapidated and had to be straight from the mid-1800s. There was a faded sign over the weathered house, which was as large as a two-story barn. The letters on the sign were so old that I couldn't make out what they once said, and the outer walls of the house were so weathered that most of the paint had flecked away, leaving gray wood beneath, its color tinged with moss and mildew. The windows were long broken, but shards of glass remained in the corners, and here and there metal trim and hinges had rusted away.

The steps leading up to the Pest House were falling apart, and the chimneys—there were two of them—were both broken, with chinks and pieces of brick scattered on the roof and on the ground below. Dark windows on the second story loomed like blank eye sockets, and every time I saw the Pest House, I could sense spirits inside, watching over the grounds.

I remembered that, as a young girl, the cockier jocks in school used to dare each other to go break into the Pest House. But as far as I recalled, nobody had ever been stupid enough to do it. For one thing, everybody knew that Veronica's lair was near there. For another, to get to the Pest House, you had to go through the Pest House Cemetery, and it was roundly accepted that the most dangerous spirits were found there.

The paths of the dead were numerous, but these spirits fell

into an odd combination of Haunts and Mournful Ones. They were so uneasy from their deaths, most of which had been painful and at the hands of neglect and disease, that they had merged into the background, intrinsically bound to the land. That happened at times, though it wasn't all that common.

When someone had been violently murdered and their body wasn't found—whether forever, or for years—this could happen. Or it could occur in cases like shipwrecks or accidents, where the deaths were violent and the bodies left behind.

When that happened, there was no exorcism possible. The spirits were there permanently, odd mutants of the astral plane who could harm others, and often reached out to do so in their anger and pain. Many of those who died in the Pest House had remained behind, and they wandered the cemetery and the old house, seeking revenge for their inhumane treatment.

As Bryan and I made our way from the car through the cemetery, past Penelope's tomb, we came to the iron gates that separated the rest of the graveyard from the Pest House Cemetery. By the looks of them, they hadn't been opened in some time. Vines were twining through the iron spikes that made up the gate and the fence. Beyond the gate, the trees seemed a bit wilder, looming darker and more unkempt. I knew for a fact that the lawn care service seldom came back to this area. They were as afraid as the rest of the town of what lay beyond the fence row.

I grabbed hold of the latch holding the gate shut and turned to Bryan. "Are you ready?"

He grimaced. "I'm as ready as I'll ever be. I know this is something you have to do, so I'll refrain from asking if you're sure you want to go gallivanting in there."

I let out a long breath. "Thank you. It would be so easy to forget this and go home. But I can't. If my grandmother had lived, I would have met Veronica by now, and I wouldn't have to cope with this fear. But I can't put it off any longer. Not with the Hounds and Magda out there."

Taking another long breath, I exhaled and pushed open the gates. Rust showered down to cover my hands as the metal gave a shriek of protest. The sidewalk was covered with debris from the windstorms. I licked my lips, then glanced over at Bryan before setting foot on the path. He swung in behind me, following close. The moment we walked through the gates I could feel the shift in energy.

It was wild here, like an injured animal hiding in the shadows to lick an infected wound. I shivered. Veronica's lair was to the right of the Pest House, and so I veered onto what I thought was the right path. It was hard to tell where the flagstones were. We were now in an area that was so overgrown and entangled that even the headstones were covered with ivy and moss. No one had been back here to tend the graves in a long time. I wondered if it would help. If we watched over the graves and remembered the dead, would that calm the unrest? But even as I asked myself the question, I knew the answer was no. No amount of remembrance, no amount of reverence would be able to pry the spirits from the land.

"There are some angry entities here," Bryan said.

"They have a right to be angry. They were tossed into this house, ill with either tubereulosis or other contagious diseases, and they were left here to die. No one came to visit them except the doctors—and they wore strange, odd outfits that made them look like aliens. The doctors spent as little time as they could checking in on the patients. And the nursing staff were a joke. They didn't want to catch what the patients had either, so they would bring a vat of soup or gruel, and a bag of bread, and drop it off. I doubt anyone here ever got proper medical attention for any wounds or for their illnesses. From what I read, when the place was closed and cleaned out, the blankets they found were mere rags, and the mattresses were nothing more than straw pallets on the floor. They made the patients bury the dead so that they wouldn't have to touch them. All in all, it's a grim reminder of how dangerous so many diseases used to be."

Bryan let out a soft breath. "I really wasn't aware of how bad it was."

I nodded. "Most people don't even know that these places existed, but they were common across Europe and—even though not quite so common here—they were found around the country. I imagine there are plenty of them around, rotting in fields, and people have no idea what they really were. They probably think they were just abandoned houses."

I stopped for a moment, holding out my hands. Bryan stood, arms crossed, keeping watch as I closed my eyes, trying to tune in to the energy of the area. A cold chill raced over me. I opened my eyes slowly, willing myself to see what there was to see.

As I glanced around, vaporous spirits appeared in my line of sight. They filled the graveyard, sitting on gravestones, wandering through the cemetery, misty forms with angry expressions. My stomach clenched as I felt their pain. Not only had they suffered the pain of their illnesses, but they had suffered neglect and malnourishment and mistreatment. From the reading I had done, I was also aware that the inmates had abused each other, the stronger ones stealing food from the weaker ones. And since men, women, and children had been forced to live together in the same houses, rape was not uncommon.

I shook my head, reaching out to Bryan to steady myself. He took my hand, kissing it gently.

"There's nothing you can do for them. You can't release them, and you can't make things any better. I'm afraid you're just going to have to accept that they will always be here, always be reliving their deaths and their lives." He wrapped his arm around my shoulder then and kissed the top of my head. "It's a painful reality, love."

I caught my breath and swallowed the tears that had welled up. I had to accept there were some things I had no control over. I could do my best to keep them from harming others, but I couldn't put them to rest and I knew it.

"I know, and thank you. Thank you for being here with me."

We passed through the graveyard then, heading toward the grassy knoll that led up to the butte overlooking the lake. It was difficult to see in the darkness here—there were no lampposts scattered around to light the way. Bryan was holding the flashlight. But up ahead, against the incline of the slope, I could see a dark opening with figures milling around it. We had reached Veronica's lair.

I froze, staring ahead as the flashlight flickered in the darkness. I had been afraid of meeting Penelope, but she was civilized, and she worked *with* the spirit shamans. Veronica, however she might have been in life, was fully one of the Unliving. While I knew she wouldn't attack me, I also knew that she could be a formidable enemy, should I get off on the wrong foot with her.

I glanced up at Bryan. "I can't believe I'm really doing this. I mean, I know I have to, but sometimes my life seems so bizarre when I stop to think about it. I am standing out here in a haunted cemetery, waiting to meet someone who is technically a monster. Why the hell did I volunteer for this job?"

Bryan let out a laugh. "The fate of your birthright, just like it's the fate of mine. Believe me, I don't relish this either. I'd rather be home, curled up with you on the sofa, watching TV and eating chips. Or in the bedroom, making love. Or even at the community center playing bingo. Right now any of the three sounds vastly more entertaining than what we are about to do. But we don't have any choice, as you so eloquently pointed out earlier."

I wanted to smack him, using my own words against me, but I settled for a long sigh, then resolutely turned toward the hillock, and marched forward to meet a dead queen.

CHAPTER 7

❧

I wasn't sure what to expect, but I was on my guard. Bryan walked stiffly behind me, and I could tell his wolf was up—listening, sensing, waiting for anybody to make the wrong move. For a moment, I thought about asking him to shift before we reached the lair, but then decided I wanted him in human form. He could listen and catch nuances I might miss. Two pairs of eyes and ears were always better than one.

As we approached, Bryan aimed the light so that the beam illuminated the ground in front of us, rather than at eye level, as a courtesy to the Unliving. They weren't all that overly fond of light. Two figures—men, by the looks of them—stopped, turning toward us, while the rest ignored us. They crossed the distance between the opening into the hill and where we were standing. They had to be the guards sent to escort us.

As they approached, I wasn't sure what to expect. My experience with the actual Unliving had been extremely limited. I was used to Haunts and the Mournful and the Wandering Ones . . . but the Unliving were a different breed. I wondered if they would wear their death masks. And even though I knew they weren't anything like what zombies were supposed to be like, my mind couldn't help but go there.

Bryan stood close enough to jump to my defense, if need be. I wasn't sure what to do next, so we just watched and waited.

The guards were twins and looked to be around fifteen—which probably meant they had died at that point in their lives. They were tow-haired, and tall. But the light in their eyes came from an unnatural fire—white flames that glimmered in the dark expanse of their eyes—and they shimmered in the darkness, their bodies sparkling with a pale green nimbus. The boys stopped in front of me, staring at me for a moment before slowly inclining their heads in a truncated show of respect. Whispers surrounded us as other members of the Unliving suddenly crowded in.

I cleared my throat. I wanted to both show respect and yet take control. I might be in Veronica's territory but my station afforded me a status over the community of the dead.

"I am Kerris Fellwater, and I'm the spirit shaman of Whisper Hollow. This is my guardian, Bryan. I have an appointment with Veronica." As my voice hit the air, it made me jump, it shattered the silence so completely. The sound of the living was always incredibly solid compared to ghostly voices.

The twins simultaneously nodded—eerie enough in itself—then, as one, they said, "Follow us." Without waiting, they turned and headed toward the entrance.

I realized we'd lose sight of them if we didn't get a move on, so I lurched forward, almost tripping over a half-buried rock, but Bryan steadied me and we followed them into the depths of the butte.

As we entered the opening, I was half expecting a gate to fall down behind us, trapping us, but instead we entered a cavern the size of a high school auditorium. Five tunnels branched off from the back wall. A flickering yellow light cast shadows on the walls, but I couldn't identify from where the diffused illumination was coming. It spread out through the entire cavern, and there seemed to be no main source.

The cavern was filled with shadows and shades—some were ghosts, outright, who paid little attention to me. Others were members of the Unliving, and they stopped, turning to watch us as we passed by. The hairs on my neck froze to attention, and I could barely catch my breath. The scent of the grave lingered here, and decay. It felt like time itself had stopped the moment we entered the lair, and the weight of dirt and stone above us weighed heavily on my shoulders, pressing down so hard that I wondered if we'd ever find our way back out.

The twins turned to the second tunnel from the left and silently led us toward it. I glanced back at Bryan, then swallowed my fear and followed them. By now, my breath was shallow, and I was sure the stench of fear was rolling off me like a noxious cloud. I tried to gather my wits.

Morrígan, Lady of Crows, Lady of the Battlefield, strengthen me.

And suddenly, from somewhere in the distance, I thought I heard the keening of a crow, long and sharp and echoing through the night.

The passage walls were polished to a high sheen, and I realized the Unliving had wandered through here year after year, using the walls for support. Years of hands smoothing the dirt had caused it to glisten like dark marble. Behind me, Bryan made sure to keep close enough so that no one could interject themselves between us.

The tunnels couldn't be terribly long, not given how little distance there was between the cemetery and the lake. And sure enough, within a few minutes, the twins stopped at an entrance to another cavern. They separated, one to each side of the tunnel, and motioned for us to enter. I wanted to ask who they were and how long they had been here as servants of Veronica—their dress gave me no clue, for they were wearing old-fashioned garments, the kind a Ren-Faire troubadour might wear. Their hair was short and curly, and the style could have been from so many eras.

As we passed by them, I paused. "Thank you." I turned to the one on my right, staring into his glittering eyes.

The fire within them flared, and a knot of fear rose in my stomach. But all he said was, "As you will," and then a slow, cruel smile spread across his thick lips, giving him a predatory look.

I swallowed again, then stepped through the opening with Bryan following.

And there she was. Sitting on a throne of bones. The bones were woven together like roots of a tree, human remains so old that I knew, just from looking, they were from centuries past.

Veronica was sitting on the throne, shoulders back, so straight she might be a statue. Her skin was almost translucent, like milk-porcelain, and her lips were ruby red. Her eyes arrested me. They weren't the black of the grave, but they were pure white, with brilliant green irises encircled by a ring of blue fire. Her hair was long and straight, jet-black and sleek as silk. Veronica was wearing a velvet dress—as white as mourning. And atop her head, she wore a diadem of gold, with an obsidian cabochon in the center. Diamonds sparkled from the circlet, scalloping the golden band.

Bryan and I approached the throne—a ring of guards watching us—and I stopped a few feet away from her, my heart in my throat.

"Well met, Kerris Fellwater, Daughter of the Morrígan, you jailor of ghosts, you demon to the dead." Her voice blew through the chamber like it was snatched up the moment after she spoke and whirled off to other lands. "So you enter my kingdom for the first time, and so you are greeted."

She stood, and I could see the throne clearly. A skeleton was embedded in it—full, arranged so that she sat on its lap, rested her head against its skull, her arms on its arms. The ghoulish nature of the scene hit me, and I had to force myself to stand my ground. I quickly looked away, taking in the rest of the room.

The chamber was of moderate size, draped in silver and black velvet, and in the center of the room a large fire pit roared with ice-blue flames, giving off the chill of etheric fire. Members of the Unliving filled the room, standing silently, waiting for Veronica to direct them.

As she descended the stairs from the throne—I counted seven—I steeled myself, feeling like I was caught in a late-night movie, a silent thriller from days gone by. But there was nothing left but to go through with the meeting.

Veronica crossed the room to me and I realized just how tall she was—far taller than Penelope, taller than anyone I had ever met. She must have been near to seven feet, towering, and her dress crested around her full breasts, the sweetheart neckline trimmed in silver. The dress flowed around her legs, shrouding her body, and the closer she got, the harder it was to focus on anything but the Queen of the Unliving standing in front of me.

"Kerrissssss . . ." My name hissed through her teeth. "I knew your grandmother. I knew your great-grandmother. I've known so many of your kind through the ages. And each spirit shaman is bound to silence, on the honor of the Morrígan's name, when I tell them my secrets. For I am as much a daughter of the Goddess of Battle as are you."

I stared at her, wondering what she meant. I had read nothing of this in Lila's Shadow Journal.

Veronica held out her arm and pulled up her sleeve. There, on her arm, was the same symbol that I had been born with. At the base of my lower back, I had a birthmark— a crow, standing on a crescent moon, the mark of the spirit shaman. The members of the Crescent Moon Society wore similar symbols as tattoos, but spirit shamans were born with it. As I stared at Veronica's wrist, I realized that it, too, was a birthmark.

I looked up at her, realizing what this meant. "That is no tattoo."

She inclined her head. "You understand."

"You were a spirit shaman."

"As are you, now."

A cold sweat broke over me and I ducked my head, not wanting to ask the question that bubbled up in me. But her gaze drew my own back up, and magnetized, I stared at her. A veil of fire flared up, flames dancing around me, consuming me with its heat. But the flames did not burn, and they seemed oddly welcoming.

"When . . . how . . . did you become . . ." My words trailed off.

She smiled, and her teeth were beautiful, needles of glistening bone that could rend and tear. Suddenly, her destructive beauty hit me full force and I found myself longing for her touch.

"Spirit shamans who turn their back on the Morrígan become the royalty of the dead. We can never escape her. Once given, vows cannot be undone. I am bound and unbound, servant and yet master, lover and betrayer of the Mother of Phantoms. One of my curses is that when asked by a spirit shaman, I must tell my story, as a warning." Her voice, so smooth and lovely, was filled with anger and I could sense the desire for destruction hovering right below the surface.

"What did you do?" I had to ask. There was no way I could leave this chamber without knowing what Veronica had done to incur this punishment.

Veronica laughed, her voice throaty and rich. "I killed my protector and my lament singer, and I handed my village over to an invading prince for diamonds and jewels. The same crown I wear here, I wore as his bride. We razed the country, tearing it to shreds . . . destroying all who lay in our path.

Until I met an army led by the Morrígan, and the Phantom Queen herself threw me down, and cursed me to forever walk the world. 'Queen you are,' she said. 'And queen you shall remain, over the dead, forever trapped in a world of your own making.' And so I became one of the Queens of the Unliving, and was sent from my home, to wander the world until I found a place to settle and make my lair."

By the way she told it, I could tell she had relayed the tale many times over, to other spirit shamans. And then— just as I was searching for something to say—a crow flew through the tunnels to land on my shoulder. It screeched in my ear.

Pay long attention, my daughter. For this is the fortune of those who betray their oaths to me. Learn, as your grandmother learned, and her mother before her, what happens to those who renege on their duties to me. Demand the vow from her.

And then, the crow vanished as if it had never been.

I swallowed again but this time I felt stronger. The Morrígan was with me, and she wouldn't let Veronica harm me if I stayed true. "The vow . . . I demand the vow."

Veronica laughed again, but this time it was short and brusque. "She's been here, I can sense her. You know, at times, the loss of her protection cuts like a knife." She paused, then cocked her head, and shrugged. "As it was, it shall always be. Hold out your hand."

I did, trepidation filling my heart. But I felt impelled, and by now I was learning to follow my instincts.

Veronica took my hand in hers, staring at it. "So soft, and so vibrant and filled with life." A hungry note entered her voice and I almost pulled away, but she held tight, using one of her long black nails to gash the pad of my palm. Then, doing the same to hers, she pressed her wound to mine.

"By the sight of the Morrígan, by the wing of crow and the kiss of magic, I bind my service to you, Kerris Fellwater, spirit shaman of Whisper Hollow, however I might help and serve. So promise and vow, I do. By my name, Veronica, Queen of the Unliving, Fallen Daughter of the Dark Mother, Watcher from the Land of the Dead, under the moonlight and wind, I give oath."

As she spoke, her voice took on a plaintive note, and I realized that tears were trailing down her cheeks. Veronica was crying, and as I held her gaze, I saw how the depths of years had weighted her down, resting on her soul and shoulders. And I saw something more—regret, and the wistful desire to let go and become vapor . . . to retreat to the Veil for good.

I brought her hand to my lips and gently kissed the top of it. "I'm sorry. I'm so sorry."

Her lip trembled. "Do not make my mistake, Kerris. Never forget the power of she whom you serve. The Morrígan is the mother of your existence. She is the brilliant queen, and she is a terrifying destroyer. She will never let you forget that you belong to her. Don't allow arrogance to rule you. It's far, far too late for me. I'll never walk again in the sunlight. I'll never cross the Gatekeeper's doorstep. I'll molder here in the depths until I wither into a husk, and then one day in the far future, the wind will blow me away, and I will finally find peace."

And then, the intimate circle surrounding us gave way and she stepped back, returning to her throne, once again the arrogant queen of the Unliving.

"What help do you seek today?"

I stared at her, looking for any semblance of the woman who knew she had made a dreadful mistake, but would forever pay for it. But the Veronica who was weary and tired had vanished, and once again, I was facing the cold visage of a long-dead ruler.

"There are Ankou in the forest up on Timber Peak. The forest Fae say you didn't summon them. I need to know if you have any clue as to who brought them forth and what they are doing here." I shored my shoulders back, feeling stronger and less afraid. I knew her secret now, and I realized she wouldn't hurt me. She *couldn't.*

Veronica shook her head, once again taking her seat on the bones of the dead. "No, I did not summon them. But the Hounds did. And their chew toy—the toy they underestimate. The old bitch of the forest is a threat, Kerris. Magda is what I sought to become. She serves a darker goddess than the Morrígan, and she seeks to destroy all that is wild and wonderful and out of her control in this town. There are fifteen witch bottles in the forest that are the summoning vehicles. Have the Matriarchs destroy them. The Ankou that run rogue carry Arawn's power, and they can and will begin harming the villagers."

She paused, then motioned to the entrance. "That is all I can do." And with that, she fell silent.

I waited, but she merely turned away and I realized the meeting was over. The twins joined us, and motioned toward the doorway. I glanced at Bryan. He was standing there, waiting, looking almost frozen as if he had no clue what had been going on. A moment later, he followed me as we turned to leave.

I glanced over my shoulder when I reached the entrance to the tunnels. Veronica was staring at me, and once again, I saw the trace of a tear on her cheek. I found myself crying, too, and I reached up, touched one of my tears, and held it up toward her. She nodded, a ghost of a smile crossing her lips, and then—before I could say another word, the light in the chamber vanished and everything went dark.

As we threaded our way out of the tunnels and found ourselves back in the Pest House Cemetery, I said nothing. All I could think of was what I had found out. Veronica had been a spirit shaman who had turned her back on the Morrígan. And this was her fate.

Bryan seemed to snap out of whatever silence he had been steeped in when we hit the graveyard, and he turned to me. "Are you all right?"

I nodded, softly. "I . . . think what she told me . . . I'll need to process it for a while."

"What she told you? That Magda is responsible for the Ankou?"

As I listened to the nuance in his voice, I realized that Bryan had no clue of what had actually transpired. I started to ask what he remembered, but then Veronica's words rang in my head. *And each spirit shaman is bound to silence, on the honor of the Morrígan's name, when I tell them my secrets.* And I knew right then that I would never be able to tell him—or anyone—Veronica's secret.

No sooner had the thought crossed my mind than a cawing echoed overhead and I glanced up to see a single crow perched on a gravestone, staring at me. The Crow Man, it was. And as the stars began to spin, I fell into his world.

The Crow Man and I were walking across a long spit of grass beside the rolling waters of the Strait of Juan de Fuca. A log, towering timber once, lay weathered, stripped of bough and limb, driftwood on the shore.

For a while, we just walked. It was nice—the weather was calm, the sky a strange blend of orange and blue shimmering against the wispy clouds, and I estimated it was near sunset. The shore was a field of pebbles, leading down to the sand and froth of water breaking against the dunes. I felt like I could breathe, that a weight had been lifted off my shoulders.

The Crow Man leaned over to pick up a sand dollar. He held it out to me, showing me both sides, then chucked it far out into the water. He shaded his eyes with his hand, staring at the rolling waves that flowed through the strait.

"The lake has been cloistered long from its sister waters." His voice was soft, echoing in the stillness of the shore. "Not all water is cleansing. Not all spirits can be cleared."

I thought of the Pest House Cemetery. "I think I understand that. Some spirits root too deep; they become part of the land itself, correct?"

He nodded. "You learn. And some spirits become part of the water—when the waters are bound against their own kind. When the lakes and ponds run deep, but not free. Energy gets trapped. Spirits become chained. There is no purification strong enough unless channels be dug and the waters washed clear."

We came to another driftwood log and I settled myself on it, staring out into the choppy waters. The wind whistled past, ruffling through my hair, blowing it every which way.

"What you are telling me . . . I cannot clear the Lady from the lake, correct?"

"Peaches are sweet, and you speak the truth." He winked at me, sitting on the end of the log, hands pressed on his knees as his headdress shaded his face. "And Veronica, she will remain in her post. You cannot help her. Don't think to try."

This was some of the clearest advice the Crow Man had ever given me, which surprised me. Usually, he spoke in riddles. I cocked my head, squinting at him with a puzzled look. "Why are you telling me this?

"Because, you are who you are, Kerris Fellwater. You might look to intervene. And that . . . would be a bad idea. Better I tell you, than you find out the hard way."

A flock of crows appeared behind us, winging their way to land near our feet. They circled him, their incessant cawing falling into silence.

I gazed at the birds. One, in particular, was watching me. As I stared back at it, I had the distinct feeling our conversation was being monitored.

"*She* sent you, didn't she? The Morrígan? To warn me."

He shrugged, but a flicker of a smile brightened his face. "She has her ways, she does. Now, Veronica was warned, as well—*Cease the warring. Go back to your post.* She ignored the signs. Three, I sent her, and three more, and three again.

She ignored them all. Those were dark days." He paused, then added, "Her name was Véronique at that time."

I pressed my lips together. That the Morrígan had warned Veronica and given nine signs and that she had ignored them was a lesson to be remembered. There would be no salvation for her, no freedom from the living death she endured. She had chosen her path and only when the Morrígan was ready, would she be freed. The Crow Man was right, I had been—in the back recesses of my mind—wondering if there was anything I could do to help the spirit.

"She seemed so remorseful . . ." I didn't phrase it as a question, but an observation. I didn't want the Morrígan thinking I was questioning her judgment.

The Crow Man shifted his foot, making a tunnel in the sand with his toe. "A bluff is as good as a trump, if you are playing with someone who trusts you to tell the truth." He held out one hand. In his fingers, he held a coin. "Heads or tails?"

"Heads." I wasn't sure what game we were playing, but I knew better than to ignore him.

He flipped it, and the coin landed tails up. "You lose. Pick up the coin."

I leaned over and fished it up. As I blew the sand off it, I saw that both sides were tails. "You cheated."

"You didn't think to ask. You accepted that I was offering you a fair choice without finding out the facts. *Always* gather your facts. *Always* question, especially when you are conversing with someone who views you as an enemy whom she cannot harm . . . outright." He laughed then and held out his hand. "My coin, please."

I softly placed the coin in his palm and for the briefest second, my finger touched his flesh and it felt like I was being sucked into a vortex of whirling energy. He quickly pulled away, tucking his coin back in his pocket.

Staring at my finger, I contemplated what he had said. "Veronica can't harm me because of the Morrígan, but she doesn't like me. She'll help because she's forced to, but I shouldn't trust her—there are ways she can still subvert the truth. Am I on the right track?"

"Like a cart set for market." And with that, he motioned for me to stand and waved his hand. The water blurred, the sandspit blurred, and the next moment . . .

. . . I was back beside Bryan, staring at a bright light. Only I was in the car, and he was gazing at me, a worried look on his face. I blinked, shaking my head as I realized it was still nighttime. The light was coming from the cab light of the car.

"Are you all right? Kerris?" He let out a sudden breath. "You're awake! Kerris, speak to me."

I winced, aching like I had been sitting in a cramped position too long. It didn't take much for me to figure out that he had put on my seat belt and it was grating into my shoulder because of the way it was positioned across my breasts. Seat belts and big breasts weren't a good mix.

"I'm okay—really. I just . . . the Crow Man took me wandering for a little while. He was just trying to help me with something." I glanced at Bryan, shifting as I unbuckled my seat belt. We were still in the cemetery, but at least we were out of the area around the Pest House. "Can we get out of here? I need to go out—get some food, be somewhere filled with people. People who are alive."

He laughed then, looking relieved. "We can do that. I wondered what had happened but figured that it was something on the order of the Morrígan or the Crow Man." He didn't ask what I had learned, or where I had been. By now I realized that Bryan was uniquely gifted in understanding that his role was one of support, at least as far as being my guardian went. He would accept what I could tell him, but not pry further.

I wanted to tell him about Veronica, but the words were

frozen. *Not your secret to tell* . . . that little inner voice whispered. Instead, I sought for what I could say.

"Veronica . . . we can trust her to help us when we ask, but I'll never fully put faith in her. There are so many layers to her story and by now you've figured out that I can't tell you everything. But . . . I will tell you when we can trust her, and when we can't. Do you remember what she said about looking for the witch bottles in the forest that Magda made?"

It was Bryan's turn to look puzzled. "Um . . . no. I don't remember hearing . . . much of anything, to be honest, after we walked into her throne room."

"I'm not surprised. Well, she told me that there are witch bottles in the forest that are the summoning vehicles for the rogue Ankou, and that we need to find them and have the Matriarchs destroy them. There are fifteen of them. How we're to find them, I don't know. And I have no idea what they look like, but I bet you anything Ivy or Oriel will know. Or Ellia, even."

Bryan sucked in a deep breath. "I really don't remember that conversation, but yeah, that sounds about right. So, she said Magda was the one who was behind this?"

I nodded. "Yes, and the Hounds still think she's . . . as Veronica put it, their chew toy. But Magda's really the one running the show. She also said that the Shadow People will start attacking the village if we don't do something soon."

"That means a trip to Timber Peak to look for those bottles. This time, we'll take the Crescent Moon Society. They're going to have to know about this." He reached across to stroke my hair back from my face. "I wish you hadn't had to go through what you did tonight. I may not remember much of it, but I remember enough to know it wasn't easy."

The softness of his voice melted my heart. In two short months, I had bonded with Bryan like I never had before with anybody. I'd dated, I'd gone out with men over the years and slept with them, but until now, nobody had ever managed to penetrate the depths of my heart. I gazed into his eyes, wanting to say so much and yet . . . it all seemed so dreamlike—so like a movie that I kept pinching myself to know that this was really happening.

"I never expected to fall for my guardian. I guess, after seeing Grandma Lila for so many years without a protector . . . I didn't think I'd have one either." My voice was shaking. I wasn't sure what was about to happen, but it felt like we were on the precipice of something so deep and powerful that we'd never make it out from the fall.

"Kerris, I told you I've been waiting for you. I knew that this was my calling in life—to be the guardian of a spirit shaman. The Morrígan told me herself. But . . . I wasn't sure what would happen either. Now I can't imagine ever being apart from you." He leaned across the seat, holding my chin firmly as he stared into my eyes. "I will always be here for you. I will always be your guardian protector."

"Never let go of me, please. Never let go."

And then, as his lips met mine, I dissolved into his kiss, holding on to the warmth of his body even as the winds rocked the car, and the spirits caught in the night wandered by.

CHAPTER 8

❧

I had a restless night, with dreams filled with fire and flame and skeletal thrones, but Bryan was there, and he woke me every time I seemed to be stressing out. We didn't make love—I was too worn out from the encounter with Veronica, and by the time we stopped for burgers, and then got back to my place, Bryan pretty much dragged my butt inside, drew me a warm bubble bath, and then put me to bed when I fell asleep in the tub.

The alarm went off at six A.M. sharp. I reached to turn it off, thinking we should just go back to sleep, but then remembered: Today was Peggin's moving day. Groaning, I pushed myself to a sitting position and, blurry-eyed, turned to stare at Bryan, who was mumbling something under his breath. I couldn't catch the words but it had to do with the alarm and ways he'd like to kill it.

Laughing, I reached over and poked him in the shoulder. "Wake up. We need to get over to Peggin's. She's providing breakfast. Get up, you." I leaned down and brushed away a stray lock of hair to kiss him on the forehead.

His eyes flew open, and he rolled over, grabbing me down on top of him, laughing. "Got you! Give me a kiss, wench."

He was tousled and sleepy and warm and I wanted to melt into his arms. I pressed my lips against his and he murmured something as he kissed me, his tongue playing over mine. My stomach tightened as a streak of desire split me in two, and before I could say a word, he pulled me up to straddle him. I said nothing, my breath shattered from the heat. The tangle of sheets got in the way and he shoved them aside so I could lean down and rub my breasts against him, my nipples stiffening as they met his broad chest.

"Ride me," he whispered, and I found myself moist and ready. I adjusted my position as he put on a condom, then eased my way down his shaft, letting out a long moan as he thrust upward, driving his hard cock into my body. I arched my back, and he eased a hand between my thighs to finger me, his fingers fluttering over my sex, sending one shiver after another racing though me. I began to ride him then, grinding against him as he bucked below me. He grabbed my hips, holding tight, and I cupped my breasts, squeezing them as he watched, the hungry look in his eyes deepening.

"Touch yourself," he said, and I did, reaching down with one hand to finger myself. As the fire spread, I circled my clit, rubbing hard and fast while I used my other hand to pinch my nipple. Bryan held me tightly, thrusting as he filled me to the core.

"Do you like it when I fuck you?" Bryan asked, his breath coming hard.

"Don't stop, please don't stop . . . *harder, please* . . . fuck me *hard*." I fell forward, my breasts pressing against him as he encircled my waist, pulling me so tight that we moved as one. He was so deep inside me that it felt like we could never break apart. He rolled me over beneath him, his hips swiveling against me as I began to peak, riding the wave as it carried me upward.

"I'm coming," I cried out, no longer in control of my voice.

Bryan shifted, pumping faster, and then, as I let out a shriek, he grunted and stiffened, arching his back as he came. A moment later, he slumped against me, reaching up to stroke my hair back and kiss me gently on the lips.

"Good morning to you," he whispered gently. "Nothing like a morning quickie to wake the blood."

"Good morning back, and you're right." I laughed. "We'd better get showered and dressed."

"And feed the cats."

"And feed the cats, yes." I glanced up to find Gabby on the bottom of the bed, staring at us. "She could burn a hole in us with that glare." Apparently Her Highness did not appreciate breakfast being delayed by a morning romp. I glanced at the clock. Ten till seven.

"Come on, missy. Get your bottom out of that bed." Bryan jumped out of bed, smacking me lightly on the ass as he did so.

We jumped in the shower together, lathering up with my honeysuckle body wash. Bryan soaped my back for me, then turned around so I could return the favor. I loved the huge shower. The baths at his house were even bigger, but my house felt cozier. I had bound my hair into a ponytail to keep it from getting wet—I washed it every three days so it wouldn't dry out and turn into frizz—but Bryan squeezed out some shampoo and began scrubbing his hair. It was shorter, though it covered the nape of his neck and his ears, and would dry quickly.

I slipped out of the shower, leaving him to finish, and toweled off, then sat at my vanity to put on my makeup. I glanced at my legs—they could use a quick shave but I'd do that in a bath tonight after helping out Peggin. By then we'd all be grubby. I popped my birth control pill into my mouth, then brushed my teeth and headed back to the bedroom to dress as Bryan stepped out of the shower. Today would be heavy work, so I chose a pair of old jeans, a pale gray sweatshirt, and a pair of low-heeled ankle boots. As I was redoing my ponytail, Bryan entered the bedroom, scrubbing the water from his hair with a towel.

"I brought my work clothes over last night," he said as he sat on the edge of the bed and slid on his briefs. Then he pulled on jeans, a sweatshirt with a Nirvana logo on the front, and his boots. "Peggin's sure she wants to do this?"

I grimaced. "Yeah, and she's already put a down payment on the place. She's able to move in so quickly because it's rent-to-own. So until the escrow goes through, she's just renting the place. I wish she'd reconsider, but Peggin's a smart woman and she knows what she's doing. I just think she underestimates the power of the area down there. Fogwhistle Pier is a freakshow place, and it's got a long history of *accidents*."

"How did the Lady . . . when did she get her start?" Bryan ran a comb through his hair and then, after we tossed our dirty clothes from the night before into the laundry, we headed into the kitchen to feed the cats.

"There are several parts to that answer, to be honest. First, there was always a creature in the lake—there are two, actually, that we know of. One's the lake monster. Totally different thing and doesn't tend to be seen around where the Lady stays. She can be all over the lake, but she primarily sticks around Whisper Hollow now. The lake monster's . . . well . . . a small cousin of Nessie, we think. But the Lady . . . she's something entirely different."

"Tell me. I should learn as much as I can about all the creatures that make this place their home, especially since you seem to be involved with all of them to some degree." He pulled out clean dishes for the cat food as I opened three cans of Fancy Feast. While I scooped the wet food into the dishes, Bryan filled another with fresh kibble and made sure their water fountain was running clean. Daphne and Agent

H paced impatiently, while Gabby leaped up on the counter to egg me on.

I frowned at her. "You know you're not supposed to be on the kitchen counters, especially when there's food up here."

"Yeah, you tell her, and just see how effective that is." Bryan snickered. He had taken a shine to my cats in a way that warmed my heart, and my cats—in return—had fallen head over heels for him, even though they seemed to sense the wolf in him. They also had taken a strong shine to Peggin. They respected my grandfather Aidan; probably sensing the lionshifter side of him brought out their obedience.

"Oh hush, you'll just encourage them." I swatted him on the arm lightly, and laughed.

"So, what else goes into making the Lady . . . *the Lady*?"

I pressed my lips together. "Well, first there is the lake spirit that's always been there—nobody knows what she is, or how she got her start. But then, over the years, she started taking people and each victim seems to strengthen her. Also, in 1937, a woman named Hallie Illingworth vanished from the area. She was constantly showing up to work with bruises, and her husband gave her more than one black eye. The cops had been called out due to their fights. But one morning in December 1937, Hallie was gone. Never seen again. Her husband told everybody she had run off."

"Somehow I don't think she ran very far, did she?"

I shook my head. "No. But nobody heard a peep from her till 1940. Two men were out fishing when they found something floating in the water. Turns out, it was Hallie. But the odd thing is, the chemicals in the lake water had turned her body into what basically amounts to . . . soap— the process is called saponification. Long story short, they discovered she had been weighted down. Her husband was eventually arrested and convicted of second-degree murder. When I was young, my grandma Lila told me about the story, and she said that Hallie's spirit had left behind an angry residue that blended with the lake's own Lady. So she, too, became part of the overall Lady. When outsiders refer to the *Lady of Crescent Lake*, they're usually talking about Hallie. But our Lady . . . she's far more insidious and dangerous than that poor murder victim."

Bryan shook his head. "The history here . . . it's ruthless at times, isn't it?"

"Oh, that's not even the half of it." I gave Gabby one last pat on the head. "Let's go. I want to get coffee on the way. I told Peggin that it would be my treat."

"Did she ever get the chimney guy in to clean out her chimney?"

"I think so—you can ask her when we get to her place." I gathered my purse and keys, and Bryan grabbed his backpack—which he'd taken to using instead of a briefcase— and we locked the door, heading out.

A long the way, we stopped for coffee. I knew what Peggin liked, and she'd assured me that Deev would drink whatever we offered him as long as it was well caffeinated. Bryan wasn't a heavy coffee drinker, but I forgave him for that. We ended up ordering three quad-shot triple-shot mochas, and one large tea for Bryan, and even though I knew Peggin was providing breakfast, I asked for four bear claws.

Peggin lived on Ravenwood Drive, on the south side of the copse where Diago hung out. I had already had one run-in with the local spirit who lurked in the hospitals, seeking out those in serious condition in order to siphon life-energy off them. He never went for the healthy, unless they tried to interfere with his feeding, but he was scary as fuck, and I really didn't look forward to any future encounters. I had hoped that we could figure out some permanent way to ban him from the hospital, but like most of the entrenched spirit-creatures in Whisper Hollow, there seemed to be no real way to get rid of him.

As we pulled into the driveway, once again I felt a sinking

feeling. The house Peggin rented was charming—a small cottage complete with a rose-covered trellis that arched over the gate leading to the front door. It looked comfy and warm and safe, and the thought of her moving into a drafty old mansion filled with spirits made me cringe.

"I wish she could buy this house, but the damned landlady . . ." I gritted my teeth, letting out a slow breath between them.

"You're going to have to let it go, Kerris. This isn't your choice. The best we can do is try to make sure Peggin stays safe." Bryan turned to me. "Promise you won't make it harder on her than it already is. I guarantee you, she's probably not jumping for joy on the inside, but she's making the best of a bad situation and you're her best friend. Don't make it worse."

I stared at him, wanting to sputter out a protest, but unfortunately, I couldn't argue with his logic. He was right, and I had to suck it up. "Fine. Come on, then. Let's get a move on." I carried the bag of bear claws while he picked up the tray of drinks.

Peggin was already hauling stuff out to the rental truck that was pulled up to the front of the garage. She grinned and waved as we headed up the drive. "Hey there, early birds. I see you didn't forget the caffeine!"

Deev joined her, carrying a box that he slid into the back of the moving van. It was one of the smaller ones, but it would fit everything she owned in a couple of trips. As Bryan handed out the coffee, taking the tea for himself, I held up the pastries.

"I brought sweets."

"I have sausage muffins inside on the kitchen table, along with hash brown cakes. It's all finger food. Let's go eat." She motioned for us to follow her and we trooped into her kitchen. It was small, but tidy, and filled with carefully marked boxes. I glanced in the living room—the same there, neat, clean, and filled with more boxes. The furniture was all covered with plastic and blankets to keep it from bumping around in the truck.

"Where are Frith and Folly?" I looked around for Peggin's ferrets.

She frowned. "I'm boarding them for a couple of days until I make sure there aren't any holes around the house for them to get out of. I want to set up a ferret room when we get there—probably one of the front parlors—so I have time to make certain there's nothing they can get into. They'll do fine once we have their toys and pens set up. But we'll have to fix a screen door on the room, because a baby gate won't work. They'll climb right over it."

One thing I had learned from our friendship—ferrets were smart. They could figure out a host of obstacles. "Never underestimate a ferret," Peggin had told me. "They'll always prove you wrong."

I opened my mouth to ask her if she was sure she wanted to go through with it, but then stopped. Bryan was right. What else was she going to do, given the short amount of time she had in which to find a new place? Instead, I picked up one of the sandwiches and bit into it, closing my eyes as the flavor hit my tongue.

"So, did you meet Veronica last night?" Peggin's voice brought me out of my food-induced reverie.

I nodded, swallowing. "Yeah, I did. Trust me, it was a lot scarier than meeting Penelope. I *like* Penelope. Veronica? Not quite so fond of. But she told me there are fifteen witch bottles out in the woods up on Timber Peak, and that's how Magda's summoning the Ankou away from Arawn. We have to find all the bottles and then Ivy, Oriel, and Ellia need to break their spell and destroy them."

Deev, who was actually sans his top hat for once, and wearing a slightly less flamboyant outfit—though now he looked a little *Mad Max*-meets steampunk—arched his eyebrows behind those goggle-like glasses.

"Ankou? The Shadow People, right? I've met several

through my life. I seem prone to drawing them in, unfortunately. I have several sculptures I made in an attempt to deal with the fear they inspire."

I stared at him. "I hope to hell those pieces never come to life. I don't think I'd want one of them running around town."

"Trust me, I keep them locked away good and tight. If they do come to life, they'll have to figure out how to get out of a padlocked barn cell." He grinned then, his teeth so white they nearly blinded me.

We chatted our way through breakfast, then got down to business. First run were the basics. Furniture, boxes of kitchen goods, anything that wasn't too terribly breakable. As I dragged out a big bag of bedding, I almost ran into Deev, who was coming back from carrying a box of pots and pans.

"Whoops! Watch out, don't want to throw you off balance," he said, stepping to the side. The man had a dexterity and grace that I found hard to pinpoint.

"Yeah, that's not hard to do." I laughed, then stopped, staring at him. "Promise me something?"

"I'll watch over her as much as I can." He stared at me, his grin falling away as well. "Kerris, you're not her mother; you can't bubble wrap all your friends."

I frowned. "That's pretty much what Bryan said."

"One thing I've learned in my life—and maybe it's because my creations are like children—is that you have to let things and people find their way in the world. Jokney, for example. I worry about the little guy every time he gets loose, but I can't tie him up for good. He never hurts anybody, and so far, nobody's ever hurt him. When he manages to get out and go wandering, I have to just trust that everything will be okay."

Whether it was his gentle tone of voice, or something in his demeanor, I relaxed. "Yeah, I can see that. I promise, I won't crowd her."

"Good, because you'll just piss her off if you do, and then I'll have to deal with the consequences." He laughed, heading back toward the house.

As I shoved the unwieldy bag of bedding into the back of the truck, I reluctantly decided that both Deev and Bryan knew what they were talking about. If Peggin thought I was hovering, she'd be pissed off. It was natural to want to protect my friends, but even if something should happen, I was realizing that being a spirit shaman didn't give me carte blanche to involve myself in everybody's decisions. If Peggin had gotten herself involved with an abusive lover, I would have tried to stop her, but this was vastly different. Feeling both chastised and grumbly, I kicked the tire of the truck, then headed back for another load.

By nine A.M., Bryan and Deev had managed to load a lot of the furniture, and we had stuffed as many boxes as we could in the truck, and in my SUV, and Peggin's car. With Deev and Bryan commandeering the moving van, and the two of us following, we eased out of the drive to make the short jaunt down toward the lakeshore, to Peggin's new house.

I expected it to be just as creepy as when I first saw it, but Peggin had hired a cleaning company to come in and scrub the place down. The windows were sparkling, the front yard had been mowed, and the porch steps had been patched.

As we stared at the house from where we had parked, I let out a sigh. Maybe it wouldn't be so bad, after all. I could still sense spirits all over the place, but they were minding their own business, at least, and given the grime and cobwebs gone from the windowpanes, the house looked like— with some TLC—it might shape up to be rather pretty.

"Okay, let's start hauling things inside." Peggin opened the door to her backseat, staring at the boxes. "How do we want to do this? Every box is labeled, by the way, for the room it goes in. I don't know if you noticed that."

"Yes, we did, Miss Organization." I grinned at her. "I have an idea. Why don't the guys haul the boxes to the front porch, and then we can carry them in from there? And they can carry in the furniture. It might be easier than all of us trying to get through the door at once." Actually, I just didn't feel like lugging heavy boxes up the steps, and since both men were fit and strong, it seemed like a good division of labor.

Bryan snorted. "You're just being lazy. But I'm too much of a gentleman to point that out."

Peggin rolled her eyes. "Yes, you are *so much* the gentleman, *however* will we stand it?" She motioned to me. "Come on, let's get ready for the big strong men." Before the guys could say another word, she looped her arm through my elbow and we sauntered up the walk to the house.

As we approached the house, I swallowed my doubts and threw myself into the task at hand. Peggin unlocked the front door and we went inside, leaving both the screen door and the front door propped wide open. It was cold, but at least there weren't any mosquitoes or flies to let in.

I stared at the gleaming floors. "You really did do a number on this place. The floors look good as new."

"No, they'll still need to be refinished, but I swear, that cleaning company? Works wonders. They spent an entire day here. And yes, they told me there were spirits here. The owner was spooked as hell when I hired them to come clean, but they sent an entire crew and they were left alone, for the most part. Only a couple times did anything out of the ordinary happen—and that was mostly when one of the crew wandered away from the others." She paused, then added, "Kerris, I know you don't like this, but thanks. Thanks for supporting me."

I blushed. "I have to tell you something. I made Deev promise to keep an eye on you."

"He told me. Thanks for that, too."

And then we were busy, carrying in boxes from the porch where the guys left them. We sorted and stacked them by room. After the guys brought in the furniture, they volunteered to go back for the second load. Peggin and I stayed behind, and started carrying the boxes destined for the upper floors up the stairs. While we were up there, since the men had brought in the furniture for her bedroom and the guest room, we dug through until we found the boxes with her sheets, and the bag of bedding, and we made both beds and arranged the furniture the way she wanted it. I plugged in the lamps and then we headed down to the kitchen to start putting away dishes and pots and pans.

"I hate living out of boxes, so I sure appreciate you giving me a hand," Peggin said.

"Not a problem." I was unwrapping plates and handing them to her as I sat at the kitchen table. "Are you going to buy a dining room table?"

"I can't afford to, unless I find one at the thrift store. I'd like to have a formal dining set, so maybe we can go bargain hunting next week. I actually need a lot of furniture to fill this house. I have enough for the living room, partial office, the kitchen, and my bedroom and guest room. Otherwise, I'm afraid it's going to be rather empty until I'm able to figure out what I want—and need." She grinned, placing the plates in the cupboard as I took the Bubble Wrap off each one. "So tell me, what was Veronica really like?"

I told her what I could—about the throne of bones, and what Veronica looked like, and the creepy-ass twins who had guided us in.

"Have you ever gone inside the Pest House?" Peggin glanced at me and I recognized the dare in her voice.

"No, and I don't plan on it."

"You should, don't you think? As spirit shaman?" The taunt was unmistakable.

I playfully glared at her. "Are you offering to go with me, then? You know that I'm not about to attempt it on my own. You want to go mucking about in that ramshackle old building? Hell, I think we should just get the town to tear the damned thing down. Why haven't they?"

"I think it's some historical marker or something. There's some reason the town council left it standing—that much I know. And no, I have no desire to go tromping through the place, but I'd love to hear about what's inside."

We had finished with the plates and saucers, and moved on to putting away the glasses and silverware.

"You just like supernatural gossip."

"Of course I do. What else is there in this town to talk about? Well, I do know a few things about the health issues of some of the members, but there's that pesky confidentiality clause, you know." She did laugh then. "Okay, time for pots and pans. By the time we finish, the men will be back with the rest of the boxes."

And they were right on schedule.

By the time we put away the last sauté pan, Deev and Bryan drove up in the moving van. We headed out to the porch to help them. This time, it was a light load—mostly books and computer gear. These boxes were heavier and my back was starting to protest as we neared the end. I'd need a long hot bath tonight, that much was for sure.

It was almost noon when I was in the living room, shoving boxes of books around to make room for more boxes, when I realized that I hadn't seen Peggin for some time. At that moment, Bryan and Deev wandered into the house.

"That's it, the last of the boxes. Now the only thing we need is to have the cleaners come in and clean out the house over on Ravenwood Street. I told Peggin I'd pay for it as a housewarming gift." Deev turned to Bryan. "Oh, by the way, I don't know if she told you, but Peggin had the chimney guy come in—everything's fine, and thanks to you, now clean as a whistle. The bricks do need shoring up on the roof, but he said we could use the fireplaces now, as long as we get them fixed soon. Peggin made an appointment to have him come back and replace the broken bricks and make sure everything is safe and snug."

"Good. Glad to hear it." Bryan glanced around. "Where is Peggin?"

I shrugged. "I think she went in the kitchen to fix lunch

or something." Although, now that I thought about it, I couldn't really remember her saying anything like that. "Come on, let's check." I dusted my hands on my pants and headed toward the kitchen, the guys following me.

As we entered the large room, I was struck by how silent it was. Everything felt hushed, as if waiting for something. A sliver of fear hit my stomach and I walked over to the sink, staring out the window. As I did, I could see a spirit standing in the yard. The spirit—a man—stared at me, then pointed toward the trees dividing the backyard from the lake. I caught my breath.

"Hell, no—oh no!" I raced to the kitchen door, flinging it open as I ran out on the back porch and slammed down the steps to the yard. The spirit was still there, still pointing, a terrified look on his face. Behind me, the men were hot on my heels.

Panicked, I raced toward the trees. "Peggin! Peggin! Where are you?"

The men were right behind me, and Bryan caught up to me and passed by. "The lake?"

I nodded, trying to keep my breathing even as I ran. Deev passed me by and I cursed the fact that I'd been too lazy to get myself to a gym. I struggled, urging myself to move faster.

As I hit the tree line, I tried to follow the path Bryan and Deev were blazing. There was, in fact, a foot trail leading through the woods, but it was overgrown and I was struggling to avoid tree roots and rocks and boughs that now littered it. The thicket was dense, but I could see the glimmer of water ahead. It would have been easier to drive a short distance to reach the pier, but I knew that Peggin hadn't done that. She had come this way—I could feel the swirl of siren song, the call that had lured her in. It was like a melody that promised peace and rest.

Suddenly, I flashed back to my dream about Peggin and the Lady.

"No!" I pushed harder, catching up to Deev, who was a

little behind Bryan. Bryan broke through the trees to the shore and in another moment, Deev and I were behind him. I glanced around, frantic. There, a few hundred yards to the right, stood Fogwhistle Pier, and at the end of the pier, Peggin was leaning down, staring into the water.

"Peggin!" My scream echoed through the air, and Peggin slowly raised her head, but she did not move. At that moment, an arm rose from the water, and then the figure of a woman clad in a long shroud, like a mummy in a cloak of muddy white. Vines draped around her neck, her arms, her waist, all trailing below the water, as though to anchor the Lady to her watery grave. Her eyes and head were covered with the white shroud, with only her mouth visible. She grabbed hold of Peggin's ankle and Peggin screamed, suddenly seeming aware of where she was and what was going on.

"Peggin!" Deev headed toward the pier, his voice thundering through the air. Bryan was by his side, and I was doing my best to catch up.

Before we could reach the pier, Peggin struggled but the Lady began to disappear below the water and, with one final jerk, she toppled Peggin over the side.

As Peggin hit the water, Bryan stripped off his sweatshirt and began unbuckling his boots, swearing as he did so. Deev ditched his coat and was untying his platform sneakers. I had it faster—I yanked down the zippers on my boots and hit the water, running.

"Kerris!" Bryan's voice echoed behind me as I dove beneath the freezing surface. Another moment and a ripple of waves told me he had joined me.

It was difficult to see, but I could make out the sparkle of the Lady's magic, and I followed the trail of glittering bubbles. I could see Peggin ahead; she was struggling against the pull of the Lady—whom I could no longer see. Bryan kicked past me and managed to reach Peggin before I did. He grabbed her arm and yanked. At that moment, Deev swam past me on the other side and caught hold of

Peggin's other arm. Together they pulled, trying to pry her away from the Lady.

I couldn't do much—I couldn't say anything, not without surfacing, but I reached out, gathered all the energy I could, and aimed it at the Lady in one violent burst. A brilliant light flared around all of us as I did so, and suddenly, Bryan and Deev had hold of Peggin and were headed toward the surface. I followed on their heels, all too aware that the Lady could—and had—killed spirit shamans before.

We struggled out of the water, back onto Fogwhistle Pier. Exhausted, but afraid that the Lady might come back, I helped Bryan and Deev carry Peggin back to land, where Deev started rescue breathing. A moment later, Peggin coughed up a lungful of water, and woozily sat up.

I glanced back at the lake. The surface was silent, but the Lady was there, watching us. I could feel her presence. Shivering and afraid, I motioned for the men to head back to the house. Bryan carried Peggin, Deev by his side.

I gathered our boots and gear from the shore. With one last glance at the lake, I whispered, "You can't have her. She belongs to us," and followed them back to Peggin's house.

CHAPTER 9

~

Deev built a fire in the fireplace as I hunted down a box with towels in it. Once we were dried off, I returned to the kitchen, where I started a pot of hot water and managed to find the tea. I set up a tray, found a half-eaten bag of chocolate chip cookies, and carried everything back to the living room.

Peggin was huddled near the fire, shivering below the blanket. She hadn't said a word since we brought her back to the house, and now she stared at the flames, her eyes haunted.

I knelt beside her. "Are you . . . are you okay? Do you need to go see Corbin? How are your lungs? The lake water's not the safest." I was hovering, I knew it, but damn it—the Lady had almost dragged her away. Of course I was going to mother-hen her.

She shook her head. "No, I think I'll be all right." She gazed into my eyes, a bleak, stark expression on her face. Then, a moment later, whatever composure she had left vanished and she fell forward into my arms, sobbing. "I thought

I was dead. I thought I was going to die. She pulled on me. I could feel her pulling me out of my body, Kerris."

I held her tight, stroking her back. The smell of lake water was thick in her hair, and for a moment, I thought I caught a whiff of something else—decay, or brine . . . something not borne from fresh water. Shivering—the scent made me wary, as though there was something hidden in the room with us—I took hold of her shoulders and pushed her back.

"I want you to remember everything you can about what happened. So few ever escape the Lady . . . the more information we have, the better off we are. Maybe someday we can fully put a stop to her attacks." I knew it sounded like a pipe dream. The Lady had been around Whisper Hollow since long before the first settlers had come in. But if we could untangle some of the spirits who had been bound to her, perhaps it would give us an even playing field on which to stand.

Peggin shivered. "I just want a hot bath first. And to be honest, I want to go home—to my other house. But I can't."

I glanced up at Bryan, feeling hopeless.

Deev spoke up. "Kerris will draw you a bubble bath. Meanwhile, I'm going to go look at that furnace and see if we can't get it to crank out some heat."

"It's new, so it should be working well. But I'm not certain where it is, or where the thermostat is." I answered for Peggin, who was leaning her head against the chair, wincing.

"Well then, we'll just have to find it." He motioned to Bryan. "Come with me?"

Bryan shifted to his feet. "Sure thing. Kerris, why don't you get Peggin into a hot bath? After she's had a soak, and washed her hair, we'll go out for a late lunch. My treat."

More grateful to the guys than I could express, I wrapped my arms around Peggin and helped her stand. She was still shaky, no wonder, given the circumstances. As I led her to the stairs, the men headed down into the basement.

Peggin undressed in her bedroom, shivering as I took the

cold, clammy clothes from her and dropped them in a laundry basket. Grateful we'd thought to make her bed already, I started to wrap her in a throw but she shook her head.

"No, I don't want the Lady's stench on it. I can smell her, Kerris. I can still smell her. The scent of rotting bodies and long-dead fish . . ."

"I think her scent got caught in your hair. We'll wash it away, don't worry." I drew the bath, filling the tub with the first bath wash I could lay my hands on—warm vanilla. The fragrant aroma filled the bathroom and I shut the door behind us to keep the warm steam in.

"I'm sorry . . . I'm sorry I was so cocky and so—"

"Stop right there." The last thing I wanted to do was have her thinking I was about to say *I told you so.* "I wish to hell I'd been wrong. As it is, now we know that the Lady lures people. It's not just bad luck. She's like a siren, you know? My guess is her voice targets anybody who's within range."

As Peggin stepped into the tub, I helped steady her with one hand. Frowning, I noticed a mark on her right inner wrist. Pointing to it, I asked, "Did you get hurt?"

She frowned and glanced at the mark. "What's . . . I don't know what that is."

"Well, get yourself into the bubbles and I'll take a closer look."

As she settled down into the water, I pulled out my phone and switched on the flashlight app. The lights in the bathroom were dim and I wanted a clear view of what that mark was. She leaned back and let out long sigh as the heat of the water began to draw the chill from her body. Peggin was plump, and curvy—typical hourglass figure, only much more Rubenesque than society approved of.

I started to reach for her hand, but she shook her head. "One minute." Taking a deep breath, she closed her eyes and slid beneath the water, popping back up after a few seconds. She took some of the bath gel—I hadn't been able to find the shampoo—and smoothed it into her hair, working it through the long red locks. Another dip beneath the water left her thoroughly lathered up.

"I couldn't take that stench any longer. At least now I smell like vanilla." She reached for the hand towel that I was holding and wiped the water out of her eyes, then handed it back to me. That done, she held up her wrist, squinting at it.

I knelt by the tub, turning the flashlight beam on her wrist. We stared at the long, black mark that looked like a streak of ink, but then I began to notice that the unsteady tendrils threading off it actually reminded me of vines.

"It looks like the start of a tattoo."

"Well, that's no tattoo I ever asked for." She squinted. "Is it a bruise? It doesn't hurt."

"Maybe . . . a blood blister?" I gently poked at it, but the mark didn't feel swollen and Peggin didn't flinch. "That doesn't hurt? Not at all?"

"No." She paused, then shrugged. "I guess we'll figure it out later. Maybe I hit it on something when I was fighting against her."

"About the Lady . . ." I didn't want to push, but the more we knew about Peggin's experience, the better.

She stared at the water, then slowly began to scrub herself with the washcloth. "I don't want to think about her, because I can still feel her there. Kerris, I feel like she's latched onto me. If I think about her too hard, it will bring her to me. Or take me to her."

I frowned. "I think we need to talk to the Matriarchs." One thing I did know. Some spirits could link into a person's aura, drawing energy from them. And if the Lady had corded into Peggin, then we needed to find the connection and sever it. Not only could a spirit—and sometimes a person—drain energy from others via psychic cords, but they could track their targets. And the last thing we wanted was for the Lady to be tracking Peggin.

Peggin glumly stared at the water. "I wish I'd never found this house. It seemed like the only way out."

"Can you still get out from under the sale? I mean, you're renting to own. What if you just find someplace else to rent—"

At that moment, I heard the men talking, their voices pitched. I motioned for Peggin to rinse her hair. "I don't trust leaving you in a bathtub filled with water while I'm out of the room. Not so soon after what happened this morning."

She pulled the plug and reluctantly stood, climbing out of the seventies retro heart-shaped jetted tub. After she took a quick rinse in the shower to wash off any residue, and I handed her a thick towel to wrap herself in, and then we stopped in the bedroom, where I managed to find her blow-dryer. She didn't bother with styling today, just hit the heat to dry out her locks, and then slid into a fresh pair of capris and a warm shirt. After she was ready, we headed downstairs to see what the commotion had been about.

Bryan and Deev were examining the mantel. I wasn't sure what they were looking for, but Deev had his head dangerously close to the flames as he gazed beneath the wide beam over the fireplace. Bryan was holding the flashlight for him.

"What's going on?" Peggin asked, forcing a smile. "You find gremlins in my fireplace, I'm going to sue you for emotional distress."

Bryan looked up. "We found something. This mantel matches some beams we found downstairs. By the way, this house is so full of ghosts I'm surprised its not labeled standing room only. We ran into a couple downstairs."

"Lovely," Peggin said, rolling her eyes. "Just what I wanted to hear. Tell me what you found—besides the spooks."

Deev stood up, abruptly bumping his head on the wooden beam. He winced, rubbing his forehead, as I pulled back from the fireplace. "What do you know about ships?"

"Ships? Starships? Sailing ships? Ships in the night?" Peggin was making an attempt at a joke, but even I could tell it was to keep herself from freaking out any more than she already had.

"Come look." Deev seemed overly excited, and I hoped to hell this wasn't a bodies-in-the-basement situation.

We followed him, with Bryan taking up the rear, toward the basement. The staircase was steep and dark, with no hand railing to hold on to. The single lightbulb that hung over the stairway was bare and flickering.

"Oh this is lovely. You need to put in a railing right away. And a light that's easier to reach. If that goes out while you're down here, how are you going to even reach that in order to change it?" I used the wall for support, grimacing at the grime that had built up over the years.

Peggin nodded. "And the list keeps growing. But you're right, these are on a priority list."

"There already was one at one time." Deev guided us down, pointing out the indentations in the wall that must have been where a railing once attached to the side.

As we entered the basement proper, I decided that if we ever wanted to murder someone, this would be the place to do it. There were three rooms in Peggin's basement—the main one in which we were standing was a larger, dimly lit room with built-in shelves along three of the walls. The shelves were deep, and it was hard to see into them. They were filled with dust and cobwebs, and boxes of junk that prior owners had left behind. I grimaced, thinking that it would be the perfect place for spiders to hide. We didn't have many poisonous ones on the west coast of Washington, but we did have hobo spiders, and black widows—so common over the mountains in eastern Washington—had been spotted around. The room was filled with broken furniture, and an old workbench with a few rusty tools on it.

But Deev ignored all of that and motioned for us to join him on one side of the room. He motioned to the wall. "See that arch?" As he shone his flashlight on it for greater visibility, I noticed that there was an archway, built of beams that curved up one wall, across the ceiling, and down the opposite wall. The wood looked worn, but there was something different about it that made it stand out from the rest of the house.

"What about it?" Peggin asked, walking over to run her hand along it. "This is smooth—it feels almost weathered. But the basement is dry—it doesn't look like there are any mold problems or flooding issues down here."

"There aren't. At least, not that we can see. But those beams? They're from a boat. This arch is built, I believe, from part of the keel beam and the ribs of a boat." Bryan crossed to stand beside Peggin, motioning for me to join them. "Look here—see those markings?"

I leaned in. Sure enough, there were letters, though they were so worn it was hard to make them out on the wood. "What do they say?"

"I think they may be a clue as to which boat these came from." Deev was touching one of the beams with what seemed almost like reverence. "They're hand carved. I can tell you that much. Whoever built this boat, built it from scratch. There's no fiberglass here, no sign that this was one of a hundred mass-produced boats of its kind. I can feel the love that went into this boat—it's radiating through the timbers. But . . . there's something else."

I joined him, placing my hand next to his. Instantly, a wave of fear and grief overwhelmed me, and I heard someone screaming. I yanked my hand away as though I'd been burned.

"Crap. What the hell happened here? There's so much fear wrapped up in this wood, no wonder the ghosts are active on this land." I stared at the beams, trying to get a sense for anything I could that might have happened.

"I'm not sure what's going on, but I'd like to know. Are there any more of these beams down here?" I cautiously passed through the arch and crossed to the other side of the room, where I peeked through the two doors against the opposite wall. One led to a grungy two-piece powder room. The other looked like it might have been a laundry room at one time, but now it just housed more boxes of junk. "You need to go through all of this stuff and clear out whatever you don't want, Peggin. There's a lot of psychic residue down here and I doubt if it's all good."

She frowned. "Boat . . . Deev, do you think you can figure out what the markings say? Do what you can—I know you have excellent vision."

I glanced at him, confused. His goggle-glasses gave me the impression he wouldn't be able to see an inch in front of his face without them. Peggin must have caught my look because she laughed.

"Deev needs his glasses, yes, but he modified them—they're enhanced. He has a microscope, a telescope, and a built-in computer in those things to aid his vision. He can see better than we can, by far."

Bryan laughed. "Leave it to the inventors and the creators of the world. It makes sense. You can't see very well? Do what you can to improve it."

Deev took the joking with good humor. "All in fun, my friends. All in good fun. But yes, pet. I'll see what I can find out. Why don't you go upstairs and get ready to leave for lunch. I'll be up in a few moments. I just need to adjust the settings on these." He reached up to the side of his goggles and I realized there were tiny knobs along the straps that held them on.

I slid my arm through Peggin's. "Come on. Let's get upstairs. It's chilly down here. Oh, did you guys even bother to check out the furnace? I think it's in that small room where the laundry used to be."

"Yes, we found it and got it started up. But this house is so drafty that it's going to take a couple hours to warm up the place. By the way, the thermostat is in the kitchen, to the left against the wall as you enter the room. I went hunting to find it." Deev shooed us out then, and we headed up the stairs.

Once we reached the living room, I noticed the heat

filtering through the vents. Deev was right—the furnace was good to go. At least one thing was working right. I made sure Peggin was comfortably ensconced in her rocking chair and moved to the side, where I put a call in to Ellia.

"We need to talk. Can you call Oriel and Ivy and meet us at the Mossy Rock Steakhouse in half an hour? Something happened this morning and we desperately need your advice."

Ellia read the tone of my voice loud and clear. "I'll be there, and I'll do my best to get the others to come."

I signed off and called the steakhouse to make reservations. As I put my phone away, Deev came bounding back up the stairs.

"Got it. One of the groupings says MS-1915 and the other . . . J. Jacobs. My guess is that's the date the ship was built, and the name of the builder."

"Well, we have something to go on. I made reservations for twenty minutes from now. Ellia will meet us, and with a little luck, Oriel and Ivy, too."

"Let me get my jacket and hat." Deev disappeared into the kitchen and when he returned, he was wearing his duster and his top hat.

"Not taking your gun to the restaurant?" It still tickled me, in an odd way, that he carried around that antique blunderbuss.

He gave me a long look and I swear, if I could have seen his eyes better, I would have probably melted under the scrutiny. "Not quite." But he chuckled, then held his arm out to Peggin. "Come on, my girl. Let's head out for food."

Bryan swung in behind us, and as we walked to the car, I felt a shiver of relief running through me. I was glad to leave the house behind us, if only for a while.

The Mossy Rock Steakhouse was fairly empty since most of the lunch crowd had thinned out, and the dinner crowd wasn't even thinking about food yet. Nadia had reserved a good table for us. I had made the reservation for seven people, in hopes that all three of the Matriarchs could make it. As we were settling in around the curved booth, Ellia and Ivy joined us.

"Oriel can't make it, she's got a meeting this afternoon, but we'll fill her in as soon as we leave." Ellia glanced at me, then over at Peggin. She stopped short, her eyes widening. "Great Mother, what happened to you, child?"

Ivy turned as Ellia said that, and gasped. "The Lady."

Peggin began to shiver, and she pulled her sweater tighter around her.

"The Lady tried to drag Peggin under about ninety minutes ago. Deev, Bryan, and I were able to save her. But . . . Peggin, show them your wrist." I motioned for her to uncover the mark.

As Peggin held out her arm, Ellia let out a soft curse and Ivy blanched.

"She's got the mark," Ivy said.

"What is that? Have you seen it before? She didn't have it on her this morning." I leaned back as the waitress appeared with a couple baskets of bread. We put in our drink orders and once she was gone, I nodded to Peggin's arm. "That appeared after the Lady dragged her under."

"How far did she get you? Into the water itself?" Ivy asked.

Peggin cleared her throat, looking all too frightened. "She took me under. I lost consciousness. When we got back to the house, as I was undressing to take a bath, I saw the mark on me. What does it mean? Do you know? Is it a bruise?"

Ellia motioned to Ivy, who reached for Peggin's arm. She held it tight, so the mark showed clearly, and gently pressed her hand against the black streak. Ellia watched dispassionately. She made no move toward them, but her gaze was fastened on the stippled line that crossed Peggin's skin. Ivy closed her eyes and softly let out a slow breath. A moment later, she shivered and abruptly let go.

"It's as I thought. The Lady has marked you. You're a target, Peggin, and she will come for you however she can. She can follow you through water; though she may not be able to directly attack you, she can use the force of water—in all its forms—to come at you." Ivy frowned, leaning back. "She's angry—so angry that you got away."

"So I was right not to leave her alone in the bathtub, then?" I wanted to know that my instincts were on point.

Ivy shuddered. "Correct. It would be easy for the Lady to reach out, lure you into sleep, then you sink below the surface of the tub while the water held you down till you drowned. Watch showers—stepping on a bar of soap is all too easy to arrange. Rain, as well. A puddle of water, a power line coming down near it . . . too many possibilities."

"Can we get rid of this mark? Is there a way to destroy or erase it?" Deev paused as the waitress brought our drinks and took our food order.

Ivy stared at Peggin as though she was trying to read what was going through her mind. After a moment, she turned to Ellia. "Would an exorcism work, do you think?"

"I don't know. Oriel might have a better idea. She understands the Lady better than any of us. We'll have to ask her. Meanwhile, is there a protection spell you can cast on her that will give her some added safety?" Ellia frowned, cocking her head to one side. "We have to do something to keep the girl safe."

Ivy took a long sip of her coffee, then grimaced and added another packet of sugar and more cream. "Bitter stuff. I never understood why Nadia insists on using such a pungent blend. The rest of her food is incredible, but her coffee-making skills could use some work." After a moment, she let out soft sigh. "I think Oriel knows a spell that might help, but it's a strong one, and will require assistance. We'll need Starlight's help—she works some incredibly powerful guardianship magic."

I jerked my head up. "Starlight Williams?" Starlight

Williams, the leader of the Crescent Moon Society, whom I had taken an instant dislike to and was polite to only because there was no choice—we had to work together.

"*Yes*, Starlight. I wish you wouldn't write her off. I know you two got off to a rocky start, but Starlight is good for this town, and she's done a remarkable job of bringing in prosperity for Whisper Hollow. She's like a beacon for those who want to spend money and attract it. And she doesn't begrudge helping out when need be."

Ivy's rebuke caught me up short. She wasn't joking, either. I might be full grown, and she might look my age, but she was still my grandmother and ever since I had returned to Whisper Hollow and met her, she had eagerly adapted to that role.

"I'm sorry. I just . . . there's something about the woman that grates on me. I don't know what it is, but she irritates the hell out of me."

Peggin finally broke her silence. "I know what it is. She reminds you of the A-list in high school." With a faint grin, she added, "In fact, if I remember right, she was on the A-list and barely even knew we were alive."

Starlight Williams was our age—in her early thirties—and she was married to Kyle Williams, a lawyer. They had two children, fourteen-year-old fraternal twins. Rachel was the teenaged queen of mean girls, and Zach was a brilliant computer student who was racking up points as a budding sociopath, according to the rumor mill.

I snorted. "Oh, she was head of the A-list. We never stood a chance around her and her hive, not that we even wanted to be part of that group."

Bryan laughed. "Ten bucks says you would have jumped at the chance. Everybody wants to be part of the A-list, even if they hate the members of it. It's human nature to want to be popular and admired. Unfortunately, at that age, a lot of the admiration is misplaced."

Peggin stuck out her tongue at him. "Oh, shut up. We did

not want to be part of their inner circle. We were in our own world. I'll have you know, I was a trendsetter back then."

"She was, I can vouch for it." I gave her a wide grin. "She started retro before retro was a thing. Well, before pinup retro was a thing. And Starlight was always jealous of Peggin because the jocks flocked around her. Men always have loved you, woman."

"You're just saying that. But say it some more." Peggin laughed and everything felt like it was almost normal. Unfortunately, Ellia brought us back to reality.

"I hate to squash the good memories, but I'm going to tell you something, Peggin, and you need to pay attention to me and not fight me on it." Ellia leaned closer. "You can't stay in that house. I don't care how much you paid, or what you think, or how independent you want to be. You stay there and the Lady's going to be on your doorstep. With that mark, the closer you are to the shore, the easier it's going to be for her to lure you in."

Peggin ducked her head. "I was afraid you were going to say that." Her gaze flickered over toward Deev, and I knew she didn't want to ask him if she could stay at his place, after all. I was about to offer my home, but Bryan spoke up first.

"You can stay at my place. It's huge, I've got a ton of space, and you can bring your ferrets." He glanced at me. "I know you were about to offer her your place, but her ferrets and your cats may not mix too well—if they do, great, but if you think that would be a problem, then take one of the empty rooms in my house."

"That's a good idea except that I don't want her alone at night. And she'll need somebody with her when she takes a bath, if what Ivy says is true. I dunno . . . what do you think, Peggin? Will Frith and Folly mind being around the cats? They're huge, but mellow, and they've been around dogs and rabbits before. I doubt they'll mind the ferrets, and we can keep your guys in the office while we're gone."

She snorted. "I think we'd be better off locking them in

the guest room or you may come home to a mass of shredded documents." She smiled at Bryan. "I really appreciate the offer but Kerris is right; if I need supervision when I'm taking a bath, I think she's better cut out for the job."

Bryan blushed. "I wasn't suggesting—" Flustered, his voice trailed away.

"I do believe that's the first time I've seen you fall all over your words," I said, laughing. "Don't sweat it. Peggin knows you weren't trying to sneak a peek. It's settled, then. We'll stop back at the house, you can pack a suitcase, and we'll head over to my place. I'm happy to have the company and we can have a slumber party, only better. With booze."

"All right, and can we pick up Frith and Folly on the way? I miss them already."

I nodded, leaning back as Nadia escorted the waitress over. The waitress was carrying a huge tray, and Nadia placed a folding rack next to the table for her to set it on. The food smelled delicious. Ivy, Ellia, Bryan, and Peggin had ordered burgers and fries. Deev and I had ordered fish and chips. The servings were generous, and as we fell to eating, I snuck a peek at Peggin. She might have been trying to make the best of the situation, but I knew that she was both terrified and unhappy. What had been such a hopeful beginning had turned into a nightmare.

A sudden thought crossed my mind. "Tell Ivy and Ellia about the ship beams!"

Deev explained what we had found.

"There's a lot of painful energy attached to those beams, too. I really didn't like touching them. I think that, after we get back to my place, we might start looking up ships in the area to see if we can figure out how those beams got in your basement," I said to Peggin, figuring that at least it would give us something to take her mind off the Lady.

Bryan cleared his throat. "There's also another matter. Shouldn't you tell them about your trip out to Veronica's?"

I blinked. In the excitement and fear of rescuing Peggin,

it had entirely slipped my mind. "Bryan's right. You know that I went out to meet Veronica last night. It was quite the experience. But long story short, she told me that there are fifteen witch bottles out in the woods on Timber Peak. Magda created them to summon the rogue Ankou that are gathering there. We need to find them, and then you, Oriel, and Ellia are to destroy them." I paused. "Won't breaking them do the trick, though?"

Ivy shook her head. "No. It takes a witch to destroy a witch bottle, especially one made by a woman as powerful as Magda. So, I guess it's another trip back to the Peak."

"Yeah, but not today." I leaned back, the food suddenly making me tired. The adrenaline of the morning was starting to wear off, and I wanted nothing so much as to go home and take a nap. The others seemed to feel the same way. We lingered at the table, ordering dessert though I doubted any of us were terribly hungry, and only after more coffee and cheesecake did we reluctantly exit the restaurant.

Peggin slipped her arm through mine. "Are you sure you don't mind me staying at your house? And the ferrets?"

"I wouldn't want anybody else." I leaned over and kissed her cheek. "Peggin, you're my best friend. I'm not about to let the Lady get a second chance at you." At her worried look, I added, "We'll find a way to break the curse. I promise you."

But inside, I wondered if I could keep that promise. And I wondered if we could keep Peggin alive until we had a chance to break the curse.

CHAPTER 10

The trip back to the house at Foggy Downs was quiet. Deev pulled Peggin to him, and she rested her head on his shoulder in the backseat. Bryan was staring at his phone, frowning over some text he had gotten. None of us felt like talking much, and I couldn't decide if it was because we were all tired, or because of all the crap that had gone down that day.

As I pulled into the driveway, I stared up at the looming Victorian. The spirits were still wandering through the yard, I could see them as plain as I could see the trees and the grass and the house itself. A brooding feeling hung over the place and I shuddered, not wanting Peggin to go back through those doors.

"I think you should let me go pack your bag. You stay here with Bryan. Deev, want to come in with me and help?" I wanted Deev with me because I wanted to have a little talk with him out of Peggin's earshot. I was done not interfering. Maybe I wasn't able to tell anyone about my dream, but I could make sure he heard what I had to say about everything else.

Deev silently unwound himself from Peggin, and followed me into the house. As I shut the door behind us, he followed me upstairs.

"I know you want to talk to me about something. What is it?" He sounded almost defensive.

"I want to make certain that you remember to keep an eye on her when you guys are alone. If you're working on a project, don't let her go off wandering. If she stays the night at your house, you need to make certain that she doesn't bathe alone. I'm just . . . a little raw."

He smiled then. "I thought you were going to blame me for what happened."

Blinking, I stared at him. "Why would I do that? You aren't the one who encouraged her to buy this house. You tried to get her to stay with you, if I remember right."

He shrugged. "I'm used to people assuming things about me, to be honest. Trust me, I know that people think I'm an odd duck, to put it mildly. I've had more than one person assume that because some of my creations come to life, that I'm deliberately messing with forces that are better left untouched. I also get a lot of comments about my braids and clothes."

I walked over to Peggin's bed and flopped down on it, shaking my head. "Oh, Deev. I know what it's like to stand out and to be talked about. Trust me on that one. But no, I'm not blaming you—it's not your fault. And as for assumptions, I never really knew you—you came to town after I left—but I'm glad to get the chance now. Because I, for one, think you're a pretty cool dude. And I also think . . ."

He sat beside me, folding his hands as he rested his elbows on his knees. "You think what?"

I wasn't sure whether I should say it or not, but decided I might as well. "I think you're good for Peggin. Anybody more mundane would cramp her style. But I know she's been lonely, to some degree, and I know that she loves with all her heart when she finally opens up to someone." I turned to him. "I also know that she refused to stay with you because she was afraid of doing something that would drive a wedge between you guys. You know . . . reality has a way of creeping in when you move in with somebody."

He shifted, his shoulders relaxing. "I see. I wondered, but I wasn't going to push her on it. I was afraid she just didn't want to live with me and didn't want to hurt my feelings about it. I wasn't ready to hear her say she wanted to take things more slowly, so I didn't ask."

A sneaking suspicion crossed my mind that they needed to quit being so afraid to talk things out, and I decided to just be blunt. "You guys can't be afraid to discuss this stuff. You're both pussyfooting around issues that could easily lead to a misunderstanding. Promise me, you won't assume? Once one of you starts talking, I'm pretty sure the other will follow suit. Peggin may seem like a tough cookie, and she is, but to be honest, she's really a big fluffball inside." I grinned at him. "But you know *that*, don't you?"

The corners of his lips turned up, and he let out a gentle laugh. "Yeah, I know it. I can see her strength, but I also know that a very sensitive nature is lurking behind all that bravado. I promise, I'll start talking to her more. Because Kerris, I *really* like Peggin. And I don't want to mess things up with her."

Satisfied, I patted him on the knee. "She told me the same thing. So you're both on the same page, at least. Now help me get some things together for her. Can you run downstairs and bag up all the food that might expire? We'll also need her ferret food and their cages, and whatever else it is that ferrets take."

"Sure thing." He obligingly took off, and as I watched the back of his duster flutter out the door, I had the feeling Peggin wasn't going to be alone again for a very long time.

I turned back to the room and picked up one of the suitcases we had emptied only a few hours ago. Time to get the show on the road. I knew Peggin loved her dresses and skirts, so I filled a garment bag with five of the dresses I knew she liked best, then added four skirts and hung the bag on the hook behind the door so the clothes wouldn't wrinkle. I tucked the suitcase full with knit tops, a couple of button-down blouses, two of her favorite corsets, several pair of shoes, underwear and bras, and then hunted around till I found her makeup-to-go bag, a scaled-down version of her vanity table cases that held scads of eye shadow and mascara.

As I was zipping the cases shut, I was startled by the door closing behind me. Thinking it was Deev, I said, "You're done already?"

No answer.

Very slowly, I turned, cautiously peeking over my back shoulder. The door was shut, but there was nobody in the room with me, at least that I could see.

"Who's there?"

No answer. But then the closet door flew open with a bang. I jumped, letting out a little shriek. As used to spirits as I was getting, they still could startle me without going to much trouble. Especially on a day like today, in a house like this one.

"Who's there? What do you want? You know I'm the spirit shaman, right? So talk to me."

Unfortunately, logic and reason didn't always work with ghosts and their ilk. The closet door began to swing wildly, slamming itself closed again and again. I backed away toward the bed, but as I did, the blinds on the window began to roll up and down, just as out of control as the door.

"Stop this. Talk to me if you have something to say. I have no patience for temper tantrums!" I put as much force into the words as I could, hoping to alleviate some of the outburst. It worked about as well as it did on a kid throwing a tantrum. Read: not at all. The door was whipping open and closed so fast that I knew if I tried to dash through it, I could easily get hurt. I shouted for Deev, hoping that he could hear me, but the house was huge and I wasn't sure how well my voice would carry. Come to think of it, was he hearing the door slamming? If so, then why the hell wasn't he up here checking on me?

I looked around for something to use as a makeshift wand. Not that I thought it would do me much good—I hadn't even mastered using the tools my grandma Lila left me yet. But if Peggin had anything that I might be able to use to channel energy . . .

And then I saw it. On her dresser, there was a large chunk of quartz crystal. I grabbed it up, surprised by the sudden current that raced through my hands. As I held it out, aiming the cluster of points toward the door as much as I could, I began to whisper the first thing that I could think of, which wasn't exactly a charm, but my heart was definitely behind it, even though my voice was shaky.

"Get the hell out of here, whoever you are. Do you hear me? I'm the spirit shaman of Whisper Hollow and you will listen to me and obey!" I headed toward the swinging door, holding the crystal out, forcing my energy through it.

The door paused for a moment, but then started up again. At that moment, a perfume bottle whirled past my head, skimming by from the vanity behind me. It barely missed me, crashing against the door as it slammed shut. Furious now, I whirled around.

"Stop this now, or I'll bring the Matriarchs out here and make your existence a living hell. *Do you understand me?*"

The door suddenly stopped, and a hairbrush that had been hovering in midair dropped to the floor. At that moment, Deev came running up the stairs.

"Kerris, are you all right? I heard noise!"

"I'm all right, but good gods, let's get the hell out of here. The spirits are up in arms and . . ." I paused. "Did you hear me calling?"

"No. I didn't hear a thing!" He grabbed the suitcase from me and headed toward the stairs. "Come on. You go first, and be cautious. If they're acting up, you don't want anybody getting the bright idea to push you down the steps."

"Good point." I clung to the railing, Peggin's makeup case slung over my shoulder. Every step, I could feel the spirits watching me, but we made it to the main floor in one piece, and then out the door without further ado.

As Deev locked the door behind him, I glanced past the house, toward the lake. There, shimmering through the trees, the water loomed like a dark force, glistening under the silver sky. We reached the cars as the rain began to splatter down, saturating the ground within seconds. Peggin slowly emerged from my SUV, where Bryan had waited with her. She silently followed Deev over to her car, and he commandeered the keys. She quietly surrendered them.

"I feel her pulling on me," she said. "I can feel her there. I don't want to drive into the water, so yeah, you drive."

I watched them get in her car, worry eating at me. That she could feel the Lady at all made me nervous, but that she had already thought of the possibility of the car going into the lake scared the hell out of me. That's how the Lady had taken my grandmother and Duvall.

Slowly, I returned to the car and looked at Bryan. "I'm so worried. Peggin feels the Lady . . . she's scared to drive. We have to do something, Bryan. Oriel has to be able to figure out a way to break the Lady's curse."

As I started the engine, Bryan leaned over to gently slide his hand along my face. "They'll make certain she's safe, love. Trust me. They'll keep her safe." But his eyes were filled with concern, too, and as I told him about the door and the perfume bottle, that concern grew. I had a horrible feeling that somehow, we weren't anywhere near fixing this. And I didn't even know if it could be fixed.

The Crescent Moon Society wouldn't be meeting until ten P.M., so I still had some time to kill. Deev and Bryan carried Peggin's luggage up to the guest room over the office. Sometimes my house reminded me of a miniature castle.

Upstairs over the master suite was my ritual room and the attic. Up a second staircase on the opposite side of the house, over the office, was my old bedroom, a guest room, and a jack-and-jill bath.

While Peggin unpacked, I decided to do a little sleuthing. She was better at computer snooping than I was by far, but I had learned a thing or two over the past couple of months. While Deev and Bryan went out to get takeout for later, I typed the name *J. Jacobs* into the search engine. After a moment I added the words *Whisper Hollow*, and *boat*. The search didn't garner many returns, but the second link told me what I wanted to know.

In 1919, in November, Joseph Jacobs and four other people vanished on Lake Crescent when their ship went down. They were never found again. The ship had been named the *Maria Susanna*. MS. Of course, the initials on the beam. The article didn't have much else to say except that Jacobs had built the *Maria Susanna* in 1915, and it had been considered extremely seaworthy. There had been a storm the night that it vanished and everyone assumed that the winds had sunk her.

I leaned back in my chair, staring at the screen. If the *Maria Susanna* had never been found, how did the keel beam and several of its ribs make their way into the Foggy Downs house? They had been adjacent the walls, but I wondered if they had been installed while the house was being built or added later on. According to the Realtor, if I remembered correctly, the house was built in 1920. I racked my brain, thinking that he had mentioned who the builder was but at the moment I couldn't bring the name to mind. Maybe Peggin would remember.

When she came downstairs a little while later, she looked calmer and a little less frightened.

"Did you get the ferrets settled in?" We had stopped on the way back to the house and picked up Frith and Folly from the kennel. When they had taken her bags up, Bryan and Deev put together the ferrets' cage.

She nodded, dropping into the chair opposite me. "Yes and they seem happy to see me again. They'll be fine up there. I can let them out when I'm in my room."

"Tomorrow we'll fix it so that my old bedroom can be the ferret room and then you can leave them out longer. We can just shut them in there and they'll be fine. There's not much they can tear up."

"Don't be so sure about that," she said with a laugh. "You haven't seen ferrets when they're on a rampage. I have to ferret proof my entire home, including most of the cupboards."

I remembered that Peggin had had childproof locks on almost all of the cupboards and drawers. "Is that why you baby proofed everything? I thought your landlord had done that."

She shook her head. "Ferrets are worse than cats in terms of getting into things, and they're smart." She glanced at the laptop. "What are you looking at?"

"I found out some information that may help us. I know what ship those beams came from." I showed her what I had found out. "Do you remember the name of the person who built the house? Your Realtor told us but I can't recall who he said the original owner was."

Peggin squinted, pushing her glasses back up her nose. She scanned the screen, biting her lip. "Well, considering four people were lost in the lake, it's not surprising that the wood would hold some pretty rough energy. Let me think . . ." After a moment she pulled out her phone. "Hey, Jack? Yeah, it's Peggin . . . Don't ask. No, my things are moved in, but I'm not staying there tonight." She paused, listening. Then, "Yeah, it is haunted. But something worse happened this morning. The Lady tried to drag me under . . . No, I'm not joking . . . We'll talk about that later, okay? Listen, Jack. You told us who the original owner of the house was. Neither Kerris nor I can remember his name. Can you please tell me who it was again?"

Another moment and she thanked him and hung up. She looked over at me. "Jack sounds a little pissed. Anyway, the

builder of the house was Herschel Dorsey. Let's take a look
and see what we find."

"Do you want some coffee while we work?"

"Do frogs eat flies?" Peggin laughed, and winked at me.
She started tapping on the keys while I moved over to the
counter and fired up the espresso machine.

"How many shots and what do you want?" We were getting low on the ground coffee so I pulled out the beans and
began grinding a new batch. With as much caffeine as I
drank, I ground enough for two to three days at a time.

"It's awfully chilly out there and I'm still cold from the
lake. How about a triple-shot peppermint mocha?"

I could tell she was already absorbed in the search because her voice drifted off. Peggin loved to snoop around
on the net and see what she could find, and she was good at
it. I pulled out two large mugs. Her suggestion was a good
one and I decided that I wanted a triple-shot peppermint
mocha as well. I pumped coffee syrup into the mugs, and
then added powdered mocha mix that I bought from the
store. As I waited for the espresso machine to heat up, I dug
out a bag of mini marshmallows. We might as well do it
right. By the time I had pulled six shots—three for Peggin,
three for me—and steamed the milk, stirring it into the
mugs, she was typing away like her fingers were on fire. I
added the mini marshmallows, and as an afterthought, hung
a miniature candy cane over the side of each mug. I carried
them to the table and put one in front of her, then sat down
by her side to watch what she was pulling up on the search.

"What did you find?" I cupped my mug with my hands,
the heat radiating through me like a warm blanket.

She paused, sitting back to sip on her mocha. She wrapped
her hands around the mug and gave a contented sigh. "This
is so nice and warm. I don't know how long it's going to
take me to get over being dragged into the lake." She glanced
at the mark on her wrist. "I wish I could scrub this off, just
make it go away."

"I know, and we'll do everything we can to find an answer for it. We're not going to let the Lady take you, Peggin. I promise you that."

"I know that you'll do everything you can," she said. "But the Lady is powerful, and I don't know many have ever survived. Can you think of anybody who she's taken and who has managed to escape?"

I struggled, trying to remember if there was anyone I had ever met who had been claimed by the Lady and gotten free of her clutches. "We can ask Ivy tonight. You should come with us to the Crescent Moon Society. You have to, anyway. After the last meeting, they made you an adjunct member." I pointed toward the screen. "So what did you find?"

"Something I really didn't want to find. It seems that Herschel Dorsey was an active member of Cú Chulainn's Hounds. Joseph Jacobs, on the other hand, was a member of the Crescent Moon Society. I'm not sure who the others in the boat were, yet, but do you want to make a bet this might have something to do with the feud?"

I frowned, thinking. "I think we need to find out from Ellia when her mother immigrated to America. Was Magda here at that point?"

"I don't think so. Ellia wasn't born until the 1940s, I believe. Her sister Penelope was born a lot earlier. Ellia was a little girl when Magda killed Penelope." She shuddered. "It's still squicks me out when I think about how Penelope died. Can you imagine how much it must have hurt with all of those nails coming out of her body? I can't imagine how powerful Magda's magic had to be to kill her in that way."

I sipped my mocha, sucking down a few of the marshmallows. "I can't imagine killing your own child, and killing them in such a horrific and painful manner. And then cursing your other child, like Magda did to Ellia? That old bitch is a horrible waste of breathing space."

"I know. I try not to think about it often because it can

give me horrendous nightmares. I wonder what Penelope feels, stuck in that tomb. Do you think she's happy?"

I frowned, mulling over my answer. After a moment, I shrugged. "I don't know. She never seems angry to me, and she doesn't seem angsty. Maybe she's just adjusted to her position. In fact, Penelope seems extremely cool—unlike Veronica. Trust me, you never want to encounter Veronica. I hope I don't have to deal with her much in the future. She's terrifying, Peggin. And I don't think she's particularly happy."

Peggin grimaced, then picked up her cup and began to drink her mocha. "I'm going to get a notebook and jot down some of this information so we can take it to the meeting tonight." She crossed the room to get her purse, pulling a small steno book out of the bag. "Thanks, again."

"For what?" I wiped the chocolate foam off my mouth with a napkin, feeling satisfied. The mocha had just the right amount of sweetness in it to tide me over.

"For everything. For helping save my life. For letting me stay in your house, for not telling me 'I told you so'—which you would have every right to." Peggin sank down in her chair, letting out a little sob. "What am I going to do? I gave Jack half of my savings as an option fee. I only have three thousand dollars left in the bank. Everything else I put into the house."

"Can you cancel the deal?" I wasn't up on my real estate law. "At least you're still on the rent-to-own basis. If you walk away, you're not going to be saddled with the rest of the house payments."

"True, but I had to sign a year's lease to start. And the option fee . . . If I walk away, I forfeit it. I'm set to lose at least a year's rent and three thousand dollars on top of that if I decide to move."

I let out a slow sigh. I hated to see her so upset. "Maybe we can take care of this. Maybe the hauntings are because of those boat beams? We might be able to exorcise the land and house. It is a pretty house—it could be beautiful if you fix it up." I wanted to make her smile, to give her some hope. She was my best friend and it hurt me to see her hurting.

"But what about the Lady?" Peggin finished making notes and then turned off my computer and pushed back.

"I don't know. I don't know what we can do. But I promise you, we will do everything we can to keep you from losing your money and your life." I carried our mugs over to the sink as Bryan and Deev returned from the store. They clattered through the living room, into the kitchen, carrying bags of takeout, which they set on the table.

"We couldn't decide whether we wanted pizza or Chinese or sub sandwiches, so we got all three. We can always eat the leftovers tomorrow." Bryan wrapped his arms around me and gave me a long kiss. "I can tell you've been into the coffee machine again."

"That's an *espresso* machine to you, bub." But I laughed, and leaned against his shoulder before extricating myself in order to unpack the bags.

Peggin moved my laptop out of the way and helped me sort out the food. Like most men, the pair had returned with enough to last us a week. There were three pizzas, two pepperoni and one with so many toppings it was hard to tell what was on there. They had also picked up large containers of fried rice, pot stickers, sweet-and-sour chicken, sweet-and-sour pork, fortune cookies, and four foot-long sandwiches, each stacked so high that I wasn't sure how we could fit them in our mouths.

I stared at the stack of food, repressing a grin. "What? Are we stocking up for the zombie apocalypse?"

"You know we're going to get hungry shortly before the meeting, and we won't have time to make anything. I figure we can just munch our way through the late afternoon and evening until the meeting tonight." Bryan shrugged, flashing me a sheepish grin.

"I think you just couldn't make up your mind so you got everything that remotely looked good." I arched an eyebrow at him. The truth was, even though we had just eaten, the food smelled good. I had a feeling stress was playing into my appetite. "We found out some interesting things while you were gone. Peggin, you want to tell them?"

"Not particularly, but I will." She laid out what we had found on the net. "So, we're thinking that maybe, just maybe, the Hounds had something to do with Jacobs's death. Or at least, *I'm* thinking. I'm not sure about Kerris." She glanced at me with a questioning look.

I nodded. "You hit my thoughts on the head. I made a note to ask Ellia tonight about when Magda was born. Whether she had anything to do with this, I'm not certain. The years don't add up. It might just be the Hounds themselves that engineered the shipwreck. I'm going to go look through my great-grandmother Mae's Shadow Journal and see if she made any mention of the *Maria Susanna*. Mae didn't emigrate from Ireland until 1936, so it was well after the ship sank. To be honest, I'm not sure who the spirit shaman was here before Great-Grandma Mae."

There was so much I felt I still needed to learn. I had no clue who had been the spirit shaman before my great-grandmother took over, and until now, it really hadn't occurred to me to find out. My great-grandparents had come over from Ireland in 1936, Great-Grandma Mae took up as spirit shaman immediately, and Great-Grandpa Tristan had worked as a logger. He had died in an accident when Grandma Lila turned thirty.

"While you do that, I think I'll take a nap. I'm tired from this morning." Peggin stood up, pushing her chair back. "Do you mind?"

"Not at all. Make yourself at home. If you need anything, I'll be upstairs in the ritual room." I turned to Bryan and Deev. "What are you guys going to do while we're busy?"

Deev cleared his throat. "I got a text while I was at the store. I've got a commissioned piece that they just moved up my deadline on. I need to go home and work on it." He turned to Peggin apologetically. "I'm afraid that this is going to keep me busy for a couple days. Will you be okay here? I'm going to have to work day and night to get it done."

"I don't mind. But check in with me before bed tonight? Just text me." Peggin looked up at Deev, who softly moved to her side, taking her in his arms. He leaned down and pressed his lips to hers. They looked so good together, and so right. They were both quirky, renegades in their own right, yet together they fit. I could see just how gentle he was with her. He stroked her hair back, cupping her face as he tipped her chin up so that she was staring into his eyes.

"Of course I'll text you. Please be careful. Do what Bryan and Kerris tell you to. You need to stay safe. *I* need you to stay safe." Even though he didn't say the words, I could hear them loud and clear beneath the surface.

Peggin nodded, reaching up to kiss him once more. "I promise. Later, monkey."

He ducked his head and laughed, then with a quick kiss to her forehead, he picked up one of the sandwiches. "Do you mind if I take this for my dinner?"

I quickly shook my head. "If you want anything else, feel free. Take a few pizza slices, too."

I found a plastic container and he filled it with pizza and a couple of pot stickers and the sandwich, snapping the lid on when he was finished. With a wave in our direction, Dr. Divine hurried out the door, the hem of his duster whirling behind him in a patchwork of color.

I filled a plate with pot stickers, two slices of pizza, and some fried rice. Grabbing a water bottle out of the fridge, I turned to Bryan and Peggin. "I'm headed up to the ritual room. I need to find my great-grandma's Shadow Journal. I think I remember seeing it on the shelf in the secret room."

Peggin yawned. "Okay, I'm going to catch some z's." She picked up a piece of pizza, eating it on the way up the stairs.

Bryan looked a little bit lonesome. "Well, given I'm the only one who *isn't* doing anything, I suppose it's a good time to start fixing some of the fence that's crumbling. I have some mortar at my house and can see about affixing the stones back in place."

Bryan had taken up fixing things around the house and yard when he noticed they needed repair. Even though I had offered to pay someone to come in to do the work, he told me no. He preferred taking on the tasks himself, and I was extremely grateful for it.

"Okay, then, we meet in the kitchen at around nine P.M. The meeting starts at ten." And with that, I carried my plate toward the opposite staircase from the one leading to Peggin's room. We had a lot of questions to answer, hopefully before the Lady made another attempt on Peggin's life.

CHAPTER 11

~

I found my great-grandmother's Shadow Journal, but quickly realized it would take some time to flip through it. As much as I loved the old leather-bound books, there were times where I wished that earlier generations had access to computers. It made searching through documents so much easier. Luckily, I was a fast reader, and began to skim the pages as I ate. An hour later I was about thirty pages through—my great-grandmother had very small handwriting and it wasn't all that easy to read—and hadn't encountered anything on the *Maria Susanna* yet.

I slid a bookmark into the journal and set it to the side. There had to be some other way. And then I remembered my grandfather's journals. Or rather, Duvall's ledgers. Grandma Lila's husband had been a member of the Hounds, and I had found the ledgers with all their information in them. It was during their attempt to get those ledgers back that we had discovered just how ruthless the Hounds could be.

Luckily, the Crescent Moon Society now possessed them,

although I had kept a photocopy hidden away in my secret room. I slid open the door and pulled the membership ledger off the shelf, along with the meeting minutes ledger. I carried them to my desk and began to flip through. Peggin was going to computerize all of the information when she had time, but for now it wasn't that difficult to pinpoint the membership list from 1919. The year the *Maria Susanna* sank.

As I skimmed through the list, I saw no mention of Magda. I jumped ahead a few years. Still no mention. Then, in 1957, her name appeared on the membership lists. By then, Ellia had left home. While she was capable of many things, I was pretty sure that Magda hadn't had anything to do with the sinking of the *Maria Susanna*.

That left the questions: Who did sink her? And why?

I thumbed through till I came to Herschel Dorsey. He had first become a member in 1912. The *Maria Susanna* had been taken down in November of 1919, so I skipped ahead in the meetings ledger to that point. All of the meeting notes were taken in longhand, and they were all photocopies, so I had to puzzle out the handwriting.

Some of the words were fuzzy, but there appeared to be some concern over the Crescent Moon Society discovering hidden accounts belonging to some of the members of Cú Chulainn's Hounds. There was also mention of a still in the woods, and apparently there had been a general discussion on how to hide it so that the Crescent Moon Society wouldn't report them to the government. I pushed the book back, and dove into the pizza again.

Perhaps the CMS had found out about an illegal still owned by the Hounds, and were going to use that information to close them down. It made sense, especially given the times. But when had Prohibition started? I had brought my laptop with me and now I opened it up and typed in the question.

Bingo! Prohibition had started in 1919 and ran through 1933. Perfect timing.

I skimmed through more of the entries during that time,

and came across Joseph Jacobs's name. It listed him as the president of the Crescent Moon Society. There was also a notation that he was trouble, and that they needed to take care of him.

Hopefully, the CMS would have records on their side that we could look at to find out the other side of the story. I replaced the ledgers and my great-grandmother's journal in the secret room and closed it. Then, taking my notes and my plate, I headed back down the stairs. I had enough to go on for the moment.

I put my plate in the sink and shrugged into my jacket, then headed out back to see how Bryan was doing.

While the sky was overcast, it wasn't raining. In fact, the temperature felt like it had dropped a few more degrees and I could almost smell snow in the air. Jamming my hands in my pockets, I walked across the yard to where Bryan was fixing the fence. He was reaching for a stone, so I picked it up and handed it to him.

"You know, I was thinking maybe we should take the fences down between our houses." He glanced sideways at me, and I realized he was actually waiting for a response.

"So that's not a rhetorical question, is it?"

"Well, it seems we're here to stay. I doubt either of us is going to move from Whisper Hollow anytime soon. And given that I'm your guardian, and you're my girlfriend, it kind of makes sense." He grinned at me, then went back to hammering nails into the boards. "Next year this will need to be replaced anyway. Whoever built it didn't use very good mortar and it's chipping away all over the place."

"Great. I don't have the money for that right now, given how big this lot is." I frowned, then shrugged. "Maybe it would make sense to take it down. After all, if for some reason we have a fight, we can always just rebuild it." I laughed, but he set down the trowel.

"Don't joke about that." He was serious, looking none too happy.

"What? I was just joking."

"Well, don't joke about that. I'm not about to break up with you, not unless you want me to leave. I'm in this for the long haul. I'm not only your lover, but I'm your guardian. I take my post seriously, and even if you . . ." He paused, his gaze flickering away. "Even if you decide you don't want to be with me, I'll be here. If we were to break up, it would be the best breakup ever."

I wanted to joke that he made it sound so good we should try it, but the look on his face stopped me. I didn't want to ruin what we had by stepping on his feelings. Even though we were still new to each other, I had to admit to myself that I was head over heels for him. I had never been in love, hadn't even had a clue of what it felt like, but now . . . now I thought I knew.

"I'm sorry. I won't joke about it. I want you here, right here. In my life, as my guardian and as my lover. And yeah, let's take down the fence. If it's that old, then we don't want it breaking apart and creating a mess. But what about my roses?" My grandmother had planted roses along the back fence—a beautiful row of climbing roses that I could hardly wait to see bloom. She had planted them after I left Whisper Hollow, so now I was looking forward to summer when the fragrant blooms would fill the yard.

"I'll figure out something. We'll make a rose garden out of them. If I work through the cold while they're dormant, I should be able to transplant them without causing a problem. We can get a picnic table or maybe—how would you like me to move the gazebo over, put it in the middle of the roses? That way we can have dinner out here on summer nights, in the gazebo, surrounded by flowers?" He made it sound so romantic, I wanted to drop everything and fall into his arms right there.

My heart leaped a beat. "It sounds wonderful. So quit trying to fix the fence. Let's start pulling it down."

"Sounds good. We can get a section down now, but I'll

have to work hard the next couple weeks to get the roses moved. I'll have my gardener come help. We'll have everything done by mid-January, in time for the roses to settle into their new soil." And with that, he wrapped his arm around my shoulder. "I wanted to show you something else while we're out here."

"It's pretty dark," I said. The light had faded and it was already twilight. I had turned on the backyard floodlight when I came out, but beyond the lights, the sky was a mournful shade of silver, with a faint glow of orange near the horizon where the sun was setting.

"That's all right." He led me over to one corner of the yard, where a raised bed filled with moss and other little leafy plants provided a nice green display for the winter. "See this? What do you think about me creating a water feature here? It would attract dragonflies in the summer, and frogs."

The realization that my boyfriend not only cared enough to protect me, but to make my yard a wildlife sanctuary, hit me square in the chest. I turned to Bryan, holding my hand out to press against his chest.

"I'm going to say something, and maybe it's too quick. If it is, then just tell me. But if I don't say it now, I'm going to blurt it out at some point when it might be more awkward." I paused as he looked at me expectantly. "I think . . . *no . . . I know* . . . I love you. I've somehow fallen head over heels in love with you. And I'm afraid to tell you this because we've only been dating a couple months, but the fact that you're my guardian makes it more complicated. I don't know—"

"Kerris . . . shush." He held one finger out to touch my lips, very gently. "I love you, too. I fell in love with you the night you almost hit me in the road. Or . . . at least . . . I fell in like with you. I already felt like I knew you because your grandmother told me so much about you. And you surpassed everything I was expecting."

I caught my breath and ducked my head, suddenly blushing. "You love me, too? No man has ever said that to me."

"Well, then . . . isn't it about time someone did?" He pulled me close, his mouth closing in on mine. "I can't believe that no one has snatched you up before now," he whispered before kissing me. I melted into his arms, leaning my head on his shoulder after he softly pulled back.

"They couldn't handle the fact that their dead relatives told me the truth about them. Or that I could see ghosts—some men were nice, but they got spooked. And some . . . they just wanted to tit-fuck me . . . fetishists." A little sob rose in my throat. I hadn't realized how lonely I had been over the years. How much I had wanted to hear someone say those words. I had steeled myself to handle life on my own, which wasn't a bad thing, but now I realized how tiring it could be.

Bryan gathered me up, looking concerned. "Here now, what's wrong, love?"

I shook my head. "Just . . . I've been alone for so long, fighting all of my battles on my own. And that's fine. We're all alone, when it comes down to the wire. But I need . . ." How could I say it? How could I say I needed someone to watch over me? To take care of me when I was sick? It seemed weak and that was the last thing I wanted to be.

"It seems like you're giving up control, doesn't it? When you fall in love? But that's okay. I'll never make you reliant on me. I'll always be here, but I'll never take away your independence, or ask you to be anything but what you are. I promise you that, Kerris." And once again, he leaned down to kiss me.

As the warmth of his words rolled through me like a wave, I whispered, "I love you, Bryan," just to see how it felt.

"I love you, too, Kerris." And with that, the fence between us really came down.

Peggin was awake when we went back inside, sitting at the table with a plate of takeout in front of her. She glanced up, a guilty smile on her face.

"Sorry, I woke up starved. I slept like the dead . . ." And

there, the smile faded. "Damn it. Now everything I say takes on a new meaning." She had applied new makeup and had changed clothes, but her voice sounded thin, almost stretched, and I realized the stress and shock of the day was going to take quite some time to fade.

"Never mind, just eat and enjoy the food. Do you want something to drink? Another mocha?"

She shook her head. "No, but some lemonade or juice would be good. So, did you find anything out about Jacobs?"

"Yeah, but let's wait till the meeting when we tell the whole group what we found out. I'm sure Starlight will pooh-pooh it as nothing important, but I'm not letting her ride over me on this one." I frowned as Peggin snorted.

"You really hate her, don't you? You feel threatened by her."

"I do not!" I glared at her, then looked away. Starlight Williams got under my skin, but not because I hated her. "In fact, I consider her irrelevant, and how can you hate someone you don't think matters?"

"Yeah, you just don't like her from high school. Why don't you give it up. She's probably too tired with her kids to continue the feud you two had going."

"We did *not* hate each other in high school. I didn't even know her very well."

Bryan was watching us with amusement. "I feel like I stumbled in on an argument that I'm best off leaving alone." Then he did something that startled me. He grabbed me around the waist, swung me around to face Peggin, and said, "I told this woman I love her today."

Peggin squeaked and clapped her hands. "I was wondering when you two would get around to that!"

"What do you mean?" I laughed, trying to break out of Bryan's embrace. "I need to get Peggin some lemonade—"

He nuzzled my neck. "She's a big girl. She can get her own lemonade." But he smacked me on the ass and let go. "All right, I relent. I think I could use some pizza right about now. And a few pot stickers."

"Save a couple more pieces of pizza for me. I want it heated up this time." While he and Peggin heated up the rest of the food, I poured lemonade all around. Wine sounded good, but wasn't a great idea right before a meeting. We gathered around the table, Peggin taking a second helping of fried rice.

"Some nights, the best thing in the world is reheated pizza and pot stickers." I closed my eyes, biting into one of the thick rolls. I loved the slightly greasy feel, the taste of the vegetables and pork mixing together along with the crispy wrapper.

At that moment, Daphne decided to join us on the table. She landed with a thud, grabbed one of the pot stickers, and took off, racing across the kitchen floor. I jumped up.

"That can't be that good for cats," I said, racing behind her. I finally cornered her, and she growled as I snatched the food from beneath her paw. "You have your own food. You don't need people food." I dumped the pot sticker in the garbage—it was gnawed on, and while I might have eaten it if I was alone, I wasn't going to do that in front of Peggin and Bryan. I refilled the cat food bowls and returned to the table. "How are Frith and Folly handling their new home?"

"They seem to be doing fine. They're happy to be out of the kennel, that's for sure." Peggin's face clouded over. "I just wish I had never found out I needed to move. Everything feels like it's ruined. I loved my life and the house I was renting. Now I'm scared and hoping I can keep myself alive." She frowned, staring at the table. "I don't suppose either one of you has a time machine I can borrow? I'd go back, tell my landlady I'd pay extra rent to stay there, and hope she agreed."

"Hey, why don't you try that? Call her up, see what she says." I gave her a hopeful look.

"Because I can't *afford* double rent, and I've got a year's payments to make on the Foggy Downs house, whether or not I live there. And you know that I'm not going to find any-body to sublet. Nobody in their right mind would touch . . ."

She trailed off, blushing. "I guess I'm not in my right mind, am I?"

Wanting to put a halt to the painful self-reflection she was going through, I held up my hand. "Stop. That's enough. I know this puts you in a bind, but we're going to figure a way out. From both that damned mark on your wrist, and from the financial pickle you're in. I refuse to let you flounder in this by yourself. We're best friends and we stick together. Do you hear me?"

She nodded, pressing her lips together. But at least there was a faint smile there.

"Good. Then enough on the angst. Maybe . . . I'll talk to your Realtor and see if there's some way you can get out of the lease. I'm good at persuading people." I wasn't, but at least I could give it a try. "I'm surprised you don't try—you charm men like the back of your hand."

"Jack is gay. He's not going to be wrapped around my finger, and before you ask, yes, he has a child. He was married before he came out. His wife was so hurt by his news that she ran off and left their kid with him. Now he and his new partner are double-dads."

Bryan laughed. "Yeah, good try, Kerris, but Peggin's charms, as remarkable as they are, won't fly with someone like that. Why don't you let me have a talk with him? I'm sure that we can come to some agreement. Give me his name and I'll call him tomorrow."

"That's wonderful . . . I appreciate your help. But that still means I have to find a new place to live." She stabbed another pot sticker. "Stupid rentals. I hate being at the mercy of somebody else's whims."

"We'll find you a place. Now can we eat and then head out? I don't want to be late. Starlight gives me nasty looks, like I don't care enough to be on time. I'd like to . . ." I stopped, looking up to see both Peggin and Bryan laughing aloud. My lip starting to twist into a frown, I finally stopped and laughed with them. Who was I kidding? Starlight was

the prom queen mean girl, and I was the geek in the corner.
That's the way it had been in high school, and that's the way
it was going to stay, it seemed.

By the time we reached the meeting, it was starting to snow.
Little flakes, very patchy, but nonetheless, it was snowing
and I was delighted. I loved snow, and wished that we got
more of it, but at least here in Whisper Hollow a few inches
usually arrived every year and stuck for a few weeks, and
that was generally enough to satisfy my snow-bunny urge.

The meetings were held at Niles's. Niles Vandyke was
the main mechanic in Whisper Hollow and he owned a large
garage. Below the garage, through a hidden entrance, was
an entire level given over to the Crescent Moon Society. The
first time I had been escorted to a meeting, I felt a little like
Batman heading into the Batcave. It was all very clandestine,
but it was also a necessity, given the ferocity and viciousness
of the Hounds. They had killed before; they wouldn't hesi-
tate to kill again.

The Morrígan and Cú Chulainn had a long-standing feud,
and the Hounds, who were dedicated to the warrior god himself, took it upon themselves to go after the followers of the
Morrígan and try to subvert them at every turn possible. On
the other hand, the sons and daughters of the Morrígan pretty
much left everybody alone—barring the spirits. Unless we
were defending ourselves. Which, at least in Whisper Hollow,
we seemed to be doing on a regular basis. The Hounds were
responsible for my mother's death, and my father's death,
and a number of others who had gotten in the way.

As we passed the guards watching over the front of Niles's
shop, they nodded us by. Gareth was sitting there. The older
biker looked as tough as he was, with a number of scars to
his credit. He was a *fixer* . . . he took care of problems for
Sophia Castillo, the chief of police, that the police couldn't
officially intervene in. Sophia couldn't be part of the Crescent

Moon Society, but she knew about us and had her fingers in the pie via one of her officers, Frank O'Conner. He worked with Gareth on the side. I wasn't sure exactly what Gareth did, but I knew that it involved some rough stuff, at times, and if I wanted someone to back me up, besides Bryan, the first place I would run would be to him.

As we entered the janitor's closet, Peggin shut the door behind us. I walked over to the back wall and pressed the second coat hook from the left. A panel slid open, and we were facing a hidden staircase. The railings helped, but the steps were at a steep incline and every time we came to a meeting, I was afraid I'd go sprawling face-first down the spiraling staircase and knock out a tooth or maybe scramble my brain.

But we descended the forty steps without incident to find ourselves in a large chamber. Two doors were placed opposite each other, on either side. In the center of the room, sitting on another stool, was Michael Brannon, the owner of the Broom & Thistle. He was holding a long sword, razor sharp, which he knew how to use with precision. One wrong move and boom, slice and dice.

"Are we late?" I asked. I usually was, and I'd started to think it was a subconscious reaction to Starlight—a little late every time just to needle her.

"For once, no." Michael nodded to the door on the right. "Go on in."

We entered the room to find a long table with chairs on all sides. Starlight was there, as was Frank. Ellia and Ivy were there, though I didn't see Oriel anywhere. Trevor, from the Vintage Bookstore, was there. Tonya Pajari—a fortune-teller—was already there, but she spoke up, saying Nathan, her husband and an ex-military man, was home sick with the flu and wouldn't be able to make it. Clinton Brady, the owner of the Fogwhistle Pub, across from the Foggy Downs subdivision where Peggin's house was, was sitting in a corner chair, nursing a beer. Nadia from the steakhouse hadn't arrived, and neither had Prague, from the Herb & Essence.

I settled into a chair, with Bryan on one side and Peggin on my other. I motioned to Ellia and she came around the table. Everybody else was chatting as we waited for the rest to arrive.

"I have some things I need to ask the Society tonight. Can you put me on the agenda?"

She frowned. "Ask Starlight. It's time you two dealt with your discomfort and started acting your ages." And with that, she abruptly returned to her seat.

I groaned. But Ellia was right, and beyond that—Ellia made it clear she wasn't going to act as a go-between any longer. Pushing back my chair, I reluctantly sauntered up to Starlight, who was busy poring over a page that looked jammed full of notes. I pulled out the chair next to her and, unasked, sat down.

"Hey, Starlight." I tried to keep my voice pleasant.

She jerked her head up, looking either annoyed or startled. I wasn't sure which. "What do you need, Kerris?"

"I need some time on the agenda. We've had several serious incidents today, one of them involving the Lady. We also have information on the Ankou, if Ellia hasn't told you yet."

She glanced over the sheet of paper. "Well, we have a full agenda tonight, but I'll fit you in. And yes, Ellia made certain to pencil in time for you. Why don't you just segue both issues together, for good measure?" She sounded surprisingly accommodating. As she glanced up, she must have seen my confusion. "Is something wrong?"

I shook my head. "I just didn't think . . ." I paused. There was no good way to say I thought she'd try to blow me off because she didn't like me. "Never mind. By the way, I met Veronica. I have information from her about the Ankou in the forest, as well."

"Good. It's important to keep relations with her on as even a keel as possible." She paused, then met my gaze, the harried irritation falling away. "I've never met her—she refuses to meet with anyone except the spirit shaman and her triad. Tell me . . . what's she like?"

A tremor filled her voice, almost reverent, and I realized that Starlight Williams was in awe of both the spirits of Whisper Hollow . . . and, by default, me. As we stared at each other, I could see that—behind the professional rich bitch—there was an insecure, wonder-filled woman inside her. I knew that Starlight had her own magic, but I didn't know exactly what it was. I figured it was time to find out.

"Veronica's frightening, to be honest. She's like . . . Morticia Addams meets Countess Báthory, I kind of think." That brought something else to mind. "Do you know why Jonah— the undertaker—was in the graveyard? I thought maybe he was checking out a spot, but I haven't heard that anybody died the past few days."

Starlight looked surprised. "No, actually. There haven't been any deaths that I know of. Not since . . . who was it that the Lady took a week or so ago?"

"Hudson Jacks. I did the ceremony to hand him over to Penelope, so he shouldn't be a problem. I was just wondering. Jonah is . . ." I paused, not knowing Starlight's relationship with the undertaker. But she just laughed.

"Jonah is a freak. Trust me, I wish his uncle was still alive. He was a good man, and he loved his job—as much as you can love a job like that. He respected his clients, both the families and the dead. I don't think I feel comfortable around Jonah." Starlight let out a little shudder.

I nodded. "I was thinking the same thing. Do you think we need to watch him?"

"Watch him? For what?" But even though she blew off the question, I could tell that I'd struck a chord, which was all I had hoped to do. Something about Jonah didn't track right with me, and I didn't want to be the only one thinking about the matter.

At that moment, Oriel and Prague entered the room, followed by Gareth and Nadia.

"We're all here now, as far as those who can make it tonight, so let's get this show on the road," Starlight said, pounding her mini-gavel for order. "We have a full agenda and I don't want to be here past midnight if we can help it. Zachary has a test coming up and we want him well rested."

Nobody said a word. Everybody in town knew that Starlight's son Zachary was trouble on legs. So far, he'd managed to get out of all his screw-ups with just a slap on the wrist, given who his mother was. One of these days, though, he was going to pull the wrong stunt on the wrong person.

"Take your seats, please. Come to order. Nadia, will you please read the minutes from our last meeting?" Without further ado, we were into minutes and agendas, and I settled back, ignoring most of the chatter, until it was my turn to talk.

Fifteen minutes later, Starlight's gavel sounded again and she said, "Tonight, Kerris has several matters to present to the group. Kerris, please tell us what you have to say."

I cleared my throat, took a sip of water, and stood. I found that people paid more attention to me when I was standing up. I launched into seeing the forest Fae, and what it had told me, then—with Ivy's help—related our trip out to Timber Peak. I then went on to tell them as much as I could about my meeting with Veronica and what she had told me about the witch bottles.

"But we have another problem, that goes beyond the Ankou. Today, the Lady tried to take Peggin."

That stopped the whispers. Everybody turned to stare at Peggin, who grimaced. She usually didn't mind being the center of attention, but this wasn't exactly the same thing as being at a party. As I launched into what we had found out about the house, and the fact that the beams belonged to the *Maria Susanna*, and that Joseph Jacobs, the builder of the ship, had been a member of the Crescent Moon Society, the room grew very still. I finished, laying everything on the table.

"I'm wondering if we have any records of who might have been in that boat with Jacobs? And whether there had been any attempts made on his life before that. If he had discovered the Hounds were running a still, and threatened to call the police . . . well . . . that might be enough right there for them to go after him."

Clinton Brady slowly cleared his throat. "Joseph Jacobs was my great-great-uncle. My mother used to talk about how he disappeared, and how his ship had been taken by the Lady. Nobody ever mentioned the ship being found, or the wood being used. This is the first I've heard of it, and now you've got me wanting to know more. He's been missing for almost one hundred years. I'd like to be able to bring him home and put him to rest, if it's possible."

As he fell silent, the room burst into conversation. I turned to Ellia, and motioned for her to follow me. "We have to get the mark off Peggin. Has Oriel found a solution?"

She frowned. "I'm not sure, but we'll ask her in a few minutes. Meanwhile, I think it's fate that Peggin moved into that house. There's more to this business with the ship than meets the eye. I can feel it in my bones."

And indeed, as she spoke, I could almost hear the Crow Man laughing from a distance. Yes, he was definitely involved. And that meant, so was I.

CHAPTER 12

A s the volume of the room grew louder, I moved off to the side. I really didn't want to deal with people at this point, or their questions. Starlight seemed to notice me sequestering myself in the corner, because she took her gavel and called for order.

"Please take your seats again. Save your questions for Kerris for later." She turned to Oriel. "Given that the forest Fae indicated that the Matriarchs were to take care of the witch bottles, are you and Ellia and Ivy prepared to go in search of them? And do you think you have the wherewithal to destroy them when you find them?"

Oriel nodded. "The hardest problem will be in finding them. You can bet that Magda didn't just set them out in plain sight or leave a treasure map leading to them. If Ivy can call up one of the forest Fae when we're out there, they may be able to help us. We'll do our best. Even if we can't find all of them, we should be able to break cycle of so many Shadow People coming in. My guess is that it takes all fifteen bottles

laid out in a particular design in order to summon the Ankou.
Even if it takes several trips, we'll find them."

"I have a question, if you don't mind." Tonya raised her
hand. Both she and her husband were from Finnish stock.
Tonya had the gift of sight and Nathan had been a military
man and was extremely precise with weaponry and tracking.
I didn't know much else about them.

"Tonya, you have the floor." Starlight waved her gavel at
Tonya.

"What happens once we break the bottles and disrupt the
spell? Won't Magda just start in building it up again? All
she'll have to do is create new witch bottles."

I rubbed my forehead. I hadn't thought that far ahead and
now I realized that it might be wise to start taking the long
view of things. Tonya's point was well made, and I wished
that I had thought of it myself.

Ellia answered for the group. "Oh, she can recast the
spell with no problem. However, making the witch bottles
needed for that spell is a long and tedious process. Unless
she has several spares made, it will take or at least another
five or six months to prepare new ones."

Tonya bit her lip, looking skeptical. "Do you really think
she's that unprepared? Look at who we are dealing with. I may
not be from Russia, but Baba Volkov is extraordinarily demand-
ing of her followers. For a priestess as powerful and prominent
as Magda is, I think that Baba Volkov would flay her alive if
she wasn't prepared with a plan B. So you know she's going to
be up to something as soon as we break the spell."

Ellia let out a soft sigh. It had to be difficult hearing
people talk about your mother like that, especially after
what Magda did to both her daughters. Though, given the
torture she put them through, I suspected there wasn't much
love lost.

"You should listen to Tonya," Ellia said. "I cannot begin
to impress upon you how powerful my mother can be. If
you think the *Hounds* are ruthless, you have no idea how

cruel and vicious Magda is. There is no forgiveness in her. No mercy. She tolerates no mistakes, and she will do her best to crush Whisper Hollow, considering she feels that the town slighted her."

Starlight gazed at Ellia for a moment, then glanced over at Tonya. She seemed to be thinking of how to respond. Oriel and Ivy said nothing. They might be the Matriarchs, but Starlight was the leader of the Crescent Moon Society and they paid her her due.

After a moment, Starlight cleared her throat. "We will keep everything you've said in mind. There isn't much we can do about potential attacks except to keep aware and alert for them. We must focus on *now*, on the present. Before I heard the news tonight, I was planning to bring up an issue. Now I see that everything seems to be related. We've been getting more reports from Whisper Hollow citizens about being attacked by the Ankou. In the past three days, Sonja has received four new reports. This seems to back up the statements the forest Fae made about Magda sending the Shadow People against the town. We have to control this situation before we entertain how to prevent future attacks. Therefore I move to include in the minutes the notation that Ellia, Ivy, and Oriel will be attending to the witch bottles tomorrow."

She waited for Trevor—who was the secretary of the Crescent Moon Society—to jot down the notes. After he nodded, she continued.

"Now, we should turn our attention to the Lady of the Lake, and what happened to Peggin, our newest member. Since there are so few survivors of the Lady's attacks, do you mind if we photograph the mark on your wrist for our records? I don't mean to seem insensitive but—"

Peggin shrugged and shook her head. "If it could help in the future, go ahead."

As Trevor pulled out his phone and began to take pictures of Peggin's wrists, Clinton Brady spoke up. "What can you tell us about the Lady? She had you in her grasp. As Starlight said, there are very few who survive her attacks. Everything we can possibly learn about her will help us in the future." Clinton's expression was sober. He had seen too many people vanish into the lake across from his pub. The Fogwhistle Pub looked directly across to the pier and more than once, he had rushed across the street, too late to save the Lady's quarry.

Peggin closed her eyes. I could tell she was struggling with the memory of her fear. Hell, I wouldn't want to remember if I were her, either. But, like a trouper, she came through.

"Honestly, it all happened so fast and I was in a trance so it's rather difficult to pinpoint anything. But . . . her song. I heard her singing. She had the most beautiful voice, until she actually got hold of me and dragged me under. Then it was dark and garbled and sounded like someone drowning. Kerris wasn't kidding when she called it siren song, because when I heard the Lady calling to me, the only thing I could think of was that I needed to go to her. I could swear that I remember her promising to make things better for me."

"How far away were you when you heard her sing?"

"Good question," I said. The distance might give us a clue as to how close one had to be in order to be in danger.

Peggin thought for a moment before answering. "Well, I was in the house when I thought I heard something. So I stepped out on the porch and that's when I heard the song." She turned to the others. "I leased a house at the Foggy Downs subdivision. The one Kerris was telling you about with the beams."

At the round of sudden gasps, Peggin winced.

"I wouldn't have done so except that I have to move within less than a month. My landlady wants her house back and I *really* don't want to live in an apartment. So I found a house that seemed perfect. It's rent-to-own, and I could afford the option fee and the rent. When I went to look at it, there was something about the house that made me want to buy it. It's a dump, but I thought . . . I still think . . . it could be beautiful if I fixed it up. I don't know whether the ghosts who live in that house were influencing me, or the Lady herself. The house is at the end of a cul-de-sac, nearest the woods that lead down to the pier."

Gareth leaned forward, propping his elbows on his knees as he fumbled with a piece of gum, unwrapping it and sticking it in his mouth. "That whole area is rife with spirits, and I think a number of them there are landlocked . . . trapped by the Lady. Not every family allows the rites that Lila . . . Kerris now . . . can offer in order to protect the spirits of the lost ones. I don't like going down there, and I'm probably one of the most head blind of this group. The entire Fogwhistle area gives me the creeps."

"I agree, and why my great-grandfather chose that area to rebuild the pub in, I have no clue." Clinton's grandfather had ordered the pub dismantled, brick by brick. It was originally built in Ireland, and was over four hundred years old. It had been rebuilt in exactly the same fashion as it was in the old country, and had its own history and spirits.

I cleared my throat. "I'm going to make a wild guess that the Lady's song can be heard up to two or three hundred yards away. Which gives her a wide berth. I'm not certain about the other parts of the Lake Crescent shoreline—she's found everywhere around the lake—but I do think that Fogwhistle Pier is her home base. And now that I think of it . . . doesn't it make sense that she's some sort of siren? Maybe a water spirit who has been empowered by all the souls that she's taken or those who've been lost in the lake through accident?"

Clinton spoke up. "Back in Ireland, they have the kelpie. It sounds like the Lady might actually be something along those lines."

"I don't know if we'll ever know, but at least we know now that she can lure people in with her song. And if they can hear her through the walls of a house, why can't they hear her through the metal of a car? Which would explain why some people go off the road when there's no reason for them to.

They just drive into her song. Like my grandmother and Duvall." I didn't like thinking about this. For one thing, it hit close to home—too close. For another, the concept of how powerful the Lady was . . . it was downright overpowering.

"If she can summon the driver of a car, she could summon the driver of a busload of people. Should we reroute buses to go another way?" Starlight's forehead wrinkled.

Cripes. Even I hadn't thought about the possibility of the Lady summoning an entire bus of people down into the dark water. Immediately, I wanted to agree with Starlight's idea, but Frank had a counterargument.

"I think that yes, she probably *can* do that and I hope to hell she never does. But what reasoning are we going to give the state Department of Transportation for rerouting buses, but not large trucks? We can't possibly tell them that we have a spirit here who is dragging people down into the depths and killing them. We'd be laughed out of their offices." He rubbed his forehead. "I can tell you right now that that's not going to fly. No. We either have to push this through under the guise of necessary roadwork—which we might be able to get away with, but then we're going to disrupt all truck traffic. And what about outside of the city limits? We can't make this happen for the entire circumference of the lake. It's just not a viable plan and, by inventing road repair work, we'll cost the city funds we don't have to spare."

Starlight cleared her throat. "Well then, I suggest we table this particular part of the discussion for later. Everybody, please . . . start thinking about potential solutions. I don't care how crazy they sound, bring them to the next meeting. But do note, this will *not* include a hunting party going after the Lady. Everyone in this room knows that we can't take her on and hope to win. She's far too powerful and she's been here far longer than we have. I have a feeling if we went out there, it would turn into a suicide mission."

Trevor noted down everything that had been said and then, again, motioned to Starlight.

She gave him a brief nod. "As to Peggin and what to do about her mark, I leave that up to the Matriarchs. Oriel has suggested a spell and I have agreed to take part, although it's not magical work that I'm comfortable with. But seeing that it's the only choice and we have to do something, it is what it is. At some point the Lady will come after Peggin again, and she may well succeed. Does anyone else have anything to add?"

Niles raised his hand. Starlight recognized him.

"As most of you know I have managed to keep the secret entrance to this chamber hidden and in good repair. Business is down lately, and we need to replace several important parts on the locking mechanisms for the doors. I need funds to do this. I can't spring for it all myself."

Starlight let out a little laugh and for once, I didn't read ridicule into it.

"Thank you, Niles, for a routine request. Talk to Frank about a purchase voucher for what you need. You'll need to get two quotes for how much it's going to cost, and submit the lower, unless it's so low that it's obviously makeshift. Frank will cut you a check to buy what you need. Now, is there anything else?"

"What about the Winter Fun Fest? Should we still proceed?" Nadia asked.

Starlight didn't bother calling for a consensus.

"I don't see why not. Yes, we are facing some tough times but the fact is we are always facing some sort of crisis. The Winter Fun Fest is a tradition here in Whisper Hollow, and I really don't want to let our traditions pass by. Our town is built on heritage and ritual, and a mutual desire to succeed and thrive. So yes, the Fun Fest will go on. Are you in charge of it this year?"

Nadia shook her head. "No, but I'm on the entertainment committee. The mayor assigned several other members; two of them belong to the Hounds, unfortunately. But since this festival benefits everybody, I don't think they'll attempt anything to stop it or screw it up."

"Then I suggest we all go out and support the festival as much as we can. With so much going on I suggest that we meet again in a week to discuss what we've learned."

As groans filled the room, Starlight banged her gavel. She seemed to enjoy pounding on the table with it. I snorted, thinking maybe she was a frustrated drummer.

"Hush! You all know how important the CMS is to this town. I *know* holidays are a busy time and we want to spend as much of it as we can with our families, but *we* are a family, too. And *our* family protects this town. So quit griping, suck it up, and mark your calendar for next Saturday for ten P.M. If there's nothing further?" She paused, waiting. Nobody said anything. "Then I declare this meeting adjourned."

As everybody milled around the room, getting ready to leave, Oriel wandered over.

"Kerris, meet us at Ivy's tomorrow morning at nine. We'll go out to Timber Peak and start hunting for the witch bottles. Tuesday night, you, Bryan, and Peggin will join us at the boardinghouse at eight. By then, we'll have everything we need arranged to perform the ritual to free Peggin from the curse. I should warn you, it's neither easy nor safe. But it's her only hope, that I can see." And with that she turned and hustled away.

We had just slipped into our jackets and were headed toward the door when Clinton Brady wandered over.

"Kerris? Why don't you drop over to the Fogwhistle Pub for an hour or so?"

"Now?"

He nodded. "Yeah. I might have some family information on Joseph Jacobs and his ship. Maybe it will help you. I can tell you the stories about him and his ships that my mother told me. Maybe something among all that scattered information will ring a bell. I'll go and dig up the pictures and family history now, if you're up for it."

I glanced at Peggin and Bryan, both of whom nodded. "Fine. We'll meet you there in twenty minutes." As we left the garage, it occurred to me that I hadn't been in the Fog-whistle Pub since before I left home, when I was eighteen and still sneaking into bars. It'd been fifteen years and what seemed like a million miles since then.

The Fogwhistle Pub really did belong out on an Irish moor, cloaked in mist and shrouded by moonlight. We had the mist, but this time of year? It was rare when the moon was able to shine through. And now, the gently falling snow just added a wonderful touch, making the entire scene seem like a Christmas card.

The pub looked as old as it actually was, weathered gray stone two stories tall. The two concessions that the Brady family had made when bringing over the pub from Ireland were to put in sturdy windows and to replace the roof with one that was far more weatherproof and less flammable. But the pub itself, and several of the old tables and benches inside, were the same as they had been over on the Emerald Isle.

As we entered through the large wooden double doors, we were greeted with a cheerful glow from the fireplace. Clinton had decked out the mantel in holly boughs and evergreens, and in the corner of the pub a large spruce stood, sparkling with red and gold ornaments and tinsel that shimmered in the glow of the firelight. The smells of cinnamon and eggnog filled the air, and as I looked around, I realized how welcoming this place was. Every table held crystal glasses filled with candy canes, and unobtrusive Celtic music played gently in the background.

Peggin and I had ventured into the pub several times when we were seventeen and eighteen. Clinton had pretty much ignored us, not bothering to card us even though he knew we were underage. We always bought one drink and stopped at that, and if we had attempted more he probably would have tossed us out on our asses.

Clinton was hustling out from the back room, his arms

filled with old photo albums and a couple of journals. The bartender—I didn't know who it was—folded the bar towel and set it on the counter, then crossed to where we were sitting.

As Clinton approached, he asked, "Would you like eggnog? I also have fresh cinnamon buns and scones."

I blinked. The thought of cinnamon buns and scones in a pub seemed odd, but then again, I was used to mainstream taverns that thrived on pretzel sticks and peanuts.

Peggin nodded. "That sounds good to me." Bryan and I agreed, and the barkeep took off toward the back to fill our order.

As we settled into our chairs, close enough to the fire to take the chill off, I glanced over at Peggin. "Remember when we came in here and tried to act so grown up? And Clinton here, he always brought us our one beer."

"You girls weren't going to get in any trouble from one drink, and I knew you both well enough that I knew you wouldn't push me any further." Clinton laughed, then shook his head. "It's hard to believe it's been fifteen years. The both of you have grown up nicely. I wish I could say that for everybody who came in here. Sometimes I hate how time changes people . . . it drains ethics, it jades idealism."

"It's been a long time, that's for certain. So much has happened since then. I had no idea back then that you were part of the Crescent Moon Society. Of course, my grandmother didn't even tell me about the society. I didn't know it existed until I returned home."

Clinton scratched the gray whiskers covering his chin. He looked like an old biker, with a bandanna wrapped around his head, in blue jeans and a flannel shirt. He was a burly man and looked like he worked out, but there was something gentle about his nature that I had always responded to. From what I knew of him, he was a trustworthy man.

"It wasn't something I aspired to but I was inducted and so here I am. And maybe your grandma just wanted to protect you for a while longer—secrets can be dangerous things to share. So, how is your real grandfather? Duvall was a son of a bitch and I'm sorry to say that I wasn't at all upset to hear that he went in the lake. But I am sorry about your grandmother. Lila was a wonderful woman, and it hurts to know that the Lady took her." He glanced over at Peggin. "We'll do every-thing we can to make certain she doesn't get you, too, girl. While I can't help with the magic, maybe I can fill in some of the blanks about that house you're living in, and encourage you to get the hell out of there as soon as possible."

A waitress brought over our drinks and pastries. The eggnog smelled so fragrant that I wanted to lap it up like a cat. The taste didn't let me down, either. As she left, Clinton spread out the journals and albums that he had brought. He opened one of the old photograph albums to a page he had marked with a Post-it note. He turned it around and shoved it across the table so we could see it. A tall man was in the photograph and he looked familiar. He was standing next to a ship. Or a boat, rather. It was a large boat and I wasn't sure exactly what kind it was, but the name on the side of the boat was clear. The *Maria Susanna*.

"This was my great-great-uncle, Joseph Jacobs. He was a boat builder back in the early 1900s in Whisper Hollow, and he built a total of seven custom boats for various mem-bers of the town. My grandmother told me that he was a confirmed bachelor, but he kept company with one of the town's most prominent feminists of the time. I guess you'd call her a suffragette, although I don't know if the term suf-fragette was even used then. She defied tradition by wearing pants, and by refusing to marry even though several men had offered. She built up quite a tidy sum for herself, and my grandmother told me that she often said, 'Why should I let any man have access to my money, when I can take care of myself?' I guess my great-great-uncle liked the fact that she wasn't looking for someone to take care of her."

"What was her name?" Bryan asked.

"Eugenie Everson. She was probably named Eugenia at birth, if you want to look her up in the records. I do know that she also belonged to the Crescent Moon Society, and that's how she met Joseph Jacobs. She was on the boat when it went down. I found this when I was digging up the photo albums." He held out a photocopy of a newspaper article. Even the photocopy looked old.

I carefully reached for it, making sure my fingers were clean. The words were a little blurry, but I could still read them.

November 8, 1919.
Last night, local shipwright and woodcarver Joseph Jacobs vanished when his ship, the Maria Susanna, is believed to have sunk due to the massive storm we had yesterday over Lake Crescent. On board with Jacobs were: Eugenie Everson, Walton Thomas, Frank Beaverton, and Walter Hanover. No sign of the ship has been found, nor have any bodies. Rescue workers are continuing to search, but all ship board members are believed to have drowned. The Maria Susanna was deemed extremely seaworthy, so questions remain. But nothing can be ascertained until the ship is found.

I looked up from the clipping. "Do we know if all of these people were part of the Crescent Moon Society?"

Clinton shrugged. "I'm not entirely certain about the other three men. But Eugenie and Joseph were. They probably got caught in a storm. The storms on Lake Crescent can be brutal. I doubt if it was the Lady, though. She couldn't very well climb aboard and take them down one by one—that's not her MO."

Peggin cleared her throat. "So what happened? Why were they out there during a storm?"

"That is a good question, and one that I'd like to see the answer to." Bryan took a sip of his eggnog.

Clinton slipped through the photo albums, showing us a

picture of Eugenie. She was a strong woman, and in her time was probably called handsome. She was tall, wearing a pair of trousers, a work shirt, and a skinny tie. Her hair was caught up in a tidy bun. He showed us another couple of pictures of the ship from various angles. It certainly looked seaworthy, at least from the old photographs.

"Your great-great-uncle looked to be a talented man. You said he was also a woodcarver?" Bryan was frowning.

"Yes, he could carve just about anything from what I gather."

"There's something I don't understand," Peggin said. "Why would someone use beams from a ship to build a house? Or in a house? And how would they get ahold of them? Is this a common occurrence?" She laughed. "I suppose that's more than one question, isn't it?"

Clinton grinned at her. He shoved another cinnamon bun in her direction. "Eat hearty, girl. I like to see women with appetites."

I realized he was flirting with Peggin but I didn't think that she noticed it. I was about to say something about Deev, but then decided that he was probably just playing around.

Clinton took a long drink of his eggnog, then motioned to the barkeep to bring more. "Okay, here's the deal. In general, using boards from a shipwreck? A design choice. But there were times when it was just cheaper to use found lumber. People did it all the time—an old barn gets razed, scavengers come through and look for all the wood that's still good to use as well as other building materials. It's nothing more than recycling."

I frowned. I knew that did happen, but something was off about it. "True, but generally, if someone finds a shipwreck, aren't they going to report it, not just scavenge through it?"

"My guess is that this Herschel Dorsey person found the wood and decided to use the lumber in his house. Maybe he thought the wreck had been reported, or maybe he just wanted free wood and didn't want to chance losing his stash.

I can't give you a pat answer," Clinton said. "But I'd like to take a look, if you'd let me. I can probably tell if those beams were built into the house when it was originally erected, or if they were added on later."

Peggin gave him a winsome smile. In the glow of fire-light, she looked warm and luscious. "Of course. Although, I'm not sure if I should go back in the house with you."

"I'd say no. I think you and Kerris here should just stay out of there. The Lady could attack you, Kerris, if she can't get to Peggin."

It made sense, in a way, though I had an odd feeling about the entire conversation.

Peggin glanced over at Bryan. "If I give you the keys, can you show Clinton around tomorrow? I don't want to impose if you're busy."

Bryan shrugged, finishing off the last bite of a cinnamon roll and licking his fingers. "I've got meetings all morning, but I'm free after one thirty. Meet me at the house at two P.M.? And I agree, Peggin. You shouldn't go back to that house until we've gotten rid of the mark on your arm. It's way too close to the lake for comfort."

Clinton gave Bryan a nod and reached out to clasp his hand. "Two o'clock is fine. I'll see you then. The house at the back end of the road, right?"

Peggin nodded. "I still think it could be a beautiful house," she said wistfully.

"I think you should cut your losses and run." Clinton offered us another cinnamon bun but we were all full.

Peggin stared at her wrist. "Do you think she'll ever really forget about me? Even if we get rid of the mark, I have this fear that she's still going to remember me, and that she's going to look for any way she can to . . ." Her voice drifted off into a choked sigh.

I reached over and took her hand in mine, squeezing hard. "We will find you a house that you'll love. I really don't think we can clear the land and house, though I can try. But there's no way we can exorcise the Lady, and with her siren song, there's nothing to stop her from calling you in again. No, I think you should move closer toward the center of town, or maybe up toward Timber Peak. At least that's away from the lake."

"I agree with Kerris. Don't go back to the house."

"You seem determined that I move out of there," Peggin said, staring at him.

Clinton's expression took on a haunted look. "I don't want to think about how many times somebody's gone over the side on Fogwhistle Pier, and I've had to run across the street to join in the search-and-rescue team. It's almost always a recovery team, by then. The Foggy Downs subdivision is a dangerous place. There are only a couple people there now, and frankly—I have no clue how they've managed to survive."

On that note, we pushed back our chairs and headed to the car.

We didn't have far to go, but we had no more than started the engine and pulled out of the parking lot onto Fogwhistle Way when Peggin shrieked. I swerved to the side, straight into a ditch, my SUV precariously tilted to one side. Bryan turned and immediately unbuckled his seat belt.

"Peggin! What the hell—"

I fumbled for my seat belt and scrambled out of the driver's door, slipping as I did so and falling into the ditch, which was covered with an inch of snow. As I struggled for my footing, I managed to land against the side of the car and found myself staring into the backseat. There, Peggin was struggling with a black silhouette. It was one of the Ankou and it was reaching for her throat as I struggled to yank open the door.

CHAPTER 13

"Peggin! Peggin! Can you get out the other side?" I was doing my best to yank open the side door on the backseat, but something seemed to be holding it closed. I didn't think it was locked, but when I touched the handle, a massive jolt, like a giant spark, flung me back and I landed against the side of the ditch, rolling toward the bottom before I could stop myself. Aching, but unhurt, I scrambled up the side, frantic.

On the other side of the car, Bryan was fighting with the other door. He was shouting, "Open, damn you! Open!" Inside, Peggin was struggling with the Ankou, which seemed to have its fingers around her throat.

There was only one thing to do. There was a series of three runes—the Void Runes—that I had learned from my grandmother's Shadow Journal, and now I held out my hands, trying to steady myself. I didn't have a wand or my dagger with me, but I focused all my energy through my fingers as I drew the runes in the air.

The first, the opening line, was a lightning bolt across a

vertical line that was almost an L shape. The second rune, to catch and shoot the energy into the abyss, was an arrow through a crescent moon. And the third rune, to suck the energy and hold it tight, was the rune of a cauldron with a skull on it.

They were complicated but I had practiced until I could draw them in my sleep. They were etched in my memory and in my muscle memory as well.

There were no words to go with these runes, but I didn't need any. As I drew the third one in the air, I aimed it at the Ankou, focusing solely on the dark silhouette. The magical arrow sprang forth. I couldn't see it, but I could feel it racing toward the Shadow Man, and it struck him in the back of his neck. An explosion of light filled the interior backseat as he let out a long shriek and vanished. Bryan suddenly fell back as the door opened and a huge cloud of black smoke poured out, caught up by the breeze to blow away to the east.

Peggin was lying across the seat, coughing and holding her throat. Bryan pulled her out, helping her to sit up against the side of the ditch. I hurried around the car, steadying myself by leaning on the side of it. At that point I realized the engine was still running, the headlights shining up toward the side of the road.

"Is she okay? Peggin, are you okay?"

She was coughing, her knees pulled up to her chest as she leaned her head against them. She nodded, looking up as I joined her and Bryan.

"Crap. Just . . . crap. That's the last thing I needed." Her voice was scratchy and she sounded like she was going to cry. But as she lifted her face to look at me, I saw she was more angry than anything else. "I am *done* being everybody's punch monkey. I want this over with."

"I know. I know, sweetie. I'm sorry." I glanced over at the car. "Bryan, can you call Niles and have them come out here with the tow truck? We aren't going to get the car out of the ditch on our own, I'll tell you that."

"I'm on it." He walked off to the side, pulling out his phone. I settled myself on the snowy ground beside Peggin. The flakes were getting thicker now, falling around us with a gentle hush. I thought about getting back in the car to get warm, but I wasn't entirely sure that the Ankou was fully gone. Then I remembered that I had a blanket in the backseat.

"Hold on, I'll be right back." I ducked into the driver's seat to turn off the car so I wouldn't drain the battery. Then I opened the back, slipping and sliding my way around the rapidly freezing ground. I had gotten inspired by Oriel's survival kit and had put a few bottles of water, some crackers and cookies, and a couple of blankets in the back of my SUV. I grabbed the blankets and stumbled around back to Peggin's side. I handed her one as I wrapped the other around myself. We huddled under the dark silvery sky.

Bryan returned. "Niles will be here shortly." He glanced up at the falling snow and, in the hush with the car turned off, the soft sound of it hitting the ground was actually soothing. "This would be pretty if we hadn't just encountered one of the Ankou."

I nodded, huddling next to Peggin for more warmth. She was in a dress so she was colder than I was.

"It's pretty, all right. But I'd rather see it from the park instead of the bottom of a ditch."

"Why do you think that thing attacked us?" Peggin asked.

"I think it was probably just random. You heard what Starlight said—she's getting reports from around town of random attacks. It's dark, we were out late on the road, apparently these things don't just enter your house." I let out a strangled laugh. "We were carjacked by a spirit."

Neither Bryan nor Peggin seem to think that was very funny. So much for my stand-up career.

Five minutes later, Niles came rolling down the road in his truck. Bryan had gone up to the side of the road to wave him down. Another fifteen minutes and my SUV was back on the pavement, with a few dents that did not make me happy. But it started right up.

"You should bring it in for an overhaul so I can ascertain whether you did any damage to the undercarriage."

I gave him a tired nod. "Yeah, I'll get into the garage at some point here. Thanks, and can you bill me? I really don't feel like standing around here any longer than necessary. By the way, if you see Starlight? Tell her that an Ankou attacked us on the way home in the car."

Niles blinked. "I'll just follow you until you reach your house," was the only thing he said.

Another five minutes and we were home. I eased into the driveway, turning off the ignition and staring at my house. Even though I had warded it heavily against the Shadow People, I still left lights on when I was gone. It just gave me added protection and peace of mind. As Niles rumbled past, waving, I turned to Bryan and Peggin.

"Well, that was an experience I don't want to repeat. Let's get inside and go to bed. I'm exhausted. Bryan, can you stay over tonight, given all that's happened the past couple days?"

"Of course," he said softly.

We trundled inside, and after feeding the cats their dinner, headed for our beds. We were all too tired to talk about what had happened. And quite frankly, the middle of the night is never the best time to talk about spirits, ghosts, and the Ankou. As I settled into restless dreams, I wondered if the rest of my life was going to be like this.

Next morning, Peggin and I showered together so that I could keep an eye on her. By the time we had dried our hair and gotten dressed, Bryan had made breakfast. I had tried to talk him into going out to Timber Peak with the

Matriarchs and me, but he reminded me he was busy all morning, and then he would be meeting Clinton in the afternoon.

I dressed for the woods, wearing old jeans and a thick sweater. It had snowed all night and we actually had about five inches on the ground, which was—for around here—a tidy snowfall. It was beautiful, but it meant that the going would be more treacherous on the mountain roads.

I turned to Peggin. "So what are you going to do today? Please promise me you won't go back to the house."

She gave me a look that said *you've got to be kidding*, and shook her head. "Not a chance. In fact, I was planning on spending the day up at the Crescent Moon Day Spa. I won't take the steam bath, or sit in the therapy pool, but I can use a haircut and a facial and a massage. A luxury, given my current situation, but I think I owe myself a little bit of pampering."

"Of course you do. I'd love to join you except that the Matriarchs are insisting I go with them. So think of me tramping through the snowy cold woods, hunting down witch bottles, while you're sitting there having somebody massage your back." I stuck my tongue out at her, laughing.

Bryan had made waffles and bacon, and we worked our way through the plates of maple-y goodness. He was in a hurry though, so he just wrapped a couple of pieces of bacon in a waffle, grabbed his jacket, and headed for the door.

"I'll keep my phone with me. I'm going to be on Skype mostly today, given the international nature of the calls. If *anything* happens and you need help, you call me or text me. Promise? Both of you?"

I nodded. "Do I get a kiss?"

He slapped his forehead and groaned. "I'm a dolt sometimes." He hurried back over to my side, leaned down, and planted a long kiss on my lips. "Love you." He whispered the words softly, but they felt as solid as the ground beneath my feet.

"Love you, too." It felt wonderful to be able to say those three words and mean them, and know they were returned just as passionately. "Go on now, get to work."

As he left the house, heading through the yard to the fence that was half down, Peggin and I finished our breakfasts.

"D-D called me last night after I got home. He said that he had a feeling something was wrong and he wanted to check up on me. I told him what happened and he offered to scrap his commission and come over and stay with me. I told him to keep working. He's an artist and he can't stop every time there's a little problem. It took a little convincing, but I promised that I'd drop over to his place today and spend an hour or so before he has to get back to work."

I reached out and took her hand, squeezing her fingers. "You know what's wonderful?" Then I shook my head. "Never mind, you'll think I'm being all girly."

"Nothing wrong with being girly. We're female, after all." She grinned. "Tell me. I want to hear."

Sheepishly, I gave her a little shrug. "It's just that . . . we're best friends and we're in love at the same time, with great guys. Did you ever think that would happen?"

She stared at me for a moment. "I think it's true. You're right. I think I'm in love." She looked like she had just made a major discovery.

I blinked. "Of course you are, it's as plain as the chunky heels on your retro pumps, my dear. It's obvious to me that you and Deev really care about each other."

"What if he doesn't love me though? What if he just likes hanging out with me?" Her voice rose and I recognized that panicked feeling of doubt. It was written all over her face.

"I don't think you have to worry about that. I really don't. Just enjoy it, and let it unfold. Don't block your emotions, because if you do, you'll make him wonder about your feelings." I couldn't resist. "Deev talked to me when we were getting your things out of your house. I think he's serious. I mean that."

Peggin let out a deep breath. "I hope you're right, because I think I am, too. I promise—I won't block my feelings. Hell, I've got enough fear coming at me from other directions now. I aim to accept whatever he can offer at this point, as long as it's offered from his heart."

Bryan had fixed our espresso, and so we cleared the table and then sat there for a little while with our coffee, enjoying what downtime we could. I glanced at the clock and groaned.

"I've got to get over there now. Promise, though. Anything happens, you text or call Bryan and me, though I don't know how cell reception is out there in the woods."

She gave me a vigorous nod and shooed me out. "I'll feed the cats and take care of their litter box and take care of a few things around the house for you. It's the least I can offer for your hospitality."

I was about to say don't worry about it, then I realized that it would give her something to do and make her feel useful. And one thing I knew about Peggin—she needed to feel like she was pulling her weight. I shrugged into my jacket, grabbed my purse and a backpack filled with some of my magical things, and headed out to my SUV, grateful that I wouldn't have to drive it up those mountain roads in a snowstorm. The dents were all too obvious in the morning light, and as I brushed the snow off the windshield I realized that somehow it had gotten cracked, as well. Groaning and wondering how much this little incident had cost me, I slid into the driver's seat, buckled my seat belt, and headed over to Ivy's.

This time when I arrived at Ivy's, all three of the older women were dressed for scouting through the woods. I was surprised to see Gareth there, as well. I glanced at him, then glanced over at Ellia with a questioning look. She motioned me off to the side.

"We decided it wouldn't hurt to have a little muscle with us, and Gareth isn't afraid to do whatever he needs to." She gave me a little smile that told me she was rather pleased about the brawn. Of course, Ellia could do a lot of damage on her own. All she had to do was take off her gloves and touch someone, and they would go spinning into a madness from which they couldn't return. A little touch—a little time spent in hell. A longer touch—lost forever in the turmoil of their own mind. A secret part of me hoped that someday she would have the chance to use that curse on her own mother, who had long ago stuck her daughter into a limbo of never being able to touch another human with her bare hands. I had never asked Ellia if she had ever had a lover, or boyfriend—or girlfriend for that matter. It somehow seemed a hurtful question and although I was curious, I wasn't about to rub salt in a very deep wound.

I waved to Gareth and settled down in a chair until everybody was ready.

"So, last night we found out that the Ankou can attack you in your car." My statement put an end to the bustle. All three of the women and Gareth turned to stare at me.

"What did you say?" Ivy settled in by my side.

"Last night, on the way home from the Fogwhistle Pub, we were attacked by one of the Ankou. It appeared in the backseat and attacked Peggin. I don't think it was connected to the Lady though. I think it was a random attack, to be honest. I used the Void Runes to dispel it, but we ended up in the ditch and had to call Niles to pull us out."

"Well, hell. This is just peachy. We can't get up on that mountain fast enough. Aidan wanted to come, so I told him we would stop on the way and pick him up." Oriel flashed me a grin. My grandfather was staying at her boardinghouse and had settled in quite nicely.

Ivy blushed. "I hope you don't mind that I suggested he come with us. I just figured that the more hands on deck, the sooner we find those bottles."

I choked back a laugh. "Oh, give it up, Grandma. You know you got the hots for my grandpa."

Ivy and Ellia burst into laughter. For one thing, I *never* called Ivy and Aidan *grandma* and *grandpa*. When your shapeshifter grandparents don't look that much older than you, it's kind of hard to refer to them by those terms. And for another thing, every time Ivy mentioned Aidan's name she blushed. I wondered if they had slept together already, but decided that asking would be going too far.

Her hands on her hips, Ivy turned to me. "Young woman, how dare you speak to me like that."

I just snorted. "So when are we getting on the road?"

"I think we're ready. We just have to stop by the boardinghouse, pick up Aidan, and then head on out." Oriel shooed us out to her monster SUV. Before we got in, I showed them the dents from where my own SUV had gone sliding off the road the night before.

Ivy put her hand on one of the dents and closed her eyes. "I can feel the residue. And you're right, I don't feel any residue of the Lady. Just of the Shadow Man. The sooner we get this done with, the better. If they are attacking random people on the road, pretty soon it won't be safe to live in Whisper Hollow."

"As beautiful as it is, Whisper Hollow has never been a safe place to live. But you're right, it's just going to get worse the longer Magda is allowed to rail against the town." I climbed into the back of the SUV, leaving the spare seat for Aidan so he could sit next to Ivy. She flashed me an annoyed grin, but said nothing.

Aidan was waiting on the corner. Oriel's boardinghouse was a beautiful three-story powder blue and white Victorian, kept thoroughly up-to-date and in perfect condition. It exuded coziness and safety, and as I stared at it, I wanted nothing more than to move in.

My grandfather tossed his backpack in the back with me, then climbed in next to Ivy. A lion shapeshifter, Aidan was a burly man, muscled, and looking around forty-five. But the expression in his eyes read far older. His hair was golden brown, and he looked like he could body-slam any wrestler to the ground. Ivy caught her breath and inclined her head as a sign of respect. When most shapeshifters first met my grandfather, the men went down on one knee and the women curtsied, for Aidan wasn't just a lion shapeshifter. He was *Lord Corcoran*, the head of the entire Corcoran pride. In other words: Aidan was a king.

I leaned over the backseat from the cargo bay and threw my arms around his neck, giving him a big kiss on the cheek. "It's been a while since I've seen you. What have you been doing with yourself? I hear you've been spending some time with my grandma." For some reason it delighted me to be able to tease the pair of them. Maybe because I'd had so few family members I could ever joke around with. Actually, when I thought about it, I had *never* had any family members I could joke around with, except for Grandma Lila. Now the only blood family that I knew of, that were alive, were Ivy and Aidan.

"You are an insolent little kitten, Kerris. You treat your grandmother and me with some respect." But the light in his eyes told me he was laughing on the inside. He returned my kiss and patted my cheek. "How is your guardian? Is he treating you right?"

I nodded. "Bryan told me he loves me." As I said the words, they came out more shyly than I had expected them to. But it felt good to be able to tell my friends.

Ivy clapped and smiled as Aidan simply nodded. "Well, you tell me if anything goes amiss. He's a good man, and I want to make certain he stays that way."

I turned around to stare out of the back window as we began the trip up to Timber Peak. The snow was coming down thicker and it looked like we were actually settling in for a bit of a storm. Feeling warm and cozy, and actually quite happy, I leaned against the backseat and spread out my legs, falling into a light slumber as we rumbled along.

* * *

I woke up somewhere between the mountain road and Lupine Valley Campground. I stretched, yawning. Ivy peeked over her shoulder at me.

"Did you know you snore?" At my horrified look, she laughed. "Not loudly, but you sounded very sniffly back there. Maybe it's the dust."

"Bryan's never complained." I really didn't want to think about snoring at the moment. I glanced out the window over her shoulder. "We're almost there, aren't we? How was the trip up here? I didn't mean to fall asleep."

"No worries," Ellia said from the front seat next to Oriel. "We'd rather have you well rested than tired."

Gareth cleared his throat. He was sitting to the left of Aidan. "There were a couple dicey moments when we almost spun off the road, but Oriel's one hell of a driver. If I were pulling a bank heist, I'd pick her as my getaway driver any day."

We all knew that was a compliment so we laughed. Gareth didn't quite have the social niceties of most people, but he was honest, and he meant what he said.

"What are we looking for, exactly? And where am I likely to find a witch's bottle?" I realized that I had no clue what we were looking for. Oh, I knew the name—but I didn't know what to expect.

Ivy fumbled in her bag and pulled out a small journal. She opened it to a page midway through the volume and handed it to me. There was a drawing of a bottle filled with threads and what looked like broken nails and other items. It could have been a wine bottle or a beer bottle, I wasn't sure which.

"So it's just a regular ordinary bottle? It looks like it's filled with garbage."

"That garbage is magical, and the contents vary depending on the intent of the bottle itself. What you're looking for will probably have snips of unexposed film, well—exposed to the light now, but it will be fresh film. I also suspect there will be charcoal, obsidian, possibly jet in the bottle. Maybe shards of broken dark glass. Possibly bone dust or bone chips. That sort of thing, and it will probably be in a wine bottle because I doubt Magda would use beer bottles. Or it may be a bottle that once contained vodka. The alcohol involved leaves an energy in the glass even after you wash it."

"What happens when we find one? Do we just pick it up and bring it over to you?" I wanted to make sure that I didn't screw anything up. Magic was very touchy, as I had been finding out, and sometimes the oddest things could make it go awry. I had no desire to somehow bind one of the Ankou to myself out of carelessness or ignorance.

She looked startled and shook her head, holding up her hands. "No, under no circumstances should you pick it up. Just plant a marker so that you can remember where it is and come get me. I brought several dozen flags." She held up bright neon orange plastic flags. They looked like construction-grade material.

Gareth frowned, staring at the markers. "Where do you think we will be most likely to find these bottles? Will they be just sitting on the ground somewhere?"

"That's going to be the harder part. I suspect she probably has hidden them in the nooks and crannies in trees, or behind boulders, maybe under nurse logs. You might also scan overhead; I can easily see her dangling them from a branch. Whatever you do, don't underestimate her intelligence. Magda is smart and cunning. Combine that with dangerous? A volatile combination," Ellia said.

Ivy glanced over at Ellia, a melancholy look on her face. "She's right. You should also be on the lookout for Sasquatch, the Gray Man, and bears. All in all, these are dangerous woods. I suggest we go in pairs. Ellia, why don't you go with Gareth. Kerris, you go with your grandfather. And I will hunt with Oriel. Here's a whistle for everyone," she said, passing out whistles on chains to each of us. "If you find a bottle or get in trouble, blow loud and clear. We need to find as many of these as we can, so don't get sidetracked, and try not to get lost. This isn't the time to look at interesting mushrooms or stop to talk to the squirrels. And by that, I mean you, Oriel." She grinned.

Oriel rolled her eyes. "Now, how many times have you seen me stop to talk to a squirrel?"

"More than I'd like to say. As soon as we get out of the car, I'll see if I can summon up one of the forest Fae and ask them to help us. Gareth, if you can manage it, try to be as unthreatening as possible, please. Some of the Fae are very skittish creatures. Others can yank your head off."

Gareth grunted, but then let out a bark of laughter. "I'll do my best."

We reached the campground and piled out into the snow. Up here, on the mountain, the snow was deeper. There must have been about eight inches. I imagined that up on Hurricane Ridge, there was a veritable deluge of the white stuff. I stamped, shivering as the cold infiltrated my jacket. I'd get used to it in a moment, but that first blast of chill air was a doozy.

Ivy walked over to one of the picnic tables and brushed the snow off, sitting on the bench with her back to the table. She closed her eyes and held out her hands, then whispered, "Ellia, the *Song of Summoning*?"

Ellia began to sing what sounded like a Celtic ballad, old and haunting. It sent a shiver up my spine and I moved closer to my grandfather, who wrapped his arm around my waist. Gareth stood back, keeping an eye over the campground. A few moments later there was a rustle in the brush and a stag slowly emerged. He was stately, gigantic with a rack that had to have at least seven tines per side. He bellowed so loud that it practically knocked the snow off the branches.

I caught my breath. He was beautiful, incredibly powerful, and there was a look in his eye that told me he was more than just an elk. He snorted, his breath coalescing into white mist.

Aidan stepped forward, motioning for me to stay where I was. He walked up to stand three yards away from the elk, then knelt and bowed his head. Ivy opened her eyes and her hand fluttered to her throat. She stood and joined Aidan, kneeling on the ground. The elk moved forward until he was standing right above them.

It was then that I could see, superimposed over the giant beast, the figure of a man rising like a ghost over the elk. He was tall, dressed in skins, and the same rack the elk bore on his head was mirrored on the man's brow. I wasn't sure who it was, but I had the same feeling that I had when the Morrígan had greeted me at Ivy's house. Then I understood. Ivy hadn't summoned one of the forest Fae at all. No, we were facing one of the gods.

Oriel stepped forward between Aidan and Ivy. She laughed, holding out her hands. The image of the god vanished as the elk nuzzled her fingers.

"Herne, my old friend! It's been far too long since we've met. Welcome to Timber Peak, although I'm sure you've been here for some time."

The stag bobbed his head, rubbing his nose against her cheek.

"Thank you for that. We need your help. We need the help of the forest Fae. We're searching for a series of witch bottles that the old crone has hidden throughout the forest. She's the one bringing dark shadows to the mountain. She has summoned the Ankou without permission from Arawn. We're seeking to break her spell, and to do so we need to find all fifteen bottles. I realized that the forest Fae may be skittish, but if they could help us even a little, we would be ever grateful."

Herne!

Now I knew who the elk was. Even though I wasn't as conversant with the Celtic gods as Ivy or Ellia, even I knew who Herne was. He was Lord of the Forest, the Woodland incarnate, the Wild God. I felt a surge of fear, mingled with awe and respect.

The elk slowly turned and loped back into the forest, but three crows flew out of the trees and landed in front of us. One took wing and landed on Ivy's shoulder. The second flew over to land on Oriel's shoulder. And the third flew toward Aidan and me. Before I knew what was happening, it landed on my shoulder. I felt a surge of energy, dark wild magic, and I could hear the Crow Man laughing in the distance. We had our guides, thanks to the Forest Lord. I wasn't sure how they would help us, but I knew that they were on our side.

CHAPTER 14

～

There was something rather surreal about hunting for witch bottles with a crow sitting on my shoulder. I was worried at first, thinking its talons might dig in too deep, but it seemed to do a pretty good job of balancing. As Aidan and I split off and headed north, toward the Screaming Tree, the crow kept silent. We'd been walking about five minutes when it suddenly set up a *caw caw cawing* in my ear. I stopped immediately.

"There's something around here that it wants me to know about. I think we're near a witch bottle. Start looking around."

Aidan and I began hunting, looking in every nook and cranny we could find. I suddenly spotted a tree that had a gap between the roots in the ground. The snow covered most of the opening, but I could see a dark hole with a buildup of detritus in front of it.

I cautiously moved into position and lowered myself to my knees, grateful that I had my gloves with me. Sticking my hand into a dark hole under a tree didn't strike me as the safest of activities, but we had no choice. I pulled out the miniature flashlight that I kept in the pocket of my jacket and shone it into the darkness. There were generally no poisonous snakes west of the Cascades, but you never knew what wildlife would make its home under a tree. I could be reaching into a bobcat's lair or a badger's den.

As I peeked into the hole and shuffled away some of the debris and snow, I saw the glint of a reflection. Sure enough, there was a glass bottle sitting in the beam of my flashlight.

"I found one!" Minding Ivy's warning, I did not touch it. Instead I just poked my head in a little further, hoping to get a better description of the bottle. From what I could tell, there appeared to be pieces of broken glass inside, and some dark liquid that had frozen. I didn't want to know what it was.

Aidan joined me, a frown on his face. After a moment we both sat back on our knees, and he pulled out one of the neon orange flags and stuck it in the ground next to the hole.

"One down, fourteen to go. You should blow your whistle." He winked at me, but behind the smile I could tell he was worried.

"Is something wrong?"

With a shrug, he glanced around the area. "I can't help but feel that they're watching us. I don't know how long they'll let us go on with this before they seek to interfere."

"They being the Ankou? Or the Hounds?"

He extended his hand to me and I took it, using him to balance as I stood. "Either. Both. I am concerned about the fact that Magda has the power to summon the Shadow People. I know she's a powerful witch, but it takes an enormous amount of skill to drive the Ankou from Arawn's grasp. The Lord of the Dead can't be happy about this, either. I would hate to see him send his own emissaries to find out what's going on. There's no telling who he might blame for this, and I would hate to be on the receiving end of his wrath."

I hadn't thought about that aspect. "Do you really think that Arawn will notice?"

Aidan stared at me for a moment, as though he were trying to figure out how to answer. "You really don't have much clue about all of this, do you?"

I wasn't sure exactly what he was talking about. "There's so much that I missed out on, and with Grandma Lila dying before I could return, there's been no one to teach me. I've been relying on her journals but they can only go so far."

"I don't think you realize the scope of our world. You lived outside of Whisper Hollow for fifteen years. During that time, had you stayed here, you would have been trained not only in your duties as a spirit shaman, but in the vast heritage you come from. You've seen the Morrígan, you know you're her daughter. And you've now encountered Herne. You talk about Arawn and you know he's the Lord of the Dead. But I don't think you realize just how incredibly powerful these entities are. And *they're* just the tip of the iceberg of our history. We are the descendants of the Tuatha de Dannan. All of this—the spirit shamans, the Crow Man, the Irish shifters, we are all part of the same magical heritage. *We* are the children of the gods."

I frowned, mulling over what he had said. "What about Ellia? She's my lament singer but she's of Russian descent and her mother is priestess to a different goddess."

Aidan bobbed his head with a smile. "The gods don't always just claim those who have the direct bloodline. If she were still in her homeland, Ellia would have probably been claimed by Baba Volkov's enemy, the goddess Morena. Remember, she's very much the Russian version of the Morrígan. And Baba Volkov hates her."

I thought crossed my mind. "Then, are Morena and the Morrígan actually the *same* being? The same goddess?"

Aidan laughed. "No, my dear granddaughter. They are not, but they are of similar stature and energy. The gods are finite, but make no mistake about the strength of their power. Which is why you can be sure that Arawn knows someone is summoning his Ankou away from his shadowy realm. And I don't think he's going to be very happy about that."

I glanced back at the tree with the witch bottle in it. Ever slowly, the scope of the world I had entered when I returned to Whisper Hollow was broadening, and even as Aidan spoke, I had the feeling I was on the outskirts of something very big and very powerful. I raised my whistle to my lips and blew loud and clear. A few minutes later Ivy appeared, Oriel trailing behind her.

"We found one, beneath that tree there." I moved back to give them room.

"That makes three. Oriel and I found two already." Ivy inched toward the hole on her hands and knees, and then—using what looked like a pair of silver tongs—fished the bottle out from the hole. Oriel held out a large padded bag, and Ivy cautiously placed the bottle inside.

"This is going to take a while, isn't it?" I asked.

Oriel rolled her eyes. "It would take far longer if we didn't have our little guides here. I think, from what we've found so far, that they're in a ring—a circle. So we have some idea of the pattern." She nodded to Ivy and their crow. "Let's get back to it."

They headed back in the direction from which they had come, as Aidan and I returned to our hunting. Ten minutes later we were standing at the Screaming Tree. It was silent, but I could feel the awareness emanating from it. The tree had eyes—both literally, with the dark socketed openings—and energetically. The Matriarchs' spell had held and whatever had dampened the tree's awareness hadn't returned.

I wanted to walk up to it and press my hands against the gnarled bark, but something stopped me. Perhaps it was Aidan's comments about being watched, or perhaps something more instinctual was prompting my caution, but either way I decided to hang back. I wasn't a child, still learning that the stove was hot. I was coming to trust myself and my instincts more and more, and if my intuition whispered that I'd get my fingers burned, I tried to listen.

Aidan joined me, staring at the tree. "Nobody really knows who woke this tree up at the beginning. Maybe it's just always been a sentinel. Whatever the case, Oriel is as tuned in to it as anybody in this neck of the woods could be."

"Tell me about the Heart of Whisper Hollow. How was she selected? Is it always a woman?"

Aidan motioned for me to follow him as we moved past the tree. "I imagine the Morrígan chooses the Heart as well, considering how intricately tied to the spirit shamans the Heart of the town has to be. Or perhaps another god or goddess the Morrígan works with is in charge of that. I really don't know much about the post, except there has to be a Heart. Whisper Hollow would wither and fold without her. And yes, as far as I know it is always a woman. I lived in Ireland you know, for several hundred years. I'm far older than your beau, as you might have guessed. All of the magical villages there have a Heart."

We skirted the tree, winding through the woodland. The snow made for difficult going, not because it was so deep but because it was slick and new and powdery. My breath came in little puffs and my nose ran from the chill. The flakes had lessened but they were still falling lightly around us. I closed my eyes for a moment, looking up into the sky as the snow drifted against my face. Even though I knew about the witch bottles and the Gray Man and Sasquatch, I still felt like I could melt right into the background, snuggle up under a tree with a blanket, and drift off secure in the cradle of the forest.

"It's in your blood," Aidan said, startling me into opening my eyes. "The forest, the very core of nature. Spirit shamans are in tune with the elements around them as much as any witch."

I smiled faintly, realizing that for the first time in a while,

I didn't have a headache. It was as though the clear air and the cool chill had washed it away, along with some of the stress that I had been feeling. I held out my hand, watching as the snowflakes fell on my glove.

"Fifteen years living in the city didn't do me any favors, that's for certain. It wasn't bad, but lonely. And I took up having to chase ghosts out of houses in order to keep my powers from imploding on myself." I looked at my grandfather. "I think sometimes I almost believed that Whisper Hollow and everything magical here was a dream. It's not that there isn't magic in the city, and I often felt the Crow Man around me—crows are everywhere. But it's hard when you're surrounded by so many people who don't believe that things like this exist. And when they find out the truth, they get afraid and back away. I guess I was really lonely there."

He wrapped his arm around my shoulders. "Trust me, I understand. When I exiled myself—or rather, your grandmother exiled me to keep me safe—I felt like I had stepped into someone else's life. The years went by, I worked, I made friends, but very few people knew who I was. I changed jobs every few years, given that I don't age the same way that humans do. It's a fine line to walk, straddling two worlds. I guess I understand you more than a lot of people would."

"I suppose large cities can't have a Heart like Whisper Hollow, or someone like me to guard the ghosts."

"Some do. You'd be surprised."

We continued searching. Every now and then a whistle would blow, and Aidan and I found two more witch bottles ourselves. By three P.M. I was freezing. Ivy called off the search. We had discovered twelve of the witch bottles, which left three that eluded us.

Oriel stared at the bag filled with dark magic. "This will be enough to disrupt her spell. I still want to find those other three, but this should send most of the Ankou back to Arawn. We need to be prepared, though. Magda is going to be seriously pissed and out for revenge. Watch your backs.

She's going to know who did this. She has enough spies in the forest to tell her."

We headed back to the SUV, soaked and chilled and tired. I gingerly crawled into the cargo bay, keeping my distance from the bag of bottles as much as I could. Aidan secured them so they couldn't roll around, for which I was eminently grateful. Nobody talked much on the way back, not until Oriel pulled into the first Starbucks we saw and we all ordered piping hot drinks. I cupped the mocha with my hands, grateful for the triple shot of caffeine. Oriel also ordered peppermint brownies, and we tore through the bag, emptying it lickety-split.

"Ivy and Ellia, I need you to help me destroy these. Aidan, Gareth, and Kerris, you can all go home. In fact it's probably better if you aren't around when we take care of this matter. I don't want any magic residue spilling off on anybody." She dropped Gareth off at Niles's garage, where he had left his car. Then she dropped me off at my house and I waved as they headed back to the boardinghouse.

I trudged inside, polishing off my mocha as I unlocked the door. Peggin looked up from the sofa, where she was curled up with the cats and a magazine. She took one long look at me and jumped up, startling Daphne as she did so.

"You look like something the cat dragged in. Here, let me take your coat. Go take a hot shower while I heat up some soup. I know you've got dinner plans tonight with Bryan, but you need something hot in your stomach. I can tell that just by looking at you."

Grateful for her mothering, I hurried to my bedroom and peeled off my clothes. The snow had soaked through, and I realized how chilled I was. As I turned on the shower and the steam began to fill the room, I let out a long sigh and gratefully stepped under the pounding spray. As the water eased the chill from my bones and the scent of amber and vanilla revitalized me, it hit me. This is what my world was: a swirl of magic and intrigue and ghosts and friends who were strange and miraculous and slightly scary. I suddenly found myself laughing. I felt right at home.

Two hours later, Ivy called to tell me that they had managed to destroy the witch bottles. By then Peggin had managed to get two mugs of soup down me, and we were playing a game of backgammon over peppermint mochas. I glanced at the clock. It was almost six, and Bryan said he would drop by at seven to pick me up. I knew that we were having dinner at the Mossy Rock Steakhouse, but he didn't know that I knew. I dressed in new black jeans, a soft blue sweater, and a silver belt.

"Say, I think tomorrow morning I'm going to go buy the Yule tree." My grandmother had brought me up celebrating the Solstice, and I loved how all the old traditions had lived on. In addition to the tree, we also had a Yule log every year when I was young, burning it for twelve nights straight as did our ancestors and then keeping bits of the charcoal to light the next year's fire. I had searched through the house, looking for the remains of last year's log, but couldn't find any, so I decided to start new this year.

"Do you have ornaments?"

"Yeah, I found Grandma Lila's stash in the attic. I think we should make an evening of it tomorrow night, decking out the house." I gave Peggin a big smile, feeling in a suddenly festive mood.

"I could get down with that," she said. "I have a few ornaments at my house, although I'm not certain we should drop by to pick them up. But I'd love to help you decorate the tree, and we could rent *Rudolph* and *How the Grinch Stole Christmas* and *It's a Wonderful Life.*"

"Sounds good to me. We can make hot cocoa and pop popcorn and just kick back. Why don't you invite Deev? By the way, did you see him today?"

She nodded, a smile spreading across her face. "He called

me and I stopped in there at around two for an hour. He's almost done with the commission; it's going faster than he thought it would. I think you're right," she said. "I think he really does care about me."

"I told you so! Anyway, I'll pick up the tree tomorrow morning and bring down the ornaments, and by the time you're home from work, I'll have dinner ready and we'll just make an evening of it." I realized that I was excited. When I lived in Seattle, I hadn't celebrated much of anything. It wasn't that I didn't enjoy the holidays, it just seemed futile when I was alone. Or, if I was honest with myself, I just hadn't felt all that festive. I tried, I had bought a small tree, but the dearth of friends and my general dissatisfaction had taken the joy out of it. I had tried to celebrate the Solstice the way my grandmother taught me, but once again—life in Whisper Hollow had seemed so much like a dream. "Do you mind if I ask Aidan? And Ivy, too?"

Peggin flashed me a soft look. "You love being back here, don't you? Even with all the problems, Whisper Hollow agrees with you, doesn't it?"

"How can you tell? Yeah, you're right. It really does. Okay then, we have a plan for tomorrow night. What do you want for dinner?"

"Oh no, you're springing for enough as it is. I'll bring dinner with me. I'll make sure there's enough for at least five. If Deev is free, I'm sure he'll join us." But she refused to tell me what she was going to bring. "Just let me surprise you for once."

We finished the backgammon game five minutes before Bryan arrived.

I held my finger to my lips as I stood to answer the door. "Remember, he doesn't know that I know about his plans. So don't say anything."

She just raised her eyebrows and grinned. "You don't have to worry about me. Enjoy yourself."

I thought I suspected a smirk hiding behind her eyes, but

I didn't have time to investigate. I answered the door and Bryan stood there, looking handsome as hell. He was wearing a snug pair of jeans, a green shirt with a black leather vest, and a very snazzy suit jacket. I blinked, not used to seeing him so dressed up.

"Are you ready?"

I shrugged into my jacket—a velvet blazer with pearl buttons. "Do I look okay?" Which was, of course, code for *am I under- or overdressed?*

"You're gorgeous, as always." He waved at Peggin, then slid his arm through mine and escorted me out to his car. He had brought his Lexus.

"Fancy ride tonight."

"Stop fishing. Our destination is a secret." He looked extremely pleased with himself.

I laughed and leaned back, staring out the window as we drove through town.

The Mossy Rock Steakhouse was at the fork of Junction Street and Fourth. We passed Diago's copse as we hung a right on Whisper Hollow Way. Turning left on Lakeshore Drive Connector, we passed the city hall, firehouse, and the police station. After the grade school we turned left onto Junction Street and then eased into the parking lot of the Mossy Rock Steakhouse. The place was jumping, and I had a feeling a lot of people wanted to eat out tonight.

I tried to act surprised. "We're having dinner here?"

"Do you mind?" Bryan look so concerned that I hurried to reassure him.

"You know I love Nadia's restaurant. The food here is wonderful. This is perfect."

We were escorted right to our table, and I ordered a strawberry daiquiri and Bryan ordered Cognac. While we were waiting for our drinks, I told him about the day.

"So Ivy and Oriel managed to destroy the twelve bottles that we found. We still have to look for the other three, but this should be enough to disrupt the spell for now. I tell you though, those woods are powerful. The magic out there is incredibly strong, and seductive in a way. I wanted to just crawl under a tree and sit there and close my eyes."

I paused while the waitress placed our drinks in front of us. After she took our order—I wanted a rib eye steak and Bryan asked for a surf and turf—I snapped my fingers. "Oh by the way, I'm getting a tree tomorrow. Do you want to come over tomorrow night and help Peggin and me decorate? We're going to watch movies and drink hot cocoa and eat popcorn."

"I would like nothing better than to join you. Anybody else going to be there?"

"Deev, if he can get away. And I'm going to ask Aidan and Ivy."

Bryan laughed. "Are we going to have a sing-along, too?" When I started to answer, flushed, he reached over and took my hands. "I was just joking! I'm teasing you, sweetheart. Get used to it. I will be there with bells on, and I will even wear an elf hat if you want me to."

I smacked his hand lightly. "Just for that, yes, I want you to wear an elf hat."

He stopped suddenly, a serious look on his face. "You know what? I was going to wait until dessert, but I have something important to talk to you about."

My laughter drained away. He sounded so serious that all I could think of was that something was wrong. "Is everything okay? Are *we* okay?"

Bryan reached into his jacket pocket and pulled out something, keeping his hand wrapped around it. "Kerris, you know I'm your guardian and I will always be here for you no matter what. But I want you to know the last couple months have been the best I've spent in . . . I don't know how many years. I've never been as happy as I am when I'm with you. I know it's only been a short time, but I love you and I want to spend my life with you. I want to spend my life guarding you, making you happy, treating you the way you should be treated. So . . ."

My eyes grew wide as he slowly opened his hand to

reveal a jewelry box. He handed it to me. I looked at him, uncertain of what do, not quite sure if he was asking what I thought he was asking.

"Open it."

I slowly opened the box to find my mother's wedding ring inside. It was the ring that Ivy had given her son—her own mother's wedding ring. Avery had proposed to my mother with it and she had been wearing it when she was killed, even though he had long disappeared. I had found it on her skeleton.

"What . . . How did you get this?"

"After you left this morning, I asked Peggin to find it. I knew you wouldn't be wearing it out to the woods. Kerris, your mother should have been able to wear this throughout a full and wonderful life. Your father should have been able to see it on her hand every day. Since they didn't get their chance, I thought . . . I talked to Ivy and she agreed that it would be appropriate if I proposed to you with it."

And then, right there in the restaurant, Bryan got down on one knee beside me. He took my hand as I watched, speechless, and said, "Kerris Fellwater, you are the one I've been waiting for. We're meant for each other, a mated pair. I want you by my side as long as we live. Will you marry me?"

Will you marry me? The words reverberated through me as I realized that this was really happening. It was soon, it was so soon, but it felt so right. He was my guardian protector, and I had fallen for him since the first night we met when I almost ran him over.

I pushed back my chair and stood, taking his hand to pull him to his feet, where I said the only words that made any sense at all to my heart. "Of course I'll marry you. I love you, and I don't ever want to lose you. And I love that you thought to give me my mother's ring." Tears running down my face, I realized that this man knew me better than anybody ever had in my life. He was my protector, and he was my mate.

"She said yes!" Bryan's sudden shout startled me, but not

as much as the influx after that. From around the corner, we were suddenly inundated with shouts of congratulations as Ivy, Oriel, Ellia, Aidan, Peggin, and Deev appeared. I realized that he had set this up better than I could ever imagine.

I turned to Peggin. "And you didn't tell me?"

She grinned. "Do you really think I'd spoil such a great surprise?"

Nadia appeared at that moment, clapping loudly as she was followed by several waiters. "The room is ready if you want to go in now."

"Room?" I looked around, but we were suddenly being herded toward the back. I realized that we were heading into one of the conference rooms that the steakhouse kept for group parties. As I entered the room, I saw a banner with our names on it over the table; balloons, bouquets of red roses filled the room, and there was a full buffet. In the center of the buffet sat a beautiful two-tiered cake, covered with white fondant and dripping with red icing roses and green vines. The words *Congratulations, Bryan and Kerris* were written across the top.

"I cannot believe you set all this up. What would you have done if I had said . . ." I stopped, then shook my head. "You knew I'd say yes. How could you expect different?"

Bryan kissed me again. "I never, ever took your answer for granted. You have no idea how nervous I was."

Everybody crowded in, taking plates and lining up for the buffet. There was steak, and fried chicken, and lobster tails, along with mashed potatoes and corn on the cob and salad. The smell of hot, yeasty rolls filled the air and my mouth began to water. The chicken noodle soup was long gone and I was starving.

I leaned my head against Bryan's shoulder as he wrapped his arm around me.

"I'm so glad you didn't make any other plans for tonight."

I didn't want to tell him that Nadia had warned me in advance, so I just smiled. "I can't believe we're engaged." I held out my hand where my mother's ring now sat on my left ring finger. I usually wore it on my right hand when I wanted to feel closer to her. "I meant what I said. This is perfect, her ring."

The band was rose gold, engraved with filigree, with a half-carat diamond in the center. It sparkled. Bryan had obviously had it cleaned today.

"I want to buy you a band to go with that. A plain rose gold band, to match. You should have one from me as well as the family ring."

"That would be perfect. We can pick out your ring to match at the same time." I paused, my mind skipping ahead. "Do you mind if we wait till the autumn to get married? When the leaves are just beginning to change and the air has that slight, bittersweet tang?"

"We can get married whenever you want. I'll be happy either way, whether it's waiting till autumn or getting married tomorrow at the courthouse. But I think it would be fun to have a big wedding. And your grandparents would like it. I know your grandfather will expect me to do right by you." Bryan's smile was infectious and I began to laugh.

"Does the Tierney clan have a tartan?"

"I'm afraid the Irish don't really have a history of tartans for each clan. We're not exactly like the Scottish. But I do have something to give you on our wedding day. It's a family necklace, emerald and diamond." Bryan gave me another squeeze and then nodded to our guests. "Why don't you go talk to your grandmother? And get some food. This is a party, woman. This is *your* party."

I snorted. "You mean it's *our* party. And don't you forget it." And with that I sashayed over to where Ivy was talking to Peggin. They both looked up as I approached. My grandmother stood and wrapped her arms around me, kissing my cheek.

"Congratulations, my dear. You don't know how happy I was when Bryan came to talk to me. You know that he got Aidan and me together, and asked our permission to marry you."

"The only permission he needed was from me. I'm a grown woman and I can make my own decisions, thank you." But secretly, the fact that he cared enough to seek out their approval made me happy. He wanted their blessing, and that said a great deal.

"Oh, *hush*. Anyway, Aidan and I were delighted to welcome him into the family."

My stomach rumbled at that point, and I realized just how starved I really was.

"I'm going to get some food, and then we're going to sit down and we're all going to have a nice long chat. By the way, I think we'll get married in the autumn. Peggin, you know you're going to be my maid of honor. And Ivy, I don't want to be given away like some piece of property, but I would love for you and Aidan to escort me down the aisle."

The rest of the evening, we spent eating and talking and planning. For once, it felt like things were going the way they should—that we had turned a corner into a brighter and better future. I wondered about Bryan's family. His father was dead but I couldn't remember if his mother was still alive. In fact, his father had been murdered in front of him when he was very young, back in 1878. And of course, I would have to meet his daughter, Juliana.

His pack was tight-knit, and I wondered how they would feel about us marrying. He'd been married before once, but it'd been an arranged marriage. In fact, I realized Bryan didn't talk much about his family in the present tense.

"You look very far away," Ellia said, and I realized that she was standing beside me.

"I was just thinking about Bryan's family and how they'll feel about me."

"If they are traditionally oriented at all, they will accept you right in. The Tierney clan is well entrenched in the service of the Morrígan." She smiled and her hand moved ever so slightly as if she was thinking of patting my shoulder. But years of practice kept her from doing so. "Everything will be fine. And for what it's worth, I'm glad he asked you. It's soon, yes, but you two were made for each other. You are destined to be together I think, the same way your mother was destined to be with Avery. Only, we'll make certain your union turns out much happier."

And with that, she returned to the buffet, and I shook off my doubts and worries. These were my people now, and they accepted me. And Bryan would be my husband, and everything would be okay.

CHAPTER 15

The next morning, we all had mild hangovers from the champagne. Peggin headed off to work, as did Bryan. He promised to talk to Peggin's Realtor that day, and I was hoping that we could have matters finished and her out of her contract by nightfall.

I settled in at the table, espresso in hand, making my list for the day. I wanted to buy the tree and pick up some new ornaments to go with the ones I had found in the attic. I also decided to stop by the bakery and pick up an assortment of cookies for tonight. Prepackaged cookies just wouldn't do for a tree-trimming ceremony.

I put a load of clothes in the washer, noting that Peggin had cleaned up the laundry room. She had also taken it upon herself to clean the bathrooms and mop the floors. Agent H rubbed around my feet, purring as I filled the food dishes.

"Yeah, it's kind of nice to have someone else around here, isn't it? Pretty soon, we'll have Bryan around all the time." All of a sudden I stopped, wondering where we were going to live. His place or mine? While I liked his estate, it wasn't very cozy.

"Well, we'll just deal with that when it comes, won't we, little guy? We've got a while until the wedding anyway." I scratched Agent H's head as he started noshing on the food. He let out a loud purr and then shook off my hand so he could concentrate on eating. Daphne and Gabby ran up, nudging him to the side so they could get at the food. I always gave them three bowls but they always gathered around one. *The cat food is always tastier in the other bowl.*

After rinsing my cup, I leaned against the counter, staring outside. It had stopped snowing, but it was still cold and the snow had stuck. I had a feeling it was here for a few weeks at least. I had a sudden urge to drive up to Hurricane Ridge. Maybe we should buy snowshoes and take to the backcountry. But before that, I'd have to hit the gym a lot harder. I was in no shape for a long snowshoeing session.

Finally, deciding to get started for the day, I gathered my purse and keys, slipped into my jacket, and headed to my car. As I stared at the dents, I remembered I should stop in at the garage to have Niles see if there'd been any underlying damage that I couldn't see.

"The damned Ankou. It's bad enough dealing with ghosts, let alone the Shadow People." At least nobody had died recently, and Ellia and I had had, for the most part, a bit of a rest. There were things I needed to do soon, but they could wait until after the holidays.

As I slid into the driver's seat and fastened my seat belt, I realized that I was slowly adapting to life back in Whisper Hollow.

I headed to the store. I had been debating whether to buy a real tree or an artificial one, but I knew that if I brought a real tree into the house, the cats would go bananas. They would climb it and tip it over, given all three were each at least eighteen pounds or more. Maine Coons were into everything, and they were smart.

I eased into a parking spot next to the door at Krugels, the local department store. For such a small town, the store was quite large, and they prided themselves on carrying just about anything from fabric to household goods to sports equipment. They had a surprisingly good selection of artificial trees, and I found one that was seven feet tall and looked real. It was American made, much to my surprise and delight. I also found a selection of delicate cat ornaments, twelve to a box. I added those to cart along with some sparkling glittery balls, garland, tinsel, and anything else that caught my eye. I deliberately avoided looking at the prices, not wanting to know how much I was spending.

Grandma Lila's ornaments were all in shades of blue and white and silver, so I decided to keep with the theme. I found little wooden birdhouse ornaments, as well as buri animals. A tiny snow village caught my eye, and then I picked up three boxes of chocolate-covered cherries, a tin of peppermint bark, and some holiday-themed paper plates and cups. For the first time in my life I was nesting, able to make my home feel like a *real* home to me

Of course, when I came to the checkout line, I went into sticker shock, but I handed over my credit card without comment and gratefully accepted help out to my car. My next stop was to pull through the drive-through window at Whidbey's Burgers. I ordered a double large cheeseburger, a mocha shake, and small fries. I was just easing into my driveway when I got a phone call. It was Peggin.

"Kerris, there's a fire! My house is on fire and everything I own is in there! I'm headed over there now. Can you please meet me?" She sounded frantic.

"Of course. I'll be there in five minutes. Don't get out of your car until I get there." I grabbed a bite of the cheeseburger and a long sip of the shake, then eased back onto the road, wondering how the hell the fire had started. Everything was wet and covered in snow, and unless somebody had broken in to torch the place, I couldn't figure out what had happened. The furnace was almost new, and the wiring was supposedly in decent condition.

I arrived at the Foggy Downs subdivision before Peggin. The fire department was already there, and I could see that the house was fully engulfed in flames. I could already tell they wouldn't be able to save it. As I eased out of the car, finishing off my cheeseburger, I could only stare at the brilliant orange glow flickering against the sky. The fire marshal came over to talk to me.

"Are you Peggin Sanderson?" he asked.

I shook my head. "No, but she's on the way. She's been staying at my house the past few days. She just moved in." I stared at the glowing flames. "We had an inspection done and they said that the furnace was new and the wiring looked pretty good. How did this start?"

"I have no idea; that will take an investigation to figure out. We got the call about fifteen minutes ago. By the time we arrived, the house was already burning at a good clip. My men are trying to control the fire so it doesn't catch into the woods but, honestly, I can't send them in there. Not unless I know there's somebody caught inside."

I let out a long sigh. "Unless someone snuck in, there shouldn't be. I will say, there are a few ghosts hanging around though." At his look I said, "I'm the spirit shaman. Kerris Fellwater." I held out my hand and he shook it.

"I don't know if ghosts can start a fire. That's not my department. But something had to have happened. We haven't had any lightning for a while, and snow doesn't usually cause a fire. Not unless there's some electrical short and the water gets on it. As I said, we'll have to do a thorough investigation. I hope your friend has insurance. Where is she?"

"She works over at the hospital with Dr. Wallace." I

paused as Peggin's car pulled into the driveway. "There she is now."

She screeched to a stop and jumped out, running over to me. "Kerris!" She turned to look at the house, which was now fully engulfed in flames. "Oh my gods, I can't believe this."

The smoke roared into the sky, turning black with soot. The smell of burning fabric and whatever chemicals might have been in the abandoned house drifted past, making my throat ache and my eyes water. The next moment, an explosion filled the air, blasting debris everywhere.

"Hell!" I grabbed Peggin and knelt close to the ground behind my car. The fire marshal joined us. A moment later, we could hear shouting as firemen raced around the house, and in the distance sirens roared, with another engine coming our way.

"What the hell just happened?" My ears were ringing as I struggled to get to my feet. I reached down and helped Peggin stand.

The fire marshal, shaking his head, staggered to his feet as well. "The furnace must have exploded. You need to back your cars out of this driveway before anything else happens." He motioned for us to move our cars further back down the cul-de-sac.

When we were far enough away to be safe, Peggin and I walked back to where he was standing, staring at the flames that had pretty much incinerated most of the house. As we watched, the roof began to ripple and firemen raced out of the way as the roof imploded in on itself.

Peggin shook her head, speechless as she watched everything she owned vanish, eaten by the fire. "All my pictures and my journals and my desktop computer . . . They're all gone. Everything I own . . . all destroyed."

I encircled her shoulders, leaning her against me as the flames gobbled what was left of the house, turning it into ash and charcoal. The firemen rushed this way and that, trying to control the burn so that it didn't get out of bounds.

I started to comfort her, to remind her that she was safe and her ferrets were safe, but then I realized that this wasn't the time for that. Peggin was watching everything she had collected and worked for go up in flames, and right now nothing I could say would make it better.

T wo hours and a dozen conversations later, Peggin and I slowly turned away.

Clinton Brady had come across the street and finally dragged us back to the pub, where he plied us with fresh bread, and brandy. Sophia and the fire marshal joined us. He had been very curious as to why Peggin was staying with me, and I had the feeling we weren't done with him. Unless, of course, he found that it was an accident. Given the age of the house, that could easily be, but somehow things never seemed to work out as simply as we wanted them to.

Jack, Peggin's Realtor, burst through the doors just as we were finishing up our drinks.

"This is going to be a mess to sort out," he said, staring at Peggin. He raised his voice just enough for the fire marshal to hear. "Especially since you wanted out of the deal. Why you had to sic your friend Bryan on me, I don't know. We could have talked this through." His voice had a nasty edge. I had a sudden vision of him backstabbing Peggin so he wouldn't be stuck with the cost.

"Do you *really* have to do this now? Right now? *Seriously?*" Hands on my hips, I stood, exasperated with him.

"Yeah, well, now nobody has to deal with the house, but somebody's going to be stuck with the cost. I have the contract right here! You signed an option to buy the house." He jabbed his finger against his briefcase, staring at her as he ignored me. "I know you wanted out. Well, I can let you off the hook for buying it—as long as you didn't torch it. But you still owe me a year's rent and you forfeit the three thousand."

"There's no house to rent. If I owe you a year's rent, it's got to be on something that I could make use of!" Peggin was getting mad now, and so was I.

The fire marshal cleared his throat. "So she doesn't officially own the house yet?"

Peggin shook her head. "I optioned to buy it, but it's rent-to-own, so I had a year to decide. I already figured out that I didn't want to live there. I called Jack to see if we could work out some arrangement but he told me I couldn't get out of the option fee or the lease for a year."

"What? Did you hate it so much that you decided to burn the fucking house down?" Yeah, Jack was playing hardball.

"What? I was *at work* when it caught on fire. I've been staying at Kerris's house the past couple days. I moved in Saturday, and that same day, the Lady almost took me down by the pier. So yeah, I decided it wasn't safe to stay there. But burn the house down? What good would that do me?" Peggin leaned across the table, glaring at Jack. I was afraid she was going to smack him across the face.

"Enough." Sophia stepped in. "Jack, you'd better not make any accusations you aren't prepared to back up. We'll wait for the fire marshal's investigation before deciding anything. So you just keep your temper under control. That goes for you, too, Peggin. I don't want to hear anything about the two of you getting into any brawls or causing any trouble. Do I make myself clear?"

"Yes ma'am," Peggin said, sitting back down in her chair.

Jack just glared at Sophia but then gave her a grudging nod. "I hear you."

And with that, Peggin and I headed back to my house. As we exited the Fogwhistle Pub's parking lot, we both took one last glance down the cul-de-sac toward the smoldering house. Luckily, no firemen had been hurt during the explosion—a minor miracle in itself. But I really didn't want to think about the cleanup ahead.

* * *

After I got Peggin calmed down, which entailed sitting guard beside her while she took a long hot bath, I bundled her into her robe with another brandy, and we curled up on the sofa.

"You don't think I had anything to do with this, do you?" The hurt in her voice told me more than her words.

"Of course I don't. My money's on one of the ghosts. I know this is bad," I added. "But you and Frith and Folly are safe. And you do have *some* clothes and your laptop. I know it's small consolation, but . . ." My voice died away. I wasn't exactly the best at comforting people.

She let out a long sigh and took a sip of the brandy. "I know," she said, hanging her head. "And believe me, I am more grateful than you can ever know that my ferrets and I are safe. Without Frith and Folly, I don't know what I'd do. But Kerris, it feels like I did something to piss off the gods. Maybe I did something horrible in another life and now karma is biting me in the butt. I don't know. If I did anything, I don't know what it is."

I let out a long sigh and enfolded my feet up on the sofa underneath me. "They say everything happens for a reason, but I'm not so sure about that. And karma . . . karma isn't what most people think it is. The concept is quite different than you reap what you sow, or everything comes around. It's a Buddhist and Hindu concept, and is far more complicated than people realize."

She frowned. "Then why did this happen?"

All I could do was shrug. "Sometimes, I think that bad things just happen to good people. Now, maybe we'll find a reason for this happening, maybe something good will come out of this. But right now, it's okay to be upset and it's okay to cry. You only wanted to make yourself a nice home. You didn't ask for any of this."

"But I should have listened to you and not moved in there

to begin with. I was just so scared about imposing on D-D and ruining our relationship. I wanted my own place and I was angry at my landlady for kicking me out. I've been a model tenant for years, I've done everything she asked me to around the place. I fixed it up, planted flowers, and then boom . . . just a 'get out' without even a thank-you or acknowledgment for what I've done. I want my own place, that nobody can take away from me." She sounded so plaintive that I wanted to gather her in my arms and let her cry it out, but I knew it would take more than tears to fix this.

I glanced over at the clock. "Do you want me to call off the party tonight? I know it's not going to be particularly cheery for you. Anything you need, just ask me."

"No," she said. "They're going to want to hear what happened anyway. I might as well tell them now, and at least I'll be among friends tonight. Maybe it will take my mind off of what happened. Waiting's going to be the difficult part. Waiting to see what the fire marshal has to say and if Jack continues to turn on me like he did. I think that hurts most of all. We've been friends for a long time, and he just turned on me like . . ."

"He betrayed you. He did something no friend should ever do. And I'm sorry about that."

We spent the rest of the afternoon watching mindless TV to take our minds off of what had happened. But I knew Peggin's thoughts were back at the house, with the charred remains of her life, and I knew it would take a long time to repair the damage that it had done.

Peggin stirred herself off the sofa. "Let's haul the tree in here. We're strong enough to do it. We don't have to wait for the men."

I glanced up at her from where I was aimlessly eating chips out of the bag. "Are you sure?" The tree was still in the back of my CR-V, along with everything else.

"I can only take so much sitting around watching *Judge Judy* before I start thinking about the fire. Do you realize the only things I have left are the clothes that you brought for me, and the ferret supplies? I don't even know if my jewelry survived. Not that I had a lot of it. Everything was still in boxes. Cardboard catches like tinder." She sounded so plaintive that I gave in. After tromping around the woods the day before, I was still sore, but if it would help Peggin, I would drag my ass out to the car and carry things in.

The manufacturer had managed to jam a seven-foot tree into a four-foot box, damned heavy and hard to manage. Somehow, we wrangled it into the living room, where we dropped it with a thud. Then we went back for the rest of the things. After we had brought in all of the packages, Peggin let out a groan.

"I forgot! I was supposed to bring dinner home for everybody."

"Don't worry about it. And don't even think about offering to go out and get it. Not after today." I moved to one side, where I called Bryan. "We need dinner for everybody. I was going to call you earlier but things got rough."

"What's going on? I've been locked up in my office all day."

"Peggin's new house caught fire. We are talking *burned to the ground*. We got over there after the firemen had arrived. The place went up like old kindling. She's lost everything except what she has at my house." I suddenly realized that Peggin hadn't called Deev. If she had, he would have been over here in a heartbeat. But then again, he was showing up in a couple of hours so maybe it didn't matter.

"Why didn't you call me? I would have been there—"

"I know, but what could you do, really? The firemen couldn't even get into the house. Then the furnace blew up, or at least we think it was the furnace, and the entire place is gone. And that prick, Jack? The Realtor? He hinted that Peggin started the fire to get out of buying the house or paying the year's lease." I was grumpy, but I couldn't help it. I was pissed out of my mind.

"Oh, *did he*? That, I can take care of."

I wasn't sure what Bryan meant but he didn't sound friendly.

"If you could do something, it would be one big worry off her mind. Jack managed to get the fire marshal's attention with his comments. Meanwhile, Peggin had planned on bringing home dinner for everybody. Would you mind picking up something?"

"Not a problem. I'll head out now and be over within the hour. Meanwhile, tell Peggin we'll make sure everything works out. Somehow, we'll manage to help her." He signed off.

I leaned back, staring at my phone. Whatever he was planning to do to Jack, I hoped it would be discreet, especially if it involved anything like a black eye. Peggin was in the kitchen, which meant she hadn't heard the conversation. Probably a good thing, actually. Deciding that I might as well make the cocoa, I pocketed my phone and headed into the kitchen.

F orty-five minutes later Bryan came in through the kitchen door, carrying bags of food, and behind him, carrying more bags, was Deev. He immediately set them down on the table and went off to find Peggin, whom I had assigned to the task of stringing some Christmas lights over the hutches so that we could have pretty lights to decorate the tree by.

Bryan set the bags down and wrapped his arms around me. "So, it sounds like it's been one hell of a day."

"You can say that again. We'll tell you what went down in a bit. I don't want Peggin to have to go through it again and again." *Like she did with her story about the Lady*, I thought.

"I brought chicken and mashed potatoes and coleslaw, baked beans and mac 'n' cheese and biscuits. Deev also thought it might be nice to add a holiday touch so we picked up some cranberry sauce at the deli, along with eggnog and Black Forest cake."

"Have I told you how wonderful you are?" I leaned into his embrace. "Thank you. At least I remembered to rent the movies this morning while I was out shopping."

"Movies are good. Music would be fine, too. Whatever works to take Peggin's mind off all of this crap." He let go of me and picked up Daphne, who had decided to investigate what smelled so good in the bags. As he set her on the floor, he said, "No, you don't, young lady. Oof, you're a big cat."

"Don't say that—she's a Maine Coon. They're supposed to be big."

"Pardon me, then. I didn't mean to insult your size, Miss Daphne. You're full-figured and gorgeous." He winked at her, and she suddenly gathered herself and leaped into his arms, knocking him back as she curled against his chest, purring so loud I could hear her from where I was standing. He laughed.

Deev and Peggin came into the kitchen, Deev's arm wrapped around her waist. "Next time Peggin forgets to call me when something like this happens, Kerris, I want you to read her the riot act. She'll listen to you."

I snorted. "Do you really think she's going to listen to anybody? You know her."

"Well, you've got me there." Deev let out a snort.

Peggin smacked his arm. "I might remind the two of you that I'm right here and can hear every word." But she was smiling, and I breathed a long sigh of relief. Deev seemed to be good for her mood no matter what was going on.

"And that's the idea," he said very softly.

Just then, the doorbell rang. I glanced at the clock. "It's a little early for people to start arriving. I asked them to come around seven o'clock and it's only six thirty." I wiped my hands on a towel and headed to the door. But, as I opened it, I realized it wasn't one of our guests. Sophia, the chief of police, was standing there.

"Hey, Kerris, is Peggin here?"

"Yeah, she is. Do you want to come in?" Concerned given what had transpired earlier, I backed up, motioning for her to come in. "Is everything all right?"

Bryan, Peggin, and Deev entered the room. Peggin's eyes widened and I knew she was as worried as I was.

Sophia nodded to everyone; she was still in uniform and had a harried look on her face. "Good evening, everybody. Peggin, I just wanted to drop by and set your mind at ease. I just took a phone call from Jack and he told me that he really doesn't believe that you started the fire. I also got a call from the fire marshal."

"And?" She tensed.

"No clear-cut answer yet, but it appears the fire started near the furnace. They found scorch marks on it that most likely indicate faulty wiring or a defective unit. I know you said that the furnace was relatively new. But that doesn't rule out that there was some malfunction that didn't show itself till now. Especially since it hadn't been used in a couple of years and you recently turned it on. Now, the home inspector that Jack hired verified that he gave it the A-OK, but he pointed out that there are often issues not visible during a cursory inspection. As to the squabble between the two of you, that's not my department and you'll have to sort that out among yourselves. But for now, the fire is being labeled as accidental. We'll know more later on in the week, but you can relax."

Peggin let out a long breath and visibly relaxed. "Can I go over tomorrow and see if I can find anything that survived? Everything I owned was in that house. Except for a suitcase full of clothing and my ferrets."

Sophia nodded. "The fire marshal said that you can come by tomorrow and look through the rubble. I warn you though, he said that there's really nothing left and it's also dangerous."

Seeing Peggin's expression fall, she softly added, "I'll have a couple of my officers come over and help you look. I'm so sorry this happened, but I'm very grateful that you and your ferrets survived." She glanced at her watch. "I've got to go. We had an incident over at the Harlequin Theatre. Apparently one of the actors in the local production of *A Christmas Carol* came to rehearsal drunk, accused the costume designer of trying to sleep with her husband, and a brawl has ensued. Several of the sets were destroyed, and Tiny Tim has a broken leg for real. I have to go sort things out."

I tried not to laugh but couldn't help myself. As I broke out in a loud guffaw, so did the others. Sophia looked put out for a moment, then joined us, shaking her head.

"I swear, this season does things to people. I see you're getting ready to trim your tree? Please, make sure not to overload any circuits or do anything stupid."

"Everything I bought for the outside is LED so it's not going to take as much juice as incandescent lights. But I refuse to use them inside—I hate that neon glow inside my house. But we'll be careful and make sure to use common sense."

"All right then, have fun. And I'll see you tomorrow, Peggin. Call me when you're planning to go over to the ruins of the house and I'll have a couple people meet you there. I don't want you hurting yourself on the debris." And with that, Sophia skedaddled.

"Well, that's a relief. At least they don't think I started the fire. But that furnace was new. And furnaces that new don't usually fail like that." Peggin twisted her lip into a frown. "At least I can go look through the remains of my life tomorrow. Corbin told me to take the week off. He's also giving me an extra week's vacation so that I won't lose out on my pay. Which is a good thing, given I have very little in my savings account right now. I don't know what the hell I'm going to do."

"I forgot, that reminds me. I have something for you." Bryan pulled out his wallet and removed a check from it, handing it to her. "This is from Jack. He wants you to have your options fee back. I ran into him at the store while I was picking up dinner. He told me it wouldn't be fair for him to keep it. He also said for you to call him tomorrow to discuss negating the lease. Obviously, there's no house for you to live in."

Peggin looked at the check suspiciously. "*Bryan*, what did you do?"

"I have no idea what you're talking about. But this is yours. It's made out for three thousand dollars plus the first month's rent. So you should be able to use it to put a down payment or first and last month's rent somewhere else." He shoved the check into her hand, folded his wallet, and slid it back into his pocket, then turned back to the kitchen. "I'll start unloading the groceries. Deev, give me a hand."

We watched them work together at the table for a moment.

"What did you have Bryan do?" Peggin asked me.

I opened one of the bags containing the new ornaments, carefully removing them from the plastic. "I have no idea what you're talking about. Now get over here and help me. I'd like to get everything set up so that when people arrive we can just eat and start decorating."

Thankfully, at that moment the doorbell rang, announcing Ivy and Aidan's arrival. Peggin gave me another smoldering look, but beneath the suspicious glare, I could see relief and the gratitude. I just smiled back as we all headed into the kitchen to grab a plate of food.

CHAPTER 16

By the end of the evening, we were all sitting around the glow of the tree. It was covered with sparkling ornaments, and everything felt soft and fuzzy and beautiful. I had turned off all the other lights, and we just finished watching *It's a Wonderful Life*.

"It's too bad that we can't summon up the Ghost of Christmas Past and have him tell us how those ship beams got there in the house. By the way, did Clinton have anything to say when you met him over there yesterday? I totally forgot that you two were meeting up, with our engagement and then the fire today."

"I forgot, too," Peggin said. "I still think he seemed awfully eager to have me move out of there, though I guess he's seen too many people sucked down by the Lady."

"What does Clinton Brady have to do with the matter?" Deev looked concerned. In fact, he looked so concerned that it caught my attention.

"Do you have something against Clinton? He's always struck me as a pretty good guy."

"I just . . . there's something odd about his pub. Every time I go in there, I feel like I'm being watched. And the pub feels haunted." Deev looked at a loss for words, which didn't surprise me. He wasn't all that chatty of a guy.

"It probably is. The place is four hundred years old," Peggin said. "Anyway, what did he have to say, Bryan?"

Bryan took on long sip of his eggnog. "He agreed that the beams probably came from the *Maria Susanna*. As to how or where the original builder of the house found them, he has no clue. The shipwreck was never found, or any part of the ship. I had a closer look at them and I swear, they look like they were built right into the house as it was erected. So I'm guessing they were there all along, though Clinton disagreed. If I'm right, that means that Herschel Dorsey had to have found some part of the ship within a year after it went down. Because he built the house in 1920, and the *Maria Susanna* went down in 1919."

"I still think that the Hounds had something to do with that shipwreck."

"Do you think that they know that we found out about it?" Bryan gave me a long look. "It could be they don't want anybody to know what really happened back then."

"I don't see why," Aidan said. "After all, anybody involved in taking the ship down would be dead by now. You can't prosecute dead men."

"I just can't shake the feeling that the Hounds are still involved and that they may have had something to do with the fire, though I don't know why." Bryan looked so worried that it began to worry me.

I was about to say something, when I heard the call of crows. Startled, I began to stand up, but the next thing I knew I was standing in front of the Crow Man, and we were looking at the remains of the house.

* * *

"There are bright glittering secrets hidden down there," the Crow Man said, pointing to the remains of the basement. "And there are hawks looking for them right now. It's a race, Kerris. And it's a race you need to win."

I glanced back at the charred foundation. "But hawks don't fly in the dark, do they?"

"Neither do crows, but I'm out and it's dark. And so are you, and you are the daughter of the Crow goddess. Sometimes birds fly at night. And old secrets could give new life to some of the battles that await in your future. Old secrets that could have helped your grandmother and great-grandmother."

The smell of burned wood drifted up to cloud my senses. I shivered. "Old secrets? How old?"

"Oh, they go back years on the family tree, to the beginning. There was a wide span between spirit shamans, and during that time Whisper Hollow was extremely vulnerable. A gift was brought from the mother country, meant to be given to your great-grandmother when she arrived. The Heart and the lament singer joined forces to protect it. But the Hounds managed to weave their own magic, and the Heart and the lament singer lost track of the gift, and it vanished, hidden away. They died without remembering their secret. But time has a way of bringing the past to surface, and those who still seek to hide misdeeds fear the revelations."

I tried to sort through the riddle. "Are you telling me there's something in that house, besides those beams, that I need to know about?"

"Perception is the beginning of wisdom." He laughed then, his voice ricocheting through the night. "I am the Crow Man. I lead the procession of the gods. I trick and I tempt. And I am the liaison of the Morrígan and her children. My messages are for you to decipher. I am not your oracle, but I am a whisper on the wind reminding you of what you once knew, of what you must know. Mind my gifts, they are only given to those who listen. But don't wait—or you will be too late."

I blinked, suddenly aware that I was back in my living room. "We have to go over to the house now. We can't wait until tomorrow. Whatever's there, and there is something hidden there, the Hounds are searching for it. They don't want me to find it."

"Let's go." My grandfather grabbed his jacket from the hall closet, handing Ivy's to her. Deev had draped his duster over the back of a kitchen chair, and now he slid into it, as Peggin grabbed her coat and my jacket from the wall pegs in the kitchen.

"We'll go in my SUV. It will hold all of us."

"No, head over to my place and we'll take my SUV. You still have to get yours serviced and checked out, and I have a feeling you didn't do that today." Bryan gave me a sideways look. "I know the dents seem superficial, but I'd rather we know that it's running in good condition before you go driving it around much more."

"I'll make an appointment tomorrow."

We trooped out of the house, stopping to unplug all of the beautiful lights. As I locked the door behind me, the snow softly began to fall again.

After a stop at Deev's to drop him and Peggin off—he wanted to get something, and he followed me in his truck from there—we eased into the driveway of the burned-out shell.

Bryan stopped a good ways before the actual house. "I don't want to accidentally drive over a nail or a piece of glass. We can walk from here. There are flashlights in the backseat."

Aidan fished around and found several flashlights in good working order. He handed one to Bryan and one to Deev, who was opening the tailgate of his truck.

Deev snapped his fingers. An odd figure, squat and short on four massive legs, eased out of the truck. Made of brass and wood, it was five feet tall, about four feet long, and looked like it had been built of metal Legos and Tinkertoys. The head was featureless but it was wearing a jaunty bowler hat of enormous size. The creature came to attention.

"What is *that*?" I cocked my head, intrigued.

"This is Kyler. Kyler came to life last night and I couldn't figure out why, but he was made to protect and to guard. When I was building him, I was focusing on the energy of a sentinel. Since he woke up last night I figured it couldn't hurt to bring him along." He smiled, sounding like a proud papa.

"Well, I doubt he can hurt matters." Bryan motioned to Deev. "Let him take the lead, if that's okay."

With Kyler in front, we gingerly proceeded. The explosion had thrown debris right and left, and before we even reached the yard, we were encountering bits of wood and charcoal. I kept my eye on Peggin, realizing how close we were to the lake. She kept lifting her head, glancing through the trees as though she were hearing something.

Kyler suddenly stopped, turning toward the tree line. One of his jointed arms reached out, pointing to the lake.

"Do you hear her calling?" I asked, suddenly going on high alert.

Peggin looked startled. "Actually, I do. I didn't realize what was happening, but you're right. I can hear her calling now. She's singing, promising me that she can put an end to my problems. That she can make everything okay again." Her voice was wistful, and I could tell she was struggling with the desire to answer the call.

The look on her face scared the hell out of me. I had never seen Peggin look so enraptured.

Deev was listening to our conversation and now he pulled up beside her and wrapped his arm around her waist. "You're not going anywhere. Not while I'm here."

She flashed him a grateful smile. "Thank you. I've never

felt like I needed a protector before, but I'm beginning to feel so helpless in the face of all of this. I hate that feeling. My life has spun out of control and all I can do is hold on while the ride takes me on a journey I never wanted to explore."

"Tomorrow night, the ritual will remove the Lady's binding from you," Ivy said. "It's a dark descent, but it should take care of the matter."

Peggin shuddered again. "I don't care what I have to go through. I want that mark off me. Every time I look at it, I can feel her watching me. And now that we're out here tonight, I can feel her calling and I don't want to hear her voice. I don't want to listen to her whispers."

"Kyler, forward."

We started up again, Deev holding tight to Peggin's waist as we approached the shell of the house. Three of the walls were partially standing, but they were leaning dangerously. The fourth was totally gone, and the upper stories of the house were nothing more than so much soot and ash. The air was filled with the smell of burnt wood, and as the snow settled down over the remains, it was starting to stick in places. I suddenly realized that the heat had been so intense that it had melted off every flake up until then.

"I think we want to go down in the basement. The Crow Man kept talking about buried secrets. That would indicate underground to me. And given that that's where the timbers were, I can't help but feel that there's something down there."

"That's going to be tricky; we'll have to watch our footing carefully or we could end up breaking our necks. For one thing the stairs are wooden and it looks like they're mostly burned away. We have to find a different way down into the basement." Bryan frowned, looking around. "I wish I had thought to bring a ladder."

"Do you have a rope?" Deev asked. "We could use it like a belay line."

"Good thought!" Bryan pulled out his keys. "I'll be back

in a moment. Don't anybody do anything stupid while I'm gone." He jogged his way back to his SUV.

I turned back to the house, realizing that there had been a reason I couldn't tell Peggin about my dream. She had needed to move into the house in order to stir this to life. Whatever *this* was. But even as I recognized the way circumstance worked, it hit me in the gut that she had to go through everything she did in order to bring me here now, tonight.

Without her moving in, without the fire, without even the Lady, we would never have been here, searching out secrets the Crow Man wanted me to find.

"I think this is what all of this is been leading up to," I said. "Sometimes the gods use us as pawns."

"Well, I jolly well would rather they use me as a queen instead." Peggin's voice was both sarcastic and wistful. "If I have to be somebody's tool, maybe they could pay me for my time and effort."

"Hear you there." I laughed. "Here comes Bryan now."

Bryan looked around for a sturdy beam he could tie the rope around, but it was hard to tell which beams would give way. "Can Kyler support weight?"

Deev shook his head. "Unfortunately, even though he's fairly strong, I made him of lightweight material and I doubt if he could keep balanced with anybody hanging off of him."

Aidan motioned to Bryan. "No worries. Give me the rope and I'll tie it around my waist and act as the fulcrum. I've got strength enough to lift anybody out of there who might need it." My grandfather wasn't just talking big. He really was the strongest of the group. I wondered if Bryan would grow into his own strength, given he was also a shifter.

Bryan handed the end of the rope to Aidan, who wrapped it around his waist and tied it off in some sort of slipknot. Most of the floor that had formed the basement's ceiling had burned away. None of us really trusted testing the rest of it. So Aidan stayed at the side on the ground, bracing himself against a large beam that had fallen. It was near enough to the hole so that we could slide over the edge and go down that way. I moved forward, but Bryan held up his hand.

"*You* are not going down there. You are going to let *me* go down there. Deev, you and Kyler watch the women and Aidan's back. If there really is a race to find something down there, we don't want be surprised if the Hounds show up."

I hadn't even thought of the possibility of the Hounds showing up while we were here. Somehow I had translated the idea in my mind to: We come out here, we find what we're looking for, and we leave. The thought that the Hounds might show up while we were in the process of our adventure set my stomach on edge.

"I'll keep watch over this way," Ivy said.

"Peggin, you stay with Deev. Don't let her out of your sight." I moved over to Aidan's side, watching as Bryan took the end of the rope and tossed it over the edge. "I don't know if I can climb down that rope or not." Considering I couldn't do a pull-up, somehow I didn't think I was going to be available to suddenly become a champion rope climber within the space of five minutes.

"As I said, you're not going down there," Bryan said. At my look, he let out a sigh. "Fine, if I *need* your help, we can tie the end of the rope around your waist and Aidan can lower you down."

Both irritated but relieved, I gave him a nod. "Just be careful. I don't know what it is we're looking for, but apparently it was important enough for the Hounds to hide it way back when this house was built."

With a nod, Bryan slowly began to lower himself into the dark hole as the snow continued to fall.

Five minutes passed, then ten. Every now and then Bryan would call up that everything was all right, to keep me calm. Meanwhile, I was keeping an eye on Deev and Peggin to make sure that she didn't try to wander off. The last thing we needed was another dip in the lake to pull her out of the Lady's grasp. Luck had been on our side the first time; I wasn't counting on it a second.

The night was far from silent. In addition to the soft skitter of snow on snow, sounds came from the trees behind us. *Scuffling and the rustling of undergrowth, and occasionally what sounded like someone tripping or falling over or the cracking of a branch.* I moderated my breath, trying to keep calm as I reached out in an attempt to connect with whatever was there. If it was a spirit or one of the Ankou, I should be able to sense it. But when I sent out feelers, I couldn't grasp hold of anything.

Another moment, and Bryan called out, "I think I found something. Kerris, have Aidan send you down."

But just as he spoke, the noise from the trees became louder. Kyler froze, pointing toward the woods, then began to lumber toward the trees.

My internal alarms went off and I screamed, "Get down," not knowing what was happening. But my instinct was to drop, and drop I did. A bullet whistled overhead as a loud crack broke the silence, and the glow of gunfire flared from one of the trees. The shot was aimed at me, and if I hadn't dropped, the bullet would have hit me.

"Kerris!" Peggin screamed, pulling away from Deev, who was shouting directions to Kyler.

Ivy whirled, racing toward me, as Aidan began to furiously pull Bryan up from the hole. I belly-crawled toward a large piece of debris, hiding behind it. As Peggin ran toward me, I motioned for her to get down.

"Down, get down now!"

She dropped to the ground and, with a loud curse, made a beeline for me. "Damned slivers. I just drove something sharp into my hand." She ducked behind the burned-out chunk of wood and crouched next to me. "What the hell is going on? Who would take potshots at us?"

"It has to be the Hounds. The Crow Man warned me they

were on the trail of the . . . well . . . whatever it is we're looking for."

"Wonderful. Couldn't he have told you about this earlier?"

I peeked around the edge of our shield. Kyler was in the
woods now. That thing could move plenty fast when the
need arose. Pulling back—we didn't know where the gun-
man had gone—I craned my neck to see how Aidan and
Bryan were doing. Ivy had managed to get behind another
piece of debris and now she waved to me to let me know
she was okay.

And then, I saw him—the ghost of Joseph Jacobs. He
looked just like his picture, and I realized he had been the
spirit who had first warned me that Peggin was headed toward
the Lady. Beside him stood Eugenie. Cloaked in a pale yellow
glow, their faces were masked with concern as they wandered
through the debris toward me. I caught my breath.

"Do you see them?"

Peggin nodded. "Yes. What do they want?"

Eugenie knelt beside us, staring at us with a curious look.
Then, she slowly reached out and brushed Peggin's hair. Of
course, her touch didn't even ruffle the strands but Peggin
still gasped.

"I can feel her—she's sad. She's so sad, but she's also
happy we can see her." She looked up at the spirit in wonder.
"Kerris, something is holding her here."

"I know, but it's not another spirit." I rose up on my
knees, still keeping myself out of the line of fire. By now,
we could hear a crashing through the woods and I figured
it was Kyler, trampling through the undergrowth. I hoped
to hell Deev had let him go alone and not tried to play hero.

Eugenie and Joseph knelt beside me, their faces intent. They
leaned in, staring at me in an uncanny way. I got neither the
sense that they were lost, nor that they were Haunts. And then
it hit me. They were here as protectors. They were guarding
something . . . and had been all these years.

"You're here to protect what the Crow Man sent me to find, aren't you?"

A light flashed through Eugenie's eyes and she leaned back, her hands resting on her knees.

At that moment, we heard a loud shout. *Deev.* Another shot rang out and Peggin screamed and jumped up. She pulled out her purse and opened it, yanking out her gun that she carried everywhere. Ever since she was mugged, she had made a point to learn how to shoot, and she could knock a fly off the ceiling. I had watched her target practice and was glad she was on my side.

"I'm not hiding here while some freak shoots at my boy-friend," she said, swinging around the barrier. I tried to stop her but before I could grab hold of her coat sleeve, she was gone.

I heard more shouts—Bryan and Aidan—and then a single shot that sounded different than the others. A loud curse . . . then a cacophony of shouts and activity.

"Stay here," I said to Eugenie and Joseph, then swung around the shield.

There, in the clearing between the tree line and where the house had stood, was a man laying facedown, with Kyler holding him down. Deev was limping, cursing under his breath.

I raced over to the scene. "What's going on? Is anybody hurt?"

"Damn it, yes. Me," Deev shouted. He groaned, then slowly folded to the ground, grabbing his leg. "He shot me in the leg." He pointed to the man on the ground. I saw *his* gun farther away, on the ground. It wasn't a handgun, but some sort of rifle with scope. He had been aiming for me, and it suddenly hit me that he had been meaning to kill me.

"Who are you? Why were you shooting at us?" I edged up close enough to shine one of the flashlights on him. He was a burly man, wearing a bandanna. As he looked up, my heart dropped through a pit in my stomach.

Clinton Brady was lying there, held down by Dr. Divine's walking statue.

W hat the . . ." But before I could even question him, I realized that I couldn't see Peggin. I screamed and headed toward the woods. "Bryan! Help me find her!"

"Ivy, look after Deev. Call the medics. And Aidan, hold him down." He frantically motioned to Clinton, then broke into a run. He caught up with me and I moved so he could go on ahead. "What if there are more of the Hounds in the woods? *Go back, Kerris.*"

"No—Peggin's in danger."

"I said *go back.*" He stopped, skidding to a halt and grabbing me by the shoulders, his eyes blazing. "I'll find her. Trust me. But you have to go back. Now."

Wanting to disobey, wanting to argue with him, I suddenly realized that he was right. If I died, the Hounds would have an easier time taking over the town. With a whimper, worried sick about Peggin, I pulled back.

The next moment, Bryan shifted and a giant wolf stood there, his brilliant white fur glowing in the night. He loped off into the woods and I realized he was following Peggin's scent. I turned, running back to Deev's side. Kneeling down, I saw that he'd been shot in the calf, but Ivy had managed to make a tourniquet.

"I've called the cops and the medics. Go see if Aidan needs help."

I nodded, moving over to Aidan's side, but he had taken the rope Bryan had been using and had trussed up Clinton tighter than a hog on butchering day.

Aidan had hold of his gun, and was examining it. "Sniper's rifle. Expensive, by the looks of it. He meant business." He turned a cold eye on Clinton. "You do realize that shooting at my granddaughter isn't the brightest move you could make."

I knelt down beside Clinton. "Why? Why the hell did you do it? You're on our side. You're part of the Crescent Moon Society." But something about the way he looked away when I spoke stopped me. I glanced over at Aidan. "He's not one of us."

Aidan gave him a long look, then shook his head. "No, I think you're right."

At that moment, Bryan shouted from the trees. I jumped up to see him struggling with Peggin, who had her gun in hand, pointed at him.

"Peggin! No! Don't shoot." I was on my feet, flying in their direction with Aidan behind me.

Peggin looked at me and I could see the confusion in her eyes. She was crying. "Don't make me. Let me go. She's calling me and I have to go to her. Don't try to stop me, please—she'll make me shoot him."

"Don't let her win, Peggin. Don't listen. Drown out her voice." I tried to think of anything that might break through the siren song that was luring Peggin in. I could hear the Lady now, faintly, but for my best friend, her voice was like a marching band.

Come to me . . . they will try to stop you . . . you must not let them . . .

I whirled around, frantic. "Aidan, help me. What can I do?"

"We have to make so much noise it will distract her. Meanwhile, Bryan, take a step back. The Lady's so strong that she will force Peggin to shoot you if you get too close."

Bryan gave him a faint nod and, hands held in the air, stepped back. "Peggin, I'm backing away, see?"

We were still in the glow of Aidan's flashlight but then, Kyler suddenly turned, and before Peggin could respond, the creature flared to life, brighter than the spotlight on a runway. Peggin shouted, dropping her gun as she tried to shield her eyes from the sudden brilliance.

As her gun hit the ground, Bryan leaped forward and knocked her to the ground, holding her down. I raced in and grabbed up her gun, cautiously pointing it toward the forest. Peggin screamed, struggling, and I heard the Lady shout— angry curses aimed toward us.

"We need to sedate her as long as she's this close to the lake." I had no clue how we were going to do so without knocking her out, but my answer pulled into the driveway with a wail of sirens. The ambulance appeared, followed by Sophia and Frank in a police car.

As the paramedics raced toward Deev, I went to meet them. "You need to sedate our friend over there. The Lady's calling her and if we don't do something, she'll either hurt herself trying to get down to the lake, or she'll hurt us trying."

One thing about the doctors and medical personnel around Whisper Hollow, they knew full well what lived in the forests and the shadows of our town. One of the EMTs immediately fished through his medical kit and pulled out a syringe. I led him over and, between Bryan and myself, held Peggin down long enough for the tech to inject her with the sedative. Within seconds, she closed her eyes, and I heard the Lady give a garbled snarl and then—the song vanished.

"What's going on?" Sophia looked at Kyler. "Dr. Divine?"

"Yeah, one of his creations. And that thing kept Clinton there from shooting me. And it helped keep Peggin from shooting Bryan."

"Peggin shooting Bryan?" Sophia let out a long sigh. "I don't think I want to know what's going on, but let's all head down to the station. Hey, Jorge?"

One of the EMTs glanced up at her from where he was attending Deev's injuries. "Yeah?"

"How is he?"

Dr. Divine groaned as they lifted him onto the stretcher. "*He* is all right. How's my girlfriend?"

"Hush." Jorge turned back to Sophia. "He's been shot, but the bullet missed anything terribly vital, though I think he's going to be on crutches for a few days. We're ready to load him in."

"Good, get the both of them into the ambulance and out of here before I leave. The Lady's on the prowl and hungry. Don't take chances, *get a move on*."

Frank had handcuffed Clinton and shoved him into the back of the police car. "He's in."

"Let's all get out of here, then. And I'm going to want an explanation of why you were out here tonight instead of waiting till tomorrow. I told you I didn't want you prowling around here without an official escort." She frowned at me, and I felt like a scolded teenager.

"We'll meet you over at the station." Bryan pushed me toward the car and motioned to Aidan and Ivy. "Let's get out of here." He glanced at Clinton. "Can he hear us from in the car?"

Looking puzzled, Sophia shook her head. "No, why?"

"Because I have what he came to prevent us from finding, though I'm not sure what it actually is. Frank, Clinton belongs to the Hounds, I think. So watch whatever you say in front of him."

"Shit." Frank let out a long sigh. "How did we not know this and how long has it been going on?"

"I have no answer for you on either question, but let's go. There may be more of them here, and the Lady is on the prowl." Bryan shooed us into the SUV and we eased out of the driveway, following Frank and Sophia, and the ambulance.

"We must perform the ritual on Peggin, there's no doubt about that," Ivy said from the backseat. "Kerris, I have to tell you this. The ritual itself could kill her. But we have no other choice. Even if we sent her away from Whisper Hollow, the Lady could still reach out, find her somehow, and bring her back."

Saying nothing, I flipped on the radio and "Bitter Sweet Symphony" came on. As the haunting tune filled the car, it drowned out the sirens as they cleared the path through the dark night.

CHAPTER 17

The police station was directly across from the fire station and the library, and one long block over from the hospital where they had taken Peggin and Deev. I wanted to be over there, keep an eye on them, but we had to sort out the mess with Clinton, and since neither Deev nor Peggin were in a life-threatening condition, I wasn't all that worried that Diago would prey on them—the spirit mostly hunted down those who had reached a crisis point.

Sophia motioned the four of us into her office, then had a quiet talk with Frank. Along with another burly officer, Frank marshaled Clinton off to a holding cell. After he was out of sight, Sophia closed the door to her office and turned to us.

"What the hell is going on? Clinton Brady, shooting at you? And Peggin shooting at Bryan? You'd better start from the beginning, and don't leave anything out." She settled in behind her desk. "On second thought, wait a minute. I need a cup of coffee. What about you?"

I nodded. "I'd love it. The stronger the better." Aidan also accepted the offer, while Bryan and Ivy shook their heads. After the receptionist, a young woman named Mandy who was looking to join the police academy in the near future, brought us our coffee, we were ready.

"Well, I assume Frank has filled you in on the Shadow People out in the forest. That Magda has been summoning them in." I knew that Sophia kept herself in the loop, even though she wasn't allowed to be a part of the Crescent Moon Society. She had to have some form of balance, given she was the chief of police, but we knew how she felt about the Hounds. Anything that was an enemy of Whisper Hollow was an enemy of hers.

She nodded. "And I gather that you all are taking care of this. I know there have been a number of attacks. And I've instructed my people to let me know every time someone makes a report. I've been feeding them to Frank and he's been giving them to Starlight. There have been at least two people who were hurt in the past week, one of them seriously. He's still in the hospital, recovering. But he was almost suffocated."

"I didn't realize it was that bad. I thought they were just scaring people. But one of them attacked Peggin the other night in my CR-V." I let out a sigh. "I'm not sure whether the influx of the Ankou has anything to do with this other issue."

I was mulling over how to approach the whole situation surrounding Peggin and the Lady and the ship beams, when suddenly I realized I was free to tell them about the dream I had had about her. My words came freely.

"When Peggin was told she had to find another place last week, she found that house. Before I even saw it, I had a horrible dream—a nightmare I couldn't tell anyone. In the dream, the Lady took Peggin into the waters, drowning her." I paused, glancing over at Bryan. "I wanted to tell someone, but both the Crow Man and the Morrígan stopped me. Now I realize that they did so for a reason. For some reason, they wanted her to buy that house. I don't know why, but it has something to do with the beams we found in the basement."

"What beams?" Sophia asked. She was recording our conversation, and I knew full well that if it contained something that shouldn't go in the records, the recording would mysteriously vanish. If she took notes, it was harder to make them go away.

We explained about the *Susanna Maria*. I took that moment to tell everyone about the ghosts I had seen of Eugenie and Joseph when we were attacked. "I think they're linked to the house in order to guard something, but I don't know what."

"I know what they were hiding. And it would never have been found if the house hadn't burned down. I still think the Hounds burned it down, by the way. I got the distinct sense when I was down in that basement hunting around that they had been hoping it would destroy something that's been hidden for many years."

We all turned to stare at Bryan, who reached inside his jacket and pulled out a slightly charred metal box. When I looked closer, I realized the box was covered with soot, but hadn't been burned itself.

"Where did you find it?"

"It was hidden in the wall behind where one of the beams was affixed. The beam had burned away, but since the foundation of the house was made from stone, this box survived inside a cubbyhole. When I went down into the remains of the basement, I saw Joseph standing beside the wall where I found this. He vanished as I headed over to him. At first I thought it might have been a trick of my imagination, but when I flashed the light over the area where he had been standing, I saw the glint of metal. I pulled it out, but I didn't have a chance to open it. But look on top of the lid." He held out the box and placed it on Sophia's desk. We all leaned in.

As I stared at the box, I realized that Bryan was right. This is what Eugenie and Joseph were guarding. On the lid, embossed in the steel, was the sign of the spirit shaman—a crow standing on a crescent moon. I caught my breath as I reached toward the box. There was something very powerful inside, something the Hounds had been hiding all those years.

"May I open it?" I looked up at him. "You're my guardian, I will listen to what you say." And right then, I realized that our roles had been fixed. He was not only my guardian, but my advisor, even though I would always have the last word when it came to our jobs.

"I think it's meant for you."

I suddenly flashed back to my conversation with the Crow Man. *"There are bright glittering secrets hidden down there,"* I whispered. *"And there are hawks looking for it. It's a race."*

"What are you talking about?" Sophia asked.

"The Crow Man. He told me that there were hidden secrets in the basement. And he said hawks were looking for it. I'm not sure why he used that as a metaphor, but I think he was talking about the Hounds." I paused, then added, "The Crow Man talks in riddles. Sometimes I have to decipher what he's actually trying to tell me."

"That's because he's a trickster," Ivy said. "He may be the voice of the Morrígan, but he's a trickster at heart. When you think about it, hawks are predators, and they are enemies of crows. Therefore the hawks are the Hounds."

"So the Hounds knew about whatever this is."

Bryan nodded. "My guess is that they used the beams as an architectural design to keep this box hidden when Herschel built the house. In fact, I would guess the beams were erected as a reminder to future generations to keep guard. But the house fell in disrepair, and generation after generation of families passed through without ever realizing what was hidden in their basement."

Sophia picked up her pencil, tapping it on her desk. "We'll probably never know the truth, unless we can somehow get the records from the Hounds—if there are any—but from what you've told me, I'd venture that they sank Joseph's ship in order to keep him from contacting the revenuers.

Prohibition had just started, and it was strictly enforced. If they did have moonshine brewing out in the woods, Joseph probably stumbled onto it. I wonder if he had told any of the other members of the CMS. I can look in the records and see if we have anything about any members of Whisper Hollow being arrested for bootlegging."

I still hadn't opened the box. I felt almost reluctant. Whatever was there had been hidden for so many years, but it was valuable enough for the Hounds to hide it from the new spirit shaman. It was valuable enough that I almost lost my life over it.

"But why *Clinton*? He's a member of the Crescent Moon Society. Why the hell would he take potshots at us? I know that he secretly works for the Hounds. I saw it in his face when we were out in the yard there. He meant to kill me. I've always liked Clinton, we've never had a problem that I knew of. But tonight he was fully prepared to *kill* me."

"If he's a double agent, then you really don't know him," Bryan said. "The Clinton you thought you knew is not the Clinton he really is. Don't beat yourself up."

"But he lost his great-great-uncle to the Hounds. He has to know that they killed Joseph. How could he do that?"

But then again, I thought, the man I had believed to be my grandfather all those years had actually killed my mother, the girl he had raised as his daughter. Duvall had belonged to the Hounds and he had married my grandma Lila. He had done so in order to prevent my mother being born. When that didn't work, when my grandmother ran off and had an affair with her lover, Aidan, and gotten pregnant, Duvall had done the unthinkable. So maybe it wasn't so strange or unusual.

I picked up the box. It was time to see what all this was about. There was a lock on it, of course. "Sophia, can you open this?"

She grinned. "No problem. I grew up learning how to pick locks. Do you think this is trapped?"

"Good question. I don't know, but it strikes me that they

had it so well hidden they probably didn't bother trapping the box. If you're uncomfortable trying to open it, tell me what to do and I will."

She shook her head. "Give it to me."

I did a double take as she pulled a set of picks out of her desk and made quick work of the lock. We all heard the little *click* as it opened. But she did not raise the lid. Instead, she slid across the table to me.

"You do the honors."

As I slowly raised the lid, a soft glint of metal caught my eye. I pushed open the box and there, nestled in a velvet cloth, was a wicked-looking dagger, its blade carved from smooth, polished smoky quartz. Etched on the bone handle was the sign of the spirit shaman—a crow standing on a Crescent moon. The eye of the Crow was an inset ruby, and around the symbol was an elegant filigree of vines and leaves. The dagger let out a long sigh, as if it were taking a deep breath, and called my name. I knew in the depths of my heart this had belonged to spirit shamans before me. I slowly reached in and took hold of the hilt, raising the blade into the air. There was a soft swish and the blade itself began to glow with a faint light.

"It looks newly made—there's no stain on it at all."

"We need to ask Oriel about this. Or . . ." I turned to Ivy. "Do you know anything about this?"

She softly shook her head. "No, but Oriel might. I'll call her and ask her to come over."

As I held the dagger, closing my eyes, I realized that it fit perfectly in my hand. It made me feel stronger, and somehow— somewhere from deep in my heart—I could hear a faint whisper coming from the blade. And I knew that it was awake, and whispering, "I'm home again. Finally, I'm home again."

Oriel hurried over as soon as she got Ivy's message. By then, Sophia had sent out for a dozen doughnuts, and Corbin had called from the hospital to tell us that Deev would be all right, and that Peggin was awake and was back to her old self. Relieved to hear both pieces of news, I was able to relax and wait for Oriel to get there.

Oriel took one look at the dagger and let out a gentle laugh. "So it's true. It does exist."

"What? What is this?" I didn't want to hand over the dagger, but finally did. I was feeling highly possessive of it, but I knew that Oriel would be able to tap into the energy as well.

She cautiously took it, then closed her eyes. "It's one of the Talons of the Morrígan. I thought as much. There are nine of these in existence. They were made for the spirit shamans, one for each of the great families. Six were lost—and five of those remain missing. Three of them are in the hands of their rightful families around the world. Two in Ireland, one in Scotland. And now . . . we have this one. Each has a special name, but the Morrígan will tell you what that is—it's not for me to say. And each has one very special ability. These daggers can dispel the Unliving. You could even destroy Veronica with this, but for that, you must have permission of the Morrígan." Oriel looked over at me. "You know why."

I nodded. "Yes, actually, I do." And that was all we said about that.

She handed the dagger back to me. "Because these daggers can dispel the Unliving, they can also dispel the Ankou. You can destroy the Shadow People with the blade, as long as you touch it into their essence. It won't work by just having it around them. You have to actually touch them with it. But it will banish them back to their realm."

I stared at the glinting edge of the blade, suddenly very appreciative. "Then I see why the Hounds hid it. They like to use the Ankou for their servants."

"And anything that gives the spirit shaman power takes power away from them. Of course they were going to hide it. My guess is that when they realized Peggin was buying the house, they knew there was a chance you might find the dagger. I'll bet you anything they are the ones who stirred up the Lady. But when you saved Peggin from going under, they had to do something else." Oriel turned to Sophia. "If the fire marshal looks for it, he should find evidence of foul play. And my guess is that Clinton has something to do with it. He was listening in at the Crescent Moon Society meeting. He knew what was happening."

Her expression fell into a frown. "I am so disappointed in him. He's been a member for years, and now I wonder how long he has been feeding them information. How long has he belonged to the Hounds? And how did they recruit him?"

Just then, Frank entered the room. "There's been a horrible accident. Clinton Brady is dead."

And that ended all speculation for the time being.

O ne of the Ankou." Oriel looked around the cell. Clinton Brady was sprawled out on his bunk. No one else had been in the cell, although Frank said there was security film footage available. Bruises around Clinton's neck showed that he had been strangled—asphyxiated. I flashed back to the other night with the Ankou in the back of my car. The Shadow People could kill, that much we knew.

Locking the door behind us to prevent anyone tampering with the murder scene, we moved to the control booth where the digital cameras had recorded everything that went on. Frank rewound to the time he put Clinton in the cell and locked the door. Then he fast-forwarded through until he suddenly hit pause.

A dark shadow had entered the holding cell, and Clinton jumped up, his hands in front of him. We couldn't hear anything, the sound was off, but Clinton looked terrified as the shadow crossed his path and reached for his neck. Clinton tried to fight back but he seemed to be grappling with air, and the Ankou wrapped its meaty hands around his neck, the dark shadows closing in tighter and tighter as

Clinton fought for breath. Another moment and it was over. Clinton lay dead on his bunk.

"So nobody saw this?" Sophia asked, turning to Frank.

Frank shook his head. "There was an alarm in another cell and there are only three of us on duty here at the station. Two of the men are out in the main office. I was guarding the cells. I ran to the other cell, only to find Stacy Johnson drunk off his ass, but in no danger. When I returned, I checked in on Clinton. I found him dead. It was just a few minutes ago."

"The Ankou can work fast." I stared at the dagger in my hand. "I wish I'd been here." But even as I said it, I wasn't sure I really meant it. Clinton was one of the Hounds and he knew our secrets. If he was prosecuted for attempted murder, there would be a good chance he would get off with a light sentence like so many criminals. The last thing I needed was to be looking over my shoulder, always wondering if he was going to come back and try again.

"So what do we do now? We know that the Hounds killed Joseph and Eugenie, and the other men aboard the ship, but whoever did it was dead long ago. Clinton attempted to kill you, but there's no way we can link him to anybody else, especially now that he's dead. As it is, I'm going to have one hell of a time explaining how he died in police custody, when nobody laid a finger on him except a shadow. I'm going to have to call on Gareth for this one." Sophia frowned. "What do we know about Gareth, for that matter? And the rest of the Crescent Moon Society? Who can we trust and how can we find out who to trust? I can't join the society, but I need to know that the entire organization is behind Whisper Hollow and not against it."

Oriel licked her lips. "Leave it to us. We'll muddle through and figure out what we can. Did Clinton have any relatives in town?"

Sophia cocked her head for a moment, thinking. "I don't think so. I think he's the last of the line. In fact, we should go through the pub before his lawyer gets a handle on it. We don't want anything to escape that might give us information on the Hounds. And because he is a suspect—make that perpetrator—in a crime, I have the right to go into his apartment if I can get a warrant. Frank." She turned to the officer.

"Already on it. I'll have the warrant in twenty minutes once I talk to Judge Aimee." And he was off.

They worked together like a well-oiled machine, each understanding their part in the relationship. Frank respected Sophia, and Sophia gave Frank enough leeway so that he could actually be useful to her.

As we returned to Sophia's office, I let out a sigh. I was tired, and the dagger felt like such a solid weight in my hand that it almost made me want to set it down and walk away. It made things real in a way that nothing else had managed.

"Once Frank gets the warrant, we'll go through the pub and through Clinton's apartment—although I think he lives in a room above the pub, actually. I can't let you guys come along; it wouldn't be proper procedure. Why don't you go over and visit Peggin and Dr. Divine in the hospital? I'll call you when Frank and I have finished our search." She paused as we headed to the door, then added, "Don't tell anybody anything yet. I want to see what we find before we go spilling the news. The media's going to have a field day with this, but maybe Gareth can take care of them, too. Oriel, can you check in on Gareth tonight so that I know I can trust him?"

Oriel nodded, turning to Aidan. "You want to help me?"

Aidan grinned at her. "It would be my pleasure."

I wanted to ask what that was all about, except part of me really didn't want to know. I decided to concentrate on Deev and Peggin and leave the strong-arming to my grandpa this time. As we headed out of Sophia's office, I realized how incredibly tired I was. And we still had to free Peggin from the Lady's mark.

Peggin was sitting by Deev. He had been confined to a wheelchair, his leg extended in front of him. He was still wearing his top hat, though they had made him exchange his duster for a hospital gown, and he was wearing regular glasses for a change, which blew my mind because I could actually see his eyes. They were extremely blue, to the point of being startling. He was complaining loudly to Corbin, who was standing next to him.

Corbin's dark eyes danced merrily, as he just stood there, arms folded over his chest, patiently listening. A tall man, Corbin had glistening skin the color of dark peat. A handsome man, his eyes were dark brown ringed with topaz, and he had been a football player in high school, and still looked the part.

I wasn't sure what his wife did, but I knew his daughter was active in the community theater. In fact, if I remembered right, she had played the lead in *Romeo and Juliet* a month ago. Peggin had told me that it was a good production, but that Kimberly, Corbin's daughter, had balked at kissing the lead who played Romeo. Apparently he had made some nasty comments about her best friend at school.

"All right, I think you have complained enough." Corbin leaned down, putting his hand on the arm of the wheelchair. "If you don't want me to keep you here, and let Nurse Reagan give you sponge baths every time she wants to, you're going to have to follow my directions. Which means you stay in this contraption until that leg heals up in a few days. Then you can move to crutches if I think it's all right. But if I hear one word about you attempting to hobble around without the chair, I'm going to slap you right back in a hospital bed, truss that leg up in the air, and let Nurse Reagan go after you. Do you understand me, Dr. Divine?"

Deev looked entirely put out, but he shrugged. "Yes, I hear you. I promise, I'll only get out of this chair when I have to go to the bathroom. I am not using the bedpan. Is that an acceptable compromise?"

Corbin cleared his throat, then gave him a short nod. "I think we can allow that, as long as you wheel up to the bathroom door and don't hobble more than a few steps. That bullet went deep, and while I got it out and I don't think there's any major structural damage, we don't want any more scar tissue forming than we have to have. I don't want a knot inside your calf."

I decided now was as good a time as any. "How are you feeling? Both of you?"

Peggin jumped up from where she had slumped down on a chair next to the arguing duo. "Kerris! I'm so glad to see you. How are you? Is Bryan okay? I'm so embarrassed about what happened."

"Don't be. It wasn't your fault. The Lady had you in her grasp, and we all know that."

Corbin's expression darkened. "Has Oriel talked to you about the ritual yet?"

Peggin and I both shook our heads.

"I didn't know you were going to be involved," Peggin said.

"There is a reason I'll be there. I don't like what it entails, I'm going to tell you that right now. But Peggin, it's the only way to get rid of that mark. I hope you trust me." Corbin gazed at her darkly, and a veiled hint of danger filled his voice.

"You're making me nervous," Peggin said.

"You're making *me* nervous, too," I said. "What are you talking about? Can you tell us about this?"

Corbin shook his head. "It's better you don't know in advance. I'll be there tomorrow night, though. We'll bring you through this. Meanwhile, how's our shooter?"

Sophia hadn't wanted us to say anything, so I shifted my eyes and stared at the clock instead. There was no way that they wouldn't be able to guess; I wasn't that good of a liar. But I could do my best. "It's getting late. We should get home. Can I take these two with me?"

Corbin tapped me on the shoulder and I turned to stare at him. It was like staring up at a tree trunk, he was so sturdy and tall.

"Clinton Brady is dead, isn't he?"

I managed to avoid blinking, and I kept my expression neutral. "You should call Sophia and talk to her if you want to know. That would probably be for the best."

"I see. She's asked you to keep quiet for now. Very well, I'll give her a call in a while. Yes, you can take these two home. Don't let either one of them out of your sight for the next twenty-four hours at least. Peggin was in shock, and Deev is hurt. Bullets are no laughing matter. I'll talk to you tomorrow night. The nurse will have their medications—I'm giving Peggin a sedative to take at night so she doesn't get up and wander away. You can give it to her if she needs it during the day, too, since we only have to get through the next twenty-four hours. Call me if you need me. My number's on the prescription."

Bryan showed up at that moment. I wasn't sure where he had been but he took over wheeling Deev toward the door as I escorted Peggin. The nurse brought us the prescriptions, and I promptly took hold of Peggin's sedatives. I didn't want the Lady encouraging her to throw them away. As we headed out to the car, I wondered how Gareth was going to spin Clinton's death. And how much had the Hounds found out about the CMS from our backstabbing friend?

I insisted that Deev stay at my house, too. "You can sleep on the living room sofa or I can make up a bed in the office for you. One way or another, I'm not letting you go home to that old barn you call a house."

I had never been inside Deev's home before, but it was huge and drafty, and from what Peggin told me there were stairs everywhere because whoever had first built it had just kept adding onto it as if it were the Winchester house.

Deev looked over at Peggin. "Is she usually this bossy?"

Peggin snorted. "She and I are par for the course. In other words: You're toast. I suggest you just acquiesce and deal with it."

Deev let out a snort. "But I'm going to need clothes, I'm not about to live in this hospital gown the entire time."

"Do you have any bell-bottoms by any chance? If they flare from the knee, then you should be okay. Otherwise we're going to have to create slits so that your calf isn't confined." I looked over at Bryan. "Maybe you can run over to his house and pick him up a few pieces of clothing?"

"I think we should just open a business. This is the second time in how many days we've gone on a clothing reconnaissance mission."

"Don't even joke, dude," Deev said. "I have no desire to see my house burned down with all my art."

"No problem. And yes I'll run over there in a little while. What time is it? It must be close to midnight." Bryan checked his watch. "Strike that. It's past two. You can wait for clothes until tomorrow morning. I think we all need some sleep."

By the time we got home, the cats were sprawled out on the sofa and looked at us like we had just caused them a major insult when I ejected them from their bed. Agent H meandered off, letting out a little grumble as he headed toward the bedroom. Daphne decided it was time for a nosh and started meowing at her food dish. And Gabby walked over to the rocking chair and hopped in that, giving me a stare like *you'd better not try it again, human.*

While Peggin fed them, Bryan got some sheets and blankets from the linen closet and made up a comfortable bed for Deev. I turned on the Christmas lights, and the soft glow wooed us all to stop what we were doing. We settled into our seats, and sat there for a few minutes in silence, as the stress from the day began to wash out.

I leaned back, thinking about the dagger that was in my handbag. I wasn't sure my grandmother had ever heard of it, but I needed to do more research. I had to learn how to use it, and I had to learn how to protect it. It was an extremely powerful piece of weaponry, and when I thought of how the Hounds had hidden it away behind the beams to keep my great-grandmother and my grandmother from finding, it made me incredibly sad and wistful.

The Crow Man was right. Great-Grandma Mae and Grandma Lila could have been so powerful with a weapon against the Ankou. The Unliving were an ever-present threat and danger. The dagger could make things so much easier.

After a few minutes, I began to yawn, the weariness setting in. I took out Peggin's sedative. It was a liquid, and I was grateful for that. It would be easier to ensure she actually took it. I poured her out the recommended dosage and handed it to her.

"I hate to act like your mother, but I need to see you drink this."

She gave me a soft smile. "I'm grateful that you are willing to oversee this. I don't trust the Lady not to influence me." She upended the medicine cup, swallowing it in one gulp. Then she opened her mouth and showed me her tongue, which was a bright cherry red.

I laughed. "Sleep deep and well."

She yawned then, stretching as she did so. "That stuff works fast," she said. I could see her unwinding, and sent her upstairs to bed.

Deev crawled under the covers, wincing. "Damn, that hurts. Can you hand me a pain pill?" Bryan brought him a bottle of water and handed him one of the pain pills, setting the rest of them beside him. Deev swallowed the pill, drinking deep to wash it down.

I left the lights on, figuring it would be easier for him to find his way to the bathroom. I set up his wheelchair next to the sofa so that he could step into it easily. Bryan headed to the bedroom and I motioned that I'd be right behind him.

Quietly, I climbed the stairs to the guest room where Peggin was staying. I knocked, softly, but there was no answer. Carefully, I opened the door and peeked in. She was curled in her blankets, snoring softly. The ferrets were playing in their cage and I made sure they had food and clean water. I crept over to Peggin's side and touched her shoulder, but she was out like a light. Checking to see that the windows were firmly shut and locked, I headed back downstairs where I locked the front door and the back, and then headed to bed. Satisfied that everyone was safe for the night, I stripped out of my clothes and crawled under the covers, falling into the deepest sleep that I'd had for a long time.

CHAPTER 18

～

The next morning—Tuesday—we were eating breakfast when Sophia called.

"We got our warrant and searched Clinton Brady's pub last night. We found a bunch of papers that indicate he's been with the Hounds for the past two years. I also found out that Clinton owed a great deal of money. Apparently he had a secret gambling habit, and had run up a bill of over one hundred thousand dollars. He had tried to take out a loan but he couldn't because he couldn't prove what the loan was for. One of the Hounds works for the bank and we think he figured it out. Apparently he saw a way to get Clinton over a barrel. The gambling debt mysteriously disappeared two months after Clinton first tried to take out the loan, but there's no indication of how he came up with the money. My guess is that the Hounds bought him off and made his little money problem vanish."

I let out a long breath. Gambling had taken a toll on a lot of people, and apparently it had destroyed Clinton as well.

It had destroyed his ethics, and it had destroyed his life in the end.

"Well I guess we know *why* he did it. The kicker is, if he would have talked to the CMS, maybe they could have helped him out." I had the feeling that somehow they would have helped him manage his way through his troubles and his addiction.

"I was thinking maybe it's best Peggin doesn't go over to the house, given how close it is to the lake. But if you want to come over today, we can sift through the rubble and see if we can find anything of hers that might still be salvageable. The place is pretty much gutted, but we might get lucky." Sophia sounded defeated. "Sometimes it's really hard being in my position. I watch the people of this town go through trauma, I watch them deal with loss and pain. I do what I can, but there's never anything I can do to solve the problem after it happens. I can only come along, pick up the pieces, and try to make things seem a little better."

I wanted to cheer her up. She did a good job and I hated to see her depressed. "Sophia, you give police a good name. Don't beat yourself up over what isn't your fault. We all respect you, and look up to you. Whisper Hollow is a magical town, and it's a dangerous town. It eats people up if they don't respect it. And you have to deal with that aspect as well. I think you do a damn good job."

She paused, then thanked me. We agreed to meet at ten A.M., and I hung up.

Peggin was still asleep; I had checked on her when I got up and she was still in bed, snuggled up under the covers. But I decided to start breakfast since it wouldn't be long before she and Deev would be waking up. Bryan had already been up and out when I woke up and took my shower. As I heated up the waffle iron, he came through the door, holding a box.

"I decided to go over to Deev's to bring him some clothes before he woke up. I can't imagine him wanting to wear that hospital gown after he takes a sponge bath. He's not supposed to take a shower for the next couple days." He set the box on the table and gave me a kiss. "How are you feeling this morning?"

"Not too bad. I just got off the phone with Sophia." I told him what she had told me. "So apparently Clinton was trying to solve his money problems, and everything got away from him. I still can't believe that he meant to shoot me down— it's just not in his nature. I think they must have had something else on him, but I don't know if we'll ever know what. Clinton was a good guy and I know it in my heart."

"Desperation can make people do the strangest things, and it can make them do things that are totally against their nature. Maybe you'll end up seeing his spirit and be able to ask him."

I cocked my head, giving him a sideways glance. "I'm not certain I really *want* to see his spirit. But some closure might be good. I wonder if Eugenie and Joseph are still there now that we found the blade. I'll find out later today when I meet Sophia at the house. We're going to look for anything that survived the fire. We both decided it wasn't a good idea to have Peggin out there. I don't think she's going to like it, but I'm going to make her take another sedative after breakfast. A little extra sleep won't hurt her at all."

As I made the waffles, Bryan took Deev's clothing in to him and helped him to the bathroom so he could take a sponge bath and get dressed. I was just finishing up the fourth waffle when Peggin yawned her way into the kitchen.

"Caffeine, *now*. If you know what's good for you, you'll give me a quad shot." She stuck her tongue out at me and I laughed but fired up the espresso machine.

"Listen, Sophia called me this morning and had some information for me." I told her what she had said. I had the feeling that I was going to end up telling the story time after time today. After I finished, I added, "She and I are going to go through the remains of your house today. *You* are not coming. You are going to take a sedative and have a nice long nap while I'm gone. And I don't want any arguments."

To my surprise, she didn't even try to put up a fight. "After I turned the gun on Bryan last night, do you really expect me to argue? That horrified me; I knew what I was doing even as I couldn't stop it. It was like something was possessing my hands. I don't ever want to be in that position again. In fact, as much as I love my gun, I'm probably going to get rid of it because I don't think I could live with myself if I ever accidentally shot one of my friends. Or if I accidentally shot anybody else who didn't deserve it."

"That sounds like a good idea to me. I like that you can shoot, and I kind of want to learn how, but the reality is that some spirits can control mortals. Around Whisper Hollow, you never know who's going to be behind the wheel. Now come help me finish these waffles while Deev finishes his sponge bath. We'll eat breakfast, and then I'm going to go meet Sophia. When I get back, I'll wake you up and we can take some time to finish trimming the house. I think we both deserve a little bit of a break." I didn't mention the meeting that night. We were already overstressed, overwhelmed, and way too tired to deal with anything else.

Sophia and I spent an hour and a half poking through the remains of the house. Very little had remained, and it broke my heart to see the broken bits of china and the charred papers and what had been the boxes that were now piles of ash. At one point Sophia suddenly stood up and called me over to her side. She had found the porcelain figure of a cat. While it was covered with soot, miraculously it was unbroken.

I slowly took the cat in my hands. "I bought this for Peggin when we were ten years old. It was my birthday present to her. Of all the things you could find, I think she'll be happy that this is one that actually survived."

We sifted through pile after pile of ash and rubble and when we were done, we had managed to find some jewelry still intact, several knickknacks that had managed to escape break-age, and the miracle of miracles—Peggin's makeup case, which must have been blown out of the window during the explosion. Some of the bottles were broken, but for the most part her thousand-dollar makeup collection was intact. By the end, we had four necklaces, three rings—all of which were diamond and gemstones—the makeup case, the porcelain cat, three pieces of Peggin's china collection, and a pile of flatware that would be good as new if it went through a thorough wash-ing. Everything else had pretty much been incinerated.

As I stared down into the basement, I thought about the blade again, and the beams from the *Susanna Maria*. This house had been cursed from the beginning.

Sophia carried the box of things back to her car while I wandered around the lot. I was looking for ghosts, but every-thing felt silent, as if the fire had wiped the slate clean. I closed my eyes and held out my hands but there was nothing here. No lost souls. No Eugenie. No Joseph. No Herschel. The land felt empty and barren.

I looked beyond the lot toward the tree line, where the lake glistened through the copse. Silent snow covered the trees and undergrowth, but when I closed my eyes and reached out I could hear a faint song and I knew it was the Lady. But she must have sensed me, for the next moment she was silent and the lake felt like a brooding lair, hushed and waiting for someone it actually wanted.

I arrived home to find Deev sitting at the kitchen table in his wheelchair, playing with Daphne. He was throwing kitty treats one by one into the living room and she was running after them. Gabby and Agent H stared at him with disdain. They ran for no person. But Daphne was quite happy to gobble up anything he offered her.

"Well, this is all we found. And we went over it pretty in-depth." I decided to wash up the silverware and the china before waking Peggin. I wanted them spotless and sparkling when she came down. As I filled the sink with soapy water, and immersed the silverware first, Deev wheeled himself over to my side.

"There's something Peggin doesn't know about me. I didn't want to tell her, because when I've told other women in the past, it's affected my relationships in bad ways." He pursed his lips, staring up at me from behind his crazy goggles. I had actually grown fond of them, and it had seemed strange to see his eyes so clearly the night before.

"Is this going to be something that's going to make me unhappy? And therefore, make *you* unhappy?" I really didn't want to hear that he was some pervert, or criminal, or anything that would make Peggin even more upset than she was.

He just grinned and shook his head. "I promise you, you aren't going to want to pop me upside the head after you hear this. I understand that tends to be your modus operandi."

"Well then, tell me what it is. I'm waiting."

"I'm rich. Peggin has no idea how much money I have. And to be honest, I never even think about it." He paused, and then added, "Where I come from, I'm pretty famous. I made a great deal of money. I can easily afford to buy Peggin any house she wants. I know she won't take it as a gift, and I know it's too early to offer it to her outright, but I was thinking that I could be her landlord. She could buy it from me at a rate she could afford, with no money down, and eventually, loans can be forgotten." Again, the edge of his lip tipped up in a quirky grin.

I wiped my hands on a dish towel and turned to him, crossing my arms across my chest as I leaned against the counter. "Where *do* you come from? Every time we've asked you, you don't seem to know the answer. I know that's your business, but Peggin is my best friend and I want to make sure she's safe. I like you, Deev. But I love Peggin."

He stared at me for a moment, and then soberly asked,

"Have you ever heard of the theory of multiple worlds? Multiple universes?"

"Are you talking about a parallel world?" It sounded preposterous on one level, but given everything we had been through, and everything that I knew about Whisper Hollow, I wasn't about to pooh-pooh anything outright.

"Sometimes, I close my eyes and I remember life in another place. And I remember seeing a spinning vortex in the woodland, and the next thing I knew, I was walking into Whisper Hollow. My first memory of Whisper Hollow is finding myself on Katega Lane. I don't remember too much beyond the spinning vortex, except that I know I've always been an artist. And I know that I came here to find something. What that *something* is, I don't know. All I do realize is that I am driven to create sculptures, and that somehow, some of them come to life."

"When did you set up your bank account?"

"Three years ago. I found that I had a check in my pocket. I'd have to go back and look at who it's from but it was cashier's check, for a great deal of money. I know the IRS investigates large deposits, but something must have checked out all right, because I was never questioned. I think I'm here from a different universe, but why? I don't know. And how do I make the sculptures that I do? Again, I don't know."

I had no clue what to say to his revelation. But something about it struck me as absolutely true. I tried to imagine what Peggin would say to it, but for once I wasn't sure.

"For now, why don't you just tell Peggin that you're more successful than she thinks you are? And that you can invest in a house, and she can rent it for as long as she likes. That might go over better." I didn't like deceiving my best friend, but until we took care of that mark on her wrist, she didn't need anything else to worry about. Deev could reveal his secrets after we were done with the ritual that night.

He gave me a long look, then nodded. "That sounds like

it might be the wisest move. And thank you, Kerris. This isn't exactly something I like to make public knowledge. For one thing, I still don't know why I'm here. And I don't want the government breathing down my neck."

With that, I heard Peggin coming down the stairs. She had woken up again, which didn't surprise me. I had given her a very mild dosage when I left with Sophia. As she entered the kitchen I went back to washing up the silverware and china. When she saw the cat, she gave a little cry and raced over.

"Kitty Kare! You found her! I can't believe that she survived." And with that, she burst into tears, and sank down on the floor weeping. The walls had come down, and the reality of her loss had settled in.

O riel had instructed Peggin to wear a simple white nightgown to the ritual and eat nothing after four P.M. She told me to dress in a black ritual dress, but I didn't have one. So far, I hadn't needed one. And since Peggin didn't have anything in white—let alone a white nightgown—we went shopping during the afternoon.

"I have to admit, I'm scared. The fact that Corbin is going to be there scares me even more. I can't see any reason for him to be, except that he's a doctor. And that means that they're right, this ritual will put my life in danger." Peggin gave me a frightened look. And she didn't frighten easily. But the last few days had shaken her to the core. I hoped we could rebuild her self-confidence without any problem.

"You'll managed to pull through this," I said. "You're a strong woman, Peggin, and I have so much faith in you. Besides, I won't let anything happen to you. You're my best friend. My BFF, and I'll always have your back." I glanced at the clock. It was two P.M. "Let's grab a bite to eat before we finish shopping. Since you can't eat after four, let's get whatever you want."

Peggin snorted." You aren't by chance offering me a last

supper, are you?" As I stammered, she rolled her eyes and waved off my protest. "Actually I am hungry. And since I have no idea what's going to happen tonight, I want fried chicken and I want an ice cream sundae. Where can we get both?"

"Lindsey's Diner, of course. She learned to make fried chicken from her mother, I gather. And you know Mary Jane's fried chicken was the best ever." When we were teenagers, we had hung out at the diner just for the fried chicken.

We bustled in, and spent an hour eating and chatting about nothing in particular. Finally, we had to get moving even though both of us were reluctant. I paid the bill, insisting to Peggin that she could pay me back later by taking me out for coffee. We stopped in at Hortense's Dress Shop, where I found a flowing long black dress that seemed like it could be used as a ritual dress, and Peggin was able to buy a white nightgown. She held up a white corset, but I shook my head.

"I don't think that's what they're talking about, and you'll make it very difficult for Corbin to do whatever he has to do." I said, giving her a grin.

"Spoilsport," she said, and chose a simple cotton shift. I wanted to believe that her joking around meant that she wasn't afraid, but I realized it was part Peggin, part bravado. I played along because there wasn't anything else I could do. She needed me to be strong so she could be strong.

We went back to my house, and I gave her and Deev some privacy. I didn't know what was going to happen, and I wanted them to have some time alone before we faced whatever it was we were going to face. I headed up to my ritual room, and knelt before the altar.

"Great Morrígan, please, whatever you do, help Peggin get through this. She may not be my lament singer, and she may not be my protector, but she is as much a part of my life as either one of them. I need her, Deev needs her, and this town needs her. Protect her and walk her through this ritual."

As I stared at the altar, at the statue of the Morrígan that was placed front and center, it began to glow with a faint light. The light began to fill the room and I felt a quiet sense of peace descend around me. It wasn't melancholy, and yet— there was a sense of loss about it.

Every time you walk through a dark pathway, you lose something. You lose a little bit of the sense that the world's fair, you lose a little bit of your naïveté. But you also gain from your journey. You gain strength, and wisdom, and the realization that you can survive more than you thought you could.

The voice drifted away and I wasn't sure whether it was my own thoughts, or whether the Morrígan had been speaking to me. Either way, I rose and silently walked out of the room. It was time to dress for the ritual.

Deev didn't like being left at home, but I gently told him that he would simply interfere with the ritual and with Peggin's ability to concentrate. Finally, he quit bothering me about it.

"Watch the cats, we'll be back as soon as we can. I promise to call when we're done." I handed him the remote and made sure he had plenty of snacks. He had actually been quite complacent about using the wheelchair and I had the feeling Corbin had him scared stiff.

When we reached the boardinghouse, I wasn't sure what to expect. I had been there a couple of times since Aidan moved there, but I had never seen Oriel's inner sanctum.

The living room had several of her guests reading the paper, watching TV—the usual. I recognized a writer who had come to Whisper Hollow to write a story about the town and never left. I couldn't remember his name, though I thought it was Shawn. He gave me a wave and went back to his book.

Oriel led Peggin and me into a back room that I knew was her own private parlor. She walked over to the grandfather clock and reached around behind it. A moment later a secret door slid back to reveal a staircase leading down. Whisper Hollow was full of secret passages, it seemed.

The stairwell was well lit, with a sturdy railing—nothing like the dark basement that had been in Peggin's house or the steep hidden stair in Niles's garage. The stairs were carpeted, probably to hush the sound of footsteps. As we headed down, the door closed behind us. Twelve steps later and we were in a private basement—in a large sitting room, with three doors off of it.

"That door leads to the restroom. The center door leads to my ritual room. The door on the left is a private chamber. Never enter it unless you have my permission. I have guardians set and they will not differentiate between friend or foe. If you have to, go ahead into the bathroom and then come on into the ritual room. I'll meet you there as soon as I am ready." She vanished into her private chamber.

"I think I need to use the bathroom," Peggin said.

I nodded. "I'll wait for you here." I settled into one of the chairs, trying to think of anything I could to take my mind off what was about to ensue. It would help if I knew what the ritual was, I thought. Then again, if it was as dangerous as Oriel and Ivy had indicated, maybe not.

A few moments later Peggin returned from the bathroom, her eyes red. I realized she'd been crying. I gave her a silent hug and we headed into the ritual room.

Bryan was already there, as were Corbin and Starlight and Ellia and Ivy. They were gathered around what appeared to be a massage table. I blinked. Somehow I didn't expect the ritual to be all that relaxing. I glanced around the room.

Oriel's ritual room was quite different than mine or Ivy's. Each wall was painted to match one of the elements. The north wall was a jungle. East was covered with clouds. South was a volcanic expanse. And west was the rolling ocean. In front of each wall stood an altar table, dedicated to the element it represented. There were crystals everywhere, from small spheres of lapis lazuli to quartz spikes the size of a small ottoman. The ceiling was painted to represent stars and galaxies, and recessed lighting provided a dizzying array of faerie lights.

Peggin gasped, lowering herself to a chair next to Corbin. "This is incredible. Can you feel the energy here? The walls are practically singing with it."

Ellia leaned forward, a gentle smile on her face. "They are singing. I could hear their voices—the ancestors live within this room. Or rather, it provides them a portal through which to speak. On the surface, the Heart of Whisper Hollow seems a gentle soul, but do not mistake that gentleness for weakness. Oriel is more powerful than all of us put together."

Starlight stood, a somber look on her face. "Ellia is right. And we are each here for a reason. This ritual can be a dangerous one, but it is also a powerful blessing. I am here to represent Starlight and the Night Sky."

Ivy stood. "And I am here to represent the Element of Water."

Ellia stood. "And I, Air. I am the breath and the song."

"And I am the Fire." Aidan stood, flashing a soft smile to Peggin.

They all looked at me, and I suddenly realized why I was there. "I suppose I represent Spirit, don't I? And Bryan—" I turned to him.

"I am the guardian and sentinel of this ritual and of the Spirit."

Oriel entered the room at that moment. She was dressed in a white gown that flowed over her curves like a Grecian toga. Around her neck she wore a cloak of fur, and around her head a circlet of woven holly. She carried a staff in one hand with a carved wooden crow affixed to the top; its sparkling eyes glittered like diamonds and might well have been.

"And I, I am the Heart and the Earth. I am she who protects the village. I'm she who embodies the essence of Whisper Hollow. I am the town incarnate, and I look after my people." She turned to Corbin and inclined her head. "And today, for this ritual, we have the spirit of Healing with us."

I glanced at Peggin, who looked absolutely petrified. Given any other day she would have probably been totally entranced, but since she was the focus of the rite, I had no doubt that she would rather be anywhere else than right here.

Oriel nodded to the massage table. "Peggin, take off all of your jewelry and your shoes and lie on your back on the table. If you have any piercings, please remove that jewelry as well," she said with a smile.

Peggin blushed. "Is there somewhere I can do that privately?"

"Ivy, please escort Peggin to the bathroom."

We waited in silence for a few moments until Peggin returned, still blushing.

"She's ready," Ivy said, retaking her position.

"Very good. Take your position on the table please, and try not to be afraid." Oriel waited until Peggin had stretched out on the table, then walked over to stand by her head. She placed a soft hand on Peggin's forehead and motioned to her wrist. "Please extend your wrist. We need to look at the mark."

Corbin walked over then, and took hold of Peggin's wrist, staring at the black filigree. "Close ranks."

Oriel motioned to the rest of us. "Take your positions. Kerris, you will stand on the other side of Peggin's head, across from me. Bryan, stand at her feet. The rest of you know the drill."

Ivy walked over to Peggin's right side, and I recognized that she was standing in the west. Ellia took her place opposite Ivy, on the left side. Aidan stood beside Bryan, in the south position. And Starlight surprised me with her agility when she climbed up to stand on a nearby dais.

"We're ready. Ellia, please do the honors."

Ellia began to sing, and her voice flowed into a field of energy that circled over to Aidan, who picked up the melody and joined her. The energy snaked around to Ivy, who added her voice to the circle, and then to Oriel, who began to sing an underlying harmony. Once again the energy moved back to Ellia to complete the circle.

The flowing current was so strong that I could see it, a

whirling ring of power, blending the green of earth and the pale gold of sunshine in early morning sky. It merged into the brilliant reds and oranges of flame, and then entered the churning currents of deep blue water. The ring of energy moved on to merge back into the green. The Elements surrounded us, circling us with a ring of protection, a ring of power and strength.

As I watched, entranced, Starlight added her voice and it felt like a rain of sparkling stars began to descend over us. Bryan began to sing, contra tone, a foundation of protection, and then—without realizing I was doing so—I added my voice, the mournful call of the spirits. We kept singing, kept the energy flowing as Corbin held out his hands, and then slowly lowered them to the edge of the massage table beside Peggin. He began to shift form, to transform into a snake, his skin taking on the scales of a diamondback rattler, as his body elongated and narrowed.

Everything took on hazy quality as I found myself drifting into the energy, and all I could hear was the calling of crows. I wasn't sure if their cry was coming from my own throat or from a long distance; I wasn't even sure what was happening except that Corbin was now a five-foot-long rattlesnake coiling on Peggin's chest. He reared up, fangs exposed, and a part of me wanted to scream and knock him away, but I knew this was all part of the ritual and it was the only thing that we could do to save Peggin from the Lady.

She lay there, silent and mesmerized, unmoving, and I wondered if she had fainted, but her eyes were wide open as she stared at the snake on her chest. The crows were screaming in my ears now as Corbin lunged, sinking his fangs into Peggin's throat. She started to scream, then suddenly fell silent as convulsions took her. Corbin slithered back, and then—in another blur—he transformed back into himself.

Peggin was foaming at the mouth, convulsing in a seizure so hard that I was worried she'd break her neck. Then, she arched, her body stiff, and collapsed.

Corbin felt for her pulse. "She's dead."

CHAPTER 19

I began to scream, but Oriel grabbed me by the shoulder.
"Hush, this needed to happen. Watch and learn."

I tried to catch my breath, tried to remain calm, but it
was difficult. I had disrupted the flow of energy and Ellia
had to start it again. When it came my turn to join in, I forced
myself to breathe, forced myself to focus on the task at hand.
Within less than a minute the circle was running again at
full speed, and I shoved my emotions down deep, watching
Corbin carefully. The realization that he was a snakeshifter
was a shock, but there was no time to think about that now,
no time to analyze what was happening.

He waited for a moment, brushing Peggin's hair back
from her face. Then he took hold of her wrist again and held
it out and as we watched, the mark faded from sight. And
then it hit me—the mark wouldn't leave until Peggin was
dead. Therefore, we had had to kill her in order to save her.

"How long?" he asked.

Oriel paused from her singing. "Ninety seconds. Give

it another minute. When three minutes are up, I will tell you."

Corbin pulled out a syringe. It was filled with a pale yellow liquid. Somehow I didn't think it was quite the same thing as snake anti-venom. He waited, poised over Peggin's arm. Time seemed to flow by so slowly that I could hear every single breath taken, every single note that was being sung. I could hear the swish as the ring of energy raced around us. I could hear my heart beating even as I joined in the song. As much as I wanted to scream *bring her back now*, I knew that it was vital that we keep up the protection around us.

"Now," Oriel finally said after what seemed like an eternity.

Corbin inserted the needle in Peggin's arm and plunged the liquid into her vein. Then, tossing the syringe to the side, he began to pat her face.

"Wake up, Peggin. Can you hear me? Peggin, I need you to wake up. Come on, girl, don't fail me now." He looked over at me. "Kerris, start talking to her. Take her other arm and began rubbing vigorously. We need to get her circulation going. Bryan, massage her feet."

As I grabbed her hand and began rubbing vigorously, calling to her as I leaned near her ear, Bryan began to rub her feet. Corbin dropped her arm and began CPR, motioning to me when it was time to breathe into her mouth.

I tipped her head back, holding her nose and making sure her throat was clear, and then fastened my mouth to hers, breathing deeply and then pulling away. We worked for what seemed like hours. Suddenly, as I was beginning to fear the worst, Peggin's chest rose, and she coughed. Corbin reached behind her shoulders to lift her into a sitting position.

"I think I'm going to throw up," she said, looking queasy. Bryan grabbed a basin that was beneath the table and handed it Corbin, who held it in front of Peggin. She clutched both sides of the tub and the next moment, was puking her guts out. The frothy matter was dark, not with blood but with what looked like seaweed and brine. It was as though I could smell the Lady again, like I had when we rescued her. I looked across at Corbin, questioning.

"The Lady got into her lungs, into her very bloodstream. This is the residue. Once she gets it out of her system, she'll be okay and no more prone to the Lady's siren song than you or me. We all have to keep our guard, and so will Peggin, but she won't be under the Lady's spell anymore."

I let out a long breath, realizing how close we'd come to losing my best friend. I also realized just how incredibly strong each person in this room was, including myself. I had so much to learn about Whisper Hollow and the people who lived here, and I had merely scraped the surface. There were so many secrets, and so many layers to this town that I wondered if anyone ever knew the true scope.

C leanup always seems easier than preparation. As we gathered in the sitting room of Oriel's inner sanctum, everyone seemed both exhausted and exhilarated. Oriel passed out food—crackers and cheese, sliced deli meat and grapes, and cookies. She made everyone take a plate, including Peggin.

"I don't care if you think you're hungry or not. You need food. The amount of energy we expended in there is tremendous, and before long you'll be incredibly light-headed and feel like you're going to faint. This goes for all of you."

I looked over at Peggin, who—for the first time in days—looked relaxed. In fact, she looked almost euphoric.

"Are you all right?" I asked her.

"Actually, I feel kind of giddy. I can't explain it, but I feel like laughing. It's like this huge weight is gone from my shoulders. I know that I died in there, you told me so, and I suppose I should feel some sense of vulnerability, but I feel almost invincible." She looked bemused as she bit into one of Oriel's thick oatmeal raisin cookies.

"I can tell you why," Corbin said. "The antidote I gave you, to bring you back, contains a euphoric. It's a magical strengthener. That's no ordinary anti-venom. Snakeshifter venom is quite different than that of a regular rattlesnake. It's far more potent, and far more deadly. And it can leave you feeling drug down for days, so when we create our anti-venom, we add a little joy juice, if you will. You'll be fine and you won't be exhausted."

"How come you kept the fact that you're a snakeshifter silent?" I was looking at the doctor with a new respect.

"How many people do you know who are afraid of snakes? Almost every snakeshifter is a healer. It's our nature—we're born to it. But people are terrified of snakes, and so we tend to keep our natures private. It's scary enough to go to the doctor, scarier still if you know your doctor is a snake." He laughed, and shook his head. "Unfortunately, we can't cure every ill, but we do our best."

"Is your daughter a snakeshifter, too? And your wife?" I was curious now, especially since I had met Corbin's wife and she was a gorgeous accountant. But I knew his daughter was following in his footsteps; she was working with herbs and learning their healing natures.

"My wife isn't, she's human. But our daughter, yes. Kimberly's a snakeshifter. And she's very interested in going into the medical field, I'm proud to say."

I nodded, promising him that I would keep their secret. As he motioned for Peggin to jump up on the table again, to check her vitals and make sure that everything was working just fine, I wandered over to Starlight. It was time to put our feud behind us. She had just helped save my best friend and that alone made me want to bury the hatchet. And this time, I didn't want to bury it in her head.

"Thank you, for helping." I held her gaze, trying to see her for who she really was.

She nodded, a soft smile playing on her lips. "Sometimes it takes danger to bring people together. I wasn't sure about you when you came back to Whisper Hollow. I suppose I felt like you had defected on us years ago. But now I understand, given what happened with your grandmother and your mother and Duvall. And seeing you now, keeping your head in a ritual that put your best friend's life in danger . . . I'll hand it to you, Kerris. I think you're going to be a wonderful spirit shaman. Whisper Hollow needs you. I'm glad you came home."

I waited, but she fell silent. After a moment, I said, "You're not going to tell me what you are, are you?"

She laughed. "I don't know you well enough yet. Someday . . . someday I will."

Corbin pronounced Peggin fit to go home. "She'll be fine. But I recommend *against* buying a new house on the lake. For anybody in this town."

Bryan and I bundled up Peggin and headed to our car after making our good-byes. As we drove home, Peggin kept giggling from the backseat. Corbin had told her she would act like she was drunk for the rest of the evening, but by tomorrow should be back to normal. I looked over at Bryan. "I'm tired and yet I feel so energized. I don't know how I can be both at once, but I am."

"I know, my love. I know," was all he said.

Three days later, I woke up to a winter wonderland. We had yet another snowfall, and there was a good eight inches in the yard. Everything was sparkling white and felt new again, and as I watched out the kitchen window, the sparrows converged on the birdfeeders. Bryan was already outside, putting up the lights on the outside of the house and trimming the trees in the front yard. He had suggested that when we got married we live here, in my house, and keep his estate for business purposes. I had agreed, content with that arrangement.

Deev and Peggin joined me as I was making peppermint mocha for breakfast.

"What can I do?" Peggin asked.

"What do you want for breakfast?"

"How about eggs and pancakes and sausage? I can start the pancakes." She moved to the cupboard and pulled out the mix, as Deev rolled over to the refrigerator and handed her eggs and milk and a package of sausage. Corbin had told him that if he was good, by the next day he'd be up on crutches and within a week he'd be walking normally again, even though he would probably need some physical therapy.

"The Winter Fun Fest begins today. I suggest we head down there this afternoon and show some community spirit. I also need to finish my shopping. Peggin, do you want to join me?"

She frowned. "Afraid my shopping this year for the holidays isn't going to be very extensive. I have to save every penny I have for a security deposit and rent."

"About that," Deev said. "I've got some news."

We both turned to look at him. For once, he was sans top hat and wearing his normal glasses rather than his goggles. His eyes still struck me as startling—they were crystal clear and as blue as the morning sky.

"I talked to your former landlady. Turns out, she's more than willing to sell the house for a good price. So I bought it. If you want to move back in, you're welcome to. I'll charge you one hundred dollars a month rent—that way you can get back on your feet and you won't have to worry about ever being kicked out. I'll give you a ninety-nine-year lease, cancelable on your end whenever you want." He grinned at Peggin, who let out a little squeal.

"You've got to be kidding! You can afford to do that? I love that house."

"It's yours for as long as you want it." He paused, then added, "I think I could come to like it, too. For now, do you want it? We can talk over the details later."

"Are you kidding? Of course I want to live there. I hated having to leave. I spent years getting that garden into the shape it's in." She wrapped her arms around his shoulders, leaning over to give him a long kiss. He reached around her, gently stroking her back.

I wondered what she would think when he told her the reality about who he was, but that could come when it came. She was recovering from the ritual rapidly, but I could still see the fear in her eyes whenever we passed the lake. Peggin wasn't going to be forgetting her experience anytime soon. But Whisper Hollow wouldn't let her go, that much I knew. It needed her as much as it needed me, although I wasn't sure just what her place was yet.

"How about some pancakes, then, now that that's settled?" I finished making our mochas and handed around the mugs, garnished with dollops of whipped cream. I set another to the side, for Bryan when he came in. In another few minutes he came stomping to the door.

"Lights are all up around the house. And the trees are covered with lights, so unless you are planning on anything else, I'm pretty much finished."

"Oh, I plan on getting some of those lighted polar bears and elk, so we're not done yet. But we'll do that this afternoon, after we check out the Winter Fun Fest."

We all pitched in to finish making breakfast, then carried our food into the living room where we settled in front of the TV. The cats sprawled on the floor at our feet as we turned on the old Alastair Sim version of *A Christmas Carol*. As the black-and-white images filled the screen, I looked outside. It was beautiful, and sparkling, and I realized that I was truly at home. I was engaged to the man I loved, with more friends than I had ever imagined having, and if that meant I walked with the dead at my shoulders and a goddess at my back, so be it. Life was a magical ride, and I never wanted it to be different.

I was standing in the middle of a forest, and the ground was covered with snow. The old crone was out there and the bloodthirsty Hounds with her. I could feel them, watching the town, waiting and biding their time. Beside me the Crow

Man stood, silent as the flock of crows gathered around our feet.

"You have the blade now," he said. "It's time you learned to use her."

I lifted up the dagger. The bone hilt and crystal blade gleamed in my hands, resonating deep within my heart and core. "This belonged to my ancestors, didn't it?"

"Yes, it was a gift from the Morrígan to the very first mother of your family line. To the very first spirit shaman, whose blood you come from. Nine great families . . . and generations past counting. You are the fiftieth generation."

"I need to know them. I need to understand."

"You feel it, then. It's time you started learning about your heritage, Kerris. It's time you started delving into the history of your kind—of the spirit shamans. There's so much that your grandmother did not know, that your great-grandmother did not know. They could not speak with me as easily as you can. Each generation loses a piece of the puzzle and one day, unless the history is pieced together, it may die out altogether."

"That's my job, isn't it? To remember the history and bring it back stronger than before." The wind whipped my hair as the Crow Man cackled.

"Yes, you are a smart one, girl. For if you were to forget, and those after you, the danger would grow stronger. The spirits will never stop walking. And the Ankou and the Hounds will never stop. For, you see, the Hounds know more of their history than you do of yours. So talk to the blade, and she will help you remember."

The crows suddenly took wing, screeching and cawing as they circled overhead. As I looked up, a giant dog formed in the sky. *The Great Hound . . . Cú Chulainn himself.* I realized that he had bigger plans than just taking over Whisper Hollow. He meant to destroy the lines of the spirit shamans, and the Morrígan herself if he could. I needed to learn, and I needed to learn fast. A shiver ran down my back.

"Will I ever meet any of the others? Perhaps if we meet, we can pool our knowledge."

"That you may. But for now you have to take care of Magda. The old crone stands between you and fulfilling your destiny. There are still three witch bottles in the woods. But she won't be making more—she is working on something far more dangerous. Talk to Veronica, talk to Penelope. Listen to the spirits and the Elements. For they are in danger as much as the living. Enjoy this brief lull, because the storm is rising and when it hits, you will need all of your reserves."

And with that he furled his cape and a swirl of color rose up to surround me, filled with snow and crows and the creaking of trees. When I opened my eyes the Crow Man was gone, and I was standing in my backyard. But a lone crow in the apple tree called to me, and I knew that the Crow Man would never be far from my side. And the Morrígan was watching and waiting for the new game to begin, between her sons and daughters and her enemies.

And the first move was mine to make.

THE PLAYLIST

I write to music quite often, and each book will have a playlist that fits the mood of the book. For *Shadow Silence*, this is the list of songs I listened to:

A. J. Roach: "Devil May Dance"

Air: "Napalm Love"

Al Stewart: "Life in Dark Water"

Android Lust: "Here and Now"; "Dragonfly"

Arcade Fire: "Abraham's Daughter"

Arch Leaves: "Nowhere to Go"

AWOLNATION: "Sail"

Beck: "Nausea"; "Broken Train"; "Think I'm In Love"

Black Angels, The: "Young Men Dead"; "Never/Ever"; "Don't Play with Guns"; "Always Maybe"

Bobbie Gentry: "Ode to Billie Joe"

Bon Jovi: "Wanted Dead or Alive"

Boom! Bap! Pow!: "Suit"

Broken Bells: "The Ghost Inside"

Celtic Woman: "The Sky and the Dawn and the Sun"; "Newgrange"

Clannad: "Banba Óir"

Crazy Town: "Butterfly"

Cream: "Strange Brew"

Damh the Bard: "Morrighan"; "Oak Broom and Meadowsweet"; "Grimspound"; "Cloak of Feathers"; "The Cauldron Born"

David Bowie: "Fame"; "Golden Years"; "Without You"

Dire Straits: "Down to the Waterline"

Dizzi: "Dizzi Jig"

Donovan: "Season of the Witch"

Eagles: "Witchy Woman"

Eastern Sun: "Beautiful Being" (Original Edit)

Fats Domino: "I Want to Walk You Home"

FC Kahuna: "Hayling"

Feeling, The: "Sewn"

Fluke: "Absurd"

Foster the People: "Pumped Up Kicks"

Garbage: "#1 Crush"; "I Think I'm Paranoid"; "Queer"

Gary Numan: "Sleep by Windows"; "Petals"; "My Breathing"; "I Am Dust"; "Everything Comes Down to This"; "Love Hurt Bleed"

Gordon Lightfoot: "The Wreck of the Edmund Fitzgerald"

Gospel Whiskey Runners: "Muddy Waters"

Hanni El Khatib: "Come Alive"

Haysi Fantayzee: "Shiny, Shiny"; "John Wayne Is Big Leggy"

Heart: "White Lightning & Wine"; "Magic Man"

Hollies, The: "Long Cool Woman"

Jay Price: "Number 13"; "Dark-Hearted Man"

Jeannie C. Riley: "Harper Valley P.T.A."

Jessica Bates: "The Hanging Tree"

Jethro Tull: "Old Ghosts"; "Dun Ringill"; "Undertow"

Johnny Otis: "Willy and the Hand Jive"

Joy Division: "Atmosphere"

Julian Cope: "Charlotte Anne"

Kills, The: "Dead Road 7"; "Sour Cherry"; "You Don't Own the Road"; "DNA"; "Nail in My Coffin"; "U.R.A. Fever"

Lorde: "Royals"; "Yellow Flicker Beat"

Low with tomandandy: "Half Light"

Mark Lanegan: "Bleeding Muddy Water"; "Riding the Nightingale"; "Mockingbirds"; "The Gravedigger's Song"

Matt Corby: "Breathe"

Mogwai: "Hungry Face"; "The Huts"

Motherdrum: "Big Stomp"

Nancy Sinatra: "The Boots Are Made for Walkin'"

Nirvana: "All Apologies"; "Lake of Fire"; "Come As You Are"

Pierces, The: "Secret"

Rachel Diggs: "Hands of Time"

Stone Temple Pilots: "Atlanta"

Sweet Talk Radio: "We All Fall Down"

Susan Enan: "Bring on the Wonder"

Syntax: "Pride"

Tamaryn: "While You're Sleeping, I'm Dreaming"; "Violet's in a Pool"

Tom Petty: "Mary Jane's Last Dance"

Toadies: "Possum Kingdom"

Tuatha Dea: "Tuatha De Danaan"; "Long Black Curl"; "Wisp of a Thing"; "Dance of the Tufa"

Verve, The: "Bitter Sweet Symphony"

Voxhaul Broadcast: "You Are the Wilderness"

Wendy Rule: "Let the Wind Blow"; "Elemental Chant"

Zero 7: "In the Waiting Line"

New York Times bestselling author **Yasmine Galenorn** writes urban fantasy, mystery, and metaphysical nonfiction, including the Whisper Hollow novels (*Autumn Thorns, Shadow Silence*), the Otherworld novels (*Darkness Raging, Panther Prowling, Priestess Dreaming*), the Indigo Court novels (*Night's End, Night Visions, Night Seeker*), and the Fly by Night novels (*Flight from Mayhem, Flight from Death*). A graduate of Evergreen State College, she majored in theater and creative writing. Yasmine has been in the Craft for more than thirty-six years and is a shamanic witch. She describes her life as a blend of teacups and tattoos, and she lives in the Seattle area with her husband, Samwise, and their cats. If you send Yasmine snail mail, please enclose a self-addressed stamped envelope if you want a reply.

Don't miss the "erotic and darkly bewitching"*
Otherworld series featuring the D'Artigo sisters:
half-human, half-Fae supernatural agents.

From *New York Times* bestselling author
Yasmine Galenorn

WITCHLING

CHANGELING

DARKLING

DRAGON WYTCH

NIGHT HUNTRESS

DEMON MISTRESS

BONE MAGIC

HARVEST HUNTING

BLOOD WYNE

COURTING DARKNESS

SHADED VISION

SHADOW RISING

HAUNTED MOON

AUTUMN WHISPERS

CRIMSON VEIL

PRIESTESS DREAMING

PANTHER PROWLING

DARKNESS RAGING

galenorn.com
penguin.com

 Penguin
BERKLEY Random
House

*Jeaniene Frost, *New York Times* bestselling author

M192AS0315